OPERATION BLACKOUT

J.L. MIDDLETON

ACKNOWLEDGEMENTS

There are many people to whom I owe my appreciation for helping make this happen. To my darling husband, Jared, you have given me much-needed support and advice, but more importantly, you have given me encouragement. Without your assistance, I would never have made it this far.

To my dear friend Krista De Los Santos, you are the reason I even embarked on this journey. You inspired me to take up writing again, and your criticisms improved the foundation on which I built this story.

To Bradley McLeod and Adam Schreiber, thank you for all the conversations and laughter we've shared over the years. Finally, to Annie Parlock, you taught me the value of good feedback, and without your input, I wouldn't have enjoyed writing nearly as much.

PROLOGUE

Due to the enigmatic and often esoteric nature of Others, it is difficult to pinpoint when they began to appear in history. There has been speculation that they are the "gods" of old, but it is possible that they appeared more recently. The first recorded instance of an Other on American soil was during the disappearance of the Roanoke Colony in 1590. The writings of John White, one of the unfortunate colonists, survive as the only narrative of the colony's ultimate fate. White wrote that in the winter of 1588, one of the settlement's infants—of which there were three, including the infamous Virginia Dare—was emitting a terrible fume that rotted organic matter that was placed too close to it. A great divide occurred within the community between those who wished to banish this child, whom they assumed was demonically possessed, and those who wished to try to exorcise the demon. Despite flared tempers, the debate remained relatively free from violence, and most of the colony chose to pack up and move, its residents refusing to kill an innocent infant but unwilling to be near its poisonous influence. White asserted that moving the child to the wilds would certainly kill it, so he stayed with the child in the abandoned colony until the end. He could not complete his narrative, as he disappeared long before a different John White, Virginia Dare's grandfather, came with relief supplies from England. But it was implied that the child's sphere of influence expanded to encompass the entire town and that the child would soon starve since no food could survive the fumes. His writings were found by White's namesake, who immediately locked them away, and they were not discovered again for another three centuries. It is assumed that this secondary White's actions occurred because the infant was, in reality, Virginia Dare, and he did not want his family's name or memory sullied. Despite the fact that the Roanoke Incident did not contribute directly to the colonists' deaths or disappearance, it is foundational to the government's fear of Others.

Further recorded incidents were isolated and few over the years, but each struck a chord with the world governments, and it became evident that the number of instances was accelerating. Notable among these were the Tunguska Event (1908), the Anjikuni Mystery (1930), the *Ourang Medan* (1948), and the Dyatlov Pass Incident (1959), and while speculations about these events have made their rounds in paranormal circles for years, only Others really know what occurred.

Unfortunately, these incidents also demonstrated to the government that Others were dangerous and had to be destroyed for the good of the people and especially for world governments. A single person with such power, even if it could be used only once, as demonstrated during the above events, posed a significant threat. The most influential governments—the United States of America, Great Britain, France, Germany, and even the USSR and China— agreed to destroy Others where they found them and to erase any evidence of their existence. This campaign would become known as Operation Blackout, and it was more than a new tool for the Cold War. Since Others could not be controlled, they were considered a time bomb more potent than nuclear weapons. Fear laid the groundwork for cooperation on a global scale, even surpassing the artificial boundaries of the Cold War.

For many years, the understood threat of Others was the widely held belief—until the Cokeville Miracle in 1986. A young couple took the occupants of Cokeville Elementary hostage and threatened to detonate a homemade gasoline bomb. Though the bomb was detonated accidentally, few victims were actually injured, and while the media focused on the mysterious "angels" who shielded the children from the blast, the US government discovered something different: a child who had used his power instinctively to defend himself but, most importantly, had not killed any bystanders in the process. The boy, Eric Dane, was removed from his parents' custody and placed in government care. He and his abilities were tirelessly researched over the years, and Dane proved to be an Other of enormous talent. But, more critically, he served as an ambassador for Others by demonstrating that they could be trained and controlled and did not need to be feared.

This led to the birth of the Bureau of Special Interests (BSI), and Dane was forever sealed within its walls. Over the years, the BSI developed its purpose, aims, and methods and created special divisions. But it is the Exceptional Division that we must fear. It is these people who sniff out Others. Their special agents come with sweet words and promises to instruct Others to use their abilities, but these are lies. It is the job of the Exceptional Division to cull the "useful" from the "dangerous." If an Other cannot be useful to the government, he will be put to death so that he cannot be a danger to the public. Many have been lured inside the walls of the BSI never to depart, and the only crime of these men and women was to be born with a power that we don't understand. They are executed without a trial, but a small percentage of traitors help to spare their lives. Be forewarned: Never take pity on an agent of the BSI. They believe that any Other, regardless of their age, is a monster or a tool and that anyone who helps them to escape is a traitor. These men destroy what they don't understand and make enemies whom they don't yet know.

— Charles Moreau
Excerpt from VSION Manifesto

————————————————————

It is the opinion of this body that the training program must be rethought and completely overhauled. While the post-1986 operation has made amazing leaps in regard to the assessment and tracking of Others, it is still failing in its primary mission: to protect the public and prevent exposure to the existence of Others. Instead of exterminating Others, BSI agents must apprehend them in a manner that makes them amiable to joining our ranks. It could be argued that this has provided propaganda fodder for the Special Interest of Others Network (SION) and opportunities for it to engage our agents and further risk exposing Blackout. The Vanguard (VSION) has become bolder and attempts to evade BSI agents by engaging them in public, where the primary directive is to preserve Blackout. Even when eliminating the terrorist element of VSION as a factor, incidents that lead to the apprehension of newly discovered Others have dangerously skirted widespread public exposure.

Regardless of the circumstances, the conversion rate of Others into useful assets is low. During our best year, in which we managed to recruit fifteen individuals into our training program, only one proved to have practical application, and the rest were released back into the civilian population to be monitored. This is a tremendous drain on our budget, and we will not always have the level of funding we currently have. Our funding was first cut following the shuffling of the bureau beneath the Department of Homeland Security's umbrella, and we have experienced slashes to our budget every year that the war in Iraq continues. We must get ahead of the curve and trim our budget before the government does it for us.

If we refocus our goals purely toward the elimination of Others, we can transfer funding from the training and monitoring programs to tracking and research. The Others in the civilian population do nothing but drain our funds. They have not encouraged undiscovered Others to seek us out or join our ranks, so they do nothing for recruitment, and SION continues to use them for its own propaganda. Therefore, I suggest we cut our losses in that department and scrap the program. Unfortunately, this means the euthanasia of the remaining subjects, but we would be better able to focus on converting Others into assets...

... Our three current assets would likely have unfavorable reactions to this shift in policy, so I suggest we do not allow them to find out. We have already placed a blind on Bloodhound, so double-blinding him would likely create no issues. He already sees Others as a danger to society and has proven himself capable of euthanizing them without prejudice. This is likely due to his ignorance of his true nature, and I strongly recommend against placing him in the training program, as any improvement in detection would likely be outweighed by a subsequent decline in performance.

Since Angel is perceptive and has been with us the longest, he is most likely to notice the policy shift first. Fortunately, he is the primary example of how we need to recruit Others at younger ages than our other two subjects, as indoctrination is more effective on preadolescent subjects. If we keep this new shift of focus from him for several months to a year, when it would become routine, I believe he would accept the change with minimal protests and even begin to advocate it if it is framed properly when presented to him.

Antithesis is likely to be the most receptive to the change because she readily embraced Operation Blackout's doctrine and incorporated it into her personal belief system. However, I still recommend withholding the change from her until the time is right and planning the revelation carefully to minimize any adverse reaction to the news. She is our greatest asset, so we must take special care of her psychological state. I also highly advise that she be separated from Agent Lawrence Johnson, as will be detailed later in this report.

—Excerpts from the Annual Performance Review, 2015
Bureau of Special Interests Archive

PART I
CODE NAME: SUPERNOVA

Cassie waited impatiently for the train to arrive. She knew that if she took out her smartphone and started playing a game, the train would arrive immediately, but if she stared at the dark tunnel instead, she would wait forever. The dilemma was partially already resolved: Her phone was buried deep in her gym bag beneath her cheerleading uniform and the kitschy shirt and apron she had to wear for work. The phone may also have migrated deeper into her gym bag to rest beneath the two schoolbooks for the homework that she didn't intend to do. She had a busy schedule, and a formal education was low on her list of priorities. She needed to remember not to bring the heavy books home next time so she could give her shoulder a break, but the looks of disappointment that she received from her older brother, Orion, always shamed her into packing the books anyway, despite having no intention of doing the homework.

They were not from a normal family: The Starrs were rich due to the unexpected success of Cassie's parents' book *Life of the Universe*, which consistently sold millions of copies each year despite having been published over ten years ago. *The New York Times* called it "the most accessible book on cosmology since *A Brief History of Time*" when assessing why it was still on the Best Seller List. Her parents were also tenured professors at Berkeley, though they had recently taken a sabbatical to accept jobs at a small observatory three hours away in northern New York. Cassie didn't understand her parents' obsession with astronomy, but she appreciated their money.

She rarely saw her parents, who had begun to take extended trips when she'd turned four, and she had no relationship with her surviving grandparents. Her parents now spent the week in Mason and commuted home on weekends if they felt so inclined, which they often didn't. She didn't understand why her parents had bothered to have children when they clearly hadn't wanted them. So, as far as family was concerned, all that was really left was her morose and serious older brother, Orion, who was attending college in Manhattan. They received a weekly allowance from their parents, which included money for groceries and utilities, but Orion had insisted that Cassie get a job if she wanted extra cash to spend. This was why she worked at Hallowed Grounds, a tacky coffeehouse that had opened during the initial zombie craze of the early 2000s. In addition to the corny name, the café was decorated in a postapocalyptic style as if the fabled Y2K had set off the zombie apocalypse. It included such fare as the "Bitten Survivor," which was a decaffeinated cappuccino, and the "Night of the Living Dead," which was three shots of espresso, strawberry flavoring, and a cheap zombie head decoration. Her bosses were a couple in their late thirties who seemed perpetually stuck in their teenage pop culture years, but they were alright, and they tried to work around her otherwise busy schedule. Immediately after school, she had cheerleading practice followed by swim team practice, and the combination sometimes kept her out until eight. She'd have to grab dinner at Hallowed Grounds to supplement the meal that Orion always packed for her, and then she would close the shop at around ten or eleven—sometimes even later, as Hallowed Grounds had no set closing hours. She would nap on the subway, thankfully never missing her stop, and then go to bed as soon as she got home.

No matter how late she was out, she could count on Orion to be waiting in the kitchen to greet her. Most days, she was met with a silent, disapproving gaze or a lecture about her doing too much, but he always made sure she was home. Likewise, he had breakfast waiting for her when she awoke, even though she seldom had time to eat it.

Orion was twenty-two and rail thin, but he appeared to be more immature due to his shy nature and tendency to slouch. He had short, curly hair, which was dirty blond like their mother's, and bags under his hazel eyes, which reflected a perpetual thousand-yard stare whenever he was not actively engaged. He preferred baggy clothes, especially his black hoodie, and because he rarely ventured from the apartment, she didn't think he had any friends. This was such a sharp contrast to Cassie that she sometimes wondered if they were actually related.

Cassie was an active sixteen-year-old with a sharp sense of style. She spent her allowance and extra earnings on the latest outfits and makeup. Her eye shadow technique was so good that nobody noticed that her eyes were a pedestrian brown, and even if they did, they didn't dare mention it to her in case they faced the wrath of her clique. Her red hair was full and wavy, not curly and challenging like her brother's, but she did share his slender build. However, she had enough friends that she didn't have to be home on any weekend that her parents chose to visit—not even for a moment—and this arrangement seemed to suit all parties, as her parents never complained. In fact, only her brother objected, and she suspected it was because he didn't want to deal with them alone.

Now that she thought about it, she hadn't seen or heard from her parents since school had begun several months ago, but she knew that they were still alive; otherwise, her allowance would have stopped by now. Since she saw them so rarely, she had only a faint impression of them when she pictured their faces: an attractive, smiling couple in their late thirties, despite the two of them being much older now. Both were tall and blond, though her mother's hair was curly and ashy compared to her father's. They seemed more like models in a department store catalogue than real people, and for much of her childhood, she'd assumed that the pictures of them adorning the walls of the apartment had been the ones that had come with the frames. The only indication of time passing was her mother's fading beauty juxtaposed with her father's baby face. After a few years, the family stopped bothering to update the photographs.

It may have been the late hour, or she may have become lost in her thoughts about school, but she didn't notice the dark man slink up behind her as she exited the subway station. She felt the knife in her back and heard a greasy voice in her ear: "Give me the money." Her heartbeat exploded as the knife tip pierced her shirt, and blood drops formed on her back. She froze, which didn't help the situation, as she held steadfastly to the gym bag that was slung over her shoulder. She didn't know why she didn't cooperate; the bag had nothing valuable in it, save for her phone and a few dollars, and she had been instructed countless times to surrender her belongings and report the theft to the police afterward.

"Give it!" the man demanded, but her paralysis held, and a struggle ensued. It was as if she'd lost control of her body, which stubbornly clung to the bag, and then the man decided that he would end the scuffle easily. She saw the blade—thin, dirty, and three inches long—grasped firmly in his meaty hand as it penetrated her side, and then the world disappeared.

Pain didn't feel the way she'd anticipated it would: sharp or numb and seeing only red and black across her vision. Instead of seeing those colors, she saw a network of impulses—the spark of combustion in the passing car engines, the incandescent glow of the streetlamps, and the electric snap of a failing outlet—and felt fire. She reached toward the burning filament in the lamp above them and brought it down onto them. The dark man disappeared in a flash of orange that was brighter than a bonfire, and her vision returned to normal. It was only when she saw the smoking heap at her feet and the weak flesh still clasped in her hands that she realized that there had been two sets of screams. His had ceased, receding into pain-filled moans, but hers continued. Then the ground came rushing up to meet her, and the cement eagerly provided her with a pillow.

Pierce Starr hacked into the flesh expertly, splitting the cartilage from the bone and separating the limb from the rest of the body. He had always hated this part of butchering; even with the blood drained and the organs removed, splash was still likely to occur, and there was only so much a plastic tarp could do to protect the surrounding surfaces. Later, he would spot clean the offending drops of blood or hunks of flesh with bleach and industrial cleaner, but there was always a chance that he could miss something, and he hated disposing of his clothes unnecessarily. Unfortunately, that was part of the deal: He and his wife, Madeleine, would kill the animal; he would clean and prepare it for storage; and she would cook it. She had gotten very good at dealing with the beast's flesh and had become adventurous with preparation, substituting normal meat with that of the animal, and he had become very fond of her newest recipe for roast, which incorporated apples and peaches.

Separating the fat and bone from the flesh was much easier. He enjoyed slicing beasts into the appropriate cuts and had studied butchering techniques especially for this purpose. Not all of his cuts corresponded perfectly with the traditional charts, but he liked the variety in tastes and tenderness that the creatures provided. While the methods that he and his wife employed necessitated the most vulnerable and sometimes sickly targets, he relished the idea of slaying a fit or well-muscled animal. Those tended to eat the healthiest, and this was reflected in the quality of their meat. Unfortunately, beggars could not be choosers, and he would rather be careful and fed than be bold and caught.

His wife appeared at the door quietly as he sliced their latest kill into pieces. She crossed her arms and wore concern on her face. She had been a real beauty once—trim and healthy with a heart-shaped face and hair that fell in soft, golden ringlets. Her nose didn't quite suit her face—it was too aquiline— and he had discovered over time that the gold came from a bottle and that her hair was naturally more ashen. But she had captured his heart with her morbid humor, she shared his interest in astronomy, and most importantly, they had the same taste in exotic foods. Her introduction to his favorite food had been their most intimate moment and had led to many more.

Regrettably, the comfort they felt around one another had nearly led to disaster. Until Orion was six, they had captured, slain, and butchered beasts in their home, but one fateful night, an animal escaped and fled into Orion's path. The creature's futile bleating roused Orion from his slumber, and he tumbled from his bed to investigate, inadvertently setting up a pending collision. The sight of the small child in his pajamas halted the creature in its tracks, and Orion naively tried to comfort it. This feisty beast was slowly bleeding out instead of having a swift death because its unnecessary struggle had prevented Pierce from inflicting the proper killing blows. The animal embraced Orion, perhaps making an attempt to carry him off in its panic to escape, but it was too wounded. Madeleine scooped up their frantic son to soothe him, and Pierce was able to finish off the beast without further incident. They cleaned up the gore once their son had fallen asleep and prepared to confront him the next morning with the truth of their habit, but he seemed to have no memory of the previous night's events. Nevertheless, it was decided that their exotic appetite needed to be curbed. Live animals were never again allowed inside the house, and after a few years of diligent work, they were able to secure a job at an observatory in Mason, which allowed them to resume their habit without the fear of being discovered.

In fact, Madeleine was supposed to be adjusting the telescope and making calculations while he did the butchering. He noticed her troubled expression, put down his tools, and removed his mask. "What's the matter, Maddie?"

"Cassie's in the hospital," Madeleine answered. "Ryan is with her, but the police want us down there as soon as possible." When Madeleine spoke, it was with a distinct detachment. Pierce had learned early on that Madeleine had been abused as a child and that subsequent caretakers had remained distant. Consequently, she had developed an unsentimental personality, which complemented Pierce's cultivated aloofness. He had acquired his exotic taste from a mysterious mentor who had shown him that it was the way to immortality. While Pierce was fifty-five years old, he appeared to be casually navigating his mid-twenties at most; in fact, generous observers often thought him to be in his late teens. Conversely, despite following the same diet faithfully alongside him, his wife found that it only retarded rather than stilled her aging. They would need to eventually part company, and he had always planned to lay the blame for their crimes at her feet. It was a partnership—a beautiful partnership that he would miss—but it was not meant to be a long-lasting one, and the unspoken distance at which they kept one another would allow him to execute his eventual escape plan without remorse.

Pierce glanced at the carcass on the tarp at his feet. "We won't be able to travel tonight. I'm halfway done with this, and I still need to store it. Plus we have to monitor the telescope. I'm not going to abandon that experiment for some fleeting family issue."

"I've already contacted Dr. Harper. He'll head up from the university in a few hours," she replied. "He'll cover us for as long as we need, but he needs to contact the administration to cancel his classes tomorrow."

He sighed in disgust; if he didn't finish his butchering, it would be a waste of perfectly good meat, and this would mean that they had risked discovery for nothing. However, he could hear his wife's unspoken reasoning. They had stayed below the radar by acting like a normal, loving couple, even if a bit absorbed in their work, and to stay in Mason now might draw suspicion. Any attention from the authorities, no matter how minute, was an unnecessary risk compared to any they took when hunting. He replaced his mask and relented. "Then help me dispose of this. We can't use the normal sites when we have this much meat left intact."

She nodded and started pulling her hair up into a ponytail. "How about that little alcove by the dam? The bears haven't gone into hibernation quite yet," she suggested as she pulled on a hairnet and tucked the last bit of ashen curls beneath the hem. She loved her long hair, even if it was a liability, but she was meticulous about controlling it. She tucked her trouser legs into her shoes and tightened any loose clothing before pulling on a pair of latex gloves.

He shook his head. "The rangers started patrolling more up there since the bear attack last year," he replied as he carefully stacked the meat into a pile. He would transfer it to a new tarp and wrap it in a bundle in a moment. He was mentally retracing his steps, trying to erase any possible evidence that might escape them, as he reviewed his memory for an appropriate dump site. "I think I saw a funeral in Bristol as we were driving up here. We might be able to dump the bones there if the soil is still loose. I might be able to salvage some meat first."

She smiled. "Try not to worry too much, dear. We'll be back up by next week, and we'll get another one," she assured him. She picked up a bundle of clothes and artifacts that had come from the beast. "I'll put these in the furnace and be right back to help you finish."

It was easy for her to tell him not to worry when the effects had clearly not worked for her, but if he didn't consume the creature at regular intervals, he was certain that he would start aging again. It was what his mentor had warned him about, and after seeing the results of consumption, he never questioned his mentor's advice. But though Madeleine's words frustrated him, they did not anger him, and he focused on the task at hand. He could never afford to become careless.

- - -

Orion's phone startled him when it rang as he left class. Hardly anyone ever called him, and he usually forgot to switch the phone to vibrate due to its lack of use. He wore an amused expression as he answered it because he didn't recognize the number and expected his sister to make an unreasonable after-hours request from a borrowed phone. But his face fell when it registered to him that it was the police station calling to inform him that his sister was in the emergency room and needed to be picked up. As his parents were three hours out of town, he was the nearest responsible agent who could assume custody of her.

The emergency room was a harrowing experience. First, because he looked like a crazed druggie due to his unkempt and gaunt appearance, he couldn't convince the night nurse that he had the right to be there. Then, when he finally obtained a room number from his sister, it was for an ICU patient who was recovering from twenty-seven stab wounds. Cassie's injuries were less severe: Between the gash in her side and the laceration from cracking her head on the pavement, she'd received twelve stitches. She also had some minor cuts and bruises, and the doctor stated that she was very fortunate that the fire had not harmed her as well; in fact, it hadn't even singed the hairs on her arms.

The policeman who had been stationed outside Cassie's room had a few words to exchange with Orion. Cassie had already given her statement: She'd been walking home from the subway station when a mugger had pulled a knife on her, and they'd struggled for a bit, resulting in her side being pierced, before the streetlamp had exploded and somehow set the mugger on fire. He was in intensive care with burns over eighty percent of his body and was not expected to last the night. A thorough investigation would be launched, and although the cop didn't say it, Orion inferred that Cassie would be interviewed further. After all, "No one lights up like that without some kind of accelerant," the cop asserted. However, he seemed particularly concerned about Cassie: why she was traveling home alone so late and why their parents were not present at the hospital. Orion explained their home situation as best he could, trying to put the cop's mind at ease, and he promised to look after his little sister. While the cop did not seem entirely convinced by his explanation, he was appeased and left, allowing Orion to finally see Cassie.

"Hey, Pickle," he greeted, using a nickname from their childhood. She had been a smart child, speaking early and expanding her vocabulary, but as soon as she had learned the word "pickle," she'd developed a fascination with it and had communicated using only that word. She spoke it in different intonations, as if it were different words, and responded only to "Pickle." So, for three months, she was "Pickle," and the name stuck.

Cassie smiled weakly, showing her naked emotions rather than her usual veneer of teenage arrogance. She was pale, despite the heavy makeup she wore, and there were dark lines beneath her eyes from where the mascara and eye shadow had run before being wiped off with a tissue. There was also a patch of clean skin on her forehead where she had been prepped for surgery, and a bandage now covered her stitches. She was wearing a borrowed set of clothes, which was most likely because hers had been ripped. She looked terrible, especially under the harsh hospital lights, but her expression turned to relief once she saw him. "Hey," she reciprocated, still shaken.

"How are you feeling?" he asked. He took a seat by her bedside. She chewed her lower lip and glanced out the door, looking for her escort. "They're gone," he assured her.

"I did something bad," she confessed ruefully. "I didn't *mean* to, but he had a hold of me, and I panicked. I… I don't know what happened." Tears started to flow down her cheeks, renewing the dark circles and tracing new lines through the foundation and blush. He took her into his arms, as he had done many times before. She was trembling, and he held her tighter as she buried her face into his chest, producing an expanding wet spot in its center. When they were little and she would awake from a nightmare, she would rouse him by crawling into his bed, and he would comfort her in this manner. But as they'd grown older, they'd also grown apart; he'd become more responsible, and she'd discovered rebellion.

The last time he had held her had been three years ago, shortly after her thirteenth birthday. He'd known that she would be offered drugs and that she would experiment, so he'd chosen to allow her to do so in an environment he could control—their apartment—with him present. One afternoon, he'd bought a dime bag of weed, locked the doors, and taught her the fine art of rolling a blunt. She'd been far from believing he was the coolest older brother ever—this was when he'd first begun to mature and become the man of the house—but she'd still respected him. Unfortunately, the experiment had ended unexpectedly when the blunt had neared her lips and had immediately gone up in flames, temporarily blinding her. They'd decided to try again, but the second time, his lighter had exploded as soon as he'd snapped the flint wheel. The tiny explosion had singed Orion while leaving Cassie unscathed, but her animal mind had nonetheless felt threatened. Before he'd been able to react, she'd reached toward the nascent flame and manipulated it subconsciously, shaping and stretching it until it became a flash fire that scorched every surface in the room.

That was when they'd realized that she had a gift. Knowing that his parents would never understand, and because her powers had scared her, Orion had forbade her from using them again. This was one of the few edicts of his that she'd willingly followed. After this incident, she'd thrown herself into being "normal": the popular cheerleader who all the guys wanted and all the girls wanted to be. It was also when she'd turned her back on him.

"It's okay. You were scared," he comforted her, stroking her hair.

"I think I killed him."

There was nothing he could say. The mugger might survive, but his concern was for his vulnerable baby sister, who feared herself. Her gift was unique; it wasn't as if he could hire a tutor for her. "We'll get you help," he promised.

"From who? It's not like it's a medical condition, Orion," she retorted, pushing him away, and she reclined on the bed again, separating herself from him. "Can we leave?" she asked, all vulnerability squelched in favor of sullen resentment; it was as if she were suddenly embarrassed to have lowered her defenses. "I don't think they said I'd have to stay overnight."

Orion sighed and nodded, tolerating her usual aloofness uncomplainingly. "Yeah. I'll find a nurse and see about getting you out of here." He patted her leg gently as he rose to leave the room. He hunched his shoulders, lowering his head as he reflected on the surfeit responsibilities he bore at his young age. He shouldn't have to deal with things like this as a college student—not until he got married and had children of his own.

"Ryan?" he heard a small voice whisper and turned around immediately.

"Yeah?" he responded. His sister studied her hands as she fiddled with the flimsy blanket that was draped over her. She seemed to want to say something, but her eyes were distant, and after a long moment of silence, she just shook her head. He hesitated before attempting to leave again, and when she made no move or sound, he left for the nurse's station. Cassie was released within the hour.

He did not own a car, so they needed to take public transport. Since taking the subway had caused the incident, he believed taking a cab would be the more sensitive course of action, and though the friendly cabbie tried to make conversation with his passengers, he was met with stony silence. Cassie stared out the window, completely withdrawn; she ignored Orion's further attempts to comfort her, leaving him to simply stare into the distance and retreat into his own thoughts. When they arrived in SoHo, she didn't even wait until he paid the fare; she simply ran up the stairs and into their apartment. He paid the driver and then followed his sister, but once he discovered that she had locked herself in her room, he gave up on trying to communicate with her any further that night.

His emotions and thoughts were too active to allow him to rest, and he didn't think he could concentrate on his homework. He threw his backpack into the space beneath the bar and crossed into the kitchen. If he couldn't sleep, he could at least still be useful and prepare food for the next day. It had been a late night, and he doubted either one of them would be cognizant enough to fix breakfast or lunch the next morning.

He retrieved fruit, carrots, and jelly from the refrigerator and peanut butter, bags, and a knife from the cupboard. He also grabbed a cutting board from the counter and placed the assembled ingredients next to it. He doubted Cassie would want a simple sandwich or vegetables, especially since they were healthy and good for her, but it was the thought that counted. Likewise, he doubted she would eat the fruit for breakfast, and he doubted he'd want strawberries in the morning either. Maybe all the food would end up in the trash can. Still, he started slicing the fruit as he considered cleaning the apartment to drown out his thoughts.

He knew better than Cassie that there was no help for her. After the first incident, he had taken to the Internet, registering on various forums to ask questions when he couldn't find information, and he'd even utilized New York City's finest libraries to do some old-fashioned research. He had come across mention of "Others"—people with extraordinary, sometimes supernatural abilities—but the only thing he'd discovered was that they were dangerous. Ancient texts matter-of-factly reported that Others self-destructed when they used their powers, often taking numerous innocents with them and mostly on their first attempt at control. In the ancient world, they were as feared as comets, which were thought to be the portents of evil, and they were seen as cursed by the gods.

Modern texts were less sensational, but they were no more educational. A speculative report on one of these Others unhappily reminded Orion of Cassie's experience with the mugger and how the incident could have gone: The Dyatlov Pass Incident was well known in paranormal circles as a mysterious event in which ten people appeared to have been killed by a supernatural force in the taiga. Most of the victims clearly fled unprepared and even barefoot into freezing conditions, driven away from their mountaineering equipment by fear, and were subsequently killed by exposure. A handful of their bodies bore signs of intense trauma, including severe skull and chest fractures, and one person was missing her eyes and tongue, but the murder instrument was never found, and the case remained unsolved. However, those who were researching Others later discovered a testimony from a lost hiker who was found in the same general area with minimal gear despite ambient temperatures being below zero. Direct interviews with her were pointless; her mind was gone. Nonetheless, the authorities managed to piece together enough from her babbling to write an official report and file it away to be forgotten. When experts on Others uncovered the report, they hypothesized that her testimony contained the missing pieces of the Dyatlov Pass Incident and explained the force that had killed the party: the lost woman, a probable cryokinetic. She had been a last-minute addition to the official party who had later become embroiled in an argument that had led to an icy confrontation with one of the women during their final night at camp. When one of the men had tried to intervene, things had escalated until the rest of the party had fled or had been killed. Panicked by the night's events, the woman had fled into the wilderness alone.

The Dyatlov Pass Incident appeared to be the norm with Others, which provoked researchers to recommend that they all be destroyed. A minority suggested that they could be trained and turned into weapons, but most saw this action as a dangerous gambit. The only hope Orion had found had been in the fleeting mentions of a group called SION, whose name echoed a rumored shadow agency called the Bureau of Special Interests (BSI), whose purpose was to exterminate Others. While the latter agency existed, its official website shed no light on its true purpose, so Orion had been unable to independently verify the sinister charge against it. In contrast, SION had been linked to terrorist activity, including purportedly causing the 2010 Deepwater Horizon oil spill by sabotaging and setting fire to the pipes. Circulated SION pamphlets insisted that the organization's cell in the area had felt pressured, that the incident was only a show of force, and that the Others should be left to live in peace. Considering the extent of economic and environmental damage to the area, the terrorism charge against SION was not implausible, and it was not the only time that the Network was associated with a widespread disaster.

Orion could not get Cassie help from characters such as these. The BSI might execute her if it caught her, and SION would indoctrinate her into its terrorist cell. He needed to find a suitable teacher for her outside of those channels, but locating an unaffiliated mentor would be difficult.

A sharp pain brought his mind back to the present and what he had been doing. Fresh blood gushed from deep wounds that he had cut into his thumb and forefinger; he figured that the gash was at least one inch deep, and he was aggravated that he had been so careless. He set the knife down and pinched the skin together, ignoring the blood spilling out and flowing over his clean hand. Instead, he closed his eyes and imagined the severed edges reaching out to each other, pulling themselves closer, and knitting together flesh, muscles, and blood vessels alike. He wiped the wasted blood away to inspect his handiwork. With a small amount of satisfaction, he began to repair the second cut. The damaged skin healed and showed no residual signs of injury, which meant that his skills were improving.

He had known of his power since they had discovered Cassie's. He estimated that she'd given him the equivalent of a second-degree sunburn all over his exposed skin. The skin that had been covered by his clothes had been only tender and dry, but the skin of the hand that had held the lighter had peeled away to reveal the layer of fat beneath it. However, he had also discovered his own reflexes: His skin had accelerated its recovery and had become pink and new within minutes, though it had also needed to be moisturized. Like Cassie, he had never used his powers for fear of losing control. He couldn't imagine what that might mean, what losing control could do, but he'd been unwilling to risk hurting Cassie, and it had instead become a secret that they shared.

He shook his head. If his thoughts were not on his actions, then he would only hurt himself if he kept using the knife. He didn't hear any movement upstairs, so it was possible that Cassie had actually gone to sleep, and this meant cleaning the kitchen might wake her. He placed the sullied cutting board and knife in the sink and the unfinished lunches in the refrigerator; he could wake up early and finish those tomorrow. His attention might be better served if he turned it to his homework, of which he had plenty. With a hefty sigh, he headed upstairs, pausing briefly at his sister's door to listen for any sound before continuing to his room.

- - -

Cassie was mortified. She lay awake in the center of her bed, sheets tangled around her legs, and stared at the ceiling. She hadn't bothered to undress, simply tossing her bag in the corner before throwing herself on the mattress.

She had never asked for her abilities. She had developed a fear of lighters and open flames since the incident with her brother and avoided anything she thought might catch fire. Perhaps it was the lingering remnants from a nightmare, but she could still see the world in fuel sources. She felt every pilot light in the building and knew every burning lamp. Her neighbors had even lit candles for a romantic evening and had allowed them to burn down to their bases. She felt their flames dying, and she knew that if she reached out, she could coax a real blaze from them. The urge to touch their heat was intense; yet, she was terrified that something bad would happen again… that she would lose control and cause the whole building to go up in an inferno.

Her brother didn't know, and she rarely admitted it to herself, but her curiosity would sometimes take hold of her, and she experimented with stretching the limits of her ability and control. These brief bouts of inquisitiveness rarely lasted long before fear set in. She would manipulate sparks and flames for hours, sometimes days, and had even once passed a week in obsession over her abilities. She had learned how to influence a fire and convince it to expand beyond the normal limitations imposed by fuel and oxygen. She could bend flames at will, but the effect never lasted; memories of the flash fire and her brother's crisp skin would resurface, and fear would consume her. Those images would now be complemented by that of the mugger: his surprise, anger, terror, and anguish. The smell of burning flesh was still in her nostrils, and the sounds of fat popping under heat resonated in her ears. She didn't even know humans could burn like that.

The flash fire had ruined her relationship with her brother. She had discovered that she was different, had nearly lost her brother, and had learned that he was also a freak all in the same afternoon. Her newfound abilities were one thing, but watching her brother heal the burns across his skin begged so many questions. If he could heal so quickly, what were his limits? Was he even human? If he wasn't human, was *she*?

She finally looked at the clock and saw that it was after two in the morning. She thought they had returned to the apartment around midnight, so it was likely that she had dozed a little. She hoped that this was indeed the case, as it would mean that she'd have gotten some rest for the following day. Her mind was buzzing, and she doubted she would return to slumber. Frustrated, she rose and turned on her computer.

During one of her experimental phases, Cassie had stumbled upon the Outcast Support Network, a candid source of information, where she'd discovered that there were more people like her who exhibited a variety of special abilities. The site had provided her with tips on how to cope with her talents, whether she chose to develop or hide them, and there had been a forum where she had been able to pose her own questions. In the latter area, she'd come across a wealth of evidence regarding a concealed war between two sides. Neither party had been named explicitly, and she'd quickly learned that anyone requesting or mentioning that information would be banned, but she'd come to realize that one side was, without a doubt, the government. While the common consensus was that the government abducted Others, there was debate over what happened to them. Supporters of the government believed that they were trained on how to use their powers, while naysayers believed that they were simply "disappeared." Regardless, the missing Others never seemed to reappear.

Cassie had soon decided not to participate in any discussions, especially since she'd never gleaned any valuable information about the sides; it had been more opinion and conjecture than facts. However, she'd still advanced her knowledge about her abilities, and she had also connected with a confidant named Sone. Although he had been unable to teach her directly and had refused to meet with her in person, she had felt comfortable speaking to him about her condition. He'd refrained from using any modern messengers or texting devices, including email, so she'd been able to contact him solely through the site. Since he was not online at the moment, she decided to compose a private message, in which she laid bare her feelings about the night's events. She feared that the mugger's image would haunt her and further undermine her rudimentary control, but she was also proud that she had employed enough discipline to defend herself without causing collateral damage to the area. She expressed concern that her reflexive action had created such a powerful response beyond the limits she'd previously been capable of. She knew that Sone would be impressed with her improved proficiency, even if he'd be a bit callous about the man's death, and would give her guidance on how to improve.

- - -

Amanda Darling-Whitcomb sat in a secluded section of the restaurant. Her vantage point not only allowed her a decent view of the city below but also enabled her to see no fewer than three television screens, all of which were tuned to different news stations. It was her habit to keep apprised of world events, especially anything that might pertain to New York City, and she often kept one station tuned to the stock exchange. It was a prudent decision for the mayor, and remaining knowledgeable about world events, developing situations, and the like would help in her bid for senator the following year.

She was not an unusual ornament in the restaurant as she enjoyed her coffee and breakfast while her staff prepared for the day. She would often dine with someone of importance, be it a fellow policy maker, a businessman, or someone else of influence, but it wasn't extraordinary to see her dining alone. She used those days to take an extra hour or two to rejuvenate herself so she could be the best she could be.

Amanda was not simply charismatic; she was special—and not just because she was born into the influential Connecticut Darlings. She had been bred to have no ambitions of her own; she was simply to marry, bear wealthy children, support her future husband's career, and continue the Darling dynasty, even if it was under another Connecticut family's name. She had obeyed these tenets for most of her adult life, meeting and marrying Johnathan Whitcomb in college and moving to New York City to support his bid for political office. Upon the birth of their first child, she immediately reported to the gym to lose weight and become flawless again, as was expected of a well-bred trophy wife.

However, fate had other plans in store for her: Around her fifth mile on the treadmill, Amanda became overwhelmed with conflicting and powerful emotions and fainted. At first, she thought she had simply overdone it after her antenatal hiatus, but as the gym staff fussed over her, she came to realize that the potent sensations she felt were coming from around her and were not a result of postnatal hormones. The subsequent weeks were equally intense, as the rest of her abilities stirred from their long dormancy. Strangers' emotional states assaulted her until she learned to filter out and diminish the flood of new information that she perceived around her. She also discovered that she could manipulate her pheromones, however slightly, and with practice, she used her newfound abilities in concert to influence the will of others. Her excellence as a wife increased to perfection as she supported and eventually began driving her husband's career from mayor to senator and, subsequently, the prime contender for running mate to the Democratic Party's presidential candidate.

Then, it came crashing down abruptly. Johnathan was mysteriously assassinated before his selection as Vice President was officially announced. The culprit fled and was killed in a violent shootout with the police. His confiscated diaries revealed a dangerously unhinged mind but offered no motive for going after the Connecticut mayor. Public sympathy was at an all-time high for the newly widowed Amanda, who reclaimed the American blue blood of her maiden name by hyphenation, and she rode the wave of empathy to the New York mayoral office. While it was a few steps down from where her husband had been, she knew how to build a power base in her own name, and in a few years, the former beauty queen could skip all the interim stepping-stones and make a run for the presidency herself.

This morning, she dined with Jack Everest, a lawyer from the prominent Milton, Chadwick, and Waters. He was not an especially tall man, and he had a slight build to match. He had boyish features with a mop of bright blond hair and piercing blue eyes, and she couldn't quite place his light English accent, which, combined with his looks, made him quite charming. Despite his charisma and popularity with those he met, she knew that he had a sinister side that belied his seemingly young age of thirty. He knew how to mine information and piece it together to construct a picture that no one else could see. He had somehow known that she would need his assistance, even before she had recognized the need herself, and he had approached her like a concerned friend or, in retrospect, more like an agent of the Devil. While she had been young and foolish to take his offer and was now in his debt, an older, wiser Amanda still considered his solution to have been the most elegant. The old Amanda would never have come up with the plan on her own, leaving her to suffer the humiliation quietly, and in the unlikely event that she had acted on her own, she would not have had the resources to conceal the crime. Jack Everest had optimized the best possible outcome for her.

He had also taught her how to become ruthless, which had helped her nascent ambition and political career. Unfortunately, his assistance had not been altruistic; it turned out that he was only an associate one makes out of necessity. She had no leverage against him and quickly learned that he was mysteriously immune to her pheromones. He was secretive, and even the numerous private investigators she'd hired had failed to ferret out any information other than what was known to the public. Yet, he continued to exploit information about her that was hard to collect. They had formed an unstable alliance over the years—uncertain for her and indiscernibly beneficial to him. This was why they were sitting together now.

For the first thirty minutes that they were together, Jack sipped his tea like a gentleman and made polite, easy conversation about topics ranging from the weather to her recent political victories. As one of her staunchest supporters, he had convinced Milton, Chadwick, and Waters, of which he was a partner, to make donations to her campaign; it was in this way that he was also an ally. He nibbled idly on the snacks accompanying their tea, speaking as eloquently as she imagined he did in court in front of the jurors. When he emptied his cup, he set it and the saucer down gently on the table, wiped his mouth with the cloth napkin, and set it beside the saucer. He had not eaten much, neither of the breakfast nor the biscuits that had come with the tea. Though he leaned against the back of his chair and draped his arms casually over its sides, he was anything but relaxed as his expression darkened and his handsome brow furrowed. "Now that we've completed the pleasantries, I think it's time we get down to the business of the day, Ms. Whitcomb," he began in an affable voice, but Amanda instinctually placed herself on edge. Despite nothing being overtly menacing about Jack's demeanor, an impalpable shift in the air caused her to recoil whenever he dropped his urbane pretext. She felt a tiny twinge of fear creep up on her, pinpricking her skin and causing the hairs on the back of her neck to stand at attention. She could never articulate what caused her apprehensive reaction, so she often chose to ignore it. What she could not ignore, however, was the loathing she felt when he made plain her subservient position, as he often did during these meetings, and she had to chastise herself since she tolerated his surreptitious torment during their frequent public encounters. A private conversation was no different, no matter how humiliated she might feel.

She nodded in response. "If you like, Mr. Everest, but I cannot tarry for more than a few more moments. I'm afraid I must leave shortly for the office, as I have a meeting with the City Authority." She kept her tone indifferent, despite the surge of emotions she felt boiling inside; it was a beneficial skill that she'd developed as a politician. "Perhaps it would be better to postpone?" she suggested hopefully.

"Unfortunately, this matter cannot wait, but I shall not keep you long," he replied politely. He shifted, steepling his fingers as he set his elbows on the armrests, and continued. "Do you remember what I told you when I first came to you?" he asked, adopting the reproachful tone of a disappointed teacher.

He must have been watching her for months, though she'd never figured out why—perhaps he'd had a vendetta against her husband, Johnathan, or the Whitcomb family—because he'd appeared within hours of her discovery of Johnathan's infidelity. In this way, he had been like a fairy godmother, and it had not taken him much effort to gain her confidence and trust during this vulnerable time. He'd then planted the seeds of ambition in her heart: Why would a woman with powers like hers waste herself with a selfish cad who was foolishly endangering his political career for a few moments of pleasure? It would be more fitting for her to seize her destiny and thrust herself into the political limelight. She could go far, utilizing her natural and supernatural abilities, which he would teach her to use with greater finesse. Most of Johnathan's political connections had originally been made by her, and it would take only a few words to convince his supporters to transfer alliances. Jack Everest had presented her with the perfect plan that would preserve the momentum of the Whitcomb political machine while transferring it to herself, and thanks to his brief tutelage, she had been able to dispose of her adulterous husband and his lover without drawing any suspicion or allowing the two deaths to be connected.

He did not give her a chance to answer, instead making his question rhetorical as he continued his reprimand. "I said that if you came across anyone like you, I had only two requests: that they be kept from public record and that you report their existence to me immediately." It had been a seemingly innocuous request and the primary payment of her debt to him, but as she'd grown to know him, she'd begun to wonder whether there was something more sinister to the arrangement than she'd originally understood. "In all the years that I have known you, you have never mentioned a single Other, and I thought that perhaps it was simply due to circumstances that I never received a report of them. But this morning, I was greeted with this." He reached for his briefcase and pulled out a single page of a police report. It detailed an incident that had occurred near midnight in which a mugger had apparently burst into flames while assaulting his victim. Jack pointed to a specific line that stated that there had been no ignition source and that no accelerants had been used. This deficit had mystified the detective on duty, as the mugger had been hospitalized with third-degree burns and was not expected to make a recovery due to the extensive injuries he'd sustained.

Amanda frowned prettily. She had been taught during her youth that ladies should always smile and that if she could not, she should at least concoct a pretty frown to enable her to keep a man. Men abandoned ugly women, and the only way to succeed was to be attractive. "What's this?"

"If you read between the lines, this Starr is clearly an Other," he explained with displeasure, "which means you failed to fulfill both of my requests. Since I have knowledge of her existence, I have clearly already completed one portion of your debt, and I expect you to rectify the situation with the authorities before someone else discovers her existence."

"How do you propose I do that?" she asked pleasantly, swallowing her critical tone reflexively; there were few times she could afford to express her emotions freely. Then, with an apologetic smile approaching a smirk, she added, "I think you overestimate my sphere of influence." Privately, she doubted it would take much effort to pull Starr's file from city records and have the detective put on disciplinary leave for his "faulty police work"; all that this would require was a simple call from the mayor's office to the chief of police. But abuses of power were always eventually found out, and she had her own plans and ambitions to secure. She wouldn't risk her position or reputation unnecessarily.

Jack scowled, his eyes cold, and his voice became low and intense, losing some of its polish. "Never mistake me for a pigeon, Ms. Whitcomb," he growled, his accent also becoming coarse. "Take care of the situation, or the police may discover new evidence in your husband's case—not enough to make you, but enough to cast suspicion in your direction and cost you next year's nomination for senator."

Loathing rose like bile in her throat, overpowering the subtle fear he inspired; he'd almost made it through one of their private discussions without resorting to coercion. She could not muster the strength to swallow her emotions this time, but she was able to school her expression into a terse nod and convey her reluctant acquiescence.

A cocky but handsome smile reappeared on his thin lips. "Brilliant. I expect to hear from you soon then." He looked at his watch casually. "I have an appointment as well, so I won't keep you any longer, Ms. Whitcomb." He snapped his briefcase shut, leaving the report to chasten her, and bid her a final jovial farewell before departing. Despite being relieved of her tormenter, Amanda's emotional state didn't improve immediately, and she decided that she needed to compose herself over her remaining coffee before heading back to the office.

- - -

Orion woke with a start, and it took a moment for his sleep-clouded mind to register what was going on. At first, he thought he was late for school, but then he remembered that he had taken the day off to take care of Cassie and allow her to recover. He stretched the knots from his lanky body and yawned as he reluctantly got out of bed and headed to the bathroom. Bleary-eyed, he examined his reflection in the mirror as he brushed his teeth, and he decided that a comb would not do much good today; the humidity was too high. He also didn't feel like shaving, and it wasn't as if his facial hair grew at an enormous speed. The combination of his youth and his blond hair, which was frustratingly lighter than that on his head, meant that no one could tell if he was growing a beard or had simply forgotten to shave that morning.

He pulled his shirt on as he descended the stairs to start making breakfast for his sister, but he soon discovered that she was already in the kitchen, dressed and eating cereal at the bar. She smiled and greeted him cheerfully. "What are you doing up so early?" he asked, puzzled; his brain was still trying to clear the cobwebs and rouse itself. Typically, the roles would have been reversed, as he was the early riser, and she usually had to be dragged from bed. On weekends, she rarely rose before noon, and it was only after a cup of coffee that she could have a civilized conversation.

"School," she replied simply. "It's past seven. I thought you might have left already or something." She rinsed out her bowl and placed it in the dishwasher.

Cassie's incongruous exuberance was certainly making it harder for his foggy brain to wake up; she was acting like his evil sister's good twin. He rubbed his eye and stifled another yawn. "No. I thought after last night, we could both take a break. I was going to let you sleep in while I made breakfast, but I guess I missed that." He sat next to her on the island.

She shrugged. "That's okay. I feel fine anyway."

He shook his head. "I still think you should stay home. You couldn't have gotten much sleep. I know I didn't."

"I've got an English test today I need to cram for," she replied, and he scowled at her immediately; she never studied and avoided mentioning tests because she knew he'd ask to see the results. "Cassie, what's wrong?" he asked seriously.

"Nothing's wrong. I just have stuff I need to do at school," she replied evasively as she rose and started heading toward the living room. "I've got to go, or I'll be late."

He stood and grabbed her arm. "Mom and Dad are coming down," he told her, and she reacted with expected distaste. Softly but firmly, as they were her parents and she had to see them, he added, "I think you can stay home today."

"Like they really care," she sneered. "If they do, they can come pick me up from school." She hoisted her gym bag onto her shoulder and began to storm out. As he trailed behind her, a stern reprimand on the tip of his tongue, the doorbell rang. He knew it couldn't be their parents since they had a key, but he nevertheless hoped it would be. The presence of their parents might actually do some good for his sister; she believed that they didn't love her, but if they arrived now, this would demonstrate that they'd driven through the night to see her. Cassie rolled her eyes, put her bag back on the chair reluctantly, and waited; she anticipated that it was probably the police doing a follow-up.

With a quick glance, Orion verified that he was properly dressed, and then he answered the door. There was a man in a suit, which appeared a little threadbare, and he wore a cleaner, newer shirt underneath with a black paisley tie knotted loosely around his neck. He had dark hair, which, like Orion's, did not react well to humidity, and he appeared to have made a cursory attempt to tame it with gel. The man nodded sharply. "Good morning. Is this the Starr residence?" he asked, revealing a barely identifiable British accent.

"Yes. How can I help you?" Something about his demeanor made Orion think he wasn't from the police department even though he wore plainclothes like a detective. While he had a worldliness about him, it didn't have the metropolitan flavor New York City cops carried with them.

"I'm Special Agent Connor," he said, briefly flashing a federal badge. "I'm here to see Cassiopeia." He smirked drolly. Some caught the pun their parents had saddled Cassie with, but others were simply confused by the length or pronunciation of her real name. "Your parents have a real interesting sense of humor, assuming you're Orion." He nodded into the apartment. "May I come in?"

"Um… sure," Orion replied, opening the door wider to allow the man access.

The agent sauntered in, taking a look around the apartment. The foyer opened into a wide shared area that encompassed an open kitchen, bar, and the living room. A set of carpeted stairs toward the back led to the second level of their home, and Orion knew most visitors to SoHo underestimated the interior size of the converted warehouse apartments. The agent whistled appreciatively and muttered, "Nice place." He laid eyes on Cassie and offered his hand. "Are you Cassiopeia?" She nodded but made no move to accept his handshake. He turned back to Orion. "Do you have somewhere we can sit and chat?"

"Why? Who are you?" Cassie asked, dropping her façade of cheerfulness. It was probably too early in the morning to remind her of the events of last night.

"Cassie," Orion scolded.

"It's alright," the agent replied. He turned to her and said, "I'm from the BSI. I'm here to talk to you about what happened."

"What's the BSI?" she demanded.

"The Bureau of Special Interests. We investigate incidents like what happened last night," the agent replied calmly. Gesturing toward the living room, he requested authoritatively, "Can we take a seat?"

Orion suddenly felt uneasy about having let this man into their home; he didn't think the agency would have found her from a simple police report. "Um, Cassie and I have to head to school."

"This will only take a few minutes," he insisted. Orion went into the living room obediently, wrapping his arm around Cassie's shoulders as they walked together. He sat next to her on the couch while the agent took a seat in the recliner across from them. He took out a small notepad, studied it for a moment, and then began. "I have the police report right here, but why don't you tell me what happened in your own words? I'd like you to clarify some things for me." As he spoke, he removed a small, shiny object from his pocket and fidgeted absently with it. It caught the light once, reflecting its silvery brilliance into Orion's eyes, and he realized that the object was a Zippo lighter. The agent continued to fiddle with the device, threading it through the fingers of his free hand like a coin as he took down Cassie's words. He seemed oblivious to the reaction he was provoking in her. Cassie clutched her pant legs, tightening her grip until her knuckles turned white, as she slowly recounted the events of the previous night. She didn't seem comfortable recalling the incident, and she either glossed over some details or omitted them completely, causing the agent to repeat some of his questions.

As Cassie reached the part where the mugger grabbed her, the agent snapped the Zippo open and brushed a finger against the thumbwheel, throwing a tiny spark from the flint. She froze suddenly, like a rabbit sighting a predator, and her eyes darted toward the spark. Orion felt his heart stop. Perhaps this man had a smoking problem and was itching for a cigarette, but Orion felt that he was endangering his life by fidgeting with the lighter now when his sister was in an agitated state. The agent remained oblivious and asked, "What was your first reaction?"

"I wanted to run. I wanted to scream, but…" She shook her head.

"But you struggled with the man instead. Why was that?" When she shrugged, he pressed, "You said he was armed, and a young girl like you usually has no chance against an armed attacker. Did you have any mace, pepper spray, or anything like that in your bag?"

"No."

The agent absently flicked the thumbwheel again, this time creating a brief, tiny flame. He clapped the lid shut, only to reignite the flame again in small spurts. "That man had a three-inch knife. You might live in a nice part of town, but do you realize what this man could have done to you?" he asked, scowling with concern. "He could have killed you, or worse, and then taken the bag," he explained. He dipped his chin, eyeing her like a disquieted parent, and demanded, "So what was so important?"

"I don't know. I just couldn't let it go," she huffed defensively. "It's just how I reacted!"

The agent nodded. "When the man was close to you, did you notice any strange smells?" He continued listing, "Gasoline? Alcohol? Maybe some natural gas?"

She shook her head. "I didn't really notice."

"So you're struggling," the agent said, maintaining unbroken eye contact with Cassie despite the constant movement of his free hand. Orion eyed the flickering flame appearing and disappearing in the agent's grip as if he was adept at sleight of hand. He thought to seize the lighter, but he wasn't bold enough to move toward the older man. "And this guy just bursts into flames." He paused his fidgeting long enough to imitate a wide fireball. "It consumes him, but you aren't even slightly harmed. And you didn't see what caused the fire." She shook her head, and he leaned forward, shutting and extinguishing the lighter with finality. He then tucked it back into his suit pocket and, with a grave expression, folded his arms in front of him. "Look at this from my perspective, Cassiopeia: You have a body in the morgue, nearly burned beyond recognition, and the only witness to the crime—the 'victim'—can't explain how the fire happened," he said. "This sounds very suspicious." Accusingly, he added, "In fact, it sounds like murder."

Cassie's eyes narrowed, and she was on her feet in seconds. "How can you say that?" Orion rose quickly as well and tried to calm her down while she screamed at the agent. She denied any malicious intent and took to insulting the agent, the government, and anyone related to either of them. The agent watched the two of them passively and took notes while Orion fought to get his fiery sister under control. In the end, he couldn't convince her to retake her seat on the couch, and she remained standing, glowering at the agent. The makeup that she had applied meticulously that morning was now streaked and running down her face.

Since his sister wouldn't allow him to comfort her, and the agent's continued presence only agitated her, Orion turned to their unwanted guest and said quietly, "I think you should leave now."

The agent nodded, yet he made no move to leave, instead perusing his notes. "Has anything like this happened to you before? The spontaneous combustion, that is." He studied each of them in turn, and while it was obvious that Cassie remained furious, Orion wasn't confident about his ability to retain a neutral expression, and he quickly looked away. "Maybe not setting fire to a person exactly, but maybe a small fire? Like a couch or some trash," he clarified, clearly fishing for a reaction. He nodded to himself again as he wrote on his notepad.

"I think you should leave," Orion repeated, this time in a stronger voice.

"Was anyone hurt the last time? Property damage?" the agent continued as if Orion hadn't spoken. The agent was actually paying attention to the two of them now rather than to his notepad, and he apparently received the answer he was seeking, because he again took brief notes before adding, "I'll keep in touch. If something else occurs, I suggest you contact me immediately." He tucked his notepad into his suit jacket and pulled out a business card, which he offered to Cassie. She refused it, and he shrugged, unoffended, before handing it to Orion instead. "I believe you wanted to show me out," he said. Orion nodded curtly and led the agent back through the living room and kitchen to the front door.

Orion felt a strange sensation creeping up the back of his neck, and he turned to face the agent before they reached the foyer. The agent was squinting as if he was trying to read something in very fine print or the sun was directly in his eyes, but otherwise, his actions seemed innocent, and Orion shook off the feeling. He opened the front door for the agent, who paused before stepping over the threshold. "If this happens again, I strongly recommend that you contact me first," he told Orion earnestly. Orion nodded, never intending to obey, but he was unnerved by the man's authority. The agent shrugged and sighed, and then he took off down the hallway toward the elevator. Orion closed the door and leaned against it in relief.

- - -

Pierce hated driving in the dawn hours. It didn't seem to matter in which direction he drove, because the car would somehow always face the rising sun, which was an annoyance that was diminished only slightly by driving with the visor down. The behavior of their planet's light source exacerbated his already palpable aggravation, and they had wasted an animal's flesh, which was practically a cardinal sin.

They hadn't left immediately after the call from home. They hadn't been able to. Madeleine had completed the core of the pictures they'd needed that night, focusing the telescope on Rho Cassiopeiae for later analysis of the supernova candidate, while he'd finished with the animal. His cuts had been quick and sloppy due to the rush, and the necessity of the slackness had clashed with his need for perfection. He'd separated the beast's parts into piles for individual disposal—especially the portions that could lead to its identification—and then he'd discarded the trash. With all the investment in killing and dumping a creature, he hated wasting the meat, but they wouldn't have time for dinner nor the time to store it properly. Once Madeleine had finished with their observations for the night, they'd packed the evidence in the car and cleaned the observatory again lest they leave behind any evidence of their hobby. Once they'd felt satisfied with their handiwork, they'd left a note for Dr. Harper, locked the observatory, and taken off. After placing the refuse in nondescript black, heavy-duty trash bags, they'd dropped off the unidentifiable trash at an apartment complex that typically had its pickup on Thursdays. Since the bags wouldn't burst, the uncategorizable meat would travel to the city dump. However, they had split the majority of the meat and bone between the loose soil of the funeral site in Bristol and a site in Johnstown that they hadn't used for a year. Johnstown had offered a nice secluded spot, but the brambles that kept it from being discovered had really torn up Pierce's arms this time around. The regular trash, which mostly consisted of soiled plastic that had been rinsed and bleached, had been left at a construction site they had passed on their commute between Mason and the city; it was a large-scale operation, and their addition would likely go unnoticed. With that business done, they'd finally been able to head home.

As he shifted the visor to blot out the sun again, Pierce thought resentfully that Cassie's situation better be dire. While it had been the couple's intent to introduce their uncivilized habit to their offspring, the incident with Orion had permanently derailed the idea, and Pierce hadn't wanted anything to do with either of his children since then. They were an inconvenience for which he paid weekly, and though he suspected that at least one of them must have inherited his ability, he could never be bothered to interact with them long enough to discern if both of them did.

Pierce's diet allowed him to heal quickly from his wounds. This ability was put to practical use whenever their meals fought back, and the night the wounded animal had escaped and tried to carry off his son, Orion had tried to help it. He had not tried to help the animal to escape—the four-year-old hadn't understood that concept—but he had attempted to assist by a different means: His will had begun to knit the beast's wounds before Pierce had been able to put a forceful and violent end to the incident. Even if his son didn't want to partake in Pierce's exotic diet, the episode had given him the knowledge that his son shared at least some part of his ability, and this meant that he still had the potential to one day join him. He'd never witnessed the same aptitude in his daughter, leading him to dismiss her as insignificant, so the interruption that she had caused in his life was met with aggravation rather than concern. While he doubted that he would ever feel true concern for his son, Orion and his untapped potential at least might be worth his time.

At around six o'clock, he hit the traffic forming on the outskirts of New York City, which is precisely what he had hoped to avoid. His displeasure grew; the morning rush hour would make his already lengthy commute even longer, and for the majority of it, he would be sitting still. He looked to his right at Madeleine, who was sound asleep beneath her jacket. She had fallen asleep just outside Bristol and had snored softly the entire way. In the morning light, with her face relaxed, the lines of age seemed to disappear and allow the ghost of her former beauty to resurface. He smiled briefly, thinking of their courtship in the fall of their junior year when he'd taken her to see *The Shining*, and he allowed nostalgia to warmly escort him the rest of the way home. Surprisingly, he found a parking spot near the entrance to their apartment and awoke Madeleine gently after he parked the car. He grabbed their small suitcase from the back seat—the trunk had been used to transport the animal and would be sanitized thoroughly during their return trip to Mason—and as they headed up to the apartment, they passed a man in the lobby. Dressed in a black suit that looked a little worse for wear, he faltered in his step, stared at Pierce for a moment, and then staggered off, causing Pierce to question whether the man was inebriated or high. He shrugged and continued up to the apartment, following closely behind his wife.

As the door to the apartment swung open, Madeleine's greeting was cut off before it began. It appeared they had interrupted something between their children. Cassie scoffed, "*Now* they show up," and then she stormed up to her room. Orion called after her, followed directly by his mother's echo, but Pierce simply slipped into the apartment, set the bag down, and secured the door.

"What happened?" Madeleine asked, confusion replacing any concern she may have had.

Orion sighed heavily. "Nothing. Another officer interviewed her this morning, and he upset her. He just left." He didn't look pleased to see them either, but Pierce dismissed his son's reaction as being due to the timing of their arrival.

Madeleine shook her head. "I'll go talk to her."

"Mom, I don't think that's a good idea. I think she—"

"Why wouldn't it be a good idea? I'm her mother!" she snapped.

Orion backed down immediately and appeasingly offered to make breakfast for all of them. He retreated into the kitchen, where he started pulling ingredients out of the cupboard and refrigerator and laying them on the counter. Since Madeleine met no more resistance, she headed up the stairs to her daughter's room, leaving Pierce alone.

Pierce did not intend to stay long, but it wouldn't hurt to unpack. It had been months since he'd been home—Madeleine often made the trip alone to avoid suspicion about his youthful appearance—and there were several items of clothing and notebooks he wanted to collect or switch out. If nothing else, he'd be able to nap in their disused bed while his wife sorted out any issues with their children.

- - -

Cassie sequestered herself in her room for the entire afternoon. Her mother had tried to reach out to her that morning, but the attempt had ended disastrously. Madeleine didn't know how to relate to her daughter any more than she could fly a plane, and every word that had tumbled from her mouth had reinforced this fact. When Cassie had been unable to stand it any longer, she'd driven her mother out of her room. Orion had come by sometime later with an offering of food, but she'd also refused to speak with him; he'd have only scolded her for disrespecting their mother, as if Madeleine hadn't only wanted to adopt a pretense of caring. No, she'd had enough of her family for the day.

For the first hour, she texted her friends, gossiping about potential boyfriends, cheerleading practice, and the upcoming game versus their rivals, the Millennium Phoenixes. She minimized the events of the previous night, admitting only that she had been mugged, and then she claimed that the reason for her continued absence was that she was still hospitalized. This lie was further elaborated by the promise that her parents would take her to see a lawyer when she recovered so that she could sue the mugger's family and the hospital. She claimed mistreatment by the staff and an accidental injection of morphine into her saline drip. The excitement of this distraction soon died when Diana's phone was confiscated by the teacher, and Kate and Natasha put theirs away to avoid a similar fate.

No longer distracted by her phone, Cassie turned to the Internet. The man who had visited that morning had claimed to work for a special government agency of some sort, but she couldn't remember its full title or even its abbreviation. Her searches weren't going any better, no matter how many tangentially related terms she attempted to add; no wonder she never did well on her research papers. Then, it dawned on her that she was missing a key term, and she finally received a hit after adding "Other" and refining the rest of her search request.

The BSI was established in 1987 under a cloak of secrecy, and while the government admitted that it existed, its true purpose remained hidden, and its vision statement was vague and blandly echoed that of the Department of Homeland Security: "To ensure a homeland that is safe, secure, and resilient against specialized agents and vectors of harm." Initially, the agency had been categorized under the Department of Defense, but after 9/11 and the creation of the DHS, it was shuffled underneath the latter's already substantial umbrella. Literature on the BSI was rare, never doing more than alluding to its function, and official documents rarely discussed how its performance affected other government agencies or what "specialized vectors" it investigated.

Cassie gleaned much more from the slew of conspiracy websites that resulted when she redefined her search. These pages seemed to have originated with the dawn of the Internet, as if she'd stumbled to the edges of its primeval past, and they reeked of craziness and paranoia. None of them appeared to have been updated recently, if at all, and she took the information they provided with a grain of salt. Nevertheless, these sites echoed everything that the Outcast Support Network had ever said about the government, and this chilled her to the bone. She learned about Eric Dane being entombed within the BSI's walls and that he had been brainwashed to persuade more of his kind to surrender to the government. Dane had claimed that those who turned themselves into the BSI were trained and given special treatment by the government, but Cassie had healthy doubts about that. She was horrified by the story of a woman named Stephanie Moreau; she was a shapeshifter who disguised herself as her son when she became suspicious of BSI's intentions. Her distrustful instincts proved valuable when she was taken into custody and euthanized so she, as her son, could be dissected. It was enough to make Cassie consider leaving the apartment that night so that the BSI couldn't track her. Unfortunately, she had nowhere to go, she had only a little money, she couldn't drive, and her parents would be of no help.

No, if the BSI were as dangerous as the sites claimed, it would have sent more than one agent and taken her into custody that morning. She was letting fear consume her, and this was how she'd gotten into this mess in the first place. She took a deep breath and calmed her mind. There was only one person she could trust.

She went to the Outcast Support Network and composed a new message to Sone in which she explained what had happened to her. She then begged him to call her, giving him her phone number even though he had strongly warned against her ever doing so. It's not as if she had anything further to lose; the BSI already knew where she was, and she was hoping to receive advice regarding her next step.

She took another deep meditative breath and refocused just as Sone had taught her to do. If she unclouded her mind and accepted the fear, rather than denying or hiding from it, everything would become clear. Sone must have told her this several times, but reaching that peaceful state was never as simple as he'd implied, and her lack of progress frustrated her. Until he responded, there was little she could do except wait, so she decided to spend the time wisely: She attempted to prevent any more incidents by reestablishing control over her ability.

If the BSI or anyone else came after her, she had to be ready, and there was only one way to do this. She needed to conquer her fear and explore and establish her limits. She could become stronger; the incident with the mugger, unpleasant as it had been, had proven that she had potential if she harnessed it.

The ghosts of fuel sources still taunted her from the edges of her senses, but they didn't interfere with her normal vision; instead, they felt like an expansion of it. She closed her eyes and breathed deeply again, consciously slowing her breath and hopefully her heart rate as well. Sone maintained that true control lay with meditative techniques, which was undoubtedly why her abilities were so wild: She moved, thought, and lived too fast. With every deliberate inhalation, she felt her connection to the network of sparks and dying flames grow until it was as plain to her as any of her mundane senses. She felt the flicker of potential fuel sources everywhere merely waiting to become useful to her.

The neighboring apartment had a burning candle in every room. The lonely housewife who lived there liked to burn them when her husband wasn't home. The smell reminded her of her mother's cooking, and carrying this memory around the house made her feel less alone. Cassie reached out toward the flame and felt its warmth as if her hand were actually hovering over it. Just then, the connection became deeper and more intimate. The fire became her limb and was just as easy to manipulate; it took only a thought, and the flame jumped to obey her orders. It grew and grew until it reached its limits and consumed all of its fuel in a dazzling burst. Though it had snuffed itself out, Cassie still smiled at her triumph. Her technique was still unsophisticated due to her inconsistent periods of practice, but with time, it could be refined. The fire had not fed on her fear and grown wild; instead, it had remained under her control. The episode gave her new confidence, and she began again with a new target.

- - -

Morgan Connor sat in front of his laptop in his hotel room. It was not the first time he'd been to New York City, and it wouldn't be the last, but the bureau had given him better accommodations on previous occasions. He assumed that this shabbier lodging was the result of the Secretary of Homeland Security's declining focus on special interests. When the Cokeville Miracle had occurred and Eric Dane had been secured, President Ronald Regan had expressed a new fascination with all kinds of extraordinary phenomena, from aliens to the supernatural, and had, therefore, created the BSI's four divisions: Paranormal, Extraterrestrial, Exceptional, and Unexplainable. While investigations had been launched, the results had been few: UFOs, ghosts, and creatures such as the kelpie had remained as elusive or unsolvable as ever. Only the Exceptional Division had yielded any results, and its usefulness had been challenged in the last decade with the appearance and strengthening of SION. The Network's supernaturally charged radicals had proven to be quite powerful and determined, leading to deaths and destruction of property, which the BSI had been created to prevent.

The BSI's job was to separate the wheat from the chaff—the trainable from the dangerous. Not all Others were destructive, but they had to learn to control their powers or they were destroyed for the good of humanity. Those who remained—the ones who completed training successfully—were allowed to live normal, albeit heavily monitored, lives. A few Others who had more useful abilities were employed by the government, often to apprehend rogue Others, but they were also sometimes used against America's enemies.

In his first year with the BSI, Connor himself had discovered twenty-two Others, which was a record for a novice agent and more than three times the annual average of seasoned agents. Seven of the Others either had abilities that had been too potent or bizarre to trust—such as the ability to apparently travel through time—or had failed the training, but he had managed to save fifteen of them from euthanasia. Most had talents that were too minor to be utilized for government work, such as the ability to glow in the dark, and he kept in touch with a handful of the younger ones. While he was uncertain as to the fate of the rest after they had successfully completed training, he knew that one of them—Emma Braddock, who was known as Antithesis due to her power-nullifying abilities—had joined Eric Dane in protecting America.

He stopped reminiscing and began to write his latest report on the girl called Cassiopeia Starr. Her ability automatically put her into the "dangerous" category because she was what was known as an elementalist—that is, an Other who could control some facet of nature. These individuals often exhibited a dearth of control and were the unequivocal justification to destroy all Others. When using their latent talent for the first time, most elementalists self-destructed and took any bystanders with them. They were considered living time bombs and had inspired the implementation of Operation Blackout.

However, the girl had shown the important capability to restrain herself. Connor had purposely baited her with inflammatory questions and accusations to judge her reactions. She had been angry, and she had lashed out with the words and surly attitude of a teenager, but she had not used her abilities to attack him, even when he had provided an ignition source. In fact, the lighter had played a key role in judging her to be trainable. Despite her brother's painfully obvious fretting, she hadn't appeared to remain cognizant of its presence after its introduction, and the sparks and flames had not reacted to her emotional state, which meant that she had a reasonable level of control over her power. Moreover, Connor hadn't felt threatened by her supernatural abilities, though she might have physically struck him during her tirade had her older brother not been present.

He knew that the immolation of the criminal during his confrontation with the young Cassiopeia Starr had been a complete accident—the result of a reflexive defensive action rather than malicious intent. In addition to being a pyrokinetic, she appeared to be immune to fire, which came in handy because abilities didn't always come in a complete set. He'd heard that the first elementalist in modern times had not been immune to his powers and had electrocuted himself on the battlefield sometime before Benjamin Franklin had begun his legendary kite experiments.

Connor's probing had also revealed that the girl's loss of control had happened before and that she had hurt someone. He doubted it had been a minor burn, judging from the strength of her reaction, but either the incident had never been reported or the signs had previously been overlooked. It had taken decades to hone the BSI's screening techniques to flag seemingly mundane accidents for investigation. Of course, such incidents had to meet specific criteria, and he was not privy to the intricacies of BSI's procedures. However, he would not be surprised if an earlier episode had slipped through the net.

With all of these factors in play, in addition to her youth, he was hesitant to recommend anything but training. Despite being an elementalist, she appeared to have enough control that she would not pose a threat to the general population if placed on parole, and if this didn't suit the BSI, she might still prove to be an asset to the government. Perhaps she could extinguish the raging autumn wild forest fires of the California hills when they occurred;

help forensics teams determine the cause of a blaze; or, better yet, prevent fires before they broke out. He had seen Others with powers as potent as hers euthanized before, so her life depended on how he wrote the report. He stressed the restraint she'd exhibited during their interview, along with the mitigating factor of imminent physical threat when she'd used her ability defensively. He then closed his report with a list of hypothetical uses for her abilities, making sure to recommend that she be taken under the BSI's wing and trained to possibly become an asset. After a hesitant moment, he added that activity related to her brother, Orion, should be flagged for future observation. His intuition told him that the young man may also be an Other, though he had no evidence to substantiate his hypothesis.

He reread his report several times, editing several sections to emphasize his point or to be more concise. He eventually revised it so many times that it barely resembled his original draft. He had an uneasy feeling about the report and did not want to submit it in its present form.

Finally, after his fifth edit, he selected the entire document and deleted it. He needed to start fresh and more critically consider the words he used to describe Cassie's case. This time, he underscored her apparent control over her abilities, stating that she had demonstrated her finesse with fire. Then, realizing that this embellishment made her sound like a murderer, he deleted it and began again. He restated the girl's words: that it had been an accident and that nothing like this had ever happened before. He retained his analysis of her apparent control while also positing that the incident had been a one-time event: Her life had been in danger, and she had reacted, but her powers were otherwise negligible, and she should be trained and then released.

He hesitated again. He could not in good conscience write that she was harmless. The corpse in the morgue testified to the fact that she wasn't, and the reactions of Cassie and her brother had revealed that her loss of control had occurred previously. Furthermore, for BSI trainers to perform their duties, they needed to be sufficiently advised about their students' abilities. Misinforming them could put their lives in danger if Cassiopeia Starr was ever stressed to her breaking point again. Connor had a duty to protect not only his agents but also the general populace. With a heavy heart, he erased the latest draft and did his best to recreate his original report. It was inarticulate in some places and needed work to adequately get his point across, but that would come tomorrow morning.

He glanced at the clock on his nightstand, which displayed the bottom of the eleventh hour, and tried to rub the fatigue from his face. He had a flight to catch in the morning and little time to make it to the airport, and he still needed to find the time to polish his report before he left. He carelessly removed his tie, which was already askew around his neck, and unbuttoned his shirt. His jacket already lay in a pile on the chair in his room, and it was soon joined by his trousers. He was not one for neatness—he had quickly tired of immaculate creases and tidy clothes during his stint in the military—and a few more wrinkles in his outfit wouldn't hurt; he'd have the suit cleaned and pressed after he'd been home for a few days. After stripping down to his boxers, he climbed into bed and turned out the light. The night terrors came under the cover of darkness, so it would be a few hours yet before he could sleep, but at least he could have some semblance of slumber.

- - -

Tom Bryerly had moved up in the world—at least by his own estimation. Nine years ago, he was a skilled locksmith—only not in the legal sense—who had a knack for making doors open spontaneously. Unfortunately, this skill was not accompanied by luck or brains. He stumbled into occupied spaces or opened empty safes just as frequently as he scored. Moreover, he was never very good at finding a trustworthy fence; more often than not, they sold him out to the cops to buy themselves more time to cover their own illicit dealings. Tom spent as much time in jail as he did on the streets, and after his first stint in juvenile hall, he was unable to find lawful employment, and the few employers who hired him did not keep him for long.

One night, Tom made the unfortunate decision to jimmy the lock on a classic red Jaguar E-Type with tinted windows that was parked just off Broadway and 53rd. Since it was during the weekend and within the Theatre District, he thought the vehicle would be an easy score—its owner would likely be occupied with a nearby event for hours, allowing him ample lead time to take the car to a chop shop. Unfortunately, the vehicle was still occupied when he opened it, and he never had a chance to run. The occupant, a young blond man of short stature, snatched him by the back of the collar. Tom didn't know how it happened—the first thing he'd learned was how to elude pursuers, and the then-young thief was quick—or even what happened. But the blond grinned, his blue eyes twinkling. "Allo, gonoph. Mighty fine talent you have," he said ominously in a thick Cockney accent.

Tom didn't know why, but the man took him off the streets and put him to work. Their "partnership" was harrowing at first: The blond, whom he knew only as Mr. Lionhart, drove him to the outskirts of the city, where Tom believed he would kill him. Instead, he forced Tom to demonstrate the true depth of his skills: While Tom could manipulate locks the old-fashioned way by hand, he learned at a young age that he could manipulate the metal so that the tumblers would simply shift to allow him entry without the need for any tools. Though his primary talent was with locks, he had limited success with other mechanical devices, and Lionhart helped him hone these abilities. When Tom graduated high school—only a year later than his peer group and with no plans, means, or motivation to head to college—the English patrician also gave him starter money for a business.

After some time and plenty of mistakes, Tom's repair shop began to make money, in no small part thanks to Lionhart. While Tom owed him a great debt, his feelings would always remain ambiguous toward his benefactor, because despite Lionhart's gentlemanly airs, he could be a sadistic brute when enraged and sometimes turned his temper on Tom. He'd gained at least one prominent scar: a six-inch gash across his temple that was partially concealed by the shaggy hair that fell from his forehead across his face and then behind his ear. Tom had received the gash from being hit with a sturdy metal pipe when he'd failed to pay Lionhart his dues on time. However, fear, resentment, and love shared equal portions of his heart; Lionhart was the only real father he had known, even if he'd filled the role belatedly, and this was the reason Tom was skulking outside the hotel room now.

He had not broken any major laws since high school. He knew how to balance his books and make sums disappear or new merchandise appear on his shelves without his distributors noticing, but he hesitated before breaking and entering. He tried to convince his nerves that he was only reliving the old anxiety that his score would be nothing despite his hard work. However, he knew that deep down, he feared being caught and sent back to jail. Real jail was different from juvie, and he had grown somewhat soft over the last nine years.

Then again, he didn't want to displease Lionhart, because associates who earned his ire met an unfortunate and often violent end. In one case that particularly haunted Tom and convinced him of his benefactor's malice, the recipient of Lionhart's anger became a dried husk that was no more recognizable than the Egyptian mummies in the city's museums. Tom didn't know how it happened, nor was he willing to find out, but the memory was enough to drive him to continue his portion of this endeavor.

The hotel door opened at his touch, and he tiptoed into the dark room, which was illuminated intermittently by reflections of streetlights breaching the closed curtains and making phantom prison bars on the walls. The ambient light was enough for him to cautiously navigate his way around the few personal effects in the room.

A glass of water and a bottle of medication rested on the nearby nightstand, and the tenant was snoring in the bed. He watched the sleeper for several moments, confirming the man was completely oblivious to his visitor before he got down to business.

Tom found the man's suitcase and began to rummage through it when he spied the laptop balanced haphazardly next to the bottle. He shifted the device gently and opened the lid to wake it. Predictably, the laptop required a password, but Lionhart had taken care of that. The jumpdrive that Tom slipped into the USB port could infect the drive without being run manually, and after a few minutes, it permitted him entry into the system. He left the drive in as he worked; not only did it need more time to complete its malicious installation, but he also needed a file that was stored on it. Luckily, the email program was still up, as was the document that he was meant to replace. The switch seemed simple enough, and he was not curious about the contents of either file. He sent the email with the altered attachment, shut the laptop, collected the hacking device, and slipped out of the room before securing the door behind him.

PART II
CODE NAME: REVENANT

"Marilyn's personal accomplishments may surprise some of the younger members of the audience, who are more familiar with her devoted service to her two children, Melissa and young Brian. Marilyn was a constant—"

There was a sudden lapse in the mourners' murmurs as a deep reverberation echoed through the funeral home. Slightly unnerved but convinced that the sound had been caused by temperature fluctuations, the pastor calmly resumed his eulogy. "She was a constant ornament in the fundraising community, assisting her daughter's soccer team and the local theater. Last winter, she became the driving force behind—"

The sound echoed again, this time deeper like a groan, and the coffin lid seemed to rise ever so slightly, as evidenced by the gentle springing motion of its flower centerpiece. This time, the pastor paused, and the silence became pregnant with expectation. The aggrieved widower stopped drying his eyes, frozen momentarily in the terrible thought that this could be a dream or a nightmare. Beside him, his daughter clutched her motionless brother tightly and murmured into his ear.

When no more activity occurred, the pastor cleared his throat. He could believe that the disturbance was a mere fantasy of grief, as he had been close to Marilyn as well. In a small town, it was easy to know one another, and her vibrant personality made her unforgettable. The terrible tragedy that had befallen her family had taken her far too soon. Composed again, he continued in his strong voice. "—the driving force behind the fundraising for Mrs. Craft and her class to visit New York City for a well-deserved vacation. I think all of us have seen the pictures. In fact, I believe this one here—"

The thick padding of the coffin could not muffle the dry gasp that emanated from within it, and if nothing else, it directed and exaggerated the desperate wheeze. Air passed over dried vocal cords, rattling them like a thunderstorm against shutters, and squeezed out through the feeble gap provided by the raised lid. Robert, the husband, sprang to his feet and threw open the casket before the person nearest him could even gather his senses. Freed, the dreadful groan grew louder, but it caused no hesitation on his part. He embraced his revived wife tearfully as the congregation fell into chaos.

- - -

John Reeves had never liked the smell of hospitals. They reeked of disinfectant and had undertones of death and sadness. The scent reminded him of his early youth spent sitting in waiting rooms while doctors spoke at great length with his parents. The two of them would reappear from private rooms like silent ghosts, and none of their conversations would be explained to him. He had known instinctually that one of them had been dying or deathly ill, but he hadn't known which one, and for the longest time, he'd imagined that it was both of them. Once, he'd fantasized that *he* had been the ill one and that this had been why his parents had kept the meetings secret. While the morbid fancy hadn't helped his developing brain, he had eventually figured out which of them had been wasting away to cancer.

Unfortunately, hospitals had become an important part of his job, as his investigations inevitably necessitated at least one visit to the emergency room or morgue. Although his district covered the northeast, some of the south, and Appalachia, he traveled only infrequently. Most of his time was spent with the handful of staff back at the office, combing through police reports, eyewitness statements, and the occasional crackpot tabloid article, rather than on the road chasing down rumors and crazy stories. He'd made the unfortunate choice to join the Paranormal Division, which never saw any real action and had thus become so stringently funded over the years that incidents that were slated for closer investigation had to be carefully selected lest the district go over budget. The only reason his department had sent him by plane this time was that it would be more cost-effective in the long run than the delays and subsequent additional fees that a bus or train ride might have generated. His department typically couldn't afford a rental car, necessitating him to pay for it out of pocket or take inefficient public transit, but the fare for the taxi ride from the regional airport would have been so exorbitant that he'd been able to convince the comptroller that it would be more economical to rent a vehicle for the short time he'd be on assignment.

"Special Agent Reeves," he said to the receptionist as he flashed his badge. "I'm here to see Mrs. Chamberlain."

She looked up languidly from the notes that she had been writing on the paper on her clipboard and scowled when she spotted his badge. "What does the FBI want with her?"

"Actually, I'm a part of the DHS," he corrected her. "They're investigating if she might have been the victim of a biological attack." Supporting his cover story, he added offhandedly, "The CDC should be by later to do their own follow-up."

She sighed heavily. "You should all just leave her alone. The family has been through enough already," she replied as she gave him the room number begrudgingly. Reeves followed the corridor to a scantly occupied private room. A woman lay sunken into the bed with blankets piled on her as if to give her more substance. Her skin was pale—almost translucent—and her eyes were clouded over as if affected by cataracts, though it had been reported that her vision had been perfect prior to the crash. Her head was bandaged, and most of her hair was shorn. Her arms rested above the covers, one in a cast and the other laying perfectly still at an odd angle. An IV provided fluids, but they seemed to collect at the entry point and then bulge beneath the skin like an angry boil. A ventilator and heart monitor kept rigid time, and if not for her open, sightless eyes, Reeves would have believed that she was sleeping.

Her husband droned on in a hypnotic voice, as if he was trying to seal himself away from reality behind a wall of sound, as he read aloud from a novel. His voice was tired, and the halting manner in which he spoke made it obvious that he didn't believe that his wife was actually listening. He had dark circles under his eyes and a few days' worth of stubble, and his rumpled clothes had probably been worn for a while. Even when Reeves knocked and introduced himself, Mr. Chamberlain didn't look up, so the curious agent picked up the patient's chart from the end of the bed and took a look at it.

"What are you doing?" chastised a nurse who had suddenly appeared behind him. "Are you supposed to be in here?"

Reeves answered her without relinquishing the chart. "I'm Special Agent Reeves. We're concerned that Mrs. Chamberlain's condition—"

The elderly nurse, whose name tag read Peggy, shushed him quickly and led him into the hallway. She also expertly regained possession of the patient's chart as stealthily as a pickpocket would. Her stern look reflected her belief that Reeves should be more mindful of the Chamberlains. "Continue," she ordered matter-of-factly.

Reeves frowned disapprovingly at her discourteous treatment, but he obliged in a professional tone. "We're concerned that Mrs. Chamberlain's condition might have been the result of a purposeful biological attack. I've been sent to assess the situation." He paused, hoping that the silence would wordlessly rebuke her for taking the chart before he had read it. She didn't yield, instead continuing to hold the chart in her crossed arms, and he allowed her to maintain the upper hand. He pressed onward, soberly prompting a continued discussion. "Could you tell me more about Mrs. Chamberlain?" he requested in a more polite voice. "Tell me the circumstances surrounding her case."

Peggy checked her surroundings cautiously before speaking in hushed tones. She explained what he already knew: Marilyn and her husband had been heading back from a party late in the evening. Wet roads had caused a semitrailer to blow a stop sign and plow into their vehicle. Marilyn had been pronounced dead at the scene due to massive trauma, and Peggy believed that her autopsy had been performed simply as evidence for possible criminal proceedings. The driver had seemed unusually unresponsive to police, but later tests had determined that he had been perfectly sober, and his odd behavior had been attributed to shock setting in. Robert had escaped with bruises, several broken ribs, and a concussion, while the driver, who had been relatively unharmed physically, had been able to resume his route within a few days when the police were finished with him. The crash had been deemed an unfortunate accident, no charges had ultimately been filed, and Robert had chosen to shift the blame to his own shoulders. "I doubt either of them were contaminated with anything, or he would be showing symptoms by now," Peggy asserted. "And he's as healthy as he can be, under the circumstances. His healing has been slow, but that's probably because he refuses to eat unless I force-feed him. That poor truck driver quit, as far as I heard, but he was healthy when he was discharged, so I don't think he was hauling anything dangerous."

The accident had been several weeks ago, which meant that there had been a substantial period during which Marilyn should have been discovered to be alive or should have died from her injuries prior to her funeral. Peggy was not the person to ask about Marilyn's postmortem state—the agent would need to head to the coroner's office for that—but he'd made the trip to the hospital, and he still had a few questions that needed to be answered.

He switched tactics, exchanging pleasantries with the nurse, and was able to persuade her to retrieve Marilyn's primary physician, Dr. Nguyen. The middle-aged doctor distanced himself so much as he described his comatose patient's disquieting medical status that he sounded as if he was recounting a strange case study from his university years rather than discussing his own patient. Marilyn barely responded to stimuli of any kind, including pain, and the nurses often moistened and closed her eyes to prevent them from becoming too dry. Her broken bones refused to knit, even her bruising didn't seem to heal, and her skin was ashen gray or black where the blood still pooled. She was fed with intravenous fluids, but she had to be carefully monitored, as injections tended not to join her slow-moving bloodstream, which was a diagnosis that Reeves felt was a euphemism for her lack of circulation. She relied heavily on a breathing machine and, to date, had not eliminated any waste, and while she had not lost weight since the autopsy, she had not gained any either. Her scans had shown no activity in her gastrointestinal system, so surgery had been decided against until her body showed signs of distress. Dr. Nguyen became agitated and hostile when Reeves tried to press him further about her intestinal enigma or any signs that she was, in fact, clinically dead. Though the conversation ended professionally, Reeves had the idea that the doctor was mentally casting profanities at him. Dr. Nguyen wanted to keep Marilyn's chart as innocuous as possible, but Reeves' questioning revealed flaws that he would have to correct on the official record. Marilyn Chamberlain simply could not be deceased, despite the clinical signs indicating otherwise.

After Dr. Nguyen departed, Peggy became forthcoming about another detail: She was the only nurse who was still willing to attend to Marilyn. At first, the nursing staff had become unnerved by her unchanging wounds. This was not because they didn't heal—which was a symptom of serious infection with which they were familiar—but because they didn't worsen either. Not only did her injuries remain static, but she also didn't develop bedsores or any other signs associated with extended bed rest. However, superstition truly began to set in when they witnessed her strange, spasmodic movements.

Before it had become obvious that Marilyn would not recover from her vegetative state, Robert had allowed his children to accompany him on his visits to encourage his wife to return to the conscious world. During these visits, the nurses had noticed Marilyn's abnormal ambulation efforts. She was not coordinated enough to get out of bed or even sit up properly, but she had nonetheless made numerous attempts. "She would place her weight on her broken arm and push behind her head with her other elbow," Peggy recalled, attempting to mimic the awkward position and failing. "Maria once said she saw her bend her knees backward beneath the sheets." While the nurses were used to odd behavior from coma patients—they tended to awake in phases rather than all at once like in the movies—the general consensus was that Marilyn was only "alive" as long as she remained on life support, from which her husband adamantly refused to remove her. "The one time she managed to sit up, she jerked her arms about like a marionette as she tried to get out of bed," Peggy continued. "She fell over and cracked her head against the rails pretty hard. She didn't bleed, even though she busted open five stitches. Her daughter screamed bloody murder, but it must have traumatized the little boy. He just kept staring at her." She shook her head. "The staff started praying for her, asking the chaplain to exorcise her."

"Did he?" Reeves asked quizzically.

Peggy chuckled. "Of course not. Don't be ridiculous. She's sick, not possessed." He made a note and, after several more minutes, ended the conversation politely.

His next stop was the county coroner's office, where he met with the chief medical examiner, Dr. Burns. Like Dr. Nguyen, she had detached herself from the reality of the situation, recalling the procedure unemotionally and avoiding questions about Marilyn's present hospital stint. According to Dr. Burns, Marilyn had severed an artery in the crash and had bled out before paramedics had arrived on the scene. Regardless, the paramedics had checked for her pulse and, despite finding none, had continued their resuscitation procedures until the ER doctor had been able to formally declare her dead. While an autopsy had been deemed unnecessary, she had nevertheless operated on Marilyn postmortem. She'd indicated her wish to be an organ donor, and there had been hope that her organs might be salvaged. While this had not been the case, her innards had not been properly realigned, as they would be removed again during the embalming process. Dr. Burns confirmed the injuries that Marilyn had sustained during the accident but curtly avoided speculating on the patient's current condition. As far as she was concerned, Marilyn had died in the car wreck.

Reeves hoped that he would find real answers at his final stop instead of more questions. Regrettably, the district could afford only a two-night stay at the hotel unless he could find compelling evidence that this case required closer scrutiny, and he could not requisition more funds unless he also identified the source causing Marilyn Chamberlain's condition, despite the evident peculiarity of the situation. When the BSI had first been established, the Paranormal Division had had unlimited funding like its sister departments, but as the years had passed with no real closure or explanation of any case, the government had begun to examine the division's spending habits, and it was now a herculean feat for a field trip to be underwritten. He had seen many one-off events that would never have become problematic and, therefore, hadn't needed anything past the initial inquiry. Such events had included supposed poltergeists who functioned only when certain people were present and psychics who couldn't perform under lab conditions. He often hoped that a pattern would emerge from the few investigations that he could conduct in person and that he might track a paranormal disturbance across the country, but the truth was that most cases were unsubstantiated or untraceable, and the Paranormal Division simply did not have a high enough success rate for the BSI to invest further resources in it.

The next morning, he arrived at the funeral home to meet with the head mortician, Derek Winchester. He was pleasant, all things considered, and had a morbid sense of humor, which Reeves couldn't help but believe was inappropriate for his line of work. Regardless, he was exceptionally cooperative when it came to his area of expertise. He detailed normal funeral embalming techniques, including the removal of internal organs and the unfortunate necessity of stuffing corpses with newspaper and other materials to mimic lifelike proportions. When he explained the replacement of bodily fluids with formaldehyde and other preservatives, Reeves knew that he had confirmed Marilyn's undead status. Unfortunately, this was also the end of his lead: Mr. Winchester assured him of the security of the funeral home, including several locks and cameras, and asserted that there had been no break-ins in the history of the home, particularly not after Marilyn's death. However, when asked if anything like the incident had happened before, Mr. Winchester hesitated and subconsciously grabbed his left hand, whose skin appeared to have been sucked dry against frail fingers, before answering in the negative. Despite Reeves' best efforts to pursue this line of questioning, Mr. Winchester sidestepped the topic using his sense of humor, and aside from a frustrated lead the mortician only alluded to, Reeves would go home empty-handed.

Marilyn Chamberlain presented real, documentable symptoms of zombiism, but Reeves would not find the necromancer with the resources at his disposal unless it happened again.

- - -

Brian missed his mother and father. They both spent so much time at the hospital these days that he was starting to forget what they looked like. His father was growing a big, messy beard, which was an odd development because his mother only allowed him to have one during the winter. He didn't know if that meant that she'd changed her mind about it, but he didn't like how it made his father look, and it was just one of the many changes that kept occurring. His mother lay in bed all day, and she wouldn't sing to him anymore. She wouldn't hug him or stroke his hair. After she fell out of bed reaching for him, his father decided that Brian and his sister could no longer visit because it disturbed their mother, and she needed her rest.

His mother definitely looked sick the last time he saw her. The makeup she had worn at her funeral was starting to rub off, and beneath it, her skin looked very gray and dry like his grandmother's hands when she didn't use enough lotion. Even her lips, which were usually bright red with lipstick that always came off on his cheek when she kissed him, were the wrong color. When she fell out of bed, he also saw some newspapers sticking out from between the stitches in her belly, and it caused his imagination to run wild. He wondered if the newspapers on their doorsteps were the same as what he'd seen inside his mother. While he'd scraped his knees before, he'd never seen anything like that in the wound. He supposed that people's insides could be different; he had an outie belly button, while his sister did not. He tried to ask his sister, Missy, about his thoughts, but she hushed him every time he mentioned anything that happened at the hospital.

Even though Nana's hands looked dry, they were soft whenever she touched him. They reminded him of his mother's hands, and he liked the way she stroked his hair as he laid his head on her lap. She spent more time with him these days, meeting him after school to walk him home, making dinner for him and his sister, and tucking him in at night. Sometimes she let him sleep on her lap while she watched TV. But as much as she tried, she could not replace his mother; she was only Nana. She was the woman who gave him extra special attention and treats, not the woman who read and sang to him at night or made his food properly and served it using the correct plates and silverware. While he loved his Nana, she was second-rate compared to his mother, and he thought he should figure out a way to show his appreciation for his mother when she returned.

In all the confusion following the accident, no one had tended to her garden, and the struggling plants were beginning to wilt or dry out. He wasn't allowed in the garden itself—his mother always said that he got dirty if she didn't watch him every second or that he liked to dig up the wrong plants—so he sat on the grass as close as he was allowed and stared into the garden's center. He imagined the tomato vines perking up, the strawberries rejuvenating, and the other greenery returning to the way he remembered it. He sat there, as motionless as a child can be, until the vegetation began to be revitalized. Although he knew that it hadn't been restored to perfection, he imagined that his mother would nonetheless appreciate his effort, especially his stylistic touches. Satisfied, he grinned; this was a great gift for his mother.

- - -

The television murmured softly in the background, reporting on a macabre discovery in upstate New York. Apparently, a skinned, dismembered body had been found by teenagers in the woods, and the police were tentatively identifying the victim as female due to the length of the hair discovered. The internal organs and the majority of the body was missing, but they were able to find pieces of scalp in the pile of body parts. The police were diligently searching the area for more of the victim's remains, especially something that might identify him or her, but the search was impeded by the thick, thorny undergrowth in which the body had been discovered.

Peggy shook her head; it wasn't the most gruesome story she'd heard during her stint as a nurse, but it was becoming harder to tolerate grisly stories as she grew older. As she turned away from the nurse's station to start her hourly rounds, she prayed silently that the victim's family would find peace.

Marilyn Chamberlain was another unfortunate victim. Peggy remembered seeing little Marilyn playing in the street when she was on her way to work. They'd lived in the same neighborhood, and though their families had not been much more than acquaintances, Peggy had kept track of Marilyn over the years and exchanged holiday cards with her parents. People were drawn to the vibrant woman, who seemed to care about everyone, and Peggy hated to see her family in its current state.

She heard Robert's loud, sporadic snoring before she turned the corner, but she was surprised to see that he was no longer alone. The stranger was dressed in what appeared to be a secondhand suit, as it was clearly showing signs of wear, and while his black hair had been gelled down in an attempt to look professional, his five o'clock shadow undermined that image. He ran a gauntlet of awareness tests, including shining a light in Marilyn's eyes, snapping in her ears, pinching her, and then slapping her smartly. The last of these actions infuriated Peggy, and she stepped in. "Who are you?" she demanded sharply.

The stranger started, turned, and reached inside his jacket. "Special Agent Connor," he replied as she studied the offered badge. Although the badge looked authentic, she still had her suspicions. It was past visiting hours, and while this wouldn't have prevented his entry, the desk staff typically informed the night nurses of visitors for security purposes. It was possible that the front desk had simply neglected to notify her, but there was something about him that she didn't trust. She felt as if he had stolen into the room rather than gaining entry legally.

"Bureau of Special Investigations?" she read from the badge.

"It's part of the DHS," he explained. "We think this might have been a biological attack."

Peggy sighed wearily and started tending to Marilyn's needs, first pulling the sheets up to her chin and then tucking her in gently. "That's what the last agent said, but we never received a follow-up visit from the CDC. What are you doing here so late?"

The agent shrugged. "I couldn't sleep."

She shook her head disapprovingly as she adjusted the IV drip. "We tested for viruses and bacteria after he brought this to our attention, and the results came back negative. It should have been in your friend's report. You didn't need to come all the way back here."

"I like to do my own investigations."

She clucked her tongue. "You need to leave the Chamberlains alone. They've been through enough." She feigned checking Marilyn's pulse, even though she knew there wouldn't be one; she had learned not to dwell on that fact after the hospital had removed her heart monitor to avoid calling attention to the lack of a steady beat. Naturally, her blood pressure was also nonexistent; nevertheless, she recorded it before moving on. The agent watched Peggy curiously, at first studying her closely, as if he were learning from her, and then distantly, as if his mind had wandered. After bringing himself back to the present, he made annotations in a tattered notepad before trying to address her again. This time, she preempted him. "Before you ask, I already told that other agent everything I know. Everything else is on her chart, and I assume you've already looked at that."

He nodded, admitting the transgression. "Actually, there's one detail that was left out that I was hoping you could fill in," he said. "When Marilyn… Mrs. Chamberlain was still, uh, *moving*, who was in the room with her?" Peggy scowled, not quite comprehending his question. "I mean, Mr. Chamberlain was there, the doctors, nurses… What are their names?"

"I'd have to check the shift schedule," she replied reluctantly. "Why does it matter?"

He hesitated. "A theory. Was there someone who was more present than the others?"

"Her primary doctor, Dr. Nguyen; myself; and the family took shifts," she replied. "Mostly Mr. Chamberlain and the boy. The daughter returned to school after the first two days. She said she had an important test coming up." She shook her head sympathetically. "It's sad sometimes how children cope. I hope she's dealing with it alright," she added, thinking about how often she'd seen the devastated looks on young children's faces. There was no easy way to break the news to a child, especially if one wanted them to understand, and each child took extended illnesses and hospitalization harshly. Some children wouldn't stop crying, while others believed they had to be strong for the family; she wondered if Marilyn's daughter fell into the latter category. "Oh, and the mother, Mrs. Peterson."

"How much time did they each spend with her?"

Peggy sighed in exasperation; it was too late for these sorts of questions. This was closer to a bureaucratic inquest than an investigation. The last time she'd had to draft and revise a timetable of the period each nurse and doctor spent with a patient, it'd been for the hospital's board members for an internal inquiry about supposed malpractice. The police usually just interviewed the nurses or doctors on shift and then left, but questioning was rarely necessary in this crime-free town, and it seemed like the agent was more interested in placing blame. "Well, I don't know. Why does it matter?" she snapped. "I suppose Mr. Chamberlain and Brian spent several hours a day with her. Dr. Nguyen checked on her during his rounds, and I did, too." She usually wasn't curt, but she didn't like this agent. Not only had she walked in on him manhandling her patient, but he was also shady; it was as if he was trying to hide something. While the previous one had simply been blunt, he had become more polite as the conversation had progressed and she hadn't been irritated by his mere presence.

"Anybody else? What about Mrs. Peterson?"

"She was only here a few days. I don't think she could bear to see her daughter like this. I think she spent most of the time at their house keeping it clean and cooking and such so they wouldn't be so stressed." Peggy made a mental note to check up on her; while Mrs. Peterson had taken her husband's death in stride, she didn't think she'd be able to weather her daughter's condition as admirably.

The agent frowned as he made another note. He stared at his pad for several moments, so Peggy assumed that she was free to leave, but he spoke up before she crossed the threshold. "One more thing: Has anything like this happened before?" He gestured toward Marilyn's bed.

Involuntarily, Peggy remembered the night Derek Winchester beat down her door. It was a warm summer evening, and the cicadas were beginning their symphony in her backyard. She'd brewed herself a small cup of tea and was set to relax on the back porch, when she heard him pounding on the front door. Old as she was, several of the senior residents preferred to see her rather than "bother" a proper doctor, and she enjoyed their trust because she'd been practicing in the town for most of their lives. She opened the door to see Derek clutching his left hand, which had warped into an atrophied, desiccated claw. Despite her protestations, she couldn't persuade him to tell her the exact nature of the accident or to go to the emergency room to seek proper care. He insisted he would be fine as long as she helped him, and knowing little else to do, she treated him for shock and gave him some painkillers that she kept in stock. Eventually, his pain subsided, but his hand never returned to normal. She now realized that the drawn, brittle skin of Derek's hand resembled Marilyn's.

"No," she replied hastily and excused herself to complete the rest of her rounds. She didn't need her concentration disturbed as she worked, and she wondered whether Marilyn's condition would evoke the memory again now that she'd made a connection between them. If that was the case, she'd learn to deal with the odd, unsettling incident; Marilyn still needed a nurse.

- - -

Robert knew that something inexplicable was happening to his wife. He couldn't recall the details of the accident: the four-way stop sign hidden by low-hanging tree branches, the bright lights blinding him through the window, or the harsh impact that had turned his reality inside out. He remembered his wife's head on his lap, her shoulder crushed against his ribs, and warm black— no, dark red—blood spreading everywhere. He knew that the truck driver had pried his crumpled door open to pull him from the car and that an ambulance technician had injected him with a cushion of detachment on the ride to the hospital. After that, there had been bright lights in his eyes and disembodied faces above him, and a cacophony had filled his head.

He'd also known when he'd woken up that Marilyn was dead. In his dreams, there had been hope that she had survived and might even be in better condition than he was, but he'd felt it in his heart as soon as he'd awoken that she had passed before he had been told. When she'd revived at her funeral, it had been a miracle—a sign from God that they should never part again.

He could overlook her pallid skin and the lack of warmth in her touch because she could still look at him, though her clouded eyes may not see him. Her head wound might refuse to heal, but when she was released from the hospital, he'd buy her a wig so beautiful that no one would ever suspect it wasn't her real hair. No one would notice her confinement to a wheelchair when she was dressed in her normal, brilliant wardrobe, although he might have to hire someone to assist her with her makeup since he had no aptitude in that regard.

No, no matter how hard he tried, the troubling parts that he could not deny were her continuing dispossession of a heartbeat and some of her interior having been supplemented by newspaper padding to mimic the plumpness of life for her funeral. By all rights, his beloved should have been in her grave and should have remained there, and medical science could not explain her presence. Eventually, someone would question her inexplicable condition to the point that she would be removed to the cemetery, and that would be the end of their unnatural reunion. In the meantime, he planned to enjoy their fleeting time together for as long as it lasted. Perhaps the sheer force of his affection would revive her permanently.

- - -

Melissa lounged half-dressed on her bed as she wasted her free time on one of her many phone apps. She'd probably download another in less than an hour; none seemed to really capture her attention like they used to, and she needed something to occupy her. The doorbell rang, and she heard Nana answer and exchange words with some man. Though she didn't recognize his lightly accented voice, he must have been a family friend, because her grandmother invited him inside. After a few more minutes, Nana called her to join them downstairs in the living room. Melissa rolled her eyes and obeyed in her own time; she might as well start the download for her next game while she got dressed and saw what Nana wanted.

A man in a suit was waiting for her. He introduced himself as a special agent, like out of the movies, and sat across the couch from her. She didn't like the way he spoke down to her as if she were still a child instead of a teenager, which she considered herself at age eleven. Nana wanted to sit in on the session with her, but the agent suggested that Melissa would speak more freely without her present and requested that she leave the room. He asked Melissa about school and her opinion on his limited knowledge of her interests until he decided to broach the real topic that was on his mind. "Tell me about the garden," he said, and she scowled, not really comprehending what it had to do with anything, until he pointed to their mother's garden. It had begun to decline since their mother's accident; yet, when she looked at it, it was not the shriveling collection that she had seen that morning. Despite brittle stalks, the tomato vines twisted around their metal stakes and bore desiccated fruit as if newly blossomed. Its neighbors yielded fuzzy gray yet plump strawberries attached to green vines. Her mother's petunias, which had long ago died of neglect, no longer drooped; they stood up, spreading what few petals that were left toward the sun. The rest of her mother's patch had undergone similar transformations, having perked up in macabre likenesses of life. However, the grass bordering the garden suffered conversely: Its vibrant green had become a mottled yellow patchwork extending a foot outward from its edge. The strange effect had been confined to a small circle; further away, the grass had remained untouched. Melissa recognized her brother's handiwork immediately.

"What about it?" she asked reticently.

The agent pointedly looked away from her, glanced back at the garden, and clarified himself. "Don't you think it's a bit odd how pert it is despite its appearance?" She shrugged, not really wishing to answer the question. It wasn't the first time she had experienced the strange phenomenon, but to her displeasure, the incidences were becoming more frequent. The agent turned his attention back to her, staring intently as he added, "A bit like your mother, eh?"

"That's not my mother!" she snapped despite herself, and he broke eye contact long enough to write in his notebook. She scowled at her outburst; despite knowing that her mother's resurrection went against nature, she didn't want to betray her brother's part in it. She denounced his talents—not him— and acknowledging the resurrection would invite investigation. She might not know how Brian had gained his talents, but she'd seen enough movies to know that the government would take him away and torture him. She'd even seen it on the evening news before her parents had changed the channel to happier family programs; the government didn't like its enemies, and due to his demonic abilities, she didn't think they would consider Brian an ally.

The agent's gaze didn't waver during the several minutes of silence between them, but he was the one to finally break it. "Do you want to explain what you mean?" She shook her head, and he set aside his notepad and pen before speaking deliberately. "Look, I know you're going through a lot. It's very sad losing your mother to an accident, and what's going on right now is scary, but I'm here to help." He gave a pained smile, attempting to express sympathy. "That's what I do: I help people in your situation. But I can't help you if you won't talk to me."

Melissa also considered what her parents always taught her: Obey the laws and authorities of the land. But once she'd reached the cusp of adolescence, they had supplemented this lesson with a seeming dichotomy: She had a civil duty to disobey rules she considered morally wrong, and she needed to develop this new moral code on her own from the foundation that her parents had provided. However, neither directive did much to aid her now. If Brian had broken the law, then the right thing to do would be to turn him over to the authorities. At the same time, wasn't she supposed to protect her own family? Which was the correct choice: turn him in or keep quiet?

"What will happen?" she asked quietly, still conflicted.

The agent's lips became a thin line. "It depends on what's happening. It can be very complex, and it varies with the situation. My agency provides training to special individuals, and it's my job to figure out who qualifies."

She looked down at her hands in her lap and studied her fingernails intently for a few minutes before taking a deep breath. She divulged her story slowly at first, as if she had to remember the words before she could speak them, but as she continued and the agent seemed to fade into the background, her memories became easier to relate.

She'd become acquainted with Brian's abilities when he'd been three years old. They'd been playing in the yard when they'd witnessed a squirrel get struck by a car. Its head had been crushed by the tires, but its legs had still twitched, and as Brian had bawled hysterically, it had risen up on its haunches and had started to stammer its way grotesquely across the street toward them. Luckily, it had been struck by another car before it had reached them, and it had not risen again.

She'd also watched her grandmother's hands shrivel as she'd turned Brian over her knee to give him a spanking. They'd returned to normal once she'd released him, but Melissa believed that her grandmother's hands aged more quickly than the rest of her body. She'd seen plants wilt and droop in Brian's presence when he'd thrown a tantrum, and he'd kept dead bugs as puppets alongside his regular figurines until she'd told him to stop. Even though she'd realized immediately what Brian had been attempting to do at their mother's funeral, she'd been unable to change his mind or stop him before the act had been completed, and while she'd initially believed that Marilyn's resurrection had been a miracle, she'd realized by her first effort at conversation with her mother that she'd been only another of her brother's dolls.

When she looked up again, she noticed that the agent wore a concerned frown. He'd scribbled most of their conversation in illegible shorthand, and she wondered now if divulging her brother's secret had been the best idea after all. Regardless, the agent caught her gaze again. "Your brother needs help," he said softly. "I need to assess him further in person. That means I'll need to talk to him."

She nodded hesitantly and led the agent to where she thought her brother would be. He was playing with his cars in the front yard, which was in easy view of their grandmother out the bedroom window. Melissa realized then that her grandmother had probably overheard her conversation with the agent, and she worried what she might think of the situation. Nana had to know about Brian, as she had experienced his sapping ability firsthand, but Melissa had never overheard her speak about it. Despite no one ever acknowledging his abilities, perhaps she should have tried to talk to Nana about it anyway. Maybe Brian's abilities were a family secret she'd misguidedly revealed to the agent.

Brian made explosive sounds as he crashed his cars into one another. Unlike other children his age, his performance delved into more detail, adding the dramatic screaming of the victims and pleading cries for help. The performance made Melissa cringe. Even though he may have watched something similar on television, it might as well have been a reenactment of their parents' car accident, and she was evidently more sensitive about it than he was; he didn't appear to notice the resemblance. A fire truck made its way to the scene, and the agent crouched down beside Brian as imaginary firemen filed out of the vehicle. "What's going on here?" asked the agent in an uncharacteristically chipper voice.

Brian eyed the agent's suit indifferently. "Did you come from a funeral? A lot of people dressed like that at Mommy's funeral," he said. When the agent replied that he had not, he followed with "Work?" After a nod, as if that meant something significant to the boy, Brian answered, "Playing with my cars."

The agent appeared uncertain and, after a brief hesitation, bent down and picked up one of the cars, but Brian slapped it out of his hand. "Mine!" he shouted angrily, seizing the fallen vehicle and clutching it to his chest possessively. Melissa chastised him for his rudeness and apologized on his behalf, but the agent seemed more diffident than offended by the outburst. Brian picked up his other car and placed both on the grass away from the agent yet still within his small reach.

The man sighed and shifted from his crouching posture to a more comfortable position on his rear. He watched Brian with a pensive expression for several quiet minutes, not even taking notes, before he made another attempt at conversation. "Do you miss your mother?" His voice was quieter, as if the conversation were to be a secret that Melissa wasn't party to.

"Mommy is at the hospital," Brian replied plainly, but his conviction to his amusement faded as he pushed his cars halfheartedly around his grass-stained knees.

"What if she were to come home?"

He shrugged. "She can't. Hospital won't let her."

"But let's say she did," he said encouragingly. "What then?"

Brian scowled, scrunching his face together until he turned red. "Missy says she already went to Heaven and that the Mommy in the hospital isn't really her," he answered, his voice becoming shriller with each word. "Nobody can bring her back because she's gone!" he screamed. Then he grabbed a car in each hand and ran toward the backyard, where he hid in his cardboard fortress.

Melissa's heart jumped into her throat, and she tried to swallow it back down. She'd done the right thing—she'd told her brother he'd created an abomination rather than resurrecting their mother—but that realization did little to ease the guilt she felt after hearing Brian's inarticulate grief. She missed their mother as much as he did, and she wished he could make her whole and truly bring her back. The agent bowed his head and retreated quietly as she deliberated on what she should do. It seemed the agent read her thoughts, for he answered her, whispering as he passed, "Don't allow him to see her again. Just let her pass peacefully." Then he departed, leaving her alone on the lawn.

- - -

It was dark—almost pitch-black. Connor didn't remember it being after nightfall. The hardened shelters were faded—not the pale gray they were at night—and the people around him were oily shadow caricatures. The sounds were muted and distorted as if his ears were filled with cotton, and he drifted on a wave of pressure whose presence reverberated at the perfect frequency to cancel out all noise. The pressure remained, driving his spine and all that it was attached to into the ground. His scream wedged in his throat, becoming a flat croak that turned into a rasp as he awoke abruptly from his nightmare. His breath and heartbeat were quick, but consciousness allowed them to slowly resume their usual rhythm as he brought them back under control.

As he began to wipe the drool from his chin, he realized that it was actually a combination of pooled condensation and spilled whiskey, and he sneered contemptuously at the mess on the table. The glass had not tipped over, as he had expected to find, but it appeared he had been careless in pouring. He grabbed a towel from the bathroom to clean it up. The remaining whiskey in the glass had become watered down, and the ice in the bucket had long ago returned to its liquid state. He wondered how long he had been out.

The television caught his eye. The newscaster was reporting that the police still hadn't identified the Johnstown victim, and it now appeared that she was merely the first victim among those found in an impromptu graveyard. The bramble patch in which her body had been found was making excavation difficult, especially since it might contain additional evidence, but there had been confirmation of recovered remains from an estimated three victims. Despite there being no official statement as to the nature of the crime, the media was already speculating about a serial killer. It was only a matter of time before they named him something ridiculously sensational and turned their wild speculations into supposed public safety announcements. Since this was a repeat of a story he had seen earlier, Connor knew that he'd slept continuously for several hours, which was a first for him.

He'd only meant to get slightly buzzed to help him write his report, but the more he'd contemplated what to write, the more alcohol he'd ended up consuming. He generally didn't drink; it aggravated his already problematic sleeping difficulties and revived thoughts he'd rather keep buried. However, this case created ethical challenges that he never thought he would encounter, including what he might do when he had Brian's powers at his personal disposal. Marilyn Chamberlain couldn't hold a conversation, but with more practice and refinement, Brian might actually be able to bring someone back to true life. If that were the case, maybe death would cease to be an insurmountable obstacle, and Brian could bring back someone who had been dead for years. This line of thinking had been a dangerous path to take, especially for Connor, and he had tried to wash it away with whiskey. But instead, he had drunk himself insensible.

He regretted receiving the tip-off from John Reeves because it had placed him in a difficult situation. Reeves had his own suspicions about Marilyn Chamberlain's resurrection, but with closely monitored resources and heavily scrutinized receipts, it had been difficult to pursue his investigation to the full extent necessary without substantial evidence. However, he had uncovered enough data to warrant a recommendation for further scrutiny by the Exceptional Division, and as they had been previously acquainted, Reeves had forwarded the case directly to Connor. The report had piqued Connor's interest, and while he had initially suspected the husband, his first visit to the hospital had dispelled this assumption.

It was true that Others tended to use their abilities for the first time in periods of heavy emotional stress, but Robert Chamberlain had been practically paralyzed by his grief, and her resurrection had only served to plant the seed for his dysfunction. Connor hadn't even tried to interview him; being in the same room had been enough to illustrate that Robert wasn't the Other, and despite Peggy's protectiveness of the Chamberlains, she hadn't fit the profile he'd expected either.

This had left him with two other suspects: Melissa and Brian. Both were young, which meant they would be more malleable for training, but Connor hadn't been comfortable with the idea of another potent young Other so soon after Cassiopeia Starr, and his uneasiness had grown as soon as he'd met Melissa. Since Marilyn's ambulation had stopped soon after Melissa's absence, he'd sincerely hoped that she had been the Other. An eleven-year-old would have been easier to deal with: less emotional, longer attention span, and more maturity. Unfortunately, he'd sensed that it hadn't been her before she'd even spoken, and her emotional detachment from the situation had confirmed his assessment.

So what would he do about Brian? He was young and still prone to tantrums. Though partial resurrection itself wasn't dangerous, his abilities seemed to stretch beyond that, and while specialists back at the BSI might be able to nail them down exactly, they would be exposed to an unquantifiable hazard in the meantime. Connor couldn't make a training recommendation without solid evidence that the staff wouldn't be placed in undue jeopardy.

Brian had touched Connor during an emotional outburst, and he hadn't suffered any ill effects. He hadn't experienced withering flesh like the grandmother, which could indicate that the boy had some measure of self-control. He also had not witnessed any life energy transfer firsthand, so he could indicate in his report that this specific danger was only related to him by secondary sources like Melissa. Except that he had observed it—the patch of dried grass near the partially revived garden, which also indicated the range of the boy's abilities. Connor suspected that if Reeves had checked the funeral home shortly after Marilyn's recovery, he would have noticed wilted flowers or some other indication of transferred life, and he wondered whether the supposed desiccation of the flowers during Brian's tantrums meant that energy had been transferred elsewhere. Connor couldn't even reliably test Brian's self-control as he had done with the Starr girl; trying to trigger the child would put him and anyone nearby at risk every time, and he knew instinctively that provocation would be disastrous in this case.

Connor had borne the heavy burden of a difficult decision before, but not with someone so young, and he wasn't yet prepared to accept responsibility for the inevitable recommendation: Brian Chamberlain was too unpredictable to train, and this meant that he had to be euthanized for the public good. Under different circumstances, perhaps the boy could have gone years without being detected and could have developed his self-control on his own so he could become a BSI asset. But Connor knew of his existence and the potential danger he posed, and there was now only one outcome. He took another swig of whiskey and began to write his report.

It took him less than an hour to complete it. Reeves' investigation had provided a good base, and Connor's account would primarily be an addendum explaining Reeves' observations in Exceptional Division terminology and outlining the steps and procedures that both men had followed. The detachment that he had keenly cultivated allowed Connor to experience a feeling of numbness as he typed the boy's death sentence, but it also provided an unexpected insight: Antithesis. The newest BSI asset could produce a field that nullified supernatural abilities, and she had been trained specifically to apprehend dangerous Others. She would be an ideal instrument to contain Brian Chamberlain's talents and the dangers they posed until the BSI could properly classify and train the boy. Unfortunately, the recommendation was a long shot: while Antithesis and Angel worked in tandem to escort Others to the Plum Island facility, her vital role was combating VSION. Taking her off the field for an extended period—however long it might take for Brian to learn to control his powers—was not strategic if his abilities weren't unmistakably advantageous to that war or Operation Blackout. Nevertheless, the proposal eased his troubled conscience.

He read and refined his report, trying to feel better about the outcome, but guilt started to eat away at him. The boy, sans ability, had the right to a long life, and the failure to save him was on Connor's shoulders. Connor was alive only because he had been saved years ago, and he needed to save as many lives as he could to repay that debt. If he didn't, Connor lost his right to live.

Conversely, it was useless to feel guilt; he couldn't change the report in good conscience, so he sent it without further review. Dwelling on that perceived failure would only cause him further distress. He stripped off his clothes to get rid of the smell of alcohol and took a quick shower. He then took a handful of his medication in the hopes that the dreamless slumber they caused would better salve his roiling emotions.

- - -

As soon as the alarm went off, Jack Everest sprang from his bed and began his morning athletic routine. He had cultivated a muscled physique to counteract his small stature, and he often thought of himself as a tiger—an unassuming creature that could strike quickly and devastatingly when it chose to. At this point in his life, brute strength was a frivolous hobby; his struggles against his larger foes took place primarily in verbal spars and could hardly be called contests. Any physical confrontations were easily ended by siphoning away the life force of his opponent, which was something he could accomplish with the slightest touch. No, his physique was compensation for when he had been William Hart, a little street urchin who'd labored to scrape together enough pence for week-old bread and who'd been too slow and hungry to catch rats. Being overweight would have been enough recompense for those lean years, but in this day and age, a healthy physique and dark complexion indicated that his wealth was enough to allow him ample leisure time, and his long years had cultivated increasing vanity as he'd gained prosperity.

The light blinked red on his phone, indicating that he had received a new email on his clandestine business account, so he logged onto his computer to find that Morgan Connor had sent another report to the BSI. Coincidentally,

Jack had also finally received the BSI's personnel file on Connor the previous night, and he meant to review it this morning. He decided to read the latest report to compare his style to the previous one on Cassiopeia Starr and to build his own profile on the agent. Connor had taken care to demonstrate Starr's trainability to his superiors, which had intrigued Jack because it was uncommon; most agents dogmatically suggested euthanasia and certainly wouldn't endanger themselves by directly evaluating an Other's abilities in person. Fortunately, the BSI would soon forget Starr's existence; the report that Jack had submitted in Connor's stead indicated that the subway incident had been a freak accident that had been exaggerated by the filing policeman.

He opened the latest report and discovered an entirely different tone from Connor. This time, the agent was clinical as he catalogued each known episode and its severity, including suspected but unconfirmed incidents that had been gleaned from previous reports. There was no impassioned plea to train the child, as there had been for Starr; Connor had devoted only one sentence to his decision, and it seemed his suggested reprieve had only been added as an afterthought. Jack didn't know who Antithesis was, but his curiosity was now piqued, and he would try to gain access to her file if the opportunity presented itself. While anyone who could restrain an Other might create a setback, it may also be an advantage if he played his cards correctly, and he usually did.

The callousness with which Connor had dictated the boy's fate titillated Jack. It displayed a sense of inhumanity that he sought in his future associates, and since he intended to keep an eye on Connor anyway, it would be more beneficial to Jack to turn him into a subordinate rather than expending resources on surveillance. He was also eager to obtain a reliable connection within the BSI. With sudden enthusiasm, he began to read Connor's file.

The file described a modern tragedy, the details of which Jack skimmed over because they bored him and reminded him of the setups of the ridiculous penny dreadfuls of his youth. Instead, his attention was caught by what appeared to be intrigue: The BSI suspected that Connor could sense Others, much like Jack could, and had opted not to inform or instruct him on improvement. This was the only way they could explain his exemplary track record without chalking it up to pure luck. Jack also subscribed to the BSI's plan: It was better to have a loyal drone to sniff out enemies than train a more efficient one who may eventually question his morals and change sides.

The revelation also altered Jack's strategy. To decrease the likelihood of being discovered, he didn't feed often, but he couldn't afford to be highly selective of his victims either. If he failed to feast on a fellow Other within a reasonable time frame, he knew that he would wither and die. Connor could find new quarry for Jack, who could then expend his freed resources elsewhere, and the agent's discoveries might improve the quality of his feasts, such as Brian Chamberlain would have. Jack couldn't harvest the child—not with the surveillance the boy was now under—but in the future, this bloodhound could uncover more tempting morsels.

PART III
CODE NAME: SONE

It had been years since Sone had gone by his given name, but he had long considered his nom de guerre his true identity. Most Others, particularly those in SION, adopted a new name to reject human society and reflect their unusual nature—Sone was no different in this regard—and it was also a reappropriation of the soulless designations that the BSI used to dehumanize Others. However, he had an additional motivation: Being Chase Moreau, the son of SION's leader, made him a higher priority for the BSI, whereas Sone was just another member of the Vanguard. His activities already made him a target, so there was no reason to give himself even greater value.

His partner, Rho, kept an easy pace beside him despite being a few years older. Sone didn't know the muscular man's real name, nor much about what he had done before he'd joined the Vanguard, but he nevertheless knew him: his loyalty, his savagery, and his intense determination to keep Others free from outside interference. Rho's ability had manifested while on a military base, of all places, and he'd had to escape utilizing his physical prowess because he hadn't yet developed control over his power. Still, Sone suspected that this wasn't the worst of his past, and Rho never delved into his personal history nor spoke of his family. The only hints of Rho's previous life lay in his long, unruly hair and the tattoos he kept shamefully covered regardless of the ambient temperature.

"I feel her closing in," Rho said in his clipped speech. Sone looked at him with concern; he could not feel anything, but he trusted his partner's senses. Rho had once described the sensation as a heavy fog drifting into the edges of his mind and making his brain feel like molasses.

"She's tracking us somehow. She's got to be," Sone replied.

"Or her handler is. We've never figured out how they find us." They stopped to rest in an alleyway. Rho leaned over and placed his hands on his knees as he sought to catch his breath. The wind kicked up, rattling cans and carrying with it the sharp scent of urine and rotting trash. "We can't make contact with her now," he panted. "Things are too hot. We'd just lead them straight to her."

Sone shook his head and drew in a long breath before replying. "They already know she exists. That's why it's so important that we get to her. We need to retrieve her before the BSI does."

Rho exhaled deeply, though Sone wasn't certain if he was sighing or simply catching his breath. Catching Sone's dark eyes, Rho knew that they were on the same wavelength. "We know how to fight them off. She doesn't," he said, voicing Sone's argument. "I don't suppose you'll wait for the situation to cool down some?" Sone shook his head. "'Course not. Then we need to evade them a bit longer—maybe get a few hours' head start and swing back 'round. Maybe they won't realize we're after her."

Sone smiled as he looked around. "This might make a good ambush point. Then we can lose them in the crowd. Use Blackout to our advantage."

Rho surveyed their alleyway as well. "The noise we make might negate their directive, and this ain't a good pinch point. But..." He closed his eyes a moment. "The subway's right below us. Give me your hand. We'll make them take the long way." Sone did as he was told, grasping Rho's offered hand tightly, but no amount of trust would quiet his anxiety about the process. He never felt the transition, and his brain could not compensate for what his eyes saw as they slid between atoms. His every cell suddenly felt as if it was filled with static; this was the best he could describe the feeling. Then, his vision returned, and they were in an alcove off a brightly lit tunnel. If anyone had witnessed their appearance, they must have quickly moved on, and the two men blended effortlessly into the subway's pedestrian traffic.

- - -

Orion grimaced as the front door slammed against the wall, knowing that the doorknob had probably dented the plaster. The doorstop had broken last week, and he hadn't yet had the chance to repair it. Under normal circumstances, he'd merely call the building super and ask him to fix it, but lately he'd been smelling smoke and finding candles with burnt-out wicks in puddles of wax around the apartment. He didn't know what his sister's thoughts were—whether she believed that she needed practice or she felt threatened by the government visit a few weeks ago—so he wanted to take care of it himself rather than risk her exposure a second time. He added patching the wall to the new list of maintenance needed.

He dumped his backpack on the floor, but as much as he wanted to, he didn't fall onto the couch for a nap. Instead, he removed his hoodie, taking the time to hang it up on its hook by the front door, and headed into the kitchen to start dinner. First, however, he grabbed a soda from the fridge and chugged it with little grace, spilling some out the side of his mouth and onto his shirt. He groaned and dabbed it with a dish towel.

He'd not slept well since the BSI agent's visit. At first, fearful imaginings had danced through his mind about what the agency might do to his sister when they came for her, but as the days had rolled on with no sign of the BSI or even a follow-up from the police department, he'd begun to think that they'd forgotten about Cassie. Unfortunately, that had not granted him the relief he'd sought, and in its stead, worries had grown about a hostile sister who barely spoke to him even when she had to. She had gone through phases since being left in his stewardship: She would reject his authority, sometimes rebelling against him as strongly as any teen against her parents, but she generally wasn't openly hostile, and since there had been a marked change in her behavior since the agent's visit, he'd decided that it was what had triggered the change.

Cassie had also always been a social butterfly, rarely roosting at home during their parents' sporadic visits, and she never wanted for companionship. Even so, she had always been respectful enough to let Orion in on her plans, especially if she was going to be gone for a long period. But as of late, she had begun to neglect this duty. It was a relief that he'd had the foresight to build a network with her friends' parents, for they were the ones who kept him updated on her whereabouts. He also knew that he could expect her home tonight, as finals were coming up, and most of her friends' parents emphasized earning decent grades. Orion knew that he should be studying for his own finals, except he wouldn't be able to concentrate until he knew his sister was sorted.

He had the night all planned out. He would sit her down to her favorite meal, which he'd prepare by hand, and then tell her how much he loved and supported her. Then he would ask her to explain her recent change in behavior, its cause, and what he could do to help her. They'd talk for an hour, or however much longer she might need, and then he'd retire to his room to study his notes and textbooks. Of course, he doubted the confrontation would go smoothly, as it never did due to her hardheadedness, but it was something he could hope for as he began his diligent efforts to make the perfect dinner.

- - -

"Did you roll your eyes at me?"

Cassie looked up and made eye contact with the customer who'd received the third wrong order in the last fifteen minutes. "No. My mascara got into my eye, and I was trying to subtly clear it, but I guess you caught me," she hissed acerbically.

"Are you being sarcastic with me, young lady?"

"Of course not," she replied sweetly. "Your order should be right back out."

"Get it right this time!" he snapped.

Maybe I would if you didn't request ten thousand modifications to a simple cup of coffee, she wanted to rebut, but she doubted her indulgent managers would appreciate her actively antagonizing their patrons. Her bosses had been supportive of her erratic schedule, and they'd let her have free food whenever she'd wanted, so she felt no need to offend the hardworking couple unnecessarily. Still, this didn't mean that she couldn't be spiteful toward the customer, and she decided that this order would now be decaffeinated. "Here you go, sir," she said as she handed the new cup to the customer with her brightest forced smile. "Enjoy!" He muttered a response that she didn't care to catch, and she turned her attention to the bell that rang when a new customer entered.

Two men entered the restaurant, took a seat by the window, and immediately drowned their attention in their phones. They might be a couple or simply friends; it was hard to tell these days since everyone, herself included, socialized over the phone. Her problem with them was that the Wi-Fi was only free to paying customers, so she had to make note of their entrance. Some customers took their seats first to wait for companions and then ordered, but others only wanted to mooch the Internet and wouldn't even place a perfunctory order. If the two men didn't order something within ten minutes, she'd have to confront them and possibly ask them to leave.

As if he could feel her gaze, the brunet with shaggy hair looked up and made eye contact, and she shuddered. While he wasn't traditionally handsome, he wasn't unattractive either, yet something about him creeped her out. Maybe it was because he was visibly scrutinizing her; most people had the good sense to realize that she was underage and, therefore, didn't blatantly leer at her. His shorter, muscled companion must have noticed his stare because he knocked on the table, diverting the brunet's attention, and shook his head reproachfully.

Cassie took the opportunity to return to work; if someone needed to approach the couple later, she'd ask Sandee to do it for her.

Her thoughts eventually turned to the past month as her body reverted to the automatic motions of working the machines and occasionally wiping the counter or refilling the cups. Though Sone had never called her, their correspondence had increased in response to her anxiety. He'd gone into depth about techniques she could utilize, such as keeping a lighter with her at all times, and he'd taught her methods to detect and evade BSI agents. Strangely, the BSI's supposed brutality did not match her experience with the agent they'd sent to her apartment, but she decided that she would have to be ready in case she needed to put up a violent defense. While she'd gotten very good at coaxing flames to do her bidding, she still could not sustain a fire for longer than a few seconds; even so, a flash fire would be enough to protect herself or enable her to make an escape.

Her newfound preparedness warred with her need for acceptance and placed her abilities on the opposite side of the spectrum. For every hour she spent practicing with fire, she spent an equal amount of time trying to blend in with her friends. What were the newest trends? She needed to acquaint herself with them before her peers did so that she could stay atop the fashion wave, and it was hard to balance this essential knowledge with her ambitious cheerleading and swimming goals. She wanted to excel—to be number one in both sports—but she needed to put in the hard work that was necessary to achieve this aim, and the effort left her with very little leisure time. She often napped in the back closet at work now, ostensibly with her managers' blessing, and she knew that refuge wouldn't last much longer; she needed to figure out a sensible pace before she burned herself out.

Closing time finally came around, and Cassie and Sandee chased out the last of the customers, including the two suspicious men. Sandee cleaned while Cassie counted the register, logged the sales for the night, and prepared the deposit bag for the morning. Ever since Cassie had been mugged, the owners had decided that none of their underage employees would carry the risk of depositing the money bag; they would ensure that this was done by legal adults only. If there were none on shift, the deposit would go in the safe and would be delivered to the bank the following morning. After Cassie secured the safe, she helped Sandee with what was left of the cleaning and then locked up. The two parted ways at the door since Sandee took a different way home, but Cassie suddenly reconsidered her route when she spotted the duo from earlier leaning against a car down the street.

With Sandee already out of sight, Cassie decided that it was best to ignore them and trudge onward. She took a deep, anxious breath, and then she quickly crossed the street away from the two men. They peeled away from the car, matching her pace conspicuously before crossing the street at the next crosswalk. She hastened her stride as she reached into her new gym bag and retrieved the pepper spray that her brother had recently procured for her. Their footsteps grew louder, and she glanced behind her to see that the gap between her and the men had closed. She then released the safety mechanism and held the device firmly in her grasp, ready to deploy it if the suspicious men threatened her. She felt a hand on her shoulder and sloppily shrugged it off as she turned around and sprayed a stream across the faces of her assailants.

Unexpectedly, the spray didn't connect with either of them. It went through the grim-faced, muscled man as if he weren't even there, despite the fact that she could plainly see him. Remarkably, she could also see the street behind him, as if he were providing little more than visual static. The brunet, who had grabbed her shoulder, must have done something, because she saw the stream of pepper spray change direction and shoot away from all of them. The muscled man wasted no time in becoming solid again and punching her square in the face. She fell backwards onto the pavement, scraping her elbows and palms as she tried to catch herself. "Rho!" the brunet chastised.

"I'm sorry, man. It was reflex." Rho began to offer her his hand, but the other man frowned at him. He withdrew the offer of his hand so that the other man could help Cassie up. She recoiled from the brunet's gentle touch, choosing instead to hold her wounded cheek gingerly, and when she did finally take his hand, he almost forced her to her feet due to her reluctance to accept his help. "I'm sorry. We're used to more violent introductions," the brunet explained. "You know, if you had used your ability instead, you wouldn't have been so caught off guard. What's the point of practicing if you're not going to use it?"

Cassie scowled, thoroughly confused by the situation. She'd thought that the two men had come to mug her or worse, and while she had been assaulted, they were now trying to hold a seemingly pleasant conversation with her. The brunet responded to her bewilderment by introducing himself. "I'm Sone. This is Rho."

"Sone?" she repeated, and then it clicked that her pen pal's name hadn't been pronounced "sun," as she'd assumed. "Sone!" she said, this time with surprise, and actually took in his appearance. The Sone she'd been imagining had been only a little older than she was and was perhaps a recent college graduate who was blessed with strong, handsome features and bright, playful eyes. The real Sone was a bit older—perhaps even twice her age—and had a lined, weathered face. He had an athletic build and an inviting smile. His fashion sense could use a little work, as he wore a nondescript T-shirt, a battered jacket, and some sort of fatigue pants and boots. She supposed that a woman his age might find him attractive, but he certainly didn't live up to her imagination, and she felt her crush deflate instantaneously. "What are you doing here?"

"You mentioned that the BSI visited you last month. I was concerned. I came as soon as I could."

Flustered, she replied, "But why? You could have called."

"To ask you to join SION," he explained. "They protect Others like us." His face softened, and his concern made him resemble her brother. "Remember what I said about the BSI? I don't want you going through that."

She took a step back from them, crossing her arms in front of her and gripping her bag tightly. "I don't either, but…" She had conducted her own research on the BSI, and she knew what the agency had done to Others; it placed its victims in modern-day internment camps, from where they disappeared forever. But she also was not ready to confront this grim reality. Practicing her abilities didn't mean that she was a freak; it meant that she was prepared to defend herself from that fate. However, willingly leaving with these two men meant acknowledging and accepting that unnatural part of her, and she couldn't. She wouldn't voluntarily become an outcast.

Besides, she barely knew Sone; she had corresponded with him about Others only, and not personal affairs, because he'd refused to disclose anything about himself. He'd supported her through her most confusing moments, but he hadn't trusted her with his personal information, so she'd only known the construct of her youthful crush. "I have cheerleading practice tomorrow," she added weakly. "And my brother is expecting me home soon."

Sone nodded. "Okay," he mollified, using his open palms to illustrate that he wasn't a threat. "We'll be around for a few days if you change your mind."

Rho hissed through clenched teeth, "We don't have time for this." He closed the distance between himself and Sone, and turning his mouth away from her, he added quietly, "Antithesis is on our trail. Why don't we just grab the girl, take her back with us, and convince her there once we're safe?"

"Because forcing her to choose would make us no better than the BSI," he replied, either for her benefit or not caring whether she overheard.

Rho balled his fists and punched the air behind the group. "We're gonna talk later," he grunted irritably and then started walking away, most likely to give them privacy.

Sone turned back to her and said, "Go home. Talk to your brother if you need to. We'll—"

She heard Rho swear, and he sprinted the few steps back to the group. "She's here," he warned, and though Cassie wanted to ask who, she was immediately distracted by an unnerving sensation. She had grown used to being able to perceive ignition sources around her, and she felt them being snuffed out like a thick, wet blanket covering the edges of her senses.

"How close?" Sone asked, his voice intensified.

His partner closed his eyes. "Two blocks," he replied. Cassie could feel the extent of the blanket's sphere of influence as it drew closer and the ignition sources denied to her shifted as if they followed an invisible force. Even though she didn't understand the phenomenon, she doubted it heralded anything pleasant.

Suddenly, the thunderous report of a pistol filled the street, and Rho briefly became ethereal as a bullet raced through his formerly occupied position. Then, the report reverberated past them again, as if the sound waves were reversing their path, and Cassie lost track of what ensued as a heavy body forced her momentarily to the ground and then dragged her into an alcove. "Stay here," Rho growled, shoving her firmly against the wall, and he rejoined his partner on the street.

"Aren't you breaking the terms?" Sone's voice boomed in the direction of their foes, but his body language didn't indicate that he had shouted. Cassie could see a dark-skinned woman sprinting toward them and taking cover behind cars as the man with the pistol kept firing. She couldn't hear the shots; she could see only the vague recoil motion of the man in the distance, and she realized that all sounds had disappeared. Unfortunately, the blanket had grown closer with the woman's approach, and disinclined to discover what happened when Others fought, she decided that she would sneak away while her footsteps were muted. She glimpsed Rho dodging the electrical probes of a Taser held by the woman while Sone seemed to keep dancing backward away from the blanket and dividing his attention between the gunman and the woman. Apparently, the woman's blanket only kept them from using their abilities within it, but it did not negate their effects entirely. Neither party had their attention on Cassie, and she quickly dashed down the street, ducking into an alleyway as soon as she could, and hurried away from the commotion. She could hear police sirens in the distance and decided to stay away from them as well.

- - -

Amanda Darling-Whitcomb was elegant as ever as she nibbled daintily at her dandelion and arugula salad; subconsciously, she knew that each pose she struck was picture perfect. "Never give your rivals any ground," her mother had always said, though her strategic scope had encompassed only competing females. However, Amanda knew that being close to flawless also made it harder for her political enemies to undermine her. Unfortunately, one of her adversary–allies was sitting across from her at the moment.

Jack Everest sported a sanguine grin as he ate and casually dabbed the corners of his mouth to catch the occasional drop of blood dripping from his juicy steak. Enthusiastically, he recounted his latest court triumph, careful to excise from the conversation any specifics that would land him in legal trouble. He seemed particularly delighted to detail how he'd twisted the words of the star witness—an upstanding society wife who'd contrived to entrap his client in an embezzlement scheme—into a dubious and unpalatable narrative. Given the way he described the woman, Amanda thought he might be making a point of how he could distort any affiliation between them to his advantage. If it came to this, she'd hire one of the partners from his own law firm; she was far more important to their business than Jack was and he'd be hung out to dry. Jack was not as clever or invulnerable as he thought, and regardless, he wouldn't ruin her appetite today.

"Honestly, though, these sorts of trials are quite dull. I'd love to become involved in a murder trial—a real one," he said, suddenly shifting topics. "Like this recent string of murders in upstate New York. I think I might even do it pro bono."

"String?" she repeated indifferently. "I thought there had been only one."

Jack's eyes lit up. "Oh, you missed it," he said eagerly. "They found a mass grave in Johnstown. The media is just eating it up. They're calling him the Bramble Butcher because he buried their remains in some sort of a briar patch." He took a sip of tea. "Of course, I'd hate to be the one in charge when they fail to convict the perpetrator. Any forensic evidence from that area is bound to be tainted since it's a cold crime scene, and it took them a while to realize there was more than one body. People trampled all through the area. Who knows what sort of missteps the investigators made in preserving the evidence?" His winsome chuckle was incongruous with the gruesome conversation topic, though he kept his tone lighthearted. "But with a prolific serial killer, such as this Bramble Butcher, it's essential to convict. Failure could destroy a political career."

Amanda gave a deep sigh of displeasure. "Yes, it would be a shame, but thankfully, Johnstown is an hour north and far outside my jurisdiction."

"For now," he replied mysteriously. As always, his expression and emotional state were inscrutable, but it was clear that he knew more than he had chosen to disclose. "Still, I would think it'd be prudent for a woman with your aspirations to have connections with other counties. It's always advantageous to have allies publicly endorse you. Your colleague might appreciate it if you reached out to him. He needn't accept your assistance for you to benefit politically from the offer."

She wished that he'd get to the point; unfortunately, he spoke plainly only when he was threatening her. "Do you know something?"

"Simply that it's not in your best interest to allow the police to investigate further and find the real culprit," he advised. "It will not turn out well for you or any politician in Johnstown."

While her intuition told her that this wasn't the entire truth, she knew better than to confront Jack directly. Perhaps he was closely connected to the murderer—an affiliation that, given enough time and information, she might use to her advantage—and if this was the case, she might be able to finally free herself of her debt to him. "What do you suggest?" she asked coyly.

"That you either sort a roadblock or a patsy for the police," he advised. "Any sort of misdirection from the real culprit."

"Again, I think you overestimate my influence, Mr. Everest," she replied pleasantly. "But I will see what I can do." She had no jurisdiction over Johnstown, which limited her sway over the proceedings. She could offer experienced detectives and forensic technicians to her counterpart, but despite involving her personnel in the investigation, she would still have no influence over it. She had no personal pull within the police department, apart from positional power, and she doubted she could use it to modify the results to Jack's liking.

"See that you do, Ms. Whitcomb," he interjected. "I'm still not pleased with your prior performance."

Composed yet placating, she replied, "I am limited in my resources. I cannot guarantee a thing other than that I will try."

"And deliver results, *Mrs. President*," he prompted. Somehow, his use of her sought title was ominous, like an implied threat. She agreed hastily despite herself, and he moved on to less provocative topics.

- - -

Rho hissed through his teeth as the sewing needle pierced his flesh. Sone tried his best to ignore his partner's reactions as he inserted the makeshift sutures, but his inexperience in this regard didn't help matters. Luckily, Rho was a good patient, only making the slightest pained sounds rather than flinching and exacerbating the wound. Sone wondered again about the mystery of his partner's past. "Decent stitching," Rho lied through a crooked grin as soon as Sone finished his work, and he wiped the wound clean again with a cloth. The black thread was crooked and had been spaced unevenly, but it had nevertheless done its job of closing the gash. Rho took an extra precaution and rolled a piece of cloth, which he'd torn from the hotel bedsheets, around his bicep to dress his injury.

Sone removed his shirt and used the mirror to examine any marks that the battle may have left. Most were just scrapes and bruises. His neck would probably become a lot darker within a few hours because Antithesis' fist had caught him just under the jaw. Although he'd lost his breath, he didn't think there would be any permanent damage to his trachea. He'd need ice to quell any subsequent swelling or bruising, so he grabbed the ice bucket and headed to the machine, only to discover that it was out of order. He used the scoop to dredge out the few ice cubes that were lodged in the reservoir and returned with this paltry prize to their room.

"She ain't worth it," Rho declared as soon as Sone re-entered their room. Rho was using the bathroom mirror to examine the hole in the side of his shirt; a bullet had probably scraped his flank as it had passed.

Sone grabbed a washcloth and began filling it with ice. "Yes, she is. We all are. We have to unite against the BSI. You know that," he reasserted as he placed the compress against his jaw.

"They were shooting at us, man. They never risk confrontation like that in a civilian center. This is generally when we cut someone loose." Rho stuck his finger through the bullet hole in his shirt and then used it to assist in taking it off. There was a corresponding angry red mark on his side, but it was no more serious than a slight burn. "Come back later and try again."

"It doesn't seem right to do that this time." Rho shot him an incredulous look, but he continued, "She's a *kid*. Most of the people we deal with are adults or have adults with them. She doesn't. I just—" Sone drew his lips together tightly, biting the insides as he thought. He couldn't explain that his mother would be disappointed in his decision to leave a child vulnerable to the BSI... that the legendary woman drilled into his head by his father's grieving devotion haunted him for the sacrifice she made for Sone. Leaving someone he had a chance to save made him culpable in that person's death. "We're in a large population center. They'll have to be more discreet, or they'll risk exposure, and we know they'll bend over backward to keep us a secret. They're not going to break Blackout over one girl."

Rho sighed. "They already broke Blackout when they fought us in an open street. It might have been midnight, but you know, this being New York, that somebody saw. Where do you think those cops came from? Nobody calls cops in the city over a few gunshots." He shook his head. "I don't think they're going to be as discreet as you think they are."

"We're also wanted criminals, Rho. And now that they've seen us with her, we've made her a target," he insisted. "We're already here. We didn't come all this way not to finish the job."

"Fine. Fine," he agreed reluctantly. "But next time, I get Antithesis, and you get to dodge the bullets." He tossed his shirt at Sone, who barely caught it before it hit him in the face. He smiled wryly yet kept a gruff voice as he added, "And practice your sewing on that! I'm hitting the shower."

- - -

Orion sat in the dimly lit kitchen as he fingered through his textbook distractedly. The dinner that he had prepared still sat in their respective containers on the table, but the food they contained had long grown cold, and the ice in the drinks had melted. He pushed the unused stack of plates to the side, where it brushed against the silverware, causing it to chime discordantly. He was certain Hallowed Grounds must have already closed for the night, so Cassie should have been home by now. Despite the attempted mugging, his first thought regarding her tardiness was that she'd decided to socialize with one of the male patrons after hours. She was currently going through a phase of pursuing "mature" older males.

He was relieved to hear his phone ring, especially when it identified the caller as his sister. "Hey, where are you?" he asked in his sternest voice.

"Ryan?" Her voice was shaky. "I'd rather not say."

He straightened immediately, leaning toward the phone and table as if the closer proximity would allow him to perceive more through the line. "Cass, what's wrong?"

"I... will you meet me at the mall?" As she spoke, he imagined her huddled in a corner, peering furtively around her.

"Why don't I just pick you up?" he offered. "Tell me where you are, and I'll grab a taxi."

"No," she replied hastily. "Just meet me there."

"They're closing soon, if they haven't already. Why don't—"

"Fine! The Rockefeller Center, Times Square, I don't care! Just some place with a lot of people. Um, a lot of people all night. Yeah."

Fear was closing around his heart. If her agitation hadn't already charged his adrenaline, her evasiveness wasn't helping matters. "Pickle, what's wrong? Are you safe?"

"Yes, Ryan, just... please just meet me somewhere public and crowded." With a jitter, she added, "And not the police station. Don't contact that detective. I don't want the government to get involved again."

His alarm became terror. "Cassiopeia—"

"I'm fine. I'll tell you about it when I see you. I promise. I just don't want another visit from *them*."

He nodded, though he didn't really agree, but if she wouldn't tell him her location, then he could only follow her instructions. Something had sparked her fright, an emotion to which she wasn't prone, and he hoped that she'd remain unharmed until she was in his custody again. He convinced her to suggest a "safe" place near her location and agreed to meet her there. After stammering some reassurances, he hung up and immediately called his parents for advice. If the government had come back to retrieve his sister, maybe his parents would know what to do. He grabbed his wallet and donned his hoodie sloppily while the phone in his hand kept ringing. He hung up and tried again, only to be greeted by the voicemail a second time. As he hurried out the door, he realized that he should have known better than to rely on his parents.

- - -

Emma Braddock was no more. She had been a fragile idealist working toward a monumental, society-changing goal, only to discover that the man whom she'd idolized—the one she would have offered herself to or died for—had been nothing more than a fraudster preying on the weak-minded. When federal agents had invaded the compound on which she had been raised, they'd arrested the adults and placed the children into foster care. People her age—adolescents on the cusp of adulthood or who had just crossed that threshold—had been siphoned into a different holding facility until they could be properly interviewed and catalogued as victims or perpetrators. After a week, she'd been rescued from the chaos by a single agent and enfolded in the structured womb of the BSI. The agent, whom she had known as Morgan Connor, had kept in touch with her on occasion, ensuring that her transition from an isolated, xenophobic, and religious upbringing to normal civil society had been smooth, but it had been the agency's staff members who had educated and transformed her. As Emma had been introduced to the modern world, she'd shed her peculiar childhood beliefs in favor of the BSI doctrine, and it had become her foundational conviction that she would stand between the weak—that is, normal human beings—and the supernatural. Thus, Emma Braddock had died, and Antithesis had been born.

"The arrogance of it all!" she exclaimed angrily, clutching the back of her head with her hands. Her fingers threaded through her tightly curled hair, dividing it into sections as she searched for the distinct sticky wetness of blood. She found none, combed her hair back in place, and started a detailed examination of the rest of her body. She was a fit young woman who had pushed her limits and honed her malnourished body to athletic heights to enable her to better combat Others, but she was still no match for sonic potency or Rho's raw strength. Though her field suppressed the use of supernatural abilities, it did not negate any effects that crossed it, nor could it compensate for natural muscle. "Engaging us in public so we can't use our full force! Using civilians as shields! They're nothing but vermin!"

"That's why we're needed," Johnson panted, hands on his hips as he bent over to catch his breath. He'd already stripped off his jacket, which had survived another encounter with the Vanguard unscathed, and his face was red from exertion. While he was by no means out of shape, their enthusiastic and singled-minded pursuit of the criminal fugitives had pushed his limits to the brink, and even though there were no visible tears in his clothing, she knew that as soon as the adrenaline abandoned them, they would be equally sore.

"I can't believe we lost them again." Her breathing had evened out, but her senses were still finely tuned, and her muscles were screaming from standing still. "Where's the nearest precinct?" she asked. While much of the BSI's ability to track Others was kept secret, even from its own agents, the agency also utilized local sources. In this case, the New York City surveillance camera network, to which the BSI had gained access by using its credentials to bully the police, had been used to track the two criminals to this location.

Johnson shook his head. "I don't think that's going to work again," he said. He inspected his appearance: His firearm was secured in his holster, and he smoothed his trousers, ignoring the new tears and scuffs; luckily, his jacket had avoided a similar fate. He tightened and fixed his tie and draped his jacket over his arm before he started on the arduous task of retrieving his emptied clips and expended shells. "We got lucky. There are thousands of cameras to search. We're going to have to figure something else out."

"Like what?" she demanded impatiently. Detective work was not her forte, nor was it expected to be, but Johnson didn't have the aptitude for it either. His job was to cover her back and direct her at a target like the spotter for a sniper. Their job was pursuit, apprehension, and transference of custody between civilian agencies and the bureau, but neither of them knew how to find a target without a support team. It was also why they were the frequent subjects of administrative discipline: Regrettably, apprehension often required the use of force, which was something that the agency mandated should be employed only sparingly in the public forum. It was too bad that the Vanguard didn't abide by these same rules, and it was only natural that she and Johnson would use equal force in pursuit of their duties. "They went that way. Maybe if I run fast enough, I could catch up and find them."

Still picking up and pocketing shells, Johnson smiled suddenly as he closed his hands around an unexpected boon. "I don't think we have to worry about it," he said and held up a small, nondescript cell phone.

- - -

As Pierce peered out the window at the lights flashing in the darkness in the field encircling the observatory, the corners of his mouth twisted into a sour frown. The police were searching the grounds in hopes of finding more evidence regarding the murder of the girl in Johnstown. From what he gathered, they had identified the victim and traced her missing cell phone via GPS to this location. This meant that he'd been sloppy. He'd thought it odd that there had been no cell phone among the personal effects of a young woman like her, but the device was still uncommon with most drifters, who may have sold it off to pay bills before becoming homeless if they'd decided that retaining it wasn't advantageous to their future situation. With the location of the missing device pinpointed, the police had obtained a warrant to search the surrounding area for further evidence, such as an actual death site. But although they had searched all day, they had yet to find anything apart from the phone, which had been trampled into the muddy road leading up to the main building. He doubted they would continue the search under the cover of darkness, so the police must be finishing up a sector before calling it quits for the night.

They had finally slipped up. The painstaking nature of Pierce's methodology—isolate a single beast, bring it to one of the kill sites, and then butcher it in the special slaughter room, where he and Madeleine could control the disposal of evidence—had been for naught. He had argued with Madeleine for the past hour about whose fault it was—who should have realized that the cell phone had existed and that it had fallen out of the animal's pocket—and she'd retired resentfully to the slaughter room. Since they were both at equal risk, he doubted she was doing little more than another deep cleaning. After she'd had a chance to cool down, he'd join her to help dispose of the most conspicuous items, such as his cleaver and knife collection.

Luckily, he'd scrubbed the trunk of their car as soon as they'd returned to Mason, so it was unlikely that the search dogs would detect the scent of the body, masked as it was now with cleaning agents and other smells. Still, it was only a matter of time before the police department would apply for a warrant to search the observatory. It was only logical; even if they had been innocent, the Starrs' statement to the police that they spent too much time in the observatory with the telescope to notice any terrestrial events was a flimsy alibi, so the law would no doubt believe that they were at least witnesses to the crime who had their own reasons for keeping silent. The uproar Madeleine raised regarding the county's imminent luminous interference with their observations served to delay the police and restrict them to daylight activity, but it didn't faze them altogether, especially because they were looking for a probable serial killer.

Pierce determined that his best chance was to leave before the police obtained their warrant. He expected to eventually end up on the wanted list, but at least he wouldn't be arrested straight away. He might be able to disappear with a decent head start, and a plan started to form in his mind. He entered the slaughter room and saw Madeleine sitting cross-legged in the center of the floor. She had taken all of his tools and separated them into piles on the floor. "What are you doing?" he asked.

"I'm figuring out which ones we need to dispose of immediately and which ones we can hide." She nodded toward one pile. "I think we can explain the plastic sheets easily enough, but the bleach will have to go. I thought about pouring it down the drain, but we'd still have the bottles."

He nodded. "I can take them with me," he offered.

She tilted her head, shifting her curls from their precarious position. Despite taking the precaution of wearing a hairnet, she hadn't secured her hair properly. "Where are you going?"

"Back to the university. I thought I'd hand-carry our results since they stopped Dr. Harper from joining us," he explained nonchalantly. "They can't prevent us from leaving if we've not been charged with anything."

"I'll go with you. I have some equipment I need to exchange," she replied, rising to her feet after some hesitancy due to her aged knees. She handed him a pair of latex gloves. "Here. Help me put these away. We'll take the rest with us," she said. She grabbed the box of latex gloves and some of the smaller knives and headed toward the kitchen. While some of their more unremarkable tools could be hidden inconspicuously around their living space, Pierce would have preferred to leave as soon as possible. But doing that might draw Madeleine's suspicion; she was intelligent and resourceful—traits that he'd once found attractive—and she would recognize the blatant attempt to leave her. If either of them went to the police now, it'd be their word against the other's, and Pierce would rather avoid the spotlight completely so that he could resume his activities in the future. He'd have to allow her to stay by his side until he found a way to unequivocally ensure her apprehension by the law. He grabbed a pair of bleach bottles, having decided that dumping their contents and burning the jugs would seem suspicious but would ultimately provide nothing for any prosecutor to use. The absence of evidence created reasonable doubt, especially if one couldn't prove what evidence had been destroyed in the first place, and since they were entering the fall months, it was conceivable that the police would believe that they were using the furnace solely to generate heat.

- - -

Sone and Rho tried to stay hidden in the darkest corner of the street, but it wasn't an easy task. Cassie Starr lived in an affluent part of the city, where the lights never dimmed and no one could enter a building without having a pass code or convincing the doorman that they were residents. Rho had noticed as much and had used it as an opportunity to suggest that Cassie wasn't as helpless as Sone believed. He wasn't wrong; her building was secure from intruders and insulated from the city's filth. But she wasn't safe. Sone had discerned her real name easily enough by tracing her IP address and had narrowed down the possibilities from there. While it had taken several hours and many illegal forays into private servers, with some determination, the data had been easy to retrieve. Once he'd discovered her real name, finding out what she looked like by hacking into the school district's database and pulling her profile had been straightforward. This had also revealed her extracurricular activities, and he knew where to find her at any given time.

The government probably already had all of Cassie's information, especially if the BSI agent had done his job properly. But to the best of his observations, the agency wasn't actively monitoring her, and she hadn't been escorted back to one of its facilities. He knew that he had to use this mysterious gap in their procedures to his advantage and retrieve Cassie as soon as possible.

"I don't think anyone's home," Rho murmured. He was leaning against the wall, obscuring his face with his shaggy locks. Both of his hands were in his pockets as he tried to seem as nonchalant as possible, but he knew that he was a suspicious figure in this neighborhood. "Light's out." He nodded toward the windows that they believed belonged to Cassie's apartment. "There's been no activity from any of the people we've seen go in, and she's not been here either."

Sone sighed as he reached into his pocket to check the time on his phone, only to realize that it wasn't there. He must have dropped it either during the fight or as they'd fled. Thankfully, it had no vital information on it, but its loss was inconvenient. "Just a few more minutes. She might not have gone straight home." But as soon as he'd voiced it, he knew that he was lying to himself.

Rho spat on the ground angrily and shook his head. He had opened his mouth to reply, when he caught sight of a movement and turned his head. Sone followed his gaze and spotted a petite woman striding purposefully toward them. She was wearing a short dress, fishnets, and high heels, and he wondered why she had decided to stalk this part of town; escorts knew to be discreet and to take a taxi to their destination. Despite her tawdry makeup and attire, the woman was trying to be inconspicuous. "Mr. Lionhart says he can get you out of the city," she whispered when she reached them. Her voice was husky, either from sickness or from having smoked too many cigarettes, and was not helped by her thick accent.

"Lady, er... Miss, we're not interested," Sone replied and turned back to look at the string of windows.

The woman licked her lips and repeated, "Mr. Lionhart says he can get you out of the city and the BSI won't know. But you have to go now."

"What?" he asked, finally catching the name that she'd repeated. His father had mentioned the name several times during SION's infancy, and the memory served to validate her message.

Her eyes flitted about nervously. "His offer's only good for now. He says if you don't come, you gotta find your own way out."

"The girl's not home. I know you don't want to, but we can always come back and try again with less heat," Rho reasoned. "This might be our only chance to escape. It's better for the girl, too."

Sone mulled over the idea, and as much as he hated to admit it, Rho had a point. They had lost Antithesis and her handler for the moment, but until they knew how they were being tracked, Sone's actions were more likely to bring the BSI down on Cassie. Antithesis might be tracking them to the SoHo apartment now. If they left the city undetected, they could regroup and maybe contact Cassie and convince her to meet them at another location. She'd clearly needed some time to think about her options, and this would allow her to do that. "Fine. Let's go," he agreed. The woman nodded nervously and started back in the direction from which she had come.

- - -

"Connor! Come with me!"

He started and looked up from his computer screen to see the face of his supervisor, William Terrance. He quickly saved the file he was working on and followed the burly man back to his office. The chair behind the desk howled as Terrance swiveled it to face him, and it squealed again in protest when he sat down. Connor took a much quieter seat across from the desk, and as he slouched into it, he folded his hands casually across his lap. "What is it, boss?"

"I know you've never been wrong before, but I think we need to reassess the Starr case," Terrance said, sliding a plain folder across the desk toward him. "Agent Johnson and Antithesis tracked VSION terrorists Sone and Rho to New York City, where they confronted them." His slight scowl was all Connor needed to see to surmise that the pursuit had been against Terrance's orders. If he remembered correctly, Sone liked to flaunt his sonic powers to bait the BSI into combat or retreat in an attempt to use Blackout as a shield; BSI agents were to avoid publicly exposing Others at any cost. "They were unable to apprehend the two, but one of the terrorists dropped a burner phone. It didn't have much on it, except for Starr's home and work addresses and her schedule," he told him. "I want to know why they were after her." He gave a casual, almost consoling shrug. "Maybe you were wrong. Maybe we should bring her in after all."

"Yes, sir," Connor replied, slightly puzzled. He'd recommended training the girl, which meant they should have already escorted her to Plum Island. It was his normal procedure to follow up on his cases and see how the subjects were adjusting to their new lives, but the Brian Chamberlain assignment had consumed his thoughts. Antithesis had personally collected the child, and without any ceremony, he had been euthanized at the containment facility. Marilyn's body had also been retrieved and would be dissected and studied alongside her son's for a brief time before its disposal. Connor had taken the next week off, determined not to learn how the death had affected the sister or father, and following all of this stress, he'd completely forgotten about Cassiopeia Starr.

Every identified Other was escorted to the facility on Plum Island to undergo a final analysis regardless of their skills or level of control. The fact that Cassie wasn't already at the facility confused him because he thought an elementalist would've been a priority for collection. It was possible that Angel and Antithesis had been otherwise engaged and that they were necessary accessories when the BSI agents took Others into custody; this was standard procedure that had been put in place to protect the staff, even if the individual accompanied them willingly.

"Is that it?" he asked.

"Yes," Terrance replied. "Take the folder with you. You might need it." He took a deep breath in an attempt to stem the disapproval that was bubbling into his voice. "Agent Johnson knows they left the area, but he lost track of them. Maybe you'll see something he missed." Connor nodded, grabbed the folder, and started to leave. "Oh, and, Connor? Sorry about the kid."

Connor hesitated in the doorway, rubbing the back of his neck briefly before replying. "Yeah? Had to be done." He didn't want to invite further conversation, so he made a quick exit. "See you, boss."

- - -

The video showed the young woman, who would be later identified as Elizabeth Singh, peering cautiously outside the elevator and studying both ends of the hallway like a timid deer. The surveillance camera was mounted in the elevator, so it did not pick up her pursuer, if there was even one. She began to press every button frantically, and she pounded on the close door mechanism, which failed to obey. She paced nervously back and forth, again peering into the hallway, and then sank into a crouch in the corner, covering her head with her hands as if to block out whatever was affecting her. Finally, she stood and sprinted into the hallway as if demons were on her tail. At this point, the video resembled another mystery that had occurred some years earlier at a different hotel across the country. The other girl, Elisa Lam, had also behaved bizarrely in an elevator before her decomposing body had been discovered in a water tank on the roof.

What the camera didn't show was Elizabeth's path after she fled the elevator. First, she took the stairs, skipping steps until she reached the roof level, and after a brief struggle with the locking mechanism, she burst into the sunlight. This is where the video resumed, though it was clearly captured by another camera that was located on the ground. Why someone was filming this might be questioned, but it would become a part of the greater mystery.

Elizabeth stood at the edge of the roof, hesitating several times. She appeared to change her mind, stepping back from the precipice, only to return shortly thereafter, almost as if it were against her will. When she stepped off, it appeared that she had been driven to do so; it was as if the great impact that awaited her was preferable to whatever had pursued her to the roof. The video also depicted her body's collision with the ground, and while the inclusion of the moment of her death was in poor taste, it ensured that the video would go viral.

Jack hoped that the media would also latch onto the story. Elizabeth Singh had been a beautiful young woman whose suicide had been dismissed when it had originally occurred years ago, but this new video evidence should inspire amateur sleuths and conspiracy theorists to reexamine the incident and create a public outcry that the case had been mishandled. Jack did not intend for the obsession to persist any longer than a few months, especially since no one would work out that a potent combination of pheromones had caused a certain young lover to jump to her death, but it would hopefully engender enough curiosity that its true message would be heard—that he had more evidence on Amanda Darling-Whitcomb's activities than she knew, and he would use it against her if she continued to be coy and uncooperative when it came to his requests.

PART IV
CODE NAME: ZENITH

Pierce had been so foolish and complacent. He had known that he would one day need to leave his current comfortable, familiar life and begin anew, but he'd always assumed that this change would be at his own discretion. He was meticulous—almost obsessive—when it came to planning his hunts, and he never believed that physical evidence would cause his downfall. According to his plan, which had now been spoilt, he would come to the decision that it was time to move on to new hunting grounds. He would take the funds he'd funneled into a private account, fake his own murder, frame Madeleine for it, and begin a new life in another country. He'd considered returning to his homeland of Britain, but he'd probably head south to Australia or another former colony; it was conceivable his earlier English crimes had been discovered during the past few decades, so it was better not to needlessly risk his freedom by returning to his mother country. Additionally, blending in with an expatriate community with similar accents might make him less conspicuous than he had been when stalking his prey in the United States. Instead, the police had somehow discovered their latest victim, and his sloppiness had allowed them to trace the trail back to their lair. It was only a matter of time before the police put the pieces together and determined that he and his wife were the perpetrators, and then after a drawn-out investigation and trial, he might be convicted or acquitted. Either way, his future hunting prospects would be ruined, and he might begin to age in the interim. Pierce needed to eschew the limelight entirely.

This was the reason he was heading back to New York City with his wife. He could diminish suspicion if he acted normally, which meant returning home to report to the university and to check on their children. However, his desire was to empty the joint account that he shared with his wife and flee before the authorities had the time to gather evidence and obtain a warrant. While not ideal, he could seek refuge in a European country that refused extradition until he could secure a new identity.

His current obstacle was the lack of a solid plan. It was clear that he still needed to frame Madeleine for his murder, but if he could pin their kills on her before he fled, this could provide additional insurance against a likely police pursuit. The challenge was how to accomplish this with the same diligence with which he'd stalked the beasts. Madeleine was intelligent and resourceful, and she was probably pondering her own escape; she'd see him coming if he wasn't cautious.

Fortunately, it took several hours to drive home, which ensured that he had enough time to formulate a new plan. He finished urinating, zipped up his pants, and started his trek back to the car where he has stopped it by the side of the road. The air was cool, the forest was still, and the fall leaves crunched under his feet as he passed through the undergrowth. One might believe that a forest would be an appealing place to conduct a hunt or butcher an animal, but it was far too open and had too many escape routes. He could also easily overlook vital evidence, as he had done with the last animal's cell phone. However, if containment wasn't an issue, he would have liked to hunt in open ground like this simply to see if he was as skilled there as he was in an urban environment. Just once, he'd have liked to see whether he could have chased down his prey instead of luring it like a spider into his web of beauty and charm.

His wife had reclined the passenger seat and had likely settled in for a nap beneath her jacket. She rarely stayed awake when he drove; she often made the trip by herself, so she especially enjoyed the occasional break that he provided when he accompanied her.

Crack! He imagined he could hear his crown breaking as his vision suddenly went black and he saw stars. *Thump!* No, it was a meaty noise reverberating directly through his skull into his eardrums and being transformed into something sharper and more fragile than the real impact. The first strike dropped him to his knees, and the second threatened to invert his world into one of pain. His wife was quick, and he could hear her soft soles scraping against the gravel as she positioned herself behind him for the killing blow. Her strikes had only stunned him without disabling him, and his vision returned in time to see the side of their car turn crimson due to the sudden spraying of his newly opened artery. Madeleine did not realize the true power of their cannibalism, for she underestimated his resilience and relinquished the tire iron in favor of a carving knife. It wasn't even a clean cut, as she'd been taught to make, and her sloppiness was likely due to the hasty nature of her assault.

She was caught unaware when he clutched her wrist, which was still clasped around the kitchen knife. She tried to move against him and drive the knife deeper, but he wrenched it free from his flesh and threw her off. If he were merely human, he knew he'd have been dead within seconds, and regrettably, even his ability to heal couldn't combat catastrophic blood loss. He covered the wound with one hand and started after Madeleine, who didn't even bother to murmur an excuse as he took the knife in his free hand. She had murder in her eyes, just as he did, and yet her participation in their hunts had never required physical confrontation. It was his job to kill and her job to cook. Even though his head still pulsed angrily and he could feel his strength draining through the warmth escaping between his fingers, she was no match for the physically younger man. Her only chance had been to take him by surprise, and she had blown it.

Their gruesome dance took them into the forest, which was now painted in various shades of scarlet. He didn't have the strength to move her body, let alone sanitize the scene, which would have proved an impossible task anyway. He could not conceal evidence this time; he could only hope that law enforcement would assume that the amount of blood he'd left at the scene was indicative of his own death. Though the bleeding had slowed, it had not stopped, and he felt faint. A desperate hunger rose within him, and he briefly considered devouring some of his former love before immediately discarding the idea. A whole body would raise fewer questions than a partially consumed one, no matter how her flesh might rejuvenate him. He would survive this if he remained patient and meticulous.

His plan was in motion, even if it was not the one he'd conceived or preferred. Another motorist would drive by the scene, see something amiss, and report it, and he would become officially dead. But he was currently unfunded and trapped within this country. He had a small window in which he could retrieve funds from his joint account without raising the suspicion of the authorities. He needed to move so he could place some distance between himself and this site. He would use the driving time to devise a cohesive plan. He was resourceful, and he would survive.

- - -

The trio had to walk a few blocks before the prostitute deemed it safe enough for them to take a cab. She smiled and tried to make small talk with the cab driver, but Sone noticed that she was still tense and that she tried to take up the least amount of space next to the two men that she could during their ride. He wondered if she knew what he and Rho were or if there was something else at play. Regardless, it wasn't his place to make her relax; if he knew how to turn fear of Others into respect, he'd be a part of the propaganda team.

When they arrived at a string of warehouses, the woman paid the cab driver and then motioned for the two of them to follow. The car's headlights briefly illuminated their path before it disappeared, leaving dingy streetlamps to do the bulk of the work. With her clicking heels echoing like a horse's slow clopping gait, she walked quickly down the long avenue. Though the briny scent of the air indicated that they were somewhere near the docks, a wall of metal shipping containers obstructed any view of the estuary that must be nearby.

When they reached their destination, the woman flung the warehouse door wide open and hastily ducked in and off to the side. Sone didn't even have time to become suspicious before he saw a small blond figure wrap his hand firmly around Rho's throat. The slight man was surprisingly strong, because Rho couldn't even put up a fight, and he didn't make a sound as the man squeezed his trachea as if he were testing the ripeness of a tomato. A dark vapor, which was perhaps a trick of the dim light and the dropping temperature, seemed to flow from Rho's body into the newcomer. As Sone watched in horror, his partner's skin became withered, and his mass seemed to evaporate.

After his initial shock passed, Sone's battle mind awoke, and he reached out to the buzzing of the streetlamps, increased its reverberation, and directed the soundwaves back at the stranger and his partner. However, the attack seemed to pass right through them, as if Rho's ability expanded to aid his assailant, and the blond man continued to drain his friend.

The incomprehensible attack seemed to last less than a minute, and the stranger discarded the corpse disdainfully and glared at Sone with steely blue eyes. "Tell your glocky blinkered scurf that New York ain't some flash house where he can cause a blasted jolly," he snarled, his face distorted with rage. "He'll not queer my pitch with his pig's ear revolution, or I'll put down on him with the coppers."

The blond's accent was heavy and almost unintelligible, and his anger was practically palpable. Though Sone didn't want to aggravate him further, he also thought figuring out his perplexing message might alleviate the situation if only he could understand him. Uncertainly, he asked, "What did you say?"

"Moreau's dogs stay out my town else they get done up like a kipper," the blond said, his accent softening into a more recognizable version of Cockney. Unfortunately, it didn't make his speech any more comprehensible, and Sone didn't have the opportunity to ask him again. He realized now that they weren't alone. While the prostitute had long disappeared, a handful of other men had stepped from the shadows. Two immediately went to Rho's corpse, barely hiding their revulsion as they wrapped its husk in a tarp for disposal.

"If you still want to scarper with my help, Javier's your man." The blond nodded to the man on his right; the lanky fellow oozed confidence despite his rather homely appearance. "He's invisible to the BSI, if you have the bottle to trust me now." The blond grinned, and it was strangely charismatic and reassuring despite his earlier show of force.

Sone looked at his offered guide and considered everything that had just occurred. Trusting him would be foolish, especially after the display, but the blond clearly wanted a message delivered to his father, and apparently, he could have defeated Sone as easily as he had killed Rho. There was no advantage in a further ruse, and while it would be in the blond man's best interest to assist Sone if he wanted his message delivered, Sone still didn't think he could accept the offer. Not only was it disrespectful to his partner, but the thought also made him ill. He shook his head. "I'll find my own way out," he replied, managing to conceal his disgust and anger.

The blond nodded. "Off you go then. And don't frig about, else you'll get brown bread too." He turned his attention away from Sone toward a dour-faced man, and it was as if Sone had disappeared as the blond focused on other business. Sone took his leave quietly, retreating through the front door, and traced his way along the warehouses. His thoughts turned toward returning home as he reached the edge of the city, and he chose to leave introspection and analysis until when he was in safe surroundings.

- - -

Unlike his female counterpart, Eric Dane had retained his given name, but it was his identity that he had lost. He retained distant memories of a normal childhood in a close-knit town in rural Wyoming, where everyone was an aunt, uncle, grandmother, or grandfather. He remembered an older brother who shoved him and called him names at home but kept him calm and safe when the Youngs entered the school and herded them into a single classroom. He remembered the worried expressions on his parents' faces, his mother's streaked mascara, and when his parents charged the police line and gathered him and his brother into their eager arms. Images of his last memory of his family were obscured by his tears as his grim-faced father, grief-stricken mother, and uncertain brother said their final goodbyes as he was taken into permanent federal custody. His father had told him that the transfer was for the best, but years later, he suspected that the Danes had received generous compensation.

He maintained those memories, but his ties to his old life nevertheless rotted. When the BSI was created, it expended adequate funds to create a comfortable lifestyle for him and any Others who might join him at the Plum Island compound. His quarters were spacious and gave him enough privacy that he didn't mind the constant video surveillance or the guards' clockwork knocks on the door. He spent his youth in the laboratory with agency scientists who sought to understand his ability and helped him to hone it. His talent could produce avian wings for shields, their luminescent appearance giving the impression of angels. But he was capable of even more, and with the bureau's guidance, he discovered that he could craft his radiance into simple physical objects, such as a hammer, sled, or even a footbridge.

He continued his education, albeit with a narrowed and sometimes heavily censored curriculum, and the bureau was forthright with its reasoning: Political ideas, cultural touchstones, and social issues only obfuscated their mission. So he learned from tutors and supplemented the lessons with readings of his own, and he didn't mind when his materials were missing a page or two or a paragraph had been blacked out. After all, the bureau provided him with ample entertainment in the form of movies and video games, and he was allowed to read newspapers and magazines whenever he wished. As he grew older, he began to request books and was able to educate himself on the philosophies of the Founding Fathers and Theodore Roosevelt and the Classics, such as Shakespeare and Mark Twain. He was free to discuss these ideas with bureau personnel and his teachers for his own edification, and no one ever denigrated his opinions or beliefs.

He was also aware of the charges that SION had laid against the bureau—that it slaughtered Others to study them like animals and that Dane had been brainwashed. Of course he knew that Others were euthanized, but this occurred only on the rare occasion that they could not develop control over their abilities. It wasn't the rule but was the final recourse after all other options had been expended, and it was a difficult decision when it was made. He was given ample opportunity to speak to captured Vanguards so that he could relay that message, but after the first few prisoners refused to listen and only spouted their own misguided propaganda at him, he stopped trying to reason with them and interacted with them only during apprehensions. Regrettably, the nonmilitant members of SION weren't any more rational or levelheaded.

For the longest time, he was alone. Discovering a preadolescent Other was atypical—a rarity that was comparable to a paragon diamond—and even mature Others didn't necessarily equal productive ones. So Dane remained unaccompanied as graduates were eventually returned to the general population, albeit in a different location from where they'd lived; this would ensure that anyone who'd witnessed the talents of the Other wouldn't have the opportunity to revisit him or her for the purposes of recording.

But Dane wasn't lonesome. Over the years, he'd acquired half a score of handlers who had continued to write him letters after they'd been rotated to new assignments, and the compound maintained twenty-four-hour staff, so there was always someone he could engage in conversation.

Then Emma Braddock arrived. She was slightly older than half his age, but she had spent her entire life sequestered from society and from any ideas that contradicted her strict religious upbringing. She was hungry for life and eager to make up for lost time. He helped mentor her, and the world now seemed smaller. The agency's focus shifted to her—on prepping her and then sending her out on raids—and Dane found that he didn't mind the lack of attention, even when she was given accolades for her role in bringing down the SION cell in San Diego and he was not. Her mere presence prevented grievous injury to their human counterparts, while he had to keep an active watch to achieve the same result. Not only would helping her mature and grow facilitate the agency's mission, but he also found that he enjoyed taking the backseat to her fire, which he had lost himself years ago. If this meant that she went out on assignments more often, so be it.

Emma—or Antithesis, as she preferred to be called—entered the lounge and began upending furniture, magazines, and any objects she could get her hands on. Her cult severely punished any deviation from "good behavior," so she had been a model citizen as a child. Upon her release, however, she'd discovered numerous feelings that she'd kept bottled up, and she did not always know how to deal with them properly. When she was angry, it was usually simple: She wanted to fight or scream, so they could point her at the Vanguard, but when no targets were available, her anger became a problem. Dane and the staff were working on teaching her healthy expression, but he needed to intervene in the interim.

"Sissy," he said warmly as he caught her latest projectile and prevented it from rebounding and hitting her. He placed his hands on her arms, gently restraining them, and said, "We talked about this. What should you be doing instead?" She clenched her fists, tensed her whole body, and then, after a few seconds, relaxed and exhaled slowly. "Good girl. Now what's wrong?"

She inhaled sharply and stiffened, but her voice was calm as she answered. "We lost them in a civilian center. They kept endangering civilians. They were using them as shields. They got a hold of this one girl..." She'd only caught a glimpse of the redhead as she and Johnson had closed in on the terrorists, and she'd seen Rho throw her into a wall, but she'd been too busy concentrating on the offensive to pay attention to any distractions. When the Taser hadn't worked, she'd closed the gap between her and the muscle and attempted to overpower him with the strength of her zeal. Unfortunately, her enthusiasm tended to override her better judgement, and Johnson soon took him off her hands.

Nevertheless, she couldn't believe she'd forgotten one of the core tenets of their mission: protect civilians. "I don't know what happened to her. I lost track of her, and then the cops showed up, so Agent Johnson had to explain what happened." Regardless of jurisdiction, the local police did not tolerate the discharge of a weapon within their gun-free city. Johnson's attempts to extricate them were rebuffed, and the two were forcibly escorted down to the precinct to explain their behavior not only to the local police chief but also to Johnson's supervisor and his boss back at BSI headquarters. It was a short reprimand, which was to be resumed at length in the BSI chief's office after the mission was over, and they were free to return to the streets after a sufficient amount of paperwork had been properly filed.

It had been hours before they'd been able to check on the girl, whose apartment had been dark and seemingly abandoned, and when they'd checked with the doorman, he hadn't seen her return that night. "After it was all over, we went to her place, but no one was there." She bit her lip and then kicked the wall. "What if something happened to her because of me? Because I didn't do my job?"

Dane pulled her close into an embrace. "VSION isn't going to target a single person," he assured her, though it wasn't necessarily true. Years ago, he had overheard two analysts discussing the record freezing temperatures in Afghanistan and the rising death toll in the region due to frostbite and exposure. One agent, a veteran local interpreter turned federal employee, had returned to his home country to collect his extended family, and neither analyst had heard from him since he'd set out on his excursion. They presumed that the agent's family had been targeted and that villages in the Herat province had simply been collateral damage. But Antithesis didn't need to know this, so he said, "She's probably shaken up and went to the police or a friend's."

She leaned into him. "Johnson said they had her address in their phone. Why would they have that?"

"I don't know, but you're home now," he replied soothingly. "The analysts will handle it, and they'll let you know," he told her, and they might if they thought it was pertinent. But they often didn't hear the resolutions of their cases because it might prove to be a distraction, and this was especially true for Antithesis, who took any failures personally.

"Do you want to watch some TV?" he asked, trying to assuage her anger and guilt by changing the subject. She gave him an unsure look before she nodded hesitantly. "How about some *Gilligan's Island*?" he suggested with a smile and popped the cassette in the VCR. He knew it never failed to cheer her up.

- - -

Reluctantly, Pierce pulled into the gas station parking lot and rolled to a stop. He reached into the back seat and snatched another article of clothing from the overnight bag. He was still bleeding, and the gash was not healing quickly enough. It was as if his body was straining to replace his traitorously escaping blood and could do no better at helping the rest of him. He felt faint, hungry, and diminished, and his reflection in the rearview mirror showed a pale man. He should have taken the time to consume Madeleine. Even a slice of her flesh might have revitalized him enough to staunch the exodus of his lifeblood.

Madeleine's flimsy scarf had already turned crimson and was becoming wet and sticky in his hand. He could tie it around his neck, but he doubted a tourniquet in that location would assist even a superior being such as himself. He threw the scarf on the back seat and grabbed another piece of clothing—this time, it was one of his good shirts—to place against his neck. No, he needed professional attention, which he could not receive without the authorities being alerted eventually.

His son suddenly entered his mind—his weak, pathetic son who would never partake in their sacred, life-sustaining meals. He remembered his last kill at their apartment and Orion's sad attempt to delay the inevitable in the cycle of life like a child freeing the dinner lobster. Orion had tried to knit the animal's wounds together, which was something that Pierce had never attempted to do to another being. Perhaps his son had abilities that differed from his, or were even stronger, and he could mend Pierce's gash. But if he could not, he knew that the spineless boy would offer little resistance in a fight and was, therefore, not a dangerous option for a last-ditch meal. Regardless, his sensitive child offered an attractive alternative to a hospital if he could summon the stamina to reach him.

The gas station attendant, an elderly man in his sixties, dropped his squeegee and raced over to the car. His face was stricken as he asked, "Are you okay? Do you need me to call someone?"

Pierce should have realized that his appearance would garner attention. He'd wiped as much of the blood off the side of the car as he could, but congealed streaks were still visible, and his clothes were torn and stained dark brown from mud and dried gore. He glanced around the parking lot, realizing that they were alone on this stretch of highway, and he had a fleeting thought of consuming this man. Although he was old and would not provide much sustenance, it might still be enough to sustain him until he secured Orion's help.

"Sir? Sir? Can you hear me?"

Pierce scowled. No, as old as the man might have been, he still appeared fit for his age and would, therefore, likely present a challenge, and Pierce didn't think he could take him down without sustaining any more injuries. It would be wiser to continue back to New York City and coerce his son to give him aid than to risk further exposure. Without a word, he started the car, backed out, and returned to the road, leaving the gas station attendant concerned and confused.

- - -

Was it a slow news week? It must have been, because the video of that wretched woman's suicide was being played on a loop on all the main city television stations. Amanda supposed it was because Hotel Carter was notorious for various reasons, and the news currently focused on the many murders and suicides that had occurred there over the years. However, she had chosen it at the time because it had been known for its unsanitary conditions and reputation—there would be countless unpleasant assumptions about the deceased found in such a tawdry place—and she'd thought that the location would alleviate the additional spite that she felt toward Elizabeth Singh, her husband's unfortunate lover.

The news stations now broadcasted theories posted on Reddit and other casual forums as if they were the gospel truth instead of some paranoid loser's rants, and while some of the readers supported the official narrative of suicide, most doggedly attached themselves to the theory that Elizabeth Singh had been murdered. Each person had a different idea as to who or what had murdered her, centering primarily around paranormal explanations. Thankfully, no one postulated that an Other could have orchestrated her death. Regardless, Amanda didn't feel safe with the face of her husband's dead lover plastered all over the news; while she'd gotten away with the murder at the time, the renewed interest in the case made her fear that someone might finally connect Elizabeth Singh to Johnathan.

Her misplaced glass fell from the table onto the floor, shattering instantly. Her mother had always taught her that a proper lady should never show strong emotion, but she suddenly found it liberating. She picked up the coffee table's centerpiece and smashed it on the floor with both hands, and like a deteriorating dam, the release she experienced overwhelmed her self-control. The next to fall victim to her anger was a vase she'd received as an engagement present. This was followed by a crystal prize that she'd received for being a political backer.

She didn't know how long her therapeutic tantrum lasted, but her apartment was trashed by the time she was finished. "Imelda!" she shrieked as she stepped gingerly around broken glass so her bare feet would not be sliced. She kept screaming, receiving no answer, and the longer she called for her housekeeper, the angrier she became. "Baines!" she shouted finally, calling for the butler, who also did not answer. She didn't even see the cook, who should have been preparing dinner, and the apparently unreliable servant had forgotten to turn off the burners and had left the knife dangling precariously on the cutting board in her haste to leave. Amanda clucked her tongue at her useless staff, not realizing that her outburst had also projected powerful pheromones and that their animalistic instincts had told them to flee. After furiously stalking the house once more to search for her neglectful staff, she decided that she'd leave the mess for them to clean when they returned and that she would take a nice shower to relax in the meantime.

- - -

A firm knock on the door roused Orion from his studying, in which he was only half invested. His professors had been kind enough to grant him an extension on his exams once he'd explained that he'd had a family emergency, but his sister hadn't been grateful enough to spare him her enmity. She was moody—almost sullen—and fought him on every subject. He'd very nearly given up on her, and at times he sympathized with animals that ate their young. His freedom came when she was absent, and he took every opportunity to study and make up for his falling grades. He was physically and emotionally exhausted, but he knew that he would make it through this trial. He had to for her sake.

He ran his fingers through his defiant curls, ensuring that his appearance was at least passable, and then he answered the door. The semi-friendly smile he'd hastily crafted fell immediately as he was greeted by the sight of the pushy BSI agent. He was still dressed in his shabby suit with the incongruously tidy shirt and tie, and although he was clean-shaven, something about him made Orion think he was running on autopilot, much like himself. His dark eyes were shadowed and distant, as if he was trying to stay focused on the now and was barely succeeding. "Oh, Special Agent…"

"Connor," he finished. He glanced around the foyer. "Mind if I come in?" Orion faltered, stammering a weak excuse about needing to study—anything to keep him out of the apartment—but the agent insisted. "Won't take but a moment."

Orion reluctantly acquiesced, inwardly resenting his irrational fear of, and inability to stand up to, authority. He was a college student; shouldn't challenging the establishment be a part of his repertoire? Yet, he could never muster an objection stronger than a meek apology. The agent strolled in, surveying the apartment for any changes that might have been made since his last visit. "Your sister around?" he asked, glancing up the stairs.

Orion coughed and shook his head. "Not very often these days."

The agent nodded and took a seat at the bar. "Probably for the best," he remarked, seemingly preoccupied. He didn't take out his notebook, nor did he fidget as he had done during their previous interview. Instead, he sat with his hands folded in his lap and his attention focused solely on Orion, who then noticed that the agent's tie was a bit looser than it had been during his previous visit and that his hair lacked its taming gel. It was as if the agent had come for a casual visit and had decided at the last minute to make it more formal. It was odd. The agent inclined his head as he addressed him earnestly. "Have you been having problems with her?"

Orion scoffed, jamming his hands into his pockets; he didn't know what else to do with them. "Aside from the fact that she's a teenager? No."

The agent smirked, nodding. "Any experimentation, like burning a few candles?" he continued probing.

Orion scowled darkly and crossed his arms. "She wasn't very encouraged by her last experience, was she?" he pointed out irritably. The recent trauma had driven a wedge between them that he had yet to remove.

"Suppose not," he conceded. "What about any new friends? Has she been meeting with anyone new? Someone you haven't met?"

"No," Orion replied coarsely, his increasing fatigue emboldening him. He was under enough stress, and he didn't think he had the fortitude to deal with this new problem. Perhaps his irritation could be fashioned into a weapon. "What's your point?" he snapped, hoping his feeble voice was like the whip crack he imagined it to be.

The agent grinned wolfishly, and there was no mirth in it—only bitterness and soured anger. "My point is that you're a terrible liar, and you'll get rid of me much quicker if you just tell me the truth. What's going on?" he barked with a level of confidence that Orion could only wish he'd someday muster.

His fragile bravado crumbled in the face of the agent's cruel amusement. Deflated, Orion shoved his hands back into his pockets, slumped his shoulders, and stared at the floor as he formulated his answer. "She's scared, but I don't know what of," he admitted quietly, finding it easier to speak to the ground. "She called me last week sounding strangely jumpy. At first, I thought maybe she'd changed her mind about coming home on the subway by herself. She'd gone back to her routine like the mugging had never even happened." He shook his head incredulously, proud of his sister's toughness and, at the same time, jealous of her strength. "But there was something off. She wanted me to meet her, just not at work. She was terrified—paranoid even. We ended up staying overnight at a hotel." He shrugged helplessly, again wishing his parents provided more emotional support than they did. "Then we stayed a few more nights until she felt safe again."

"What scared her?" asked the agent with concern that seemed genuine.

"I don't know. She wouldn't tell me. She just didn't want anyone involved." He sighed deeply. "But she is scared of you… I mean, the BSI. She'd freak out if she knew I was speaking to you." He stole a nervous glance upstairs, hoping his guest wouldn't notice.

The agent shook his head contritely. "We're still the proper authorities, and we will help your sister," he asserted firmly. "It's better for you to contact me over anyone else. They might not understand the delicate nature of your situation, and you don't want to make it any worse for her. She's got enough on her plate." His expression had become frank, as if he didn't expect Orion to trust him but he empathized nevertheless. "So do you, mate. You don't need to shoulder all the burden."

The corners of Orion's lips twitched upward; he was entertained by the unexpected commiseration, but it didn't change his circumstances or opinions. "I'll keep that in mind if I find out anything," he promised, assuming it was what the agent wanted to hear.

Silence blanketed the room, and despite the agent's struggle to wear an encouraging expression, Orion did not want to break it. He wanted the uncomfortable encounter to end, and after several minutes, it became apparent to the agent that he would get no further. He stood, readjusting his suit to give Orion a longer opportunity to speak, and pointed at the door. "Guess I'll be going," he concluded with disappointment.

Someone fumbled with the lock, jamming the key into it sloppily and activating the tumblers. The door swung open, bearing the weight of Orion's father, who resembled a stumbling survivor of a manmade disaster. One bloodstained fist held Pierce's keys against the doorknob as he tried ineptly to shut the door behind him. His other hand was clamped firmly over his neck, and more blood leaked through his pallid fingers. The agent reacted immediately, rushing to his side and offering his support, while Orion could only shout at his father in alarm. The agent braced Pierce so he wouldn't fall, attempted to navigate him to a chair, reached for the makeshift bandage so he could examine his neck, and calmly announced that he knew first aid and could help him if he could see the wound.

Orion didn't know what happened next. There was a clap of thunder, distorted and deafening in the small space, and his ears rang. The agent fell away, and as scarlet began to blossom from his stomach, he grunted. But Orion hadn't heard the sound. Instead, he saw his father point the stolen weapon in his direction, and his heart began to pound loudly in his ears. It must have drowned out the sound of his sister's rushing footsteps, for she was suddenly on the stairs behind him, and he froze. He couldn't possibly move quickly enough to protect his sister, but he couldn't face his father either. Pierce was pale—almost as white as the kitchen tiles—but he still projected unyielding strength. Orion was cemented to the spot.

Pierce switched his aim from his son to his daughter. Despite having staggered into their apartment, adrenaline steadied his feet beneath him, and his eyes were steel. He spoke slowly and deliberately as if each word drained some of his vitality. "Help me like you did that beast that night. Make me whole."

Confused, Orion tilted his head and replied, "What?"

"Make me whole," Pierce growled again. "Close up my wound, or I'll shoot her… and then you." Using the appropriated gun to emphasize his point, he added, "This makes it a lot easier to kill you."

Perhaps his sister had fewer qualms about confronting their father or had honed her skills, because Orion knew that what followed was the result of her actions. The florescent lights flickered and then exploded as they must have on the night of the mugging. The fragments showered the two of them, pricking Orion like glass rain. Incandescence engulfed their father and transmuted into a warm yellow flame that danced over his form and quickly faded, leaving behind raw, wine-colored flesh. All of his hair was singed away, and his clothes turned to ash, but the flame must not have been searing enough to heat the gun. Pierce sneered, likely from the pain, and pulled the trigger, though Orion didn't know whether the action was the result of reflex or malice. His heart stopped when Cassie's body was suddenly propelled backward against the wall before she tumbled down the stairs. He briefly felt a second flash of heat as the paralysis of his legs suddenly lifted, and he sprinted to his sister's side. He caught her awkwardly, her fingers and hand already twisted beneath her in an attempt to stop her fall and her head an inch away from impact with the carpeted stairs. He cradled her limp body against his, negating the remainder of her inertia. There were already tears streaming down her face, and she was wailing and sobbing like the child she still was.

He laid his sister on the floor tenderly while murmuring half-spoken prayers and reassurances; some were in her direction, but they were mostly for his own benefit. Her panic rose as she saw the blood soaking into their respective clothes, and he caressed her red hair softly in an effort to reassure her. He thought that if her anxiety increased, she might go into shock. "It's not bad. Some wounds just bleed a lot," he whispered, hoping it was the truth. He knew that areas of the human body were more prone to superficial yet unpleasant-looking damage. "You just need to relax, Pickle. Breathe in and out," he coached. His heart broke, and he felt helpless against her pain.

She moaned, and in her distress, she clenched her fists and tried to tear his shirt. "I don't think it's one of those places, Ryan," she whimpered. He shushed her gently, stroking her as if she were a frightened animal, and then laid her across his lap. His hands searched out the edges of the wound beneath her shirt, and he shut his eyes, closing out the world, save for his sister's breath and body. His senses extended until he could feel the inside of her wound as clearly as a surgeon would see it, and he carefully called her flesh into service. Muscle and soft tissue began to knit back together, slowly reversing the paths of the fractured bullet, while separated bone interlaced again and produced new plasma. Her pallid complexion paled further, but this would only be a temporary loss of constitution that could be replaced by a robust meal and a full night's rest. Her death grip loosened as she drifted into a peaceful slumber and started to snore softly. With a relieved smile, he kissed her forehead, tucking strands of her hair out of the way, and laid her gently on the floor.

Knowing that this wasn't the end of it, Orion rose and approached the agent, who'd shifted onto his back with his knees bent and his hands pressed firmly against his abdomen. Tears streamed down his face, and he was muttering to himself as he stared at the ceiling.

Orion hesitated. The puddle of blood was growing, and the agent would soon bleed out. The right thing to do would be to treat him as he had his precious sister, but the threat of the BSI loomed in the back of his mind. If he let this man die, would the threat die with him?

The agent's gaze turned to meet his, and he swallowed hard. "Stern," he breathed in anguish. The sudden regret in his brown eyes stirred deep recognition in Orion's breast, though he could not identify the feeling. The man's inhalations became labored, and he was almost wheezing, signaling that the end was near. Orion knelt beside him immediately; he couldn't be callous. He placed his hand on the agent's skin, which was now slippery with blood, and willed the wound to heal. The bullet had remained whole, so he would not need to force its pieces through innumerable ruptures, and the majority of the damage it had caused was a nicked vein rather than shredded entrails. As with his sister, he forced bone marrow to create new platelets and plasma, and then he repaired any superficial damage to the agent's internal organs. His patient's breathing eased and normalized, and he sat up unsteadily, reeling from his sudden lightheadedness.

"Whoa, lie down," Orion cautioned him, but the agent shook his head. His balance was shaky as he rose to his feet, and his legs wobbled as he stepped closer to the corpse. Pierce's leathery skin had become patched with black, waxy white, and brown and had peeled down to the fatty layer in some places. This was not the flash burn that Cassie had initially created; it must have been the result of the second wave of heat that he'd felt. The agent reached down for his weapon, and upon trying to take it from Pierce's grasp, he discovered that it had become fused with his flesh. Nevertheless, he pried it free with disgust and fired once into the remains of Pierce's blackened skull. When Orion looked to him for an explanation, he shrugged and said, "Zombies." He then dropped the gun as his legs failed him, and he collapsed onto the floor. Like Cassie, he fell into a deep slumber, leaving Orion alone with his thoughts as sirens sounded in the distance.

- - -

The water had begun to turn cold; nevertheless, Connor didn't move. He allowed the spray to spill over him, hoping that the water would penetrate his skin and somehow warm his soul. He had nearly died for the second time, and his survival had yet again depended on an Other. It seemed his fate was forever tied to the offspring of chance and the strange tendency of the human genome to mutate. He'd saved this one though. Orion Starr and his sister were safe—or at least as safe as they could be under the unfortunate circumstances.

He'd been unconscious when the police had arrived but had revived as the paramedics had pulled up. When he'd tried to secure the scene on his own, he'd been overridden by an officer with a more intact awareness who'd insisted that Connor travel to the hospital to be evaluated more thoroughly. The paramedics had then loaded him onto a stretcher and took him away. He had been fortunate enough to be able to use his cell phone in the ambulance, and due to his forewarning, the BSI had been able to contain the quickly developing situation. Their federal agents had been able to shut out local law enforcement and had changed the facts to suit their needs while sticking close to the truth: Pierce Starr had died in a shootout with Special Agent Morgan Connor, who'd happened to be on site following up on a previous case. The expertise of the first responders had allowed Connor to survive, but they had been unable to save Pierce Starr. There had been no mention of his massive burns or his daughter's wound, and the scene had been scrubbed clean by the bureau, further burying any evidence that might have contradicted the official narrative.

As soon as Connor had regained full use of his faculties, he'd located the Starr siblings, and thankfully, they had only been processed into custody at the Plum Island facility. He'd testified to Containment that Cassie had again only acted in self-defense, saving her from being considered for euthanasia, and he'd reiterated that despite being an elementalist, she was trainable and could become a valuable asset.

Within hours of his release from the hospital, Connor had learned the probable circumstances of Pierce's grave injury, though it had been primarily through the lens of the story-driven, embellishment-hungry media, who had already tried and convicted him postmortem. It appeared that the adult Starrs had left their post at the observatory to return to New York City, only to fall into squabbling midway. Pierce had slain his wife, who had managed to inflict a grievous wound before her death. Their flight had clearly demonstrated guilt of some kind regarding the Johnstown victim, and a warrant obtained shortly thereafter had revealed that the observatory had hidden an amateur slaughterhouse. The Bramble Butcher quickly became a plural title applied to the Starrs, who had formerly been best known for their writing skills and interest in astronomy. While Connor still had reservations about the incredible leaps of logic that the media had made, he'd realized the difficulty that this community verdict would create for the Starr children.

Connor had secured a private meeting with his boss, and he'd been able to negotiate what he'd considered a good deal on behalf of the siblings, despite the rather conservative nature of the BSI. Initially disbelieving in his own eloquence, he'd apparently found the appropriate words to convince Terrance to offer a deal: If Orion came to work for the bureau, he and Cassie would be spared the media circus that would follow the postmortem conviction of their already famous father. Cassie would be tutored by the BSI on how to use her abilities safely and then given the choice to join as an agent or return to civilian life. If she chose the latter, she would be given a new identity free from the taint of their parents. But Cassie had seemed less than pleased with the arrangement, and while her brother had been similarly unenthused, he'd nevertheless accepted gracefully.

So why, then, did Connor feel cold? A postmortem had been conducted on the adult Starrs: Madeleine had been entirely human, while her husband's results had been indeterminate. Connor had surmised that Pierce must have had some ability if he'd been able to travel as far as he had without succumbing to his mortal injuries. So while he had been in a direct confrontation with an Other and he'd been on the receiving end of another one's talent, it had still been one of the better encounters that he'd experienced. He'd also saved the girl from being euthanized, which is what he'd wanted since he'd met her, and her brother, too, as a bonus.

The water felt as if it had turned to ice and was now leeching warmth from his pores. He shut off the faucet and began to towel off. Deep down, he knew why he felt the chill: What if, like Brian Chamberlain, Orion Starr's ability could be used to bring back the dead? Surely, Connor had been on death's doorstep, if he hadn't actually crossed the threshold, and Orion had been able to bring him back from the brink. His memories had grown fuzzy sometime after the first gunshot, and despite being told of his single-mindedness to secure the scene, he did not really recall any of the subsequent events in detail.

The chill in his bones and the frost in his blood he felt were the reality that he'd died and had been brought back to life with no memory of the other side. No Heaven. No Hell. Nothing.

He discarded the towel on the floor and decided to focus on other matters. He poured himself a drink before even getting dressed, and he let it sit while he found a clean pair of pants to wear. Orion Starr was to become a new type of resource—not a field agent like Connor nor a traditional asset to be kept locked up at Plum Island—and it was Connor's job to test him under duress. A boy—man, he supposed—with his talent to heal was vital against his kind since most of them had destructive capabilities, and his worth on the battlefield was incalculable, provided he could handle the stress. So Connor was to allow Orion to accompany him as he investigated potential Others, assess his willingness to help the government combat his kind, and teach him the basics of becoming a field agent. Orion seemed to have a gentle soul, one that easily bowed to stronger wills, and Connor didn't think he should be anywhere but in a safe laboratory; but it wasn't his decision to make. The boy had to become an asset like Angel and Antithesis or be euthanized; he couldn't be allowed to fall into SION's hands. Orion didn't know this, of course, and Connor presumed that he wasn't supposed to know either, but it was the logical conclusion should Orion make the wrong decision. This made it Connor's job to ensure that he made the right one.

- - -

Jack stared at his manicured hand and flexed it experimentally, watching his fingers expand and contract as if they were new appendages. The pulse of his victim raced through his veins, and he could almost hear the terrified voice of the VSION hooligan as his soul and life force were being slowly absorbed by Jack's superior mind. His skin felt electrified, and sights and sounds became more vibrant. He always felt more alive after a feeding, but it had been years since he'd claimed sustenance from an Other. The sensations that accompanied the forfeited essence made his head swim, much like the effects of the opium and laudanum medicines of old. This had been an unscheduled feeding, and it had been a boon. He could sustain himself for several years—perhaps even decades—without consuming an Other, and his occasional penchant to feast upon incompetent humans in his employ enabled him to stretch that time even further.

Even so, harvest time was drawing near for Pierce Starr. He did not want his progeny to learn too much—that there were others like him and that feasting upon them would have an even greater effect. And as with any harvest, planting season would soon follow. He'd kept his eyes on Pierce's brood, and while both had shown potential, he knew that Cassiopeia was now on the government's radar, and this automatically disqualified her as her father's successor. The government did not know about his existence, and he intended to keep it that way, which meant that Orion would inherit his father's mantle if he had the same potential with his abilities. Very soon, Jack would reap the bountiful harvest of the human souls that Pierce had consumed, and he would then instruct Orion how to sustain his life force in the same manner.

Now that Jack had fed on the VSION operative, he felt less threatened. Even though his food source was still not secure, it was not as immediate a concern as it had been. The unexpected snack had taken the edge off his appetite and allowed him time to conceive a skillful plan to extricate Pierce from the circling authorities long enough for him to be harvested, at which time his son would disappear from the world without a trace.

Jack turned his hand and allowed his fingers to become transparent like the ghosts of Charles Dickens. This acquired skill was not the ability to become invisible, though he might nevertheless be able to utilize his newfound power in such a way. He recalled that the other VSION hoodlum had lobbed something at him, and it had gone straight through him and his victim. Experimentally, he tried to return his arm to its place on the armrest, but instead, it flowed straight through the surface as if neither one truly existed. Grinning, he opened his palm and found that the formerly solid object was as easy to navigate as smoke. So his last meal had been able to manipulate his cells to some extent.

He had a thought as he removed his arm from the recliner and decided to imagine himself as heavy as lead. As he felt himself sink further into the cushions, the wooden frame began to buckle under his new intense weight, and his grin widened. He didn't know how this new ability would benefit him, but it would certainly prove interesting.

He noticed one of his underlings hovering near the doorway wringing his hands in distress so hard within his jacket pockets that he may well soon tear the cloth in half. The lower echelons of his hired help were not known for their constitution, and rumors had spread about the nature of Jack's appetite. He'd heard a masterful fictional account of his disappointment and the subsequent torture of the underling who had failed him, so he was not unaccustomed to them experiencing apprehension in his presence. Mercifully, his enforcers and managers were made of sterner stuff.

"What is it?" he asked the assistant, whom he assumed was new. The man shook as ridiculously as any new hire who'd heard the legends. They didn't last long; they either developed steel nerves, or they ended up dead by some means or another.

"I have bad news," he replied reluctantly.

Jack felt his feeding euphoria begin to fade in the face of his building irritation. "Spit it out then."

"Starr is dead. The police killed him." He held out the report, which he was unfortunate enough to be the one to deliver. Jack didn't even look at him, his attention now on the document, and the man slowly backed away as he would from a grizzly bear.

Anger flooded into Jack, turning his veins into fire. How complacent he had been! He'd sat here with a full stomach, practically bursting and desire sated, and he'd allowed his harvest to be spoiled while he'd lounged in his post-meal bliss. Even if there were a way to salvage Pierce's yield, Jack did not have the connections to access his corpse in the morgue. "Find his blooming chavies. If either of them have been nibbed, the lot of you get lavendered, and I start a jemmier crew," he growled. His transitory guttural accent obscured his words but not his rage or meaning. Decades' worth of planning had been derailed in an instant because his bastard hadn't had the brains to properly cover his tracks.

PART V
CODE NAMES: SUCCUBUS & ECHO

The sour smell of wasted beer permeates the room and lingers in the air, although she doesn't allow it to draw her attention. Instead, her nose picks up the woody scent of a man's cologne and she doesn't like the smell but hides her distaste behind a meticulously crafted smile.

There is a pale stripe on a hand—a man's well-worn and callused hand—and this finger's girth is smaller than its companions. Something resided there for a long time and is now gone. Whether this is a temporary or permanent absence, she does not know, and she doesn't believe it would matter to him either way.

The music is low, soft, and unintrusive, and there are chapped lips and warm breaths on her neck like a secret being spoken directly to her. He has to bend down to whisper into her ear, and she leans away and places a covered hand on his chest flirtatiously to encourage him to keep a teasing distance. Her hands are small and almost childlike, and her fingers are thin. Her satin gloves extend past her elbows, and despite being more congruent in high-fashion parties, here in this low setting, they lend her an air of mystery and sophistication.

She stirs her drink daintily as she pulls away from her partner, and he subconsciously follows her incline, captured by the gravity of her charms. He is entangled in her web, where she has complete control, and it is a wonderful feeling that eclipses the disgust that she feels when she tolerates his revolting touch.

Lena Malmkvist awoke and quickly tried to latch onto the last tendrils of the dream before they evaporated into the conscious world. This was different from the peaceful nocturnal resetting of the brain; this was her hunter's sense honing in on her next target. The hunt always began with these thin wisps of impressions as she slid gradually into the demon's body and saw through its eyes. They were precognitions, a chance to stop the crime before it happened, and the path to redemption. When she'd first experienced these visions, she'd believed them to be the normal substance of nightmares, and she had not acted. But once she'd had to stand in the charred wreckage of her former home, she'd finally recognized the new path set before her and had accepted it zealously.

She pulled her long blonde hair into a ponytail and knelt on the floor as she got into the pushup position. She pressured her mind into amassing details as she trained her body. What did she recall? Her hands were small and her legs slender, her hair was long, and the man's hand felt large on her back, so it was likely that this demon was female.

Her muscled arms pumped rhythmically, rarely straining as she formed images in her mind. The victim had fresh stubble growing on his chiseled chin, but this detail would not yet help her; she needed to first synchronize with the demon's mind by emulating her, and then she could focus on locating the victim and the future scene of the crime.

The drink, which had been sweetened, had only a hint of alcohol; the demon had wanted to remain aware of her surroundings and to be able to guide her victim into her web. It had been a mixed drink, composed more of pineapple and sprite than vodka, and it had been garnished with a cherry that she'd coyly sucked on when she hadn't wanted to drink. Black gloves had enveloped her thin elbows and disappeared into her sleeves somewhere around her slight biceps. She'd covered her body with a black form-fitting pantsuit that had revealed many of her curves without exposing anything but impressions; it had hugged her like a second skin and had felt like armor protecting her.

Lena got up and wiped her hands on her thighs. The first order of business would be to find that outfit, feel it against her real skin, and be embraced by it like the demon. Then she'd mix the same drink and sample it as she tried to imagine why the demon preferred its taste. These were small details, and they did not narrow down much about the incident, but she had discovered that evidence built up over time and helped her better channel the visions.

- - -

Orion Starr had researched how to cope with the new stressors in his life—leaving school, having a new job, no longer being the caretaker for his sister, and trying to integrate into a new world—but putting these skills into practice was another ordeal entirely. He felt sweat begin to bead on his skin as he nervously followed Morgan Connor into the azure brick building that served as the Office of the Chief Medical Examiner. He chafed against the rough weave of his suit collar; while he could have afforded a better suit—he was now the sole executor of his parents' non-seized assets—he was too overwhelmed to spend the proper time on choosing the right cut, gentle fabrics, and complementary colors. He was satisfied that he'd found suits that didn't require any altering to be decently comfortable, though he now regretted his hasty decision.

The agent spoke to the receptionist with confidence despite his ungainly mannerisms, and though Orion knew he could learn from his lead, he was soon distracted by how welcoming the lobby looked. If he hadn't known better, he would have thought that he was in the reception room at a normal medical clinic or office space rather than the one at the city morgue. He shifted uncomfortably on his feet; he was still in the city, which only served to heighten his anxiety. When he'd asked Connor about the situation, the agent had told him that there were enough cases in New York to allow him to stay there indefinitely while he showed Orion the ropes. He had assured him that the familiarity of his surroundings would help him absorb the training more quickly, as he wouldn't be distracted constantly by new scenery. But instead, Orion looked over his shoulder continually, expecting to see a classmate or neighbor who was ready to confront him about his parents' supposed activities. Since there had been no one left to attend trial, the media had quickly released every publicly known fact about the Bramble Butchers and had interviewed their colleagues. Once the story had run its course, interest in it had died down as the nation had turned its attention to the next headline. He was grateful that he'd been able to spare his sister the media circus, and though the BSI had protected him from harassment, the incident had still left its mark. It didn't help that the thought of seeing a corpse made him feel queasy, and his partner didn't seem to spare a thought for his comfort.

A sudden pat on his back jolted him from his thoughts, and he turned to see Connor's wide grin. "Don't worry, mate. It's just a dead body. It won't hurt you," he assured him with insincere friendliness. Connor wrapped his arm around Orion's shoulder to lead him as they followed the receptionist. "'Sides, your cologne will cover up the worst of the smell," he teased. "You really should look into wearing less. It's meant to be a hint, not a substitute." Before Orion could respond that he didn't wear cologne, he continued, "You look like the sort of lad who was into *The X-Files*, so this'll be right up your alley… though it's a bit dodgier in real life."

Orion grimaced. Connor—or "the agent," as he still referred to him mentally—was beginning to charm him, if by nothing more than the careful application of Stockholm syndrome. He checked up on Orion regularly, bringing him food—generally ramen and instant mac and cheese—or smaller comfort items for the apartment, though the younger man didn't really think he needed that many sponges or toothbrushes. Orion had practically lived on his own since he'd been ten years old, so he knew how to run a household. Connor would also hang around for a half hour or so making awkward small talk before clumsily taking his leave. Their interactions almost felt like those that would occur between estranged family members—like a father or older brother who was making an effort to be a mentor but failing—and while Orion didn't know what to make of it, he discovered that he appreciated someone trying to look after him for once, even if that someone tended to act like an annoying prick.

Television police procedurals had not prepared Orion for the smell. The room was cold and clean, but beneath the sharp tang of disinfectants and the stale odor of refrigeration, he could detect a musk blended with pungent, earthy scents. All were repugnant but were easy to filter out if he breathed through his mouth; the drawback was that the air also had an unidentifiable aftertaste. Connor hesitated as he entered the room, swallowing briefly before recovering his composure, and Orion felt satisfied that even the experienced man could submit to nerves.

Connor had re-explained their modus operandi before they'd set out that morning: The home office would comb through assorted reports originating from the police, media, medical professionals, or even blogs and forums and would flag incidents for field agents to investigate personally. When not in the field, the agents would also assist with this process and might seek out several similar episodes in an area to piece a case together before setting out. His plan was to demonstrate how events usually unfurled in the field rather than coming together by exceptional good luck, so he'd guide Orion step by step. Because the body had been found after the crime and no one had come forward as a witness, their first move was to examine it and then interview the coroner.

Connor spoke confidently to the female medical examiner, almost flirting with her as he asked what she had discovered. Orion listened absently to their conversation and began to drift away as he stood over the corpse. It was naked, its modesty preserved by only a thin paper sheet, and its head was wrapped with gauze, securing its jaw shut. Though its eyes were closed, Orion knew enough about the real world to guess that they'd been sealed shut somehow, and he was relieved that he wouldn't have to see its clouded eyes. The wrinkled face sagged and was sorely creased, as if its owner had smoked too many cigarettes over the years or had spent too much time sunbathing without the proper protection.

This was the closest that Orion had ever been to a corpse, save for his father's, and he kept his distance as if it might spring back to life and grab him. He had a fleeting thought that this had happened to him before, though he knew it was impossible; yet, he still took a disquieted step back. He didn't notice anything remarkable about the corpse.

Connor shoved a clipboard into his hands and hissed, "Pay attention." He then flashed the medical examiner a cocky smile. She remarked that this was the third body she'd seen in five years with abnormal damage to the head and that while the cause hadn't been determined, she was fairly certain that it hadn't been a contagion. However, due to the prolonged time between incidents, she wasn't even certain they were related. He thanked her, and she affirmed that she'd be around if he had any further questions.

The agent nodded to the chart. "So, what did you learn?" he asked, but Orion simply pulled a face expressing his directionlessness. Connor snickered and relieved him of the clipboard. He squinted a bit at the script and then pronounced, "After a while, you sorta learn how to read these things. There's abbreviations and shorthand and terrible handwriting, but..." He trailed off as he concentrated. "So, this is the part that drew our attention," he said, pointing at the chart as he explained. For lack of a better term, the coroner had listed the cause of death as "old age"—which was not a recognized medical diagnosis—despite the victim's official record declaring that he had been only thirty-eight. When the medical examiner had asked for clarification from the coroner, the explanation had involved the same kind of multiple organ failure associated with the elderly at the end stages of life. Even the victim's skin had lost its elasticity and had sagged and shriveled around his facial area. However, his body weight and musculature had remained normal, and tissue samples had returned without anomaly, leaving officials baffled as they had quietly changed his cause of death to the more formal "unknown."

"That's all in there?" Orion asked incredulously.

Connor shrugged. "Mostly. I also read the BSI report on the way over. The medical examiner confirmed it though, which you might have picked up had you been listening," he replied. "Bodies like this turn up about every year and a half, and they never know what to make of it, but the victims are of the same age range, physical type, race, and that sort of thing, which would indicate a serial killer if not for the odd method of death."

Orion scowled. "So, who did it?"

"That's what we're here to figure out, mate," he replied cheekily. "If we're lucky, we can figure out what kind of Other it is before we head into the field, like we did with your sister, but that's not the typical routine." He explained that while the latest murder had happened recently, he and Orion were still pursuing what was practically a cold case: Their target apparently had their powers under control and only struck intermittently. Headquarters saw it as a good start for Orion, as it allowed him to put his toe in the water and learn the ropes while not being under intense pressure to solve the case; more experienced agents than he had failed, so there would be no administrative repercussions if he made no progress.

"Since this is a relatively dead end, our next step is to interview the guy who found the body." Connor cocked a grin. "I hope you were paying attention. It's your turn to do the interview."

Orion's face contorted with dismay. He was not ready to speak with another stranger today; he had been anxious enough coming into the building. Interviewing for a job after his college graduation had been one of his greatest fears, and even though he'd be on the other side of the metaphorical table, he did not feel any more self-assured. Connor's grin split wider, showing his teeth. "I'm joshing you. You should see your face," he teased. He placed his arm around Orion's shoulder and pulled him close as they left. "This is great! I don't know why I didn't pick up a partner earlier." Orion simply cursed inwardly and mused that he'd liked the aloof, borderline-rude agent better than the boisterous version with whom he now appeared to be stuck.

- - -

Jody Barles was no longer a young woman. She was now entering what was considered middle age, but her short stature and chubby face often made men underestimate her maturity. She appeared to be on the cusp of jail bait, and she knew that this appealed to most men. In conjunction with her light skin and dark hair, her Filipina blood softened her features, further muddying her age. As she sat on the stool and sipped the establishment's version of a Barbie—which was mostly sweeteners, such as pineapple and sprite, with a dash of vodka—she mused that she had never really dated anyone. But this was probably for the best, as in her experience, men were after only one thing, which was fine because so was she.

She'd chosen this bar because it attracted the type of men she targeted:

primarily lowlifes who had either just gotten out of jail or hadn't yet been caught, though a few seemed to be genuinely down on their luck and poverty-stricken. There were drug dealers, carjackers, gamblers, and petty thieves. She hated pimps the most, but they seemed to avoid this bar; maybe it was out of their territory, or she hadn't attracted the attention of any yet.

She caught the eye of the bartender and gestured for another drink. Despite the alcoholic mix being a bit extravagant for her surroundings, she was beginning to blend in and become a regular, which was a bit of a problem as well. Anonymity was her ally, and an attractive woman was easily recognized—especially one who was meticulous about keeping her fair skin covered whenever she went in public—and her gloved hands were exceptionally conspicuous. She spoke to no one, save the bartender, and contentedly observed the patrons in silence night after night until she found a target. She generally didn't need to find one more frequently than every few years, but her last encounter had left her unsatisfied and had initiated a creeping doubt that she'd been misguided in her selection and execution. After seeking out a similar hunting ground, she was shortly able to find a new target, and this bolstered her conviction that she and her mission were righteous.

She surveyed the room again, more slowly this time, and sighed heavily when she confirmed her target's absence; this was the third time in a row that he had failed to show. She casually shifted her weight to one foot as she stood and paid her tab after a few unhurried minutes. She knew that he would return in a few days, as she had observed him and his routines for some time; she just needed to remind herself to be patient and that waiting was an inevitable part of the process.

When she left the bar, the streets were dark, with only a few scattered, dim streetlights to illuminate her path. The city had stopped trying to replace the lamps after they'd kept breaking mysteriously less than a week after their installation; if this neighborhood wanted darkness, there was no reason to waste funds on replacement lights when there were thousands of other items on the budget competing for attention. The darkness didn't bother Jody like it used to when she was a child. She knew now that she was the most powerful creature on the streets, and confidence oozed from her pores like a protective layer.

There were quiet voices whispering to her left, and she didn't deign them with a glance. The criminal elements tensed, but perhaps sensing there was something wrong with the situation—no unescorted woman should be so self-assured in that neighborhood late at night without a reason—they did nothing, and she passed by unharassed. She supposed that's why she never had any trouble at the bar with any supposed pimps; she was a "trap" no one could figure out. She snickered at the small gang's timidity and continued on her way. If this street was full of predators, then she was the apex and not the prey.

- - -

Sone thought he'd hidden fairly well by taking refuge in the supply closet. It smelled stale, the redolent cardboard boxes obscuring the lingering scents from chemicals, old files, and assorted equipment. He sat behind one of the metal shelves, knees up to his chest, and let his mind drift. He heard the faint whine of rusted hinges and the scrape of footsteps across the cement, but he disregarded the sounds until a feminine head appeared around the corner. "That's what I thought," she said.

Naught was approximately his age, though one would not have guessed it by her appearance. Her eyes always seemed to harbor dark shadows beneath them, and the thin streaks of white that ran through her hair seemed to testify to the hard life she'd lived. Her minor medical knowledge had been put to good use as the facility's unofficial medic, and she'd become affectionately known as "Doc" around the canteen. Through their limited interactions, Sone had come to know her as a kind and compassionate individual, despite her reluctance to socialize, and she'd made an effort to seek him out once she'd learned of Rho's death. Since she was not gifted with tact, she'd blurted out that she'd heard the news, but the subsequent conversation had been salvaged by her genuine concern, and they had struck up a burgeoning friendship.

She inhaled sharply, plopped down in front of him, and crossed her arms. "What happened back there?"

Sone snorted dismissively. He did not like speaking specifically about himself; his father had instilled in him the knowledge that he was only a cog in a greater machine and that as his son, he would never simply be a person. He was a symbol: He represented SION and, by extension, all Others. Sone had taken this doctrine to mean that his personal life—and, in particular, his emotional well-being—was secondary to the cause. His silence was met with wide, expectant eyes, and he eventually relented to her bated breath.

"I froze," he admitted softly. "That's the first time he ever invited me to speak about her." Her kindhearted expression transformed into one of surprise, and he just shook his head. "Stephanie Moreau and the mother I remember are two completely different women. He's always *told* me about her. Lectured.

Placed her up on a pedestal. It's the same speech he gives everyone else, but it's supposed to have special meaning for me because her sacrifice was *for me*." Though Charles Moreau hadn't spoken to his son about his mother at first, Sone had begun inquiring more insistently as he'd grown older, and he'd received the same recycled speech that Moreau gave his flock. Stephanie had been held up as an impossible martyr, and her real memory had slowly faded.

"But that's not how I remember her. She was either a stay-at-home mom, or she worked from home. I don't know, but she was always in the other room while I played on the floor in the living room." Sone continued to speak, easily recalling to his receptive and supportive audience the things that a six-year-old comprehended. When they'd thought that he'd been asleep, his parents had fought, mostly about how frustrated she had been about caring for Sone alone all day and never being able to leave the house to socialize. While their voices had carried through the walls, it had been only the sound that had scared him; her malcontent, if it had existed, had been hidden in the daylight, and his young mind had not known the concept of divorce. She had baked and cooked with him and had sometimes partaken in his games of pretend. She had been his only playmate for a long time because he hadn't attended public school, which was a fact that his father had later attributed to his mother's supposed insight that Sone was an Other.

Naught smiled supportively. "I think that would have been a fitting tribute," she said. "You remember her as she was: human—not a hero. It makes her more real, and it doesn't knock her off her pedestal, if that's what you're afraid of. People aren't perfect, and neither are their relationships."

He shook his head; she didn't understand the legend that had been drilled into his head. Stephanie Moreau had been a saint and the epitome of Others: different but flawlessly integrated into society instead of posing a threat. His father wouldn't agree with Naught's appraisal.

"In any case, Dr. Moreau recovered just fine," she continued. "He probably should've warned you about having to give a speech in the first place." She punched him in the shoulder playfully. "So don't worry about it." When she didn't receive the anticipated response, she became serious and asked, "Does it still hurt?"

He looked at her, considering. While they had spoken about Rho's loss, he had seen it as a relationship that had been forged out of convenience: He'd needed to talk to someone, and she'd been available. Her further attempts to connect with him were not unexpected or unwelcome, but he wasn't certain how to proceed. Despite sharing a partnership, he and Rho had rarely spoken of their pasts or their thoughts beyond superficial gossip and conversation, and even though he'd considered Rho his best friend, in retrospect, they hadn't been as close as they could have been. Before that, he'd had only his father—a man who should have nurtured him but who was instead a distant figure who preached that Sone needed to be strong to avenge his mother, and so he was. Naught's continued concern about his feelings was as alien to him as affection. "I'm fine," he replied, probably cutting off any future connection.

"Ah," she said, perhaps disappointed, and rocked back on her heels. They sat in silence for a few more moments before she quietly excused herself and left. He sighed deeply, steeled himself, and also chose to return to the rest of the world.

- - -

They stood in the faintly musty hallway of a typical apartment complex. Wearing suits, with their hands in their pockets, they tried to look casual—or at least Orion did. He didn't know what to do, so he tried crossing his hands in front of him, and then he folded them as well, but he decided that this looked too aggressive and uncrossed them. He felt like an unwanted missionary waiting on a doorstep, and he hoped the tenant would answer soon.

Connor knocked again, and there was a muffled "I'm coming!" followed by shuffling. A bleary-eyed man opened the door and peered at them through half-closed lids. With his mussed hair and the partially soiled work clothes twisted about him, he appeared to have just woken up. He scratched his chin absently as he yawned. "Yeah?"

The agent nodded before officially introducing himself and then Orion as his assistant. After making certain that they were speaking to Lance Trainor, the sanitation worker who had discovered the body, Connor began to clarify statements from the report. Orion noticed that when Connor smiled, the expression was strained, but he seemed to be making a genuinely affable effort, and he wondered if he hadn't noticed it previously at his doorstep because he'd been intimidated by the agent's presence. In any case, he scrutinized his body language, the way he held himself so naturally, and he doubted he'd be able to match the agent's self-security; Orion's stomach was still in knots despite him being one of the authority figures in the situation.

Lance shrugged and then shook his head. "It was the damnedest thing," he confessed, breathing heavily. "He weren't even hidden... just lying against the wall." At first, he'd thought that the man had simply been a drunk who'd passed out in the alley or a recently homeless man, but he'd decided to investigate further because something had seemed off about the situation. On closer inspection, he'd realized that the victim's clumsy positioning had been due to rigor mortis setting in and not to excessive alcohol consumption. He described the victim in much the same way that he'd appeared when they had seen him in the morgue: a tall, middle-aged white male with nothing evidently wrong with his body. "But I ain't gonna forget his face," he added and shuddered. He insinuated that it had resembled cured meat, but he didn't venture into details, and Connor refrained from pressing him further. Orion didn't think the body's appearance had been that unnerving, and he wondered which of the two of them were experiencing the incorrect reaction to the corpse. He'd watched his father die, so maybe that event had rendered him incapable of having the proper response. "That's why I been taking off early when I feel like. Boss thinks if he gives me enough time off, I won't sue for any kinda emotional damages. He don't know this ain't the first body I seen on the job."

The agent was uncharacteristically quiet and attentive during the interview, listening patiently to Lance's words and taking notes as he had done in Orion's apartment that first day. After clarifying any lingering details, he concluded the engagement by thanking Lance for his time. Lance simply shrugged again and slammed the door. Connor turned to Orion and deadpanned, "So, what did you observe?"

Orion pressed his lips together tightly in frustration; he was quickly learning that the older man was not much of a teacher. He crossed his arms as a delaying tactic while he reflected on the interview and what his partner had been trying to impart. "How to persuade a witness to talk to you in a casual setting?" he mumbled hesitantly.

Connor snorted acerbically. "Well, yeah, but that wasn't what I was going for," he replied. "Did you notice his body language? How relaxed he was?" After barely pausing, he explained, "It means he wasn't lying."

"Why would he lie?"

He shrugged. "Lots of reasons. Maybe he'd been drinking on the job. Maybe he tampered with the evidence." He chuffed. "Hell, he could have even been our Other. I don't really know," he scoffed cynically. "The point is that we need to focus on reading between the lines and not just on the words they're saying. Sometimes it's how they say it, and sometimes it's their body language. If I thought he was lying or hiding something, then I would've pressed him for details to see if he knew anything. That's how I caught you and your sister." He smirked wickedly. "You've got a tell." Even though Orion's lips twisted into a frown, he didn't rise to the bait.

"Normally, this is a dead end," Connor continued to lecture. "A cold case. The witness doesn't really know anything useful, and there were no substantial clues left at the scene. But…" He produced his smartphone from his pocket and showed him the screen, whose lettering Orion couldn't read at a glance. It appeared to be a document, and Connor scrolled through it casually as he spoke. "… the police managed to trace the victim's footsteps back to a bar, where he was seen with a woman." He paused on a fairly nondescript police sketch of a woman of undeterminable ethnicity and scowled. "Well, these things aren't really accurate," he commented dismissively. "Anyway, the other victims were also seen in different bars with a woman who matched this description, and all three victims left with her, so that means there's a pattern that matches an MO. However, since the crimes took place years apart and in different precincts, the police never made a connection, but we did." He smirked. "Well, our analysts compiled the cases over time. I just used the database to properly connect them."

Orion crossed his arms and ended up hugging them closer to his chest. "If you knew all that, why did we even come here?" He was starting to feel as if Connor was purposely withholding information, though he didn't know to what effect. Because he was artistically inclined, socially withdrawn, and managing a household, he tended to shy away from straight intellectual challenges; he found that he was generally too fatigued to attempt them, and he felt that his energy reserves were better kept for his daily tasks. Being Connor's partner was exhausting enough, and the gauntlet of new information, techniques, and problems to be solved was starting to push him over the edge. This training was like college on steroids, only he was starting as a senior and not a freshman, and an inkling that he wasn't up to the task was starting to eat away at him, further feeding into his anxieties.

"To teach you some skills," Connor quipped as he pocketed his phone. "Besides, it's not like I knew it was going to be a dead end when I brought you here. Mr. Trainor might've known something and cracked the case wide open. We're the first BSI agents to interview him." He paused briefly, absorbing Orion's posture, and then observed, "You're acting sullen. You're not picking up your sister's personality, are you?" Not even waiting for a reply—which probably wouldn't have come, despite how much Orion wanted to rebuke the agent for his teaching style—he continued, "At any rate, our next step is to regroup. I've got hard copies back in the room, so you can look over them and tell me what to do next."

While Cassie would've had a snappy retort about Connor's mentorship skills, Orion could only nod passively as they departed. If he could survive his sister's capricious moods, he could tolerate the agent's feeble attempts at clever banter and rapport.

- - -

She finally exits the bar, her gloved hands wrapped tightly around his arm. He leans in to kiss her, as he has all night, and she pulls away coyly, telling him to wait just a bit longer as she caresses his face with her gloved hand. They pass through the acrid smell of cigarettes and duck into a darkened alleyway. She rests her hands on his shirt collar, which is dirty and in need of a wash by knowledgeable hands, and she inhales his woody cologne again. This time, she pushes through the sour cloud clinging to him, grips his collar tightly, and presses her lips firmly against his. His reaction is delayed by the expected pleasure of her touch, but panic quickly sets in as he feels something being drained out of him. She is certain that it is his life force or some intangible part of his soul, and she always imagined it to be his power. She is seizing back her power from him and letting it fill her core. Her revenge electrifies her skin, and she feels as if she can do anything. She feels alive!

Lena started awake. She could still feel the pulsating of his energy beneath her skin, as if it were flowing through her veins now and not the demon's. It was intoxicating, and it was almost as if she could understand the demon's need to hunt men.

She rolled out of bed abruptly, purposely landing hard on the floor in the pushup position to jolt her thoughts from the dream and reject its siren song. She remembered releasing his empty husk and watching it fall unnoticed to the pavement. She was sweaty, despite the night's coolness, and she decided to put the dampness to use. She skipped the pushups, instead opting to pull herself up in the doorway where a metal bar hung, and she continued until her cold perspiration was replaced by heat and stickiness.

Hunts were always difficult: Immersing oneself in a demon without losing one's purpose was a challenge. Her senses worked by honing in on the demons and slipping into their minds slowly before an event so she could locate them easily and stop any crime from occurring. Sometimes, she was unlucky—she didn't always piece the clues together in time—but even when she failed, she still saw the next kill through the demons' eyes. Most of them were bloodthirsty killers who were little better than animals as they stalked their prey in small towns, cities, and other places where they could live undetected. She wished that they would congregate in a den instead of living individually; it would be expeditious to kill several demons at once, and she could potentially save many more lives if she didn't have to hunt down each one separately.

The demons' methods of killing were strangely human. After tricking their prey into trusting them, they often resorted to mediocre means of disposal, such as strangling or stabbing their victims, and none seemed to know what to expect of Lena when she confronted them. Once cornered, all animals choose to fight back if given the chance, and demons were no exception. Some fled, hoping that their victims would provide a roadblock, but she single-mindedly chased the demons down like a hound and slew them. Others fought back using improvised weaponry—a knife, a discarded plank of wood, or even a length of pipe— but they rarely chose to use their infernal abilities.

In fact, she had encountered only one individual who had, and she had been fortunate enough to corner him alone in his lair. He'd pitched a strange semifluid substance like melting snowballs at her, and it had sizzled without heat against everything it had touched, bubbling and hissing against corrugated walls and cheap floor tiles and gutting pitted surfaces. The viscous material had eaten through her jacket, which she'd quickly shrugged off before it had been able to burn her newly exposed skin. She'd taken cover behind a wall, shot the monster in the head with her gun, and watched as it had exploded, splashing the angry liquid everywhere. This demon matched the nightmares that haunted her: creatures who used a supernatural power, which was an unearthly magic that they could twist to their will.

Lena lifted her body and twisted until her calves were secure between the bar and the lintel. She crossed her muscled arms over her chest and breathed deeply before she pulled her torso up, exercising her abs. This hunt felt different. Whenever she completed her connection with a demon, she was able to push its feelings to the back of her mind; she was only a spectator searching for clues. But this one—this woman—made her empathize, and yet she couldn't glean as much information as she normally did at this stage. Lena must not be focusing hard enough. The "woman" was a demon who fed on men; she had witnessed this and felt the hunger herself. There was no justification for the murder of humans, no matter how it made "her" feel.

She jumped down after unhooking her legs and went into the next room to tire herself out with the punching bag. She had dyed her hair jet-black like the demon's, and she had bought and worn the same brands of makeup in an effort to generate clearer nocturnal visions. Despite knowing the entire murder—from the moment the demon confronted the victim to his helpless death at her hands—she had lacked the essential details to narrow her search properly. After listening to accents and examining the news station on the bar's television, she'd determined that she was in New York City. Unfortunately, there had been several bars called Red Bull, a name that she'd managed to pull off a napkin, and searches had been further confused by the energy drink and a New York-based soccer team. But despite the difficulty of her search, she had managed to narrow down the demon's hunting ground to a handful of bars and she raced the invisible countdown to the demon's slaughter to stop her before it was committed. Now, she also had to contend with the insidious notion that she may not want to kill this demon.

- - -

Orion heaved a heavy sigh as he shifted his weight and stretched his shoulders. He leaned over a map of the city that was spread out over his kitchen table. The places where the bodies had been found had been marked in red, and the victims' paths from the bar that they had left with the mystery woman had been traced in black. One of them had strolled a significant distance before he'd reached a sufficiently isolated alleyway, while the other two had been found less than a block away from their respective bars. He ran his hand through his rough curls, and they came to rest on the nape of his neck, which he began to massage to ease his frustration. He couldn't see a pattern, despite Connor's insistence that there would be one. He read over the reports repeatedly, looking for any additional clues he may have missed; they reminded him of the logic puzzles his mother would do on lazy Sundays when he'd been a child. She'd tried to interest him in them as well, but he'd preferred crossword puzzles and Connecting the Dots; the latter was ironic since he was failing to do so now.

He looked up at the agent, who was likewise bent over the map; his jaw was set, and he wore an intense expression. He was scowling, which Orion had come to realize was his resting face, and his hands were stretched out on each side; one hand brushed against a cold, forgotten cup of coffee. He'd loosened his tie, which hung like a noose against his unbuttoned shirt, and his dark hair seemed to have relaxed as well, the gel loosening its hold on the unruly strands and allowing wisps to curl in the humidity. He was muttering to himself while tracing lines with his finger and staring intently at signs that only his expert eyes saw. Orion found himself wondering if the older man had ever been married; he had yet to mention a past relationship, and though his left hand was distinctively unmarked, he decided the real giveaway was Connor's messy appearance. Orion was no neat freak himself, but maintaining a clean apartment made herding his sister a lot easier and generally improved his mood.

He wondered how his precious sister was adapting to her new life. He'd been warned not to contact her until the media frenzy surrounding their parents' deaths had subsided. While she was hidden from the limelight, he was easier to track down, and through him, the media could potentially locate her. He'd declined any interviews, regardless of the payday involved. This was due not only to his own social anxiety but also to the fact that he wasn't emotionally ready to confront the repulsive truth about his parents' double lives, and he'd decided to focus on saving his sister instead. For the first few weeks, he'd written his thoughts in a journal with the intent to share them with Cassie later. Even though she was at the age where she wanted to reject the values of their parents—in this case, it would be his—he thought the tragedy that had befallen them would instead bring her closer to him, so he waited patiently until he felt it was safe to contact her.

Cassie had been placed in Pennsylvania with another professional couple, although this pair worked directly for the government; he forgot exactly how, but one worked for the local police department, and the other held some sort of administrative position with the DHS in Washington, D.C. He'd insisted that he had to approve of Cassie's new caretakers, as he was technically her guardian now, and the couple had seemed nice when they'd met. Timothy and Charlene Vicker were older and apparently experienced parents, though their son had died in a car accident four years ago. The three of them discussed Cassie's health and what Orion expected for her, and they seemed to be the parents the two siblings should have had. Unsurprisingly, Cassie expressed contempt toward the Vickers, but he suspected that she was secretly grateful for the chance at normalcy and a loving home.

"So what now?" he asked, breaking the silence.

The agent looked up at him. "We're still looking," he grunted.

Orion sighed again. "I mean, we've been staring at the map for hours, and we haven't made any progress. What's the next step? I don't see a pattern here," he declared, his frustration evident. "You don't have to do this every time, do you?"

"No," Connor acknowledged. "Most of the time, I'm not assigned to cold cases, and make no mistake: That's what this is, even if we've got a corpse in the morgue. If I am, I usually have backup, like an analyst of some sort," he said. He reiterated that this case was meant to teach Orion what field conditions could be like, but it was just as likely that he would be doing work similar to this when he was reassigned back to the home office on Plum Island as a new type of analyst. Orion wasn't happy with this revelation, but he refrained from expressing it, aside from a dejected grimace. Connor went on to explain that he'd purposely chosen a slow, likely unsolvable case to allow Orion to learn the techniques in a comfortable environment—namely, his hometown. Orion abstained from informing him that New York City was decidedly an uncomfortable environment for him at the moment.

"There will be a lot of dead ends," the agent assured him. "Even with the BSI's considerable resources, we can't always track down an Other on the first try. If they aren't out there exposing themselves, it could take years. Our techniques are improving, though. A few years ago, I'd probably have to wait for this to all arrive by mail or fax instead of a handy-dandy download." He grinned with typical snarkiness. "Or I could've brought it with me, but you know how airlines overcharge for luggage these days." He looked down at the map and studied it for a moment, brushing his hand across its surface. His fingers hesitated, and then he pointed at a small, hole-in-the-wall bar in a part of town that Orion knew to avoid, especially after dark. "I think we should visit here tonight. Have ourselves a little stakeout."

Orion moved so that he could see the map from the agent's angle, but he didn't see any pattern that might connect to the rest of the murders. "Why?"

"Because these are her hunting grounds, so to speak, and we'll get a feel of it and maybe where to head next." His half-cocked grin widened. "And because you also need to learn to function on little sleep and being stuck for hours on end with someone you can't stand," he quipped. "Besides, it'll do you some good to get out once in a while and have some fun."

Orion groaned. "I thought stakeouts were conducted with advanced planning," he said, pointedly meaning the need to have adequate sleep. It was still early evening, but the bars in the city tended to never close. He'd managed to be invited to a few in his first year of college, but disgusted by the clouds of smoke and the obnoxious behavior of the other patrons, he hadn't been back since. Besides, he couldn't be responsible for his sister if he was drunk, and it was easier to be constantly available for her just in case than to try to live his own life.

The agent nodded. "That's the idea, but we don't always have that luxury. Besides, it'll be like a night on the town. We'll get in a few drinks and see if we can pick up that special someone. Hell, we might even get lucky." He winked cheekily.

- - -

The bitter flood of adrenaline hit her veins the moment Jody saw him. She had been strolling casually toward her hunting grounds to waste another night lying in wait, when he crossed the street in front of her. The tall man straddled the boundary of forty, but the lines in his face aged him by decades, and his soldierly bearing revealed the cause to those who'd also experienced life in the service. His dark brown hair was just a quarter inch too long, and his strong jaw was masked by stubble, which he rubbed with irritation and undoubtedly felt the need to shave, even though no regulation required him to anymore. He wore jeans and a tattered shirt and moved through the dangerous neighborhood with unconcerned ease. Despite all of her careful investigation—the nights spent stalking him silently from the bar to his residence and the mornings when she observed him stumbling between work and infuriating visits to the local veteran's office—she could not guess why he had chosen this bar as his haunt.

It didn't matter to her anyway. In all likelihood, the crime-infested neighborhood reminded him of his glory days and placed him into the element in which he was most comfortable. He sauntered with confidence, but not the same that she exuded; his was that of an alpha who dared anyone to challenge his dominance. She knew instinctually that he could put down men like dogs and force women to submit to his will. He belonged in the perpetual war of violent streets, not the civility of the modern First World.

Her hatred for him had been honed into a weapon in the weeks since she'd first spotted him in the bar. She had only observed him from a distance and had seen how well he'd treated those around him and how he'd blended into both civilization and gangland with ease. When she had seen enough, she'd decided that this target had to be the next animal she crushed.

He entered the bar, and she was only minutes behind him. Her entrance was unremarkable, and she sat down alone and bided her time until the moment was right. A combination of sweet innocence and coquettish naughtiness, she was all smiles when she sashayed up to him. She caressed his shirt coyly with her gloved hands, deflecting his comment about their oddity with a quip about eccentricity and secret fetishes. Even though her skin crawled with revulsion, the fabrics between them protected her from harm, and she suppressed any non-seductive expressions. Finally, after enough teasing and a staunch affirmation that any act between them did not require an exchange of currency, she convinced him to follow her back to her apartment. She hooked her satin-covered arm around his while her free hand traced lines into his shirt, and she carefully ensured that only her breath touched his ear.

- - -

Lena knew that it was the demon as soon as she walked into the room. She saw the evil of its aura surround her like a dark cocoon concealing a full monster soon ready to emerge from its chrysalis. Unlike the demons who had preceded her, the woman was almost unremarkable; yes, she exuded innocence in an adorable way, but she also lacked the marked deformations: the snaggletooth, monobrow, unnaturally long fingers, or other signs that Lena had gleaned from folklore, old wives tales, and esoteric texts. She was small—almost like a malnourished child—and it struck a chord of sympathy in Lena's hardened heart. The demon sat alone at the bar, and Lena had half a mind to sit next to her and strike up a conversation. She already knew her target intimately, so maybe she could persuade her to cease her lethal activities through simple dialogue rather than violent confrontation. Considering how harmless the child-demon appeared, it was possible that this would be her first murder, and Lena could set her on a path away from wickedness.

Lena took a seat in a corner booth and tried to hide in the shadows. In an effort to drown her newfound compassion, she ordered a drink; it was the first time that she had done so while on a hunt. No matter how weak or pitiable the demon appeared, Lena could not allow this compassion to take root. She'd seen the demon take a life in her visions, and it had been done without remorse. She had seen firsthand the destruction that a demon could do—what one had done to her childhood home—when left unsupervised and not confronted. If she left this one alone now, this demonling would only develop into a time bomb that would later explode elsewhere. The blood that was spilled later would be on her hands, just as the blood of her family had been.

Lena watched the demon as she flirted with her victim, whom she recognized easily from her vision. The demon had targeted this man specifically not because of something he had previously done to her but because he reminded her of someone else—the true object of her hatred. Lena struggled to remain objective; through her link to the demon, the man incited the same anger in her breast, despite the knowledge that he was blameless in all of this. He spoke to the demon about his recent divorce, unloading his troubles as easily as he would have to a dear friend, and she listened with feigned sympathy. She really knew how to draw victims into trusting her.

Lena had hoped that the demon would excuse herself to go to the restroom at some point before their rendezvous so she could intervene, but the demon never left her victim's side. She watched as the two of them exited the bar. They were physically clinging to one another, yet the demon still managed to keep him at a safe distance. Lena left money on the table—hopefully enough to pay the bill—and discreetly exited a side door to trail the couple into the alleyway.

With the man now secured in the demon's fatal grasp, the attack was underway. Her lips pressed tightly against his and she drained him, causing his skin to rapidly become ashen and his body lifeless. Jody drank her fill within seconds and then let his corpse fall as soon as he could no longer support his own weight; she was too petite to hold it herself. Jody's keyed-up emotions flooded Lena's senses, causing her to falter, stagger a few steps, and fall to her knees. It wasn't just that Jody needed to feel strong or that she was addicted to the rush; she was also reclaiming her power from her abuser, who was encapsulated in this unfortunate surrogate. This was not the first time that she had killed, nor would it be the last if she continued unchecked. Years of unwelcome touching had cultivated her strange power so that she could finally fight back, but it had not been enough; she saw her father everywhere more and more often now, and she would have her revenge even though the real perpetrator was long dead.

As her euphoria began to subside, and sensing that she was no longer alone, Jody turned and noticed the formidable woman kneeling behind her. The pseudo-current flowed through her veins, making her invulnerable, but she could also feel a tug in the direction of the stranger, and she approached Lena cautiously. This woman, who was tall, tough, and everything that Jody was not, gazed at her, and yet her blue eyes were not focused on her; in fact, they were not focused on anything, and as Jody tilted her head curiously, she realized that the stranger was enthralled by her, as her movements echoed her own. She felt a call, as if she needed to complete a circuit, and she approached the mesmerized woman cautiously as she removed the glove from her right hand. Delicately, almost in a tender caress, she touched Lena's cheek and felt the circuit complete. She was in her head. She understood her and her cause. She was a kindred!

Lena felt the shock of betrayal course through Jody's mind as her blade pierced the demon's abdomen, digging deep within her stomach and slicing apart its innards. It had been hard to resist the siren call of this woman, who could touch her without draining her and whose mind was a field of sorrow, pain, and revenge just like Lena's. She had felt herself echo the demon's sentiments and realized that she could even resonate, borrow, or even build on her unnatural abilities, but against great pain, she had chosen forbearance. She escaped the siren allure of this new possible life by replacing the surrogate image of the now dead male victim with one of her own: her father. He must have confronted the traitorous demon in his household as his family had perished in the inferno. Had she been there, would she have empathized with that demon then? No, she would not and could not if she wanted to achieve redemption for her childhood failure.

Jody's hand fell away from her cheek as Lena rose, and they switched positions: She was standing, while Jody lay on the cold pavement. With steely determination, she stood on Jody's uncovered hand with the boot of her heel, placing enough weight on it to protect herself without being thrown off balance, and sliced the demon's throat cleanly. As Jody flailed, trying to staunch the flow of blood, and the light of her dark eyes faded, Lena knew that she had done the right thing, because she was a hunter, and Jody was a monster.

- - -

The bar smelled, though Orion couldn't pinpoint what exactly the stench was; he guessed from its sourness that it was someone's old vomit, but it could just as easily have been spilled liquor or urine. He tried not to think about the floor's stickiness and what it would do to his shoes. As someone passed behind him, Orion leaned forward and barely missed upsetting the glass of alcohol in front of him. He winced in disgust at the lukewarm swill; even if he had chosen to imbibe alcohol, this would not have been his choice, as it reminded him more of rubbing alcohol than the consumable kind. He glanced across the table at his partner, whose languid body language belied his watchful gaze. One arm was propped on the back of the chair, and his face was set in a leer. Sat half-turned away from the table, Connor swirled the untouched drink in his hand lazily while listening to the lone ice cube clinking in the glass. By now, his dark hair had won its war against domestication and had begun a mutiny against good taste, led by a cowlick at his crown. He'd suggested wearing casual clothes so as not to draw unnecessary attention to themselves and had changed into jeans and a T-shirt, neither of which helped him blend in.

Orion fared better only by mishap: His usual baggy clothes, hoodie, and gaunt face made him resemble a druggie looking for his next fix. He supposed that Connor's sloppy appearance might be having a similar effect, only that he'd resemble someone who was merely a casual user. Orion's inability to relax made it difficult for him to blend in as easily as the agent did. Maybe that would make his role as a druggie seem more authentic.

Connor glanced at his drink, clearly contemplating taking a swig of it, but he swished it around again and placed it on the table. Orion didn't know why he didn't imbibe; the agent had informed him that a drink or two would make them less conspicuous as long as he didn't drink enough to be impaired. While Orion had considered taking a few sips, he wasn't overly confident in his alcohol tolerance because it had been months—maybe a year—since his last drink.

The agent's attention was abruptly seized by a woman as she stumbled into the bar. Her face was haggard, her dark hair greasy and tangled, and her clothes mismatched and disheveled as if she were wearing her only outfit and couldn't afford to wash it. She appeared older than the median age of the establishment, but since many patrons were also drug users, it was difficult to determine maturity based on appearance alone. Connor watched her drink for a while, almost drowning herself in alcohol, and he seemed to suddenly lose focus and turn inward. He finally took a generous swig of his beverage, shook his head in revulsion at the quality of the concoction, and refocused. He turned his back on the newcomer and set his face in a cynical, lopsided smirk. "So, why don't you tell me about your family, yeah?" he said suddenly. "Stuff I can't just read in your report."

Orion couldn't tell if the interest was genuine and the request had been tactlessly made or if he was somehow being mocked. He did not understand Connor's most recent shift in personality. The agent kept up a façade of casual, almost slapdash professionalism, but he was certainly more proficient than he appeared; Orion didn't know whether this was a purposeful attempt to make people underestimate him. Despite the regular annoyance that he provided at Orion's apartment, he'd also shown concern about his well-being—something that he certainly appreciated experiencing for once—but he felt that there was something more to Connor's visits. He raised an eyebrow and asked cautiously, "What kind of 'stuff'?"

He shrugged. "Girlfriend. Hobbies. Favorite color," he replied. "Typical small talk." He leisurely took another mouthful, this time swallowing as if he were pacing himself.

Orion assumed that they had drained the well of casual conversations over the many visits to his apartment, but evidently Connor believed that there were more topics to mine. "I don't like talking about myself," he complained.

Connor's cocky grin widened. "Ah, mate, that's something you're going to have to learn to do if you want to get anywhere in this world," he lectured almost contemptuously. "You've got to have confidence, and what better way to demonstrate it than by talking about yourself for hours on end?" He raised his glass in a toasting motion for emphasis.

"Then tell me about yourself," Orion retorted flatly.

Connor's smile faltered, twisting momentarily into a hostile scowl, but it quickly rebounded as if Orion had only imagined it. "Fair enough," he said and began to tick off his fingers. "No girlfriend—not for years, I like to knit, and my favorite color is blue." When Orion's only response was to be markedly unamused, he demanded, "Fine! What would you like to know? Oh, I know: We're both orphans." His inimical tone was unwelcome, which Orion showed with a scowl, and Connor relented reluctantly. "Alright, that wasn't very nice..." He drained his glass, slammed it on the table, and leaned in conspiratorially. His tone was quiet yet sharp like slivers of busted glass. "I'll tell you a little secret: I wish I was an orphan. Mamgu raised me for a few years, then she off and died and left me back with my mum." He focused on a point in the distance, as if he had lost his center, and in contrast with his previous affected disengagement, his painful digs appeared to be legitimate attempts to stay detached from personal entanglements. When his distraction passed and he returned to reality, his manner was more accessible but no less mordant. "That's enough of that, though. And now you know where the accent is from," he concluded, even though this didn't explain anything to Orion. "It's your turn."

Though Orion wasn't usually one to be distracted by an attractive woman, the slight figure lingering at the entrance recaptured his attention. Despite being covered from head to toe, every inch of her alluring body was hugged by black spandex, which served more to accentuate her curves than to conceal them. Cassie had dressed this way once before he'd set her straight, so Orion

JL MIDDLETON

immediately assumed that the lady was a teenager like his sister, and he could now fathom why she'd sneaked into a shady bar: It was a cheap thrill to be somewhere forbidden, even though the neighborhood was too dangerous for someone her age. Cassie knew better, but the lack of forethought about personal safety wasn't beyond some of her friends.

"Come on, now," Connor persisted. "If we're going to be partners, we need to get to know each other."

Orion was debating whether the girl needed a lecture, when he saw her leave on the arm of a much older man. Though the man was heavily intoxicated, he was the pillar of strength, and his hands wandered all over her concealed body, probing her limits. She encouraged him by moving the offending appendages teasingly to more publicly appropriate areas. "Agent Connor," Orion interjected, pointing at the departing couple, "what was the victim's profile?"

"You don't get out of it that easily," Connor chastised, but he followed Orion's gaze to the door. His eyes flowed over the man, noting the similarities in his physique to the corpse in the morgue, and then continued onto the woman to make the same assessment. "Shit," he cursed as he realized his error. His voice was tight, matching his expression, as the tension spread to the rest of his body. His hand reached under his shirt subconsciously to pat his weapon, which had been returned to him despite its recent betrayal, and then it dropped away without touching the recently installed security strap and leash. The woman, whom they had both dismissed because she'd only vaguely resembled their ambiguous police sketch, was leaving with a man who was the very definition of the perpetrator's victim profile. Orion wondered whether Connor knew for certain that this was their culprit or whether the alcohol had prejudiced him toward rushing into action.

Connor was on his feet and poised to dash after their target when Orion asked, "What do I do?" He hadn't been issued a firearm, nor had he been given any combat training of any kind; he was still a civilian and he probably would've refused a weapon had it been offered.

The agent's attention snapped back to him, and he grimaced in distinct annoyance. "Follow me," he growled, instantly causing Orion to recoil. Hoping to avoid further incitement of Connor's displeasure, Orion quickly and quietly followed him out the front door, and thankfully, the other patrons ignored their hasty departure. The agent hesitated on the street, scouting for their target's probable course, and then tread down a side street with swift footsteps. Orion followed as closely as he could, his sneakers scuffing noisily against the pavement, and he tried to reassure himself that Connor, being a member of law enforcement, would protect him if the confrontation turned violent. He halted hastily, barely avoiding running into Connor's back as the latter drew his firearm and peered around the corner cautiously. He drew a bead on his target as he simultaneously entered the alley and bellowed, "Freeze! BSI!" Orion followed gingerly.

To their surprise, another young woman was in the alley. Crouch notwithstanding, she appeared to be tall, athletic, and not much older than Orion. The blood that sullied her blonde hair and nonstandard fatigues drew Orion's eyes to the rest of the scene. She rose, revealing her victim to be the young brunette from the bar. Her throat had been sliced, and her arterial bleed faintly painted the scene, including the newcomer. Unfortunately, the man was slumped behind the two women, and his wan countenance confirmed his likely demise. The blonde deliberately held the bloodied knife out to her side and dropped it as she raised her hands over her head and shifted her weight as if to kneel. Her blue eyes suddenly glinted, as if they'd become reflective by a trick of the light, and her posture turned from unconditional surrender to wariness. Her scrutiny enveloped them as if she was hunting for something that only she could see, and her formidable gaze locked onto Orion, forcing him to eventually avert his eyes.

"What is BSI?" she inquired suspiciously. Rather than adopting the broad stance that she had taken earlier, she turned her body so she became a profile. Although her hands were still in the air, she had lowered her arms to be more level with her body. As far as Orion could tell, she was still not a threat, though she might become one.

Connor's aim never faltered. "The Bureau of Special Interests," he explained. "We police Others. We try to stop things like this from happening." His eyes indicated the unlucky man.

"Others?" she echoed. "Do you mean the demons?" Pointedly, she narrowed her gaze on Orion, and he shrank away.

"If that's what you call them," Connor replied calmly.

She snickered bitterly. "I hate them," she said quietly. "There is no policing them. They should all be destroyed."

"There are good Others," he interjected. He leaned toward Orion slightly, as if to prepare himself for possible interposition if she decided to go on the offensive. "They hunt the bad ones... the ones you would call demons. Mr. Starr here helps us apprehend the bad ones before they harm people. You could too, if you wanted. We always need help from those who know about Others and aren't afraid to deal with them." Slowly, he transferred his weapon to a single hand and used the free one to retrieve his badge from his back pocket. Unfolding it, he presented it to her as harmlessly as he could.

Her gaze shifted to Connor, and her eyes gleamed again briefly before lowering to examine the proffered badge. "Good Others," she mused skeptically, her focus squarely on him. She paused as she deliberated internally, and she gradually relaxed the tension in her body and adopted a more neutral stance. Whatever was going through her mind, she kept it to herself, but she surrendered without further incident.

- - -

The blonde turned out to be a woman named Lena Malmkvist, and she decided to join the BSI's ranks after being connected with headquarters and being convinced that the bureau wasn't a front for the demons she hunted. Not only had Connor brought her to their attention, but he had also seen her on the field, and they wanted his evaluation. So he wrote a statement in addition to the initial incident report. He couldn't tell them about much, other than the attitude he'd sensed: She was willing to take the hard road when it came to euthanizing Others while still using prudence. She seemed capable, both in investigative techniques and the ability to take care of herself, and it turned out that she had been hunting Others for years, believing that she was a lone soldier in a battle against evil. It would take a while to expunge years of prejudice, but it would be worth it. Cross-examination revealed that she had taken down several bad individuals, but despite her assertions, Connor was uncertain they had all been Others.

Processing her at Plum Island generated two additional interesting facts, one of which he'd already suspected: She was an Other herself. He couldn't pinpoint when he'd developed the hypothesis, but it had made sense against the background of her testimony, and despite the fact that her clairvoyance would normally divert her to Paranormal's jurisdiction, further testing had revealed that her ability ran deeper than that. Granted enough time, she could mimic and utilize another Other's power simply by being in their proximity, and after generous training, she would be a valuable asset to the bureau. Connor hadn't asked how she'd taken the revelation given how she felt about Others, but he had a feeling her path would be difficult until she accepted it.

Instead, Connor dealt with the fallout from the second grain of truth.

It seemed that Lena had been motivated by a childhood trauma that had been unearthed as soon as her name had been placed in the database. While Lena had been away at a boarding school, one of her family's employees, a pyrokinetic designated Tinder, had set fire to the house, and her family and all the inhabitants, including Tinder, had been killed in the ensuing inferno. Lena had not been given more than a precursory interview to assess her threat to Blackout, and since she had not been present during the incident, she had been filed away and forgotten.

Connor and Orion returned to Plum Island so that the latter could experience processing from the other side since he would be working in the office environment rather than in the field. Unfortunately, this meant that Orion was present when Malmkvist cross-referenced "Code Name: Tinder" in the system. Owing to the name's pyric connotation, the younger man became obsessed with the blonde and her childhood incident until Connor made the regrettable decision to allow him to access the file. Orion studied it, rereading it until he practically memorized it. His introverted nature notwithstanding, he became even quieter and more introspective, and he withdrew from his training. Connor's frequent visits to Orion's apartment no longer elicited a reaction, despite the agent's best efforts at goading him into one, and he decided to confront the situation directly.

One night, after bringing a new offering of Chicago-style pizza, Connor took an aggressive stance. "So, that incident with Tinder was mighty unfortunate, yeah? Burned the whole family to bits, save for that one poor girl, and that was only 'cause she wasn't present," he scoffed, baiting Orion intentionally. Having endured countless years of absorbing his mother's animosity, he'd learned how to get under someone's skin; it was not a skill that he used often, as it pushed witnesses to be defiantly uncooperative, but it was nevertheless a valuable tool in his kit, and he wielded it now. "Thinking that could have been you, eh? Or maybe some of your sister's friends?"

When he received no response, he leaned forward into Orion's space, knowing how much he disliked it, and added icily, "Maybe this whole building with everyone in it, including your parents, though I suppose you'd be better off in the latter respect, eh?" The mention of the Starrs earned a fixed, angry stare, but still, no words came. Connor had been certain that this would have been the correct button to push to force a dialogue. "Ah, now there's a response," he taunted. "Maybe you'd like to elaborate?"

As Orion's silence continued impressively, Connor leaned back in his chair, lifted its legs off the floor, and reclined in a cavalier fashion. "You don't have to, of course," he mocked. "I could just talk for hours and make wild assumptions and accusations to entertain myself, but I'm not going to leave until I get an answer." As if to emphasize his point, he slammed the chair legs down, propped his arm on the table, and started drumming his fingers in a quick, irregular pattern. He could see Orion's annoyance rising and his resolve cracking, but hesitance still sheltered behind the bulwark of his stubbornness. Connor decided to give him one last push and grinned sardonically as he badgered, "Come on, then! It's only going to get worse from here."

The younger man scowled. "This was a bad choice."

"What was?"

"You," he replied pointedly, adding, "them... whatever you want to call this." As he averted his gaze to the table's surface, his eyes lost their focus, and his mouth tightened angrily. Connor recognized bitterness when he saw it, but he wasn't going to allow the conversation to fizzle there. "Don't make me drag this out of you, mate," he warned.

Orion tensed further, turning his mouth into a pale line and giving him the appearance of a brooding teenager. "You're right," he said angrily, his voice even and steady despite the cutting tone, and the self-control he demonstrated emphasized his forced maturity. "I was thinking that case could have been us, only not the way you think. Clara..." He used Tinder's real name, possibly in an effort to humanize her; in contrast, Connor found it easier to perform his duties by referring to Others by their database designations if he knew them. "Clara lost control, but Cassie's never been like that, even if she's had an accident or two."

Connor would hardly characterize Cassie's track record as clean. She'd caused two deaths, earning a respite only because she had acted in self-defense, and he knew that she had caused as-yet-unidentified harm in the past. The BSI's belief that she could become a threat to public safety wasn't without merit, but making a verbal assertion in this regard wouldn't facilitate continued discussion with her brother.

"Now if she has an accident, you'll look at her just like Clara and..." The dam finally broke, and his emotions overtook him. The fear and love that he felt for his sister were enviable, but they were also a heavy burden. Self-consciously, he wiped away the few tears that had dared to manifest and continued as if nothing had happened, but his voice betrayed him and cracked as he spoke. "You'll kill her. There aren't any second chances. I never should have made this deal," he lamented, rubbing the nape of his neck in tiny circles with his fingers as if doing so would somehow present him with a solution. "I should have just taken her and run."

All the affected smugness and arrogance drained from Connor's face as he adopted a solemn posture. He exhaled through his nose, folded his arms, and said gravely, "You couldn't have done that, lad. You'd have been found, and Cassie would have been euthanized for sure." The search wouldn't have taken much time or effort either; with her parents wanted for murder, state and local law enforcement would want to locate the Starr siblings to determine whether they had been among the victim count, and their faces would have been plastered everywhere. Fugitives lost the chance for clemency, so by surrendering to Connor in their apartment, Orion had ensured Cassie's continued survival.

Connor decided that Orion deserved to hear the full truth, no matter how brutal it was, because he'd proven that he could make difficult choices. "Look, it's a raw deal, mate, but you made the right decision," he continued grimly and maintained full eye contact so that Orion would pay attention to his message. "You didn't fail your sister by coming to work for us. You gave her a chance, but now the onus is on her. *She's* got to do well. She's got to pass her training and maintain her control, or else she'll be considered a danger just like Tinder. *And there's nothing you can do.*"

Connor watched for his reaction, and Orion seemed to be absorbing the lesson as he sat motionless, except for an imperceptible nod. He clapped him on the shoulder supportively and attempted to reassure him as he closed the conversation. "There comes a time when a parent has to let their children make their own way, and that's how it's got to be with her." He found it ironic that he was giving a lecture on parental concerns when neither of them had ever had stellar role models. Nevertheless, he knew that Orion needed to hear it, as he'd borne the responsibility of parenting for over a decade. "You can't protect her any more than you already have, and you can't influence the amount of control she has. Only she can do that, mate." He squeezed Orion's shoulder, hoping that if he'd heard only a portion of the conversation, he would remember that part. "The best thing you can do for her is keep doing your job. Doing your job well means she can live in anonymity because the government is reassured that Others don't pose a danger to public safety."

Orion didn't like his answer, and it strained their nascent partnership. They didn't discuss his sister, Tinder, or euthanasia any further, but Connor suspected that Orion would eventually accept and internalize the unforgiving reality that his family's existence had created. The Starr siblings' lives depended on it, and Orion was sensible enough to do what it took to protect his sister.

Mercifully, Orion was more willing to discuss the other matter that bothered him, even though it took several nights of sitting in purposely uncomfortable silence for Connor to finally pry it out of him. "Are all of them like that?" Orion asked softly when he finally yielded. "Do you always have to draw your gun? You didn't with us."

Connor studied him, his eyes sliding over the slight, hunched body. Orion was lanky, but he knew how to make himself appear smaller, and he almost shrank into his baggy clothes. Even though he was twenty-two, he seemed at least a decade younger, as if the maturity that had been forced upon him in his early years had stunted the development of the other aspects of his personality. Connor had also had a difficult childhood, and he empathized, even though Orion's suffering had occurred in plusher surroundings. "No, I didn't need to with you, and I normally don't have to," he replied. "I'm an investigator. I just have the weapon in case something goes wrong." Privately, he thought about the fact that it hadn't assisted him much in his confrontation with Pierce Starr.

"You would have shot her if she hadn't surrendered." It wasn't a question.

"Yes," he admitted, and he wouldn't have hesitated. He hadn't known that she was an Other, but she'd clearly murdered at least one person and had conceivably still posed a threat without her knife. The military had taught him to shoot to kill and the BSI advocated the same escalation of force in order to prevent unnecessary harm to its agents or nearby civilians. It was also fortunate that New York City vigorously enforced its anti-gun laws, which had discouraged Lena from carrying hers, or the night might have ended in another shootout instead of being resolving semi-peacefully.

Orion shook his head. "I don't think I could do it."

Connor frowned. "And you won't," he replied, trying to sound reassuring. "Confrontation isn't our wheelhouse, mate. That's for special teams. The closest you should be getting to a fight is the aftermath. Your ability is more valuable during the cleanup." He clapped him on the back. "Just remember: I'm showing you the ropes so you understand what we go through, not because you'll be doing it on a daily basis." He considered the young man again. He was going through a confusing stage in his life; it was a time when he should have been in college and experimenting with the adult he wanted to be, not minding his sister or mourning estranged parents. It should have been his discovery phase, but that had been stolen from him and replaced with a set path from which he couldn't deviate, and it was Connor's solemn duty to help him realize this and guide him to make the right decisions.

Connor sighed deeply. "Look, mate. No one's expecting you to accept this overnight. It will be difficult, but you'll get through this. No one's going to make you do anything you don't want to do." He knew that this was a lie when he said it, and it hurt; the program itself was something that Orion didn't want to do, but he doubted the BSI would ever confront him with the ethical problems that Connor had to ponder, as they did not want to risk alienating Others in their service, especially when the numbers remained critically low. "I'll be here to help you, so don't worry about things you can't change."

The younger man shook his head, simultaneously rejecting and accepting the course of his life. In the end, he didn't speak again and looked up at Connor with a ghost of understanding. Connor nodded in turn and left noiselessly. Orion had to make the right decisions.

PART VI
CODE NAME: PHOBOS

Lewis huffed, hands on his knees as he bent over, and then took his pulse as soon as he caught his breath. His speed was improving, though it was his heart rate and recovery time that he was really concerned with. He and his wife had made a New Year's pact to drop their respective vices for the sake of their children. To hold up his end of the deal, he needed to stop smoking. He was down to a pack a month, which was better than the several he used to have per day, but since he couldn't quite succeed at this endeavor, he'd compromised by attempting to improve other aspects of his lifestyle in keeping with the spirit of the agreement. This had led to a promise to run a marathon in October, and while he didn't believe that he would be ready within the next month, he was determined to keep his word this time. He'd disappointed his family too often in the past, and redeeming himself was a private resolution.

After another moment of rest, he decided that he'd earned his cigarette for the day, and he took a seat on a nearby bench. As he lit up, he watched children across the way running around the playground under the watchful eyes of their mothers, and he thought about his own children, who were probably walking home from the bus stop now. He might return with the youngest one after dinner so she could release her excess energy before bath time and bed.

A woman entered his vision, but it was her bullmastiff that caught his eye, and he flinched instinctively when the dog glanced his way. His nerves unsteadied, he took a long drag of his cigarette and tried to relax into the bench. He closed his eyes, and when he reopened them, the landscape had changed so much that he immediately wondered whether he'd fallen asleep. The children were no longer playing and shouting; instead, their motionless bodies were scattered across the ground, bleeding from holes in their chests, heads, or limbs. The other patrons had disappeared, blanketing the sunny park in an eerie silence, and then his vision swam with ribbons of darkness that fled to the edges of his senses. He thought that he heard the children laughing again and that he saw their vague shapes dashing across the empty park toward him, but as the shadows grew nearer, he realized that they were actually large, prowling dogs. The ebony hellhounds' muzzles were covered in foam, and they showed every inch of their sharp teeth. Lewis drew his legs up onto the bench slowly and stood on its surface in an attempt to put some distance between himself and the beasts as they continued to close in on him. He glanced at the nearest tree, which was more than a few paces away, and knew that he would never make it there and into the safety of its branches. His heart was pounding in his ears while he searched desperately for a solution, and finally, instinct took over. He leapt over the forming pack and fled toward his house, where he hoped to find shelter. He heard the hounds baying hatefully behind him and felt teeth nipping at his heels. He did not make it more than a few yards before the hell beasts overtook him. As he fell to the ground and felt their heavy bodies pinning him down, the pain he experienced as dagger-like teeth rent his flesh soon caused him to lose consciousness.

- - -

Connor thumped the front door energetically and was greeted less than enthusiastically by Orion, whose ambivalent expression was becoming increasingly familiar. "Good morning, lad! Sleep well?"

Orion grunted. In a sick way, he was beginning to miss his sister's sullenness in the face of his partner's capricious moods; he never knew whether he should expect mordant enthusiasm, pitiable instruction, or a graceless wellness check. He stepped away and shuffled toward the kitchen, trusting Connor to shut the door behind him. Despite knowing that very few items currently resided in his fridge, Orion checked it in an effort to give himself something to do aside from stare at his partner while he delivered his lesson brief for the day. Sustained eye contact bothered him, and in particular, Connor always seemed to be scrutinizing him. Accordingly, he looked away so that he wouldn't be overly mindful of Connor's assessment.

Since the refrigerator didn't provide an adequate distraction, Orion turned to the countertops and started wiping down the surfaces with a spare cloth in an obvious effort to keep his hands busy. But because the kitchen already looked spotless, his attempts were evident to Connor, even though he often proved to be oblivious to Orion's discomfort. While the police had been kind enough to refer Orion to a few crime scene cleaners, he had chosen to undertake the task himself as he'd felt responsible for the whole situation. He had failed to protect his sister from the government and from their father, so a part of his penance was to tidy up the mess that had been left behind. It had taken significant effort to scrub the bloodstains from the floor, which nonetheless retained a faint umber hue, and it had been even more difficult to find and clean the stray spots of blood along the stairwell, steps, and landing. The place where his father's body had lain remained a blemish, albeit a sanitized one; in his zeal to remove the charring, he'd scrubbed and bleached it so thoroughly that it was distinctly lighter in color than the surrounding area. Nevertheless, his effort had made it nearly impossible to tell that a death and two attempted murders had occurred in his kitchen, and his apartment now seemed emptier—almost uninhabited—thanks to the absence of his sister.

Connor entered the apartment, stopping to grin smugly in the foyer after he shut the front door. "Hope so, because you're in for a treat," he quipped. "We've got to head up to Scotts Ridge."

Orion nodded absently, and then he paused when his mind caught up with the conversation. "Wait. That's not within city limits," he remarked, and Connor gave an indifferent shrug. Suddenly confused, he remarked, "I thought we were staying in the city for my training."

"Things change," he replied without concern. "There was an incident up north. HQ thinks it might have been a terrorist act, but it doesn't match the MO of any known Other in the database," he explained. "Since I'm so 'lucky' when it comes to finding Others, they want me on the job, so you're along for the ride."

"Terrorists?" Orion repeated, imagining the worst.

Connor chuckled derisively. "It's not as dramatic as that. 'Other' terrorists— not the jihadist kind," he replied insouciantly. "If it's VSION, things might get hairy, but they usually stage an incident then cut and run. They're more the violent 'activist' sort than killers, and they tend to avoid direct confrontation." What Connor didn't mention was that "direct confrontation" generally involved bullets, as impressive abilities notwithstanding, very few Others could stop modern technology. In posing a threat to Blackout, they forfeited clemency with the BSI and its international sister agencies.

"That makes me feel better…"

Connor grinned, beguiling witticism on the tip of his tongue, and then froze abruptly as a vision replayed itself in his mind's eye: Orion lies on the polished wood floor of an abandoned house, his neck at a regrettable angle and his body wracked with spasms, and he is covered in a layer of coarse white dust. He's only a few feet away, yet Connor can't seem to reach or even perceive him.

It was only a nightmare—an almost welcome change from his normal repertoire of night terrors—and yet he suddenly no longer wanted Orion to accompany him. Pushing the irrational concern aside, he continued, "You'll be fine. Just duck behind a car or something." He paused, and then added semi-facetiously, "Or identify yourself as a fellow Other. That might make 'em hesitate as long as you don't tell them you're with the BSI, too."

Orion sighed deeply; his exasperation was palpable, and he wished Connor could be completely serious for even one conversation. "So why do you have to go? I thought the point was for you to keep out of danger."

Connor nodded. "'S true, but I'm also the best at ferreting out Others. If this is a new one, I have the best chance of unmasking him, and if the bloke's unaffiliated, then we need to get him off the streets immediately." He chuckled again, and self-aware, he acknowledged, "A lot of 'ifs' there. Anyway, think of this as your next phase of training—just quite a bit earlier." He smiled reassuringly, quirking the corners of his mouth up and thereby undermining any sincerity in the action. "Trust me, you're overthinking it. You'll be fine," he said, slapping Orion's shoulder smartly. Then, in a tone that really didn't invite disagreement, he commanded, "Now go pack some snacks. Scotts Ridge is an hour and a half away on a good day. Let's not overcomplicate this trip any more than we have to. It's bad enough we'll have to switch trains three times just to get to the car rental agency. I don't want to have to make a detour for a decent sandwich."

- - -

Their drive to Scotts Ridge was uncharacteristically silent. Orion didn't have to suffer through awkward conversation or Connor's attempts to tease him, as the latter appeared to be lost in deep thought aside from the odd furtive glance. Connor never asked him to take over the driving, for which Orion was grateful, because although he technically knew how to drive, he'd only received his license last month at Connor's request, and he had zero confidence in his new abilities.

Instead, Connor had him review the file for the case they were currently working on. The attack, as it had been tentatively classified, had involved several victims spread across a small city park. Witnesses had given confusing, often conflicting accounts of the incident: Many had described a horde of spiders swarming up their bodies, beneath their clothes, and into their mouths, while others had claimed to suddenly find themselves in freefall or trapped in enclosed spaces. Some had been more specific, such as animal attacks in which the description of the animal or animals had varied widely, spanning from snakes to dogs to a bear. One individual had even stated that a particularly fierce clown had chased him across the square that covered the park. The handful of children present had become practically catatonic, choosing only to cling to childhood objects such as stuffed toys while refusing to speak or close their eyes for even a moment.

Additionally, there was a common thread among the adults: They had each seen the children's massacred bodies lying across the playground and had then heard them giggling before suffering their respective hallucinated assaults. The city authorities seemed stunned, as no signs of disease or biological weaponry had been found in the area, and while shaken, the adults seemed to have recovered. However, it was expected that the children would require intense therapy to restore their responsiveness.

When Connor pulled up to the park, which was now taped off as a crime scene, he left the car without a word and walked slowly across the grass while examining every inch of it. Orion followed him dutifully, observing his movements, but he quickly grew impatient with the lack of conversation or even acknowledgement from his partner. Because Connor had given him the file to read, he'd expected an explanation or an irritating, smug, one-sided dialogue when they reached their destination, but instead, he was being met with indifference. Deciding that he wasn't going to get anywhere if he just waited, he steeled himself against his anxiety and asked, "What are we looking at here?"

While Connor didn't quite start, he seemed to have temporarily forgotten Orion's presence. He stopped examining the grass, stood up from his kneeling position, cleared his throat, and replied, "All those witness statements, yet they can't agree on what they saw." He pointed a few feet from them at an upset wooden seat flanked by two trash cans. "A man said a pack of 'hellhounds' attacked him by that bench." He indicated the curb opposite their car at the boundary of the yellow crime scene tape. "A woman saw the ground drop out from beneath her. She said a cliff suddenly appeared at her feet, and she was prevented from backing away from its edge." He turned around and pointed at the playground where swings, seesaws, and slides sat abandoned. Its sawdust had been trampled flat by many feet and then piled to the side when investigators had decided to examine its plastic bed for evidence. "The children were playing over there. Nothing reported outside the bounds of this park." He sniffed the handful of grass in his hands and then brushed it off into the breeze when it yielded no noteworthy clues. "I just wanted to see what it was like before we checked into the hotel."

Orion's stomach dropped. "Hotel?" He instantly started to wonder if he'd secured the apartment properly and shut off all the lights. His mind started deliberating which arrangements to make for Cassie—which friend's parents would be home and receptive to an impromptu sleepover on a school night—when he remembered that it was no longer necessary. Cassie was in Pennsylvania with the Vickers, and he was absolved of daily responsibility for her, but his mind still substituted their old situation out of habit: Cassie was merely out with friends, sullenly checking in to appease him, and would return home after her school and work obligations were fulfilled. It wasn't until late at night when it was evident that she wouldn't be returning that he remembered their new circumstances. He'd once called her new number to talk to her and find out how she was settling in, but there had been no answer, and she had yet to respond to his voicemail. That was reasonable; she was probably still processing the events herself, and it would take her a while to adjust to her new circumstances and accept their parents' actions. He didn't mind giving her space and time to adjust, or more optimistically, he figured that she was busy with her new family and school and hadn't noticed the message he'd left.

"Yeah. We're staying the night," Connor replied confidently.

"Of course we are," Orion grumbled. He decided against asking why this hadn't been mentioned previously because he knew that Connor would roguishly state that he had already told him and that he should have deduced this result given that Scotts Ridge was so far away. He sighed and continued to observe Connor. The senior agent retraced the steps of the victims, trying to recreate their viewpoints based on their various accounts, and he would stop occasionally to examine the ground or the odd landmark. Orion didn't always follow his reasoning or methods, but one thing was certain: Connor wasn't making light of the situation, as he had done with the previous case. His demeanor was grave, and Orion realized that Connor hadn't been purposely ignoring him; rather, he had been concentrating, and Orion had been merely background noise.

- - -

Aaron felt sick to his stomach. His anxiety had increased of late, exacerbating his aversion to the outside world, and he'd allowed himself to grow lax when it came to his usually strict routine of making daily forays to the park. After the commotion the day prior, he'd completely forgotten to eat or even pick up his prescription; his mind had been preoccupied with returning home as soon as possible to recuperate. Familiar with his medication's withdrawal symptoms—namely, nausea and dizziness—he knew that he should remedy the latter problem before even thinking of eating a meal this morning. If he'd only preserved his routine as he'd been instructed by his therapist, he'd have collected his refill before, but he now had less than a handful to ration, which was the reason for his current desperation.

His vision swam, and he paused to lean on the automatic door for support, accidentally upsetting the mechanism from its jamb. The ache in his legs was also renewed as he barked his shin on the frame and stumbled away. He must have injured himself more than he'd thought when he'd fled the scene yesterday; since his self-exile, he'd rarely left the house on long trips, and his stamina and physique had consequently degenerated.

The store was moderately populated for the afternoon, and he muttered halfhearted greetings to other patrons as he made his pained way toward the pharmacy at the back of the store. During his third brief exchange, he noticed that the shadows were gathering, pooling, and coalescing just at the edge of his peripheral vision. He averted his gaze, opting to ignore the phenomenon, until he heard a shriek that confirmed that his perception was reality. He quickly crouched, taking shelter near a display. Clearly frightened figures huddled together across the aisle, and he wanted to send them a signal of reassurance, but he could not get their attention.

Beads of sweat started to form on his brow. He had not carried a firearm for years—he had been forbidden to—but he had his special tactics training to fall back on, making him the hostages' only chance; he had to take control of the situation. He paused, shook his head to clear it, and inhaled a deep, calming breath. How did he know that there were hostages or a hostage situation? There had been no gunshots or orders issued, and he had not seen any gunmen. He needed to stay grounded in the present.

As if to answer his dilemma, light footsteps passed his position and turned the corner. She was a petite blonde who was probably lovely under the layer of grime that seemed to cling to her enraged form, and despite the sorrow etched into her features, there was an all too familiar fury in her eyes. She raised her weapon, which he knew instinctively was her father's hunting rifle, but she aimed it at a cowering woman and the children she sheltered. Aaron knew that he had to act. He shoved the barrel away and toward the floor, and though he desperately wanted to be the hero—to correct his past failure—his feet instead propelled him past the slip of a girl and out the door of their own accord. He could not save the hostages— thought maybe he could have once long ago—and his terror insisted that he could save only himself as he fled into the afternoon sun. His feet pounded across the parking lot pavement and continued unabated until he reached the safety of his cozy cottage apartment.

- - -

Even though each man had his own room, Connor ended up invading Orion's, but he found that he didn't mind the agent's company this time. Since they'd arrived in town, he'd been watching Connor, trying to figure out this new beast and how he worked. The case file lay open, and dossiers were scattered across the table and their folder. Connor had loosened his tie, unbuttoned his collar, and rolled up his sleeves as he'd rearranged them, and their new order was a mystery to Orion.

A mess of Chinese takeout cartons was also spread between them. Connor's mouth, when unoccupied by food, no longer stretched into a sly smirk but set into a dogged scowl, and the agent scanned each report periodically between bites. While Connor hadn't tried to stop Orion from taking any of the dossiers, he didn't feel it would be a welcomed action, and now that he realized that Connor wouldn't actively teach him, he concentrated on learning through observation. The agent had behaved exactly as Orion had expected any investigator to act—poring through files and examining evidence himself—and somehow, Orion felt less anxious during this investigation than he had during the previous case. Maybe because he wasn't being pressured into providing answers or taking actions when he wasn't ready and was instead moving at his own pace. Then again, Connor was still driving their momentum steadily forward, but this time, he wasn't showboating and grandstanding at every opportunity, and this might have made the difference when it came to his teaching technique.

"Okay. For the sake of argument," Connor said suddenly, breaking the silence that had descended between them, "this was some sort of attack and not a psychic event, because if it was, then the DHS would have sprung for the Paranormal Division to come instead." The latter sounded like an aside, so Orion merely nodded encouragingly over his chow mein and made a note to inquire later about the Paranormal Division and why it hadn't been partnered with them on the investigation. He'd skimmed the missions of the other departments and gathered that they weren't as successful at the BSI, but he didn't really understand how the other departments were expected to operate on a shoestring budget and still deliver results.

"So we've got to assume that this is the work of an Other—not something else." Connor placed his carton on the table abruptly and cleared off the paperwork. He rearranged the remaining utensils and cartons—even claiming Orion's against his soft protests—to construct a makeshift replica of the crime scene. "This is the park," he continued, muttering more to himself than to his companion, "and this is where the attack was. The perimeter is fairly circular if we make a few assumptions—traffic on this street prevents any victims from standing here, so the theory holds true—and it doesn't match up with the boundaries of the park, so that means there was an epicenter." His eyes moved across the map, and his voice became more rapid. His finger traced along the outermost victims, standing near what he'd newly established as the perimeter, and then began to spiral into the interior. "These people," he continued before pausing over a cluster of three adults, "reported vision lengths up to five minutes, and the lengths seemed to diminish further out, which supports that there was a central location."

Orion looked at the map. "That's near the playground," he observed. "Could it have been one of the children? It might have been an accident." He chewed on his lower lip, biting back the rest of his line of thought. Despite being reassured that his membership of the BSI protected his sister, his fraternal instinct advised against exposing her further. Still, he knew that he had something relevant to add to the conversation, so he disclosed timidly, "I mean, Cassie's first time had a lot of power behind it. She didn't know she had it, so she really couldn't control it." Hastily, and possibly unnecessarily, he added, "At the time."

Connor shook his head vigorously. "Normally, I'd agree, so your analyzing skills are improving," he replied absently, as if the praise were an afterthought, and continued, "but the vision of dead children doesn't make sense for a child. Most American children have never seen such a thing, so they couldn't project it onto an adult." He sighed unhappily. "It must have been something an adult saw…" He trailed off, his eyes lost focus momentarily, and his face became blank as he suddenly turned inward.

Orion had spent enough time with Connor to recognize brooding, though he'd yet to broach the issue of why it happened or what triggered it; their relationship wasn't genial enough for that, and he honestly doubted it would ever be. If he didn't feel comfortable speaking to him about his sister or family life, he couldn't expect Connor to confide in him. To coax him back to the present and hopefully follow his train of thought, Orion remarked, "I thought you said it wasn't a psychic event."

Initially, Connor didn't respond, but his consciousness gradually resurfaced, and he began muttering to himself. "Spiders. Hellhounds… Hell… hounds. Hounds." He slowed, brows knit together, and deliberately enunciated each word. "Dogs. Snakes. Coffin. Heights. Freefall." He snorted suddenly, almost coughing, as if his amusement surprised him, too. "Clowns." He grinned as realization settled in. "Fears," he announced confidently. "They're fears, which explains why the children are catatonic. Everything is scary to them. Adults know how to deal with their fear." He shrugged and added, "Most do, anyway."

"That's rough," Orion commented, but it didn't seem like his prompting was still necessary, as Connor simply continued. The agent leaned over the map, pointing excitedly at its landmarks, and let Orion be his sounding board. "The children were here. Duration diminished outward but increased along this way. These three were near the center, but they weren't on it, according to the discrepancies in their vision lengths. The playground is over here, boxing in the other side, which means…" He quickly switched over to the file and shuffled through the pages. When he didn't find what he was looking for, he went through them again and then twice more. "No one was standing there," he grunted with frustration. He sighed heavily, rearranged the files, and began again from the beginning, pointing out the facts he knew. "Okay. She was here. He was here. He was here," he said, indicating the cluster of three near the epicenter, and then he continued pointing while muttering to himself. When his repetition did not yield new results, he shook his head and rested his hands on the edge of the table. "Someone had to be here, so someone else had to have seen him, which means we need better witness statements," he declared. He relinquished his dominion over the table and sank into a chair. Then the corners of his lips quirked up, and reclaiming his food carton as he propped his feet upon the table, he asked smugly, "How would you like to conduct some interviews tomorrow?"

- - -

Sone and Fission were having a quiet but intense conversation, to the extent that they were ignoring their respective meals, when Naught entered the canteen. She was honestly surprised that Fission continued to remain among their number: the shy young man of Japanese descent had been sent by SION to be an ambassador during the Tōhoku earthquake and had narrowly dodged interception by the BSI's Japanese counterparts when he'd used his abilities to assist with the nuclear cleanup. Since Naught had signed on, Fission had been kept on quieter assignments, primarily teaching their newest recruits how to safely control themselves, but he had still been the primary candidate when the Nepalese earthquake had struck the previous year. During his Japanese trip, he had garnered experience with relief workers, and he knew how to establish rapport with survivors, even if his supernatural power could not provide succor this time. After he'd spent several relatively quiet months in Nepal, he'd again run afoul of international Blackout enforcers when he'd discovered a Nepali Other named Hira. While Naught wasn't privy to the specifics of the resulting confrontation, she knew that Hira had not accompanied him home, and Fission had refused to speak of his time in the Kathmandu Valley. The introvert she'd met had become even more reserved and soon developed pacifist and even nihilist tendencies. Although SION was meant to be a refuge—not a bastion of warriors—each of them expected that they would need to defend themselves against the BSI one day. VSION protected them but couldn't be everywhere.

As she did not want to interrupt them, Naught claimed a seat a few feet away, but she could still overhear their conversation.

"Come on," Sone insisted. "You'll be safe with me."

Fission scoffed. "There's no such thing as 'safe' for us. You're asking me to directly confront the BSI." His voice was tight, his fists clenched, and his fingers tense, their knuckles pressed together in an effort to prevent his hands from shaking.

"Not directly," Sone said, speaking slowly as he determined the most tactful path to take, "but they may be there."

Fission's light eyes went to the television playing in the corner. "I'd say it's a definite," he replied pointedly. Naught turned her attention to the device, which was tuned to a news station that was currently running the headlines. Patrons of a drugstore had suffered a disturbing, terrifying, semi-collective delirium while shopping at their local chain. While the media provided vivid witness accounts—though the details varied—the story's denouement was a video caught by the store's cameras that showed the victims reacting simultaneously to absolutely nothing. Initially, it was believed by the authorities that it was some sort of mass hysteria, the cause of which they could only speculate, but a reporter had managed to connect the event to a similar incident in a city park the day prior, and it was then assumed that the two attacks had been related and that they had been the result of terrorist activity. The scaremongering had continued with conjecture that Scotts Ridge had been the test bed for some sort of bioweapon and had been the precursor to a nationwide campaign.

Frustrated, Sone sighed heavily. "That's why we need you, Fission. Vanguard numbers are dwindling," he explained carefully, and it was true: VSION's effectiveness as a fighting force had been dissolved in the short time since Antithesis had been introduced to the field. All Others were helpless against her ability to nullify powers, and she'd helped the BSI make short work of their base in San Diego. Members of the Vanguard had stayed to cover the retreat of the noncombatants, and all of them had been captured or killed. The defeat had dealt a harsh blow to SION morale. "We need your combat experience."

Fission scowled angrily. "Don't you know what radiation does to people? What radiation poison is?" he growled. Like a steadfast mountain, he declared, "I'm not going."

Naught's ears were still intruding upon their conversation while her eyes soaked in the images from the news program. They played the same images over and over: men, women, and children in concert taking cover, crouching, or freezing in fear. They cried, screamed, or threw stock from store shelves in an attempt to fight back, and one individual sprinted from the store. The newscaster explained in her voiceover what viewers were seeing and the top speculations of experts, complete with handy arrows, boxes, or circles around evidence to prompt viewers to agree. It was through this helpful lens that Naught noticed another detail. Squinting briefly, she realized that she recognized the man who had sprinted out of the store. "Aaron?"

Sone continued his lecture. "Don't you know the damage this Other could do to our image? We're already labeled as terrorists. This could change the government's minds about even bothering to spare our kind. The danger we pose would far outweigh any use the government would manufacture for us. This is Eric Dane all over again, but he's not a poster child for clemency this time." He pointed at the screen, which was now showing a tearful woman recalling her personal vision, which she said echoed a traumatic event that was the worst night of her life.

Sone hesitated, grinding his teeth as he contemplated sharing what was on his mind. It was not a popular opinion, especially among the refugee-like main body of SION, but because Fission had also suffered the darker side of the BSI, he didn't think he needed to pull punches when it came to talking about taking the offense. "Besides, do you know what someone like that on our side could do? He or she could be our Antithesis. You wouldn't ever have to go into combat again."

"I'm already not," Fission replied flatly.

A new clip played, this time from another angle and with a recitation of witness statements. As Naught listened to the commonalities between them, she realized that there was a familiarity to their words. The visions echoed Aaron's late-night confessions to her when he'd woken from his nightmares: his heavy guilt manifested in the guise of elementary schoolchildren stripped of their innocence and forced into shadowy, spectral forms who laughed at him for his failure. Her stomach dropped as her mind resisted the conclusion, but she knew the truth. This was Aaron's fault. He carried a heavy burden and had somehow learned to share his torment with others over the interceding years.

It also meant that she was in the best position to help him. She was familiar with his suffering, and perhaps this time, she could ease it; she owed it to him. "I'll go," she volunteered.

Sone gave her an incredulous look. "What? No, we need you here, Doc," he said and then turned to Fission. Deliberately and with a healthy dose of reproach, he continued, utilizing her interjection to support his argument, "We can't expect our only doctor to leave. What if something happens like in San Diego? We need her here to attend to patients."

She cut in again. "We both know I'm not a real doctor."

Realizing he was now fighting on two fronts, Sone granted her his full attention. "You're the closest thing we have to one," he argued.

"I know him," she said persuasively and indicated the screen again, pointing out the fleeing man. "That's our guy. That's Aaron Grimm. We used to date. Don't you think that will make it easier to recruit him?"

"How was the breakup?" Sone asked skeptically.

"Amicable enough." It was only partially a lie. In the months leading up to her departure, their relationship had become strained, causing long bouts of silence. Neither of them had the energy to work through their problems, and they'd each known that the relationship was ending.

As a last-ditch effort to dissuade her, Sone asked, "What about your experiment?"

She scowled disapprovingly, recognizing his efforts at deterrence and misdirection. "There's a small likelihood that the new protocol will even work, even if I were a real doctor. I have to wait for Dr. Moreau to secure new supplies to continue the trial, and we both know that we can't afford them without new funding. Millions of dollars of funding," she responded curtly. She believed that she'd uncovered the gene responsible for the manifestation of their abilities, and with SION's blessing, she'd begun experimentation on how to suppress it. The quality of life for many Others diminished once their talent surfaced, and many would appreciate the better control that her treatment might bring. However, her research had progressed at a snail's pace between her inexpertise and the lack of proper equipment. "Any other reservations you'd like to air or fabricate?"

"No, Doc," he replied, defeated.

Her expression relaxed slightly, and her voice lost its edge. "I lived in Scotts Ridge with Aaron, so I know where we can probably find him," she reasoned. "I'm a better choice for this mission than Fission, and you know I wouldn't volunteer for the hell of it. I like my cozy lab and my lack of involvement with VSION."

He nodded slowly, acquiescing to her request. "Sorry, Fission," he apologized softly. Fission's response was a terse nod, and he favored her with a faint, grateful smile as he left the table. Sone shook his head, either at Fission's prior refusal or at his attempts to pressure him into action, and he reset his body from a confrontational to a receptive posture. "What can you tell me about this guy? Why do you think it's him?" he asked encouragingly. She recited her reasoning and then began to recall their relationship as an impromptu dossier.

- - -

Connor smiled warmly. "Thanks again for your cooperation, ma'am," he said to the woman as they stood on her doorstep. It'd taken some time that morning to convince Orion that he hadn't been joking about who would be conducting the interviews, but the delay to prep him for the process had been unexpectedly fortuitous. Another incident had occurred during their commute to Scotts Ridge, and the related information, which had needed to percolate through BSI channels before getting to them, had arrived via email while Connor had been coaching his protégé in interview techniques. The two of them had reviewed the videos captured by internal cameras and the dossiers that had been speedily established by headquarters, and Connor had concluded that one of the recorded patrons must be their Other.

Despite Orion's nervous inexperience, they had been able to conduct several interviews that morning, and this woman, who was a part of the triad that Connor was certain had seen the perpetrator, had recognized the man fleeing the pharmacy as their missing perpetrator from the park. Even though the BSI had been unable to identify him, they were one step closer to tracking down their target.

The woman nodded a weak reply. There were dark circles under her eyes, and she kept her arms wrapped firmly around herself. Orion fumbled, uncertain how to conclude the interaction, and half-bowed feebly before retreating down the stairs. Before Connor also took his leave, albeit more gracefully, he made a mental note to make Orion see a therapist about his social anxiety. The woman withdrew into her apartment and shut the door as Connor met Orion on the sidewalk. "You're improving, mate. You just need to work on that confidence." He clapped him on the shoulder.

The younger man gave him a sideways glance and was forming a retort when Connor spotted a familiar figure across the road. "Sam?" he muttered, his brain trying to recollect her proper name. When his memory clicked, he called more confidently, "Sam!" The blonde still didn't turn her attention from her companion, who was getting into the passenger side of a car, so he commanded loudly, "Sam Anderson!"

It took a few moments for Naught to register that her given name was being shouted, and when she looked for the source of the sound, she was genuinely surprised to see an old college friend rapidly approaching her. "Morgan?" she exclaimed and stopped mid-motion, half in the car and half out, to embrace him. "Look at you! I never thought I'd see you in a suit," she beamed. Sure, the suit appeared a bit worn, but so had most of their clothes in college, and the look flattered him; he'd cleaned up handsomely from the stressed, emotionally starved student she'd known.

"Yeah, well... goes with the territory," he replied sheepishly. "I ended up being a government stooge after all."

Her grin widened. "You can still take down the establishment from the inside."

Exchanging an equally mischievous smile, he indicated the long locks of white that framed her face and temples and teased, "Is that what the hair's about?"

She shook her head, her expression dampening slightly, but her tone remained light. "No, that's natural… unfortunately." She noticed a young man in their company. He was quiet, flaxen-haired like her, and dressed in a properly fitted new suit in contrast to his companion. He also hung back several feet, not intruding on the conversation but also not wanting to become involved. Naught decided that wouldn't do, so she stepped around Connor and offered Orion her hand. "Hi, I'm Sam," she said, introducing herself.

He hesitated, regarding her hand as if her gesture might be a trick of some sort, and finally took it in a malleable grasp. "Uh, I'm Orion, Morgan's partner."

She smirked. "Awfully young for you, isn't he?" she teased Connor.

"*Work* partner," Connor replied firmly. "We work together."

She chuckled fleetingly but quickly cleared her throat and became appropriately shamefaced. "Oh, sorry," she said to Orion while attempting to hide her amusement.

Changing the topic, Connor asked, "What have you been up to?"

"Oh, I'm still a free spirit, you know," she replied flippantly, and the simple phrase put Connor on guard. Something was off. Maybe it was the tone of voice she'd used or the way she'd rubbed her eye when she'd said it, but it had been subtle like a signal of some kind. "Maybe a little more maturity… a little less partying," she continued. "Anyway, we're in town visiting a friend, so we should probably get going." Her clever grin reappeared; it was so much like the one he often wore, and it was likely that she had influenced him during their years together. "It's nice seeing you again. Glad you made it. You deserve it," she said sincerely. She gave him one last hug and then got in the car, where her companion was waiting patiently.

"Thanks," he replied, speaking to her through the door. As she shut it, he leaned in and slyly kept his hand on the car door, preventing her from moving away too soon. "You take care, Sam," he said deliberately.

"You too," she replied with a smile. Since she hadn't done anything further to trigger his vigilance and she hadn't directly asked for his assistance, he didn't have much choice but to let her go. Maybe he'd imagined a problem; it had been years since he'd seen her, and her body language had probably changed. He waved briefly at the dark-haired man in the passenger seat and stepped away from the car. Seconds later, she drove off, and Connor turned to Orion. "Ready to head to the police station and follow up on this lead?" he asked, his tone businesslike, and Orion merely nodded his agreement; he was already practicing what he'd say to the authorities, because he knew that Connor would make him do the talking again.

- - -

Sone watched the two of them suspiciously in the side mirror as they drove away. "They were BSI," he stated matter-of-factly when they had put enough distance between them and the agents as if the latter might have overheard.

"Morgan?" she chuckled incredulously. "No. Definitely not."

Certain, he nodded sharply. "Remember the girl Rho and I went after? That blond guy was her brother. I bet dollars to donuts that after the incident with her father, they went in and scooped both of them up. They were already watching her and the house." Naught switched her gaze to her former friend, whose form was retreating in the rearview mirror, and felt uncertainty creep up on her. While Sone had been in this game longer than she had and was, therefore, more knowledgeable about the people and players involved, she couldn't help but believe that his conclusion about her former friend was incorrect.

She and Morgan Connor had belonged to the same social circle: children, often damaged in some fashion, who had miraculously escaped poverty through the magic of a college acceptance letter. While Naught had embraced her newfound freedom, her stunted ambition and lack of maturity had been an obstacle that she had been unable to surmount long enough to enable her to graduate. She had wanted so badly to get out of her house that she hadn't given much thought to what she would do once she'd accomplished this goal. Morgan, conversely, had worked hard—the hardest of those in their circle, in fact—and had been kind and generous with his time, if not his money. He hadn't spoken much about his family, aside from vague allusions to a dead father and his mother's dependence on drugs and alcohol. When he'd left abruptly in the middle of his junior year to return home to his mother, who'd suffered some sort of not-quite-medical emergency, Naught had known that he'd been pulled back into his toxic situation. Since she'd left soon after his departure, she hadn't known what had happened to him, but based on his clean, professional appearance, it was clear that he'd managed to improve his situation, and if he was anything like his past self, Morgan was not capable of the evil she knew the BSI committed.

"And I haven't heard from her since that night," Sone added.

She shook her head and sighed heavily. She was not quite convinced—it would take more than a quick verdict, even if she trusted Sone's judgement—but she did not want to continue the conversation. "Okay," she acquiesced. "Then we'd better find Aaron before they do, if that's the case."

Their search had been frustrating so far. Aaron hadn't left a forwarding address at his last residence—the duplex that they'd shared and she'd just departed—and after she'd left, she hadn't kept tabs on him like she should have. She racked her brain for mutual acquaintances who might still be in town and hoped that they'd maintained contact with him. The closest contact lived five minutes away, so she turned the car and headed there.

- - -

The gunmen from the store had followed Aaron home, and he didn't know why. He may have confronted the girl, but he hadn't really meant to; she had been about to shoot those people, and he'd needed to escape. It had simply been a moment of opportunity, and he'd purposely avoided heroics. Now the two of them had decided to stake out his house instead of fulfilling their plan for the pharmacy, and he didn't know what to do.

Sweat was dripping off him, running in rivulets from his brow and across his chest and soaking into his clothes, and his endless pacing across the living room to check the opposing windows was making his discomfort no easier. He could not be placed in this situation again. He could not confront the two student shooters again.

Looking between the slats in the blinds, he could see the two dark figures. They were pacing slowly on the lawn like guards, and yet their demeanor was oddly calm, as if they were waiting for something. The girl, whose face had become obscured by an ever-thickening layer of grime, took something out from her vest and raised her clutched fist high into the air, where he could see it clearly. It was a signal. It must have been, for other figures began to draw toward her, taking form from the shadows as they came closer. Children—laughing, cherub-faced children. But when they directed their gazes toward him, their eyes harbored the same accusatory rage as the girl's.

Aaron flinched under their collective anger and drew away from the window. Belatedly, he realized how foolish he was acting: He'd tried to ration his medication out until he knew he'd be able to cultivate the courage to confront the outside world, but he now had only three pills left. The pharmacy may have been anxiety-inducing, but it was ultimately harmless; there had been no incident there, aside from his panicked flight. There were no shadows collecting outside his apartment, just like there were no such things as ghosts. He knew this place—he knew Scotts Ridge—and this was why he'd returned here. His familiarity with the area made it easier for him to differentiate between his reality and his hallucinations.

His therapist, whom he couldn't afford to see as often as he needed, had provided various techniques for his attacks when they came. He inhaled deeply, counted to ten, and then did it again until his heart rate slowed and his agitation decreased. He reminded himself of the facts he knew. He was Aaron Jason Grimm. He was thirty-two, and he lived alone. His mother had died when he'd been young, and his father had passed last year in a car accident. He lived at 4 Meadow Lane in the guesthouse behind the Primrose Bed & Breakfast, where he worked as caretaker. He was good with his hands and had taught himself several skills.

As he recited abstract concepts about his life, he also busied his hands. There was a repair job—several, in fact—that needed to be done before the bed-and-breakfast could be reopened. There was a short in the electricity, and after consulting with the owner, they were going to replace the wiring for the whole house. The owner could have hired a professional, but Aaron had shown his competence by remodeling the place, and he was allowed to undertake this job as well. He'd replaced most of the old-fashioned wiring, and work was coming to its completion. Only the living room and foyer remained, and this was where he was now headed. The single-mindedness of the task allowed him to stroll past the shadow children and not acknowledge their hateful, spectral presence on his way into the main house, where he now knelt on the floor with his hands on the wires and his tools at his side. He was fine, and in a few hours, he'd be able to attempt another expedition to the pharmacy.

- - -

True to form, Connor made Orion speak to the desk clerk when they arrived at the police station, and though he stumbled at first, he gained enough confidence throughout the exchange to realize that the experience hadn't been nearly as harrowing as he'd kept telling himself. Connor had assisted by flashing his badge, proving that he was a special agent, and Orion had been able to negotiate an interview with an officer. While they were waiting, Connor smiled and gave him an encouraging pat on the back, which he tolerated sheepishly. Orion knew that his partner's social attempts were genuine, but his attention, positive though it may be, still made him uncomfortable. It was the inverse of his parental relationship, and he preferred the quiet that he'd experienced earlier in their case when Orion had merely existed.

When the sergeant came to greet them, Orion almost didn't realize that she was an officer. Due to her short stature, she appeared young, but the lines etched into her face indicated experience. She led them back to a private office and offered them seats; in the city, she would likely have been allotted only a desk. Her nameplate introduced her as Alejandra Luna. "Brown says you boys are federal, but you just need an ID on a suspect?" she said, adjusting her glasses. "That's a bit unusual. Pardon me, but normally when you boys roll into town, you want to take over the investigation."

Connor nodded and straightened his posture to speak. "We came to town because of the incident, but we're not going to get in your way or anything. Wouldn't want to intrude on your investigation." A bit of sarcasm crept into his tone, despite his best efforts, but he pressed ahead. Although he had been raised to have a healthy respect for the law, it was hard to maintain this reverence when the local police and even other federal agents dealt with only the mundane and were often skeptical or unhelpful when he needed help tracking down Others. "We've got our own leads to follow," he said, hoping candor would help grease the wheels. Headquarters had worked quickly and had isolated the best still of their person of interest to send to him. He pulled up the snapshot on his phone and showed it to the sergeant. "We just want to talk to this guy."

As soon as she saw the picture, Luna's expression changed from civil disinterest to brief surprise before her face set in a disapproving scowl. "What do you want with him?" she asked, an edge suddenly in her voice.

"We think he might know something," Connor replied calmly. Recognizing the building tension, he leaned back, allowing her to continue holding the phone, and added amenably, "He's not a suspect or anything. We just think he might have seen something the others didn't."

She sank back into her chair, folded her arms, and spoke grudgingly. "You boys should really just leave him alone. Anything he knows probably wouldn't be worth anything." She shook her head and added, "It definitely wouldn't hold up in court."

Orion frowned. "What do you mean?"

"Well, that's Aaron Grimm," she explained, identifying him reluctantly. His case was a sore point for the department, not because of something he'd done—they all respected him—but due to his discharge from and subsequent treatment by the government. "I'm pretty sure he's been diagnosed with schizophrenia, but with health insurance being what it is, it's probably an unofficial diagnosis. I know he's definitely got PTSD. We all tend to look the other way when he gets his prescription filled, or we get called to escort him home because he's caused a disturbance." She explained that the pharmacy charged him a nominal fee, mostly to keep their records in order for inventory and tax purposes, but the town provided the rest of the funding through sporadic donation drives.

Orion risked a sidelong glance in Connor's direction, attempting to ascertain his reaction, and saw that he was troubled. In lieu of taking notes, Connor twirled his pen in tight, controlled motions as he tried to formulate a line of inquiry. Thankfully, Luna continued her story without being prompted. "A few years ago, when school shootings weren't quite yet the norm, he was the first cop on the scene. He managed to secure the area and even subdue one of the shooters, all without his sidearm, but these were different from the normal rampaging shooters." She seemed to age visibly as she added, "They had a plan. They were going to ensure there were no survivors by blowing up the school."

Orion winced and shifted uneasily. "Oh yeah, I remember. Sarles Elementary, right?" he asked. When Luna confirmed, he turned to Connor to explain since the incident had been quickly and regrettably preempted on national news by the Deepwater Horizon spill. "They rigged the whole school with explosives. One of the shooters had a jacket with a dead-man switch. When she died, her body blew up, and she took half the hostages with her." He shuddered at the memory. Cassie had been the same age as the victims, and though she'd attended a private school—a place that his absentee parents had deemed safe—the attack had been on the heels of a car bomb that had been detonated in Times Square. It was the first time that he'd realized how fragile their lives were, and he'd also firmly comprehended how little he and his sister meant to their parents because they refused to return early from a work trip to comfort their anxious children. "I was scared to let Cassie go to school for a week after that," he admitted. Then, he addressed the sergeant. "Didn't the officer get crucified?"

Luna's frown deepened. "He did his best under the circumstances, as far as we were concerned. It was the media who put him on trial," she replied bitterly. "No, he stayed on for a few weeks afterward, but I guess it was too much for him, and he ended up quitting. He started having his episodes a couple weeks later." She sobered, making eye contact with each of them separately. "That's why we look out for him now," she said deliberately. "It could have been any one of us."

Connor nodded sympathetically. "Do you know where we could find him?"

"He works as a caretaker for the old bed-and-breakfast up on the hill," she replied, picking up her pen and writing the address and directions on a notepad. "Folks say it's haunted now, which is a load of nonsense. Nothing's ever happened up there—no murders, kidnappings, or any of that 'violent crime' garbage. It keeps him employed, and I guess it keeps him busy. Phil—he runs the hardware store in town— Phil says he's been doing a lot of repairs to the place, maybe even remodeling. Maybe they'll reopen someday. It always looked like a nice place to live." She held out the address and then snatched the paper away as Connor reached for it. Grimly, she warned, "Now, you two better be nice to him. He gets disorientated easily, and if I hear that you've upset him, I can make your stay in town very unpleasant. I don't care what your jurisdiction is here."

Connor smiled winningly. "Of course. We'll be perfect gentlemen," he promised, and she relinquished the paper. He glanced at it before tucking it in his pocket and asking casually, "Say, why do people think the place 's haunted?"

Her initial response was a dubious look, as if she wanted to recheck their credentials; while a fair share of people in the state believed in the supernatural, in her experience, most professionals eschewed those beliefs, and she certainly didn't think anyone at the federal level had the mental wherewithal left for it; surely they spent all their intellectual capacity coming up with new bureaucratic ways to interfere with state jurisdiction. "Folks who spent the night there claimed to hear children laughing. A few said they saw shadows or strange visions," she explained, her skepticism clear. "It's a load of hooey. It's an old building. It settles at night, and people have overactive imaginations, especially when there's no one else in the building." She shook her head. "Bunch of trespassing kids with nothing better to do."

Connor cast Orion a significant glance before smiling and offering his hand to Luna. "Thank you, officer," he said, excusing himself. She nodded curtly, and the two men quickly exited.

- - -

The car stopped, and Naught put on the parking brake, but she found herself unwilling to move and placed her hands on the steering wheel again. Apart from her initial view of the building as she'd pulled up, she couldn't make herself look at the Primrose Bed & Breakfast. Afraid that she might catch a glimpse of Aaron through the naked windows, she instead opted to stare ahead through the windshield. "We didn't really break up," she confessed finally. "I was a coward, and I left in the middle of the night. I just didn't want to risk a confrontation. He tended to get unpredictable… sometimes violent." She'd been woken up several times to the bed shaking or to screaming, and she'd had to coax him awake from his nightmares to calm him down. Other times, she'd turn over and feel how cold his side of the bed was and realize that he'd been there only long enough for her to fall asleep. Just as often, she'd hear him sobbing softly, only for him to deny it had happened when she'd inquired about it. Once, she hadn't been careful enough in rousing him, and he'd slugged her for her trouble, giving her a black eye. He'd apologized profusely, but it had nevertheless pushed her toward the breaking point. "I just got tired of dealing with it… with him," she admitted, and her whole body felt weary. "His episodes were exhausting."

"Can you still talk to him?" Sone's tone was ambivalent; they shared a bond—one that he wished to develop—but they also had a job to do, and that came first. He wished that she'd informed him of this complication prior to their arrival so that he could have devised a contingency plan.

"Yeah," she replied. She pressed her palms into her eyes, paused, and then rubbed them before favoring him with a sad smirk. "I mean, we both knew it was ending. I just made the first move." She swiftly slid her palms across one another, mimicking a jet taking off, to emphasize her point.

He hesitated unexpectedly as a thought occurred to him. Naught didn't seem like the kind of woman who would meekly suffer abuse, but he knew nothing of her past, except that she'd had a difficult life. It was possible that there was something more to the episode with Aaron, including her apparent reluctance to confront him now. Then again, she'd practically begged to come on this mission, and that action wasn't consistent with his new hypothesis. "Are you sure?" he asked uncertainly.

"Totally," she replied, her somber tone shifting toward lightheartedness. "You'll see. You ready?" She paused, steeling herself against the steering wheel, and plastered a smile on her face as the two of them exited the car.

In decades past, the Primrose Bed & Breakfast had been a vast estate, and it still maintained echoes of that majesty. The front of the house sported a beautiful view over the valley, as well as the front yard. The garden, which had once been carefully manicured, had been portioned off and sold to developers, who had created smaller residences with similar views along the switchback street that led up to the place. The guesthouse windows were bare—the drapes that formerly adorned them had been stashed safely in storage while renovations were underway—and it was visible through the windows that scant pieces of furniture had been thrust against the walls and covered in heavy canvas. Gypsum dust and debris peppered the emptied floors alongside toolboxes and various electrical cords.

The veranda had been partially refurbished and expanded into a receiving area complete with a trellised overhang; in the summers, its vines would flower, welcoming customers as they dropped off their luggage, but only a specter of its majesty remained as winter inched closer. The sidewalk had retained its original patterned stones, and Naught stopped to admire its intricacy. She was lingering intentionally, delaying the inevitable as she tried to piece together what she would say to Aaron when she saw him. The video hadn't revealed much change, though he had grown thinner, and she had only the information that her friend had provided. How would Aaron react after all this time, and what if he hadn't taken the breakup as well as she'd assumed?

There was no point in speculation, especially when she and Sone were standing on his doorstep. She gave herself a once-over, running her fingers through her hair and adjusting her clothes, and then knocked boldly on the front door before stepping back. Sone stood behind her, ostensibly to give her some privacy, but he didn't seem like he was willing to avert his eyes and instead seemed ready to intercede if the reunion turned sour.

They didn't have to wait long; Aaron was soon peering hesitantly through the door. "Aaron!" Naught greeted cheerily, outstretching her arms.

"Samantha... ?" He opened the door wider and accepted her embrace reluctantly. She held him tight, as if the interceding years hadn't occurred. "Are you real?"

"Of course I am," she replied, her smile faltering slightly. "Can we come inside?"

"All hallucinations say that," he stated, yet he still stepped aside to allow the two of them entrance, and a feeling of unease bubbled up from her stomach. He regarded her skeptically from head to toe, inventorying differences, before his eyes settled on her face. Gingerly, he touched her whitened locks. "You've changed."

She forced a smile as she covered his hand with hers and moved them both toward her cheek. "Only a little," she said sadly and squeezed before relinquishing her grip to introduce her companion. "This is my friend Sone. We're here to help you. We're part of this organization—"

"I should get back to work," Aaron interjected. Grudgingly, he dropped his hand from her face and then curtly shut the door behind them before walking deeper into the house.

"… that helps people like you," she finished. It was not like him to simply brush her off, but it had been years since they'd spoken, so she couldn't blame him for being unsociable. Regardless, she'd come to have this conversation, and she wasn't going to allow him to leave it so easily. She followed him, and Sone, who was judging her wordlessly, trailed behind. Sone paused, his attention caught briefly by something she didn't see, and then joined them with a bemused expression on his face. He didn't offer an explanation and she didn't bother to ask; her attention remained on Aaron.

The extent of the construction had been only partially visible from the outside. The interior plaster had been torn away to expose old copper wiring, which Aaron had slowly begun to replace by hand with modern insulated wiring. Some of his completed work was also visible in the form of new drywall installations and unopened kits of molding, mud, and primer paint, while the unfinished sections revealed a rat's nest of archaic supply and return wires covered by powdered gypsum chunks. "Yeah, you've done a great job, from what I hear," she said, deciding that compliments might help reestablish their rapport. "Have you been taking classes? I didn't know you knew so much about carpen—"

"This is the first time you've talked to me," he stated straightforwardly. He picked up a pair of pliers and began stripping some wires in the wall. She thought about following him, moving into his space so that her voice wouldn't be muffled, but then she recognized that her interference near a possibly live wire wouldn't be welcome, and she kept her distance.

"I know. I'm sorry," she apologized. "I should have—"

"Don't know who that other guy is supposed to be," he said, evidently ignoring his presence.

"Sone. He's a friend," she repeated. She sighed deeply, steeling herself again for what would come next. She was terrible with words, especially when it came to her own emotions, and her apology was something that needed to be done. She wanted to make amends for abandoning him; if only she could find the right words. "I should have spoken to you earlier or before I left, but I didn't know how to deal with it. I mean, I still don't, but I want to give it a try." She dared to touch him, caressing his back lightly so as not to distract him.

"At least the two of you are a welcome change," he muttered into the wall. His callused fingers were carefully working the wiring away from the wall, isolating the K&T wiring from the brackets and washers that were meant to anchor it in place. The section he was working on was small but tangled, and the worn wires were sometimes patched with tape, which had long lost its adhesion.

Sone pawed at her shoulder, unintentionally shoving her into the rough surface of the wall sealant. "Naught—"

She ignored the interruption and straightened, addressing Aaron. "I know this is sudden. I know I have no right to come back into your life again, but I promise you that I'm not going to leave again," she continued. Memories of the night she left came flooding back to her. He'd been asleep on the couch with a half-empty beer bottle in his hand; she'd known that if she'd plied him with alcohol, he would sleep more soundly. She had planned to take only one bag, which had already been packed and hidden in the bedroom closet ready to go. While retrieving it, she'd paused to take one last account of the items she'd felt that she would have needed or would have been leaving behind when she'd heard a crash coming from the living room. She'd known instinctively that he'd fallen onto the floor and that he would have woken back up if she'd gone to check on him, so she'd left through a side window instead. She hadn't even left the note that she'd promised herself she would write.

"I'm going to work through it," she promised. "I mean, we are, and we'll get you help for the other thing. The organization I'm with—"

"Naught!" Sone repeated more urgently, making contact with her shoulder with greater force. She'd half turned to identify the source of the interruption, when Aaron suddenly dropped his tools and buried his face in his hands. She could see his lips moving and hear the slight whisper of words, but she caught only the odd syllable. As she started to lean down to check on him, she noted an odd creeping movement at the edges of her vision as if something lingered just out of view. When she turned her head to see it better, it danced away from sight and then abruptly changed direction, landing haphazardly on the floor with a splash. The shadows in the room had liquefied and were coming for them.

- - -

"Looks like someone beat us here," Orion said as they pulled up, commenting on the car parked in the receiving area. "Isn't that your friend's car?"

Connor pulled their vehicle beside it and parked. He scrutinized the car's exterior, but since it was a common model and color and he hadn't paid close attention to it earlier, he couldn't be certain. "Might be," he agreed.

"What is she doing here?"

He shrugged as the two of them exited the car and met at its front bumper. He hadn't spoken to her since college, and she could have been there for any number of reasons, but the why really didn't matter; her presence alone made him change his game plan. Luna had mentioned a small backyard cottage that had been converted to an apartment, which was where Aaron lived. While it was the logical place to check for a mentally ill recluse, and a confrontation there would minimize collateral damage, Connor needed to place the safety of the apparent bystanders first.

Based on probability, the house was the most plausible destination. If Aaron was receiving visitors, the guesthouse or the manor would be equally credible choices given that the latter was also his place of work. However, if Sam were one of the caretaker staff and Luna had simply forgotten to mention her, then she would head to the house, and any visitors—likely de jure trespassers—would choose to explore the house if they were seeking ghosts. This meant that Connor should adjust his strategy and search the house first to divest himself of any civilians before confronting Aaron.

Having made this decision, he turned to Orion, who awaited his direction uncomplainingly. Orion was a good, obedient kid, and he hoped that the situation with his sister would be resolved without issue because he deserved better than the hand he'd been dealt. He considered instructing Orion to remain behind him, which would enable Connor to shield him from harm, as he had done during the previous confrontation with Lena Malmkvist, but the broad range of this Other's ability gave him pause. The hallucinations had affected an entire park, and it was just as likely that the two of them might be overtaken by phantom images, so concern for Orion's safety might be moot; if it was not a directed attack, neither of them could take shelter.

In following his train of thought, Connor also realized that his sidearm would become a liability in the imminent encounter. None of the previous victims had been armed—though some had tried to fight their visions and had injured bystanders—and he couldn't guarantee that he wouldn't try to employ his firearm. Therefore, it behooved him to remove it from his possession, and he reached for his belt to disengage the holster. Abruptly, Orion shuddered in a false start, and his eyes became wide with panic. "Cassie!" he screamed in a frenzied voice and took off toward the house before Connor could stop him or even incite caution. Without breaking his stride, Orion burst through the unlocked front door and disappeared into the house. Driven by concern for his young partner, Connor went against his better judgment and took off at a jog up the sidewalk with his hand pinned firmly against his holster.

A burning wave broke over Connor, stealing his legs from beneath him and sending him flat onto his back. A sharp reverberation chased it like thunder and lightning cracking the sky open. His head struck the pavement hard, causing him to see stars, and he shut his eyes against the splintered wood and glass that shot across his vision. Debris bit into his exposed flesh, and when the cloud settled, he quickly found his feet again and rushed to survey the wreckage that had formerly been the manor.

The scene reminded him of a bomb detonation, and he was doubtful he'd find survivors as he made his way cautiously through the rubble. "Orion!" he shouted, making the young man his priority. He saw movement beneath some loose planks of wood and rushed to uncover the victim. He began digging, carefully removing each fragment so as not to cause a collapse and further injury, and he focused on exposing Orion's head. His progress was swift, but it halted instantly the moment he recognized the casualty's face.

His chubby cheeks were obscured by blood and dirt, and gypsum dusted the ridiculous wisp of a mustache on his upper lip. His tight dark curls had been sheared to the scalp in deference to easier style management, but Connor recalled its wild appearance in the weeks between trims. Connor could even see glimpses of his desert uniform between chunks of rubble. All was as he had remembered it—frozen in time since the last day he'd seen him… the last day he'd been alive. It was not Orion, as he had hoped, nor Sam Anderson, nor even another bystander. It was Jacob Stern—his best buddy during deployment and the first Other he had ever met—who had sacrificed his life so that Connor would survive.

Terrified, he recoiled instantly and retreated, losing his footing in his haste as his heel caught on a loose board. Compounding his ill luck, he was jarred into a different direction as he fell, and he could only imagine that it was a secondary detonation and that they were still under artillery fire. He wanted to save Stern—to drag his body to safety in one of the hardened shelters—but he knew that he was dead; he'd used his supernatural ability to create some sort of domed shield and sealed the primary blast in with him. Stern's body was in pieces, and he was rapidly bleeding out, if he hadn't already; no amount of first aid instruction had prepared Connor for the reality of this moment. Other artillery strikes were still incoming, and he needed to make it beneath hardened cover before the next hit, or Stern's sacrifice would be for nothing.

- - -

Naught became conscious of a blanket of silence swallowing all sounds, and she knew then that Sone had taken charge of the situation. Given his experience as a leader of the Vanguard, this was to be expected, and the idea of seeing him in action appealed to her curiosity. She was aware of his aptitude with sound, although she had never seen it demonstrated, and she wondered how much she could perceive on the visible spectrum.

She, contrastingly, would be useless in this fight. SION had been sympathetic to her plight when she'd first arrived among their ranks, but its leadership had also shown enthusiasm about her ability and had immediately solicited her to join the Vanguard. In comic books, the superheroes who exhibit enhanced speed are never affected by the adverse effects of moving quicker than the eye can see; but this was not true in her case. The wind blinded her when she was moving at top speed, which was something that she quickly learned to combat with goggles, and no pair of athletic shoes, let alone normal clothing fabrics, survived the stress she placed on them. She had "reappeared" naked more than once, and this was only one among the practical problems. Through her experiments, she'd begun to realize that her body could not cope with the speeds at which she was capable of moving; rather, enhanced speed accelerated the wear and tear on her ligaments, tendons, and joints, and her internal organs often expressed their displeasure within a few minutes. Her metabolism also increased, which thankfully spared her from dieting but increased her grocery bill. She'd also discovered that she had become proof of Einstein's theory of relativity: The quicker she moved in relevance to the world, the faster she aged. She could live hours in the span of a few nanoseconds, and her ability didn't spare her from time's wrath. Once she'd discovered that she had not been born with a complete set of powers, she'd stopped using her abilities and had instead learned to rely on her mind and practical self-defense techniques as a contingency plan against the BSI.

Sone took an aggressive posture, and she mimicked him, deciding to interpose herself between Aaron and any harm; furthermore, having her back to the wall was prudent. She knew that the BSI employed Others—why they chose to betray their own kind was a quandary for another time—but she had reservations about the coming confrontation. She'd believed that she'd be able to convince Aaron to join her without encountering any agents, and she didn't want to injure anyone unless her life was at stake.

The liquid shadows crept forward, first rising into columns and then refining their shapes into those of small children. They kept their distance, forming a semicircle around the three of them, and despite the dark clouded pools where their eyes should have been, she could feel their judgmental stares. She looked to Sone for his expertise, but he seemed as stunned as she was.

She felt the vibrations of the frenetic impact from the front of the house, followed by the erratic tremor of light feet running across springy floorboards, and the young blond man appeared in the room. His face was ashen and panic-stricken, and he threw himself onto his knees a distance away, sobbing and rambling inaudibly through his tears. Stunned by his arrival and subsequent strange behavior, she leaned forward and squinted, trying to see beyond her normal perception. Her attention was violently seized by one of the shadow children, who grabbed her chin in its small hands and forced her to meet its corrupted gaze. Its touch was cold, inspiring revulsion, and she instinctively resisted its unnaturally strong grip, but her animal strength was not enough, and she looked it in the face.

She had been tossed around as a youth and knew how to swallow fear in favor of survival, so she was able to look past its absent eyes and see its whole visage. It was not a child, as she had believed; no, it had the square jaw and sunken eyes of a grown man, and worse yet, the longer she stared into the abyss, the more she realized that its forebear must have been Aaron. She tore her eyes away from its face to examine the other children, who were closing their circle, and she confirmed that they all bore a striking resemblance to her ex-boyfriend. She felt her stomach drop and her heart skip a beat. She wrenched her head free from the child's fierce grip and gaped at Aaron, who was still kneeling on the floor behind her; he had barely moved, only to curl himself up further, and he pulled his knees to his chest. The heels of his hands were still in his eyes, and his lips moved intermittently as he murmured noiselessly into his kneecaps.

Movement at the front of the house diverted her attention, and Connor stumbled in, exaggerating the placement of his feet as if the ground were carpeted with broken glass and he was barefoot. He settled into a spot near

Orion and, like his partner, behaved peculiarly by pantomiming the stacking of invisible objects.

Out of the corner of her eyes, she saw an eruption of powder like fine snow and felt heavy, granular debris strike her face and exposed skin. The overhead fixture slanted violently, shattering the unlit bulbs it contained. "Sone, what are you doing?" she chastised him, and when she failed to hear her own voice, she realized that his absolute silence had not been lifted. He did not react to her outburst and continued his seemingly undirected acoustic onslaught.

Her awareness broadened as she tracked each person simultaneously. Connor staggered backward, tripping over Orion's extended heel as he backpedaled unexpectedly. Sone's plaster sonotechnics continued, the bursts leveling out and becoming more controlled, and she realized that Connor was in the middle of his strike path. She sprinted toward him, accelerating her body just beyond the speed of sound, and jerked him clear of the destruction, mindful to support his neck and not jolt him too severely with her velocity. She overlooked Orion's existence—perhaps because she had met him only briefly—and the sound wave collided with his head, whipping it backward violently. The cavitation further traumatized his brain, if not his viscera as well, and the burst lifted his body and propelled it across the room and through an exposed wall before burying him in the rubble.

Knowing that she had to neutralize the crisis before it escalated further, she released Connor to the floor, where he fell with a thump, and she focused on Aaron.

The children had swarmed his contracted body, transforming into a writhing mass from which faces surfaced sporadically. She swallowed her disgust and reached into the inhuman mound in an effort to uncover Aaron. It was cold and endless, and she thought she might lose herself in it. Her mind turned to the times she'd pretended that his night terrors hadn't disturbed her and to the days when she'd wished that he was normal. Whenever she hadn't been able to deal with it anymore, she had run away and found activities that had kept her out of the house until he had already fallen into a drunken stupor. Even though she'd loved him, she'd come to resent the amount of care and understanding he'd needed, but she had been the one to let him down. He had been dealing with an illness, and instead of assisting him in the healing process, she had exacerbated the situation by chiding him for not dealing with it better. She had been a vital part of his support network, and she had abandoned him.

Her fingers wrapped around a wrist and followed the arm until she found his shoulder. She caressed his back, pulling him into a hug as her other arm found his body, too. She was pressed against him, cradling his head against her shoulder, and she stroked his hair as she whispered comforting words he couldn't hear. She willed the warmth of her body to envelope them both in a protective bubble, and she wrapped him in a blanket of affection. She felt his tears begin to soak through her shirt and his ragged breath become even again, and she knew that he would be OK because she would make his recovery her mission.

After what seemed like hours, their intimate reconciliation was interrupted by Connor's unsteady yet firm voice: "Sam, please step aside. It's time for us to go." She became aware that the other noises of the world—from the settling of the house to the distant hum of an airplane—were pouring into the room. She took in more of her environment. The shadows had dispersed, lightening to pale shades and returning to their corners. The room was spattered with plaster and littered with misplaced tools, but there was no sign of the children's invasion, save for the shattered wall beneath which Orion's body lay. Beside her, Sone had regained his senses and was standing, seemingly waiting to follow her lead.

With his hand on his firearm and his feet in a shooter's stance, Connor was immovable, and yet he was making a conscious effort to be otherwise nonthreatening and approachable. He retrieved his badge with his free hand and displayed it briefly before replacing it in his inner jacket pocket. Sone had been correct; he was a member of the dreaded BSI, although he was being more evenhanded than his peers, who would have shot the three of them without initiating dialogue. "It occurs to me that the two of you are here to collect Mr. Grimm," he said, inferring their SION membership. "I'm willing to overlook your presence here, Sam, if you'll just step aside so I can take him in and get him help."

She gave him a dirty look because she knew that he was lying. "You're not going to get him help. You're going to kill him."

He nodded slowly. "That's probably true," he admitted, "but he's a danger to public safety." Though his posture remained resolute and unyielding, his soft brown eyes found hers, and he spoke to her directly. "He's got no control," he reasoned. "He's traumatized a park and a pharmacy, and he's just killed my partner." He paused, biting back anger or tears, and the corners of his mouth tightened and then twisted. "I can't say he's a prime subject for rehabilitation," he hissed, undoubtedly with more acidity than he had intended.

"Aaron needs help, and he's not going to get it from you," she replied protectively; this was the path she had chosen, and she would stick with it to the end if that's what it took for redemption. "Now, I don't want to hurt you, but I will if I have to," she continued. "You're reasonable, so just leave, and we'll call it even."

"You're right. I am reasonable, but he's a time bomb," he asserted in a small, tense voice. As he continued, he made grand gestures with his free hand, attempting to distract her from his tightening grip on his weapon. "An episode like this on a larger scale could kill more. SION claims it saves Others' lives, but he killed one just now. That park was full of children, and so was the pharmacy." He scowled, his brow furrowing like it once had when he'd lectured her in college after an ill-advised drunken night out. "Next time, we might not be so lucky, and there'll be a death count. Now, I don't want to use force, but you have to admit this situation warrants it," he remarked sardonically. "All I'm asking is that you step—"

Risking extreme speed one last time, she relocated to Connor's position and removed his hand from his weapon. She didn't know much about firearms, and it took her several attempts to dismantle it fully before she allowed the stripped pieces to fall from her hands along with the unexpended ammo, which had been unburdened from its clip. She then returned to her place beside Aaron, not allowing his body to waver due to her transitory lack of support.

When time returned to normal, the disassembled firearm clattered to the floor and startled both Connor and Sone, who had likewise never seen her ability demonstrated. "He's coming with us, Morgan," she said resolutely. Powerlessly, Connor looked at the pieces scattered across the floor and reassessed the two foes before him. Acknowledging that he was disarmed and outnumbered, he prudently spread his arms in submission. "Alright, but if he kills anyone, those deaths are on your head, Sam," he warned and retreated.

Now that the threat had passed, she returned her attention to Aaron. His recovery from his episode had progressed further, and he seemed aware of his surroundings. She kissed his forehead, reassuring him of her presence in reality, and murmured comforting words. Sone interjected urgently, "We should go," and he helped her support Aaron as they left.

- - -

Orion inhaled deeply, hungrily, as if his lungs had finally found air after a long time underwater. The adrenaline in his veins forced his eyes open wide so that they could catch any hint of danger. He was lying on his back, and he could see only an enormous carved ceiling overhead.

He tried to piece together how he'd arrived at his present location. He remembered that they'd driven up to the house on Meadow Lane and that he'd waited outside for Connor's direction. While he'd anticipated a confrontation, he hadn't known what to expect. Would it be potentially violent, as Lena Malmkvist had threatened, or would the Other come along quietly, as he had? Connor had seemed wary, but he hadn't said anything.

Casually, he'd glanced through the windows of Primrose and glimpsed his sister lying in a pool of blood. Even though he'd known that his sister was safe with the Vickers in Pennsylvania, no amount of logic had been able to eradicate the fear that he'd felt during that moment, and he'd run to her without a moment's hesitance. Her body had been warm—so warm—as if he'd just missed her assassin, and the gaping hole in her chest had testified to the fact that it had been her blood on the floor. He'd known intuitively that he had failed to protect her from their father, who had returned to exact his revenge on his own family. Orion had closed his eyes and willed her flesh to answer his call, but her body had remained inert no matter how hard he'd concentrated.

He felt a sharp twinge and an enormous, bludgeoning pain that engulfed his whole body, and then there was darkness. When his vision returned, Cassie stood before him with her arms wide, welcoming him. Her red hair was tamed, and she wore a long white dress that suited her age rather than the adult she desperately desired to be. She was angelic and beautiful, and she was also his little sister and not the rebellious teenager. He took her hand and followed her from this place. The light was dim, as if he wore shades, and everything was covered in a fine, gray mist. He could not see more than twenty feet ahead, let alone where she was taking him, but he wasn't worried; she was unharmed, and she was with him.

He did not remember leaving the mist nor returning to this place, but the ceiling resembled Primrose's style. His body no longer ached, and as the adrenaline fled his body, he realized that he felt rested as if he'd had a full night's sleep. Perhaps it had been a dream—or more likely a nightmare, given his energetic awakening—but he did not have long to ponder the situation, as Connor's face soon appeared in his field of vision.

The muscles of his face were tight, and his eyebrows were knitted together. "How ya feeling there, lad?" Connor asked soberly, offering his hand; he seemed worried but unable or unwilling to properly express it. Orion accepted his aid and the older man helped him into a sitting position. Orion was covered in grainy residue, which he recognized as the chalky remains of the walls, and he dusted himself off.

"Fine," he answered uncertainly. He felt great, all things considered, but Connor's expression hinted that this might not have been the correct response.

"You took a pretty bad blow. I wouldn't say you're fine," Connor said, and Orion could only shrug. The lines in Connor's face deepened, and he cocked his head as he quirked his lips. He still hadn't released him, and though there was no pressure, he had the feeling that Connor wouldn't allow him to stand on his own yet. "Are you sure nothing hurts? Not even a little?" he pressed. "Maybe we should take you to the hospital just in case. Get you checked out with an MRI or something."

"I don't need doctors, remember?"

"Right," he remarked, unconvinced, and the gap that followed was oppressive. Gradually, Connor moved his hands and assisted him to his feet, bracing him awkwardly in case he lost his balance. Orion felt no different as a result of the change in elevation, but he suspected that Connor had expected the worst.

They were now in uncomfortably close proximity, and Orion began to feel self-conscious. He shifted away, and Connor reluctantly released his supporting grasp, allowing him to stand on his own. "What happened?" he asked, breaking the silence.

Connor immediately looked away toward the center of the house. "They got away," he said. He then flipped a mental switch and gave a conceited smirk, curling his lips wickedly in Orion's direction. "Looks like you've got your first failure." Though he'd spoken the words aloud, Orion didn't believe he was speaking to him, and his fleeting glibness evaporated unexpectedly.

"'They'?"

He ignored him. "But it's a great learning opportunity, isn't it?" he scoffed, mocking their normal teacher–student relationship. He was sour and angry, and Orion didn't know what he'd done to provoke him. One moment, Connor was fuming, twisting his expression into ambivalence, and then his perplexing episode ended, and he sighed deeply as he relinquished whatever negative energy he'd amassed. He gathered himself, and when he met Orion's gaze, his face showed sheer exhaustion. When he spoke, his tone was apologetic, and he clapped him on the shoulder again. "Let's head back to the hotel, eh? 'S been a long day."

- - -

Connor spent the entire evening monitoring Orion, watching for an irregularities. At first, he doubted the young man's healing abilities, examining him every so often in search of a fractured skull or tender rib. He tested his vision, forced him through motor control exercises, and quizzed his memory in an attempt to diagnose him with a concussion, but Orion passed and showed no signs of brain injury. He even checked his temperature, looking for signs of infection. Eventually, Orion tired of his obsessive attention, and Connor had to shift to subtler observational techniques.

He tried without success to persuade him to discuss the incident, but it seemed Orion was a master of evasion. This skill was likely a result of years of having to avoid answering uncomfortable questions about the whereabouts of his parents, and Connor felt no strong need to relive the day himself. Without Orion's input, he could rely only on his own recollection of the events, and though the memories unsettled him, he could only press Orion so hard without drawing suspicion. His vision, along with what followed, would become the standard narrative, and he changed the topic.

In the end, he found no evidence of harm, and at Connor's insistence, Orion settled in the agent's bed. Connor took the armchair, using the excuse that he would work on their report; while true, he also wasn't ready to let the boy out of his sight. Connor couldn't shake what he had seen at Primrose, even if the boy was alive and well now.

It was late when he began the report, but it was easy to write. Despite the positive identification of the Other, he had failed to take Aaron Grimm into custody, and worse yet, he'd allowed him to fall into the hands of VSION. Connor took full responsibility. He had no doubt that the individuals he had encountered were members of the Vanguard, given their coincidental appearance and preparedness to fight him, and accessing the BSI's database confirmed it: The dark-haired man was Sone, a known terrorist. There was not much that Connor could add to his file, even to pad it out. Instead, he built dossiers on the other two. He knew about the first, Aaron Grimm, thanks to Sergeant Luna and her unwitting provision of his file, which Connor had requested from the local station's Human Resources under her name. His undiagnosed schizophrenia, compounded by his post-traumatic stress, was a potent and deadly combination; an episode could be triggered at any point in time, and now that he was in the hands of VSION, he could be honed into a weapon.

However, the inclusion of Sam Anderson saddened him. As kindred spirits, they had once been drawn together, and he could not imagine her as an adversary creating disasters and murdering innocent people simply to send a declaration of "freedom" for her kind. He checked for her in the database after he found Sone, and she was absent from its catalogue, but now that he had engaged her, he was obligated to complete a dossier on her. This meant that she would be classified as a high-value target like any other member of the Vanguard. He tried not to think too hard about it as he wrote her biography and psychological profile.

The report became more difficult once the dossiers were completed. To properly document the case, he had to record all the events that had occurred. He did it primarily to help future investigators learn from his methods: how to find an Other, determine its abilities, and bring it into custody. This time, they would learn from his failures.

He thought it might be useful to describe his vision—the details and differences from reality—but he could not progress past his departure from the car at Primrose. Years prior, he had recounted a similar event to military investigators in a desert thousands of miles away. His words had been mechanical, as if he had been reciting from a script, and had even included the fantasy of Stern's telekinetic shield, and his thoughts had never truly entered the moment. Now, however, his mind would not permit him to leave the bumper of their rental car and continue down the trellised sidewalk toward the house. He knew what had happened then—a terrible reenactment of the airstrike that had almost killed him—yet he could not recall one moment of the episode; his brain shut it down, instead forwarding to his confrontation with Sam, so he had no choice but to continue from there and leave the delirious period a blank.

His recollection of that moment was scrambled, mixing his vision with bodily sensations and glimpses of the intact room, so he was not entirely certain when he returned to reality. He had seen Orion thrown through one of the walls and watched the collapsing weight crush his body. The BSI database described the power of Sone's sound waves as reaching the pulverizing force of a freight train, and he didn't believe Orion could withstand the impact, even with his extraordinary regeneration. Yet, Orion was unharmed and sleeping in his bed, which meant that he had somehow survived.

The ability to recover from catastrophic wounds was different from being an exceptional healer. People—even the good ones—still needed to die to maintain the natural balance, and the BSI wouldn't permit the existence of an Other who could upset the balance too much. Even if this Other never fell into SION's hands, there were elements in the government who would misuse effective immortality, which meant that the Other had to be terminated to prevent a quandary; the BSI's rules were very black and white.

The moral choice was to recommend Orion's immediate euthanasia, even though he couldn't prove definitively that a resurrection had occurred; he couldn't risk this possibility, and the BSI's rules mandated the elimination of threats before they became problematic. Nevertheless, he could not avoid his personal feelings on the matter. He had come to know Orion and appreciate his circumstances, from his difficult relationship with his sister to his nigh-abusive childhood of neglect; he had done well raising himself and his sister, superseding his selfish parents, and he was genuinely a nice kid. He had taken Orion under his wing, just as he had been instructed, and they had forged a bond, unsteady though it might be.

It was an agonizing decision. Shortly after meeting the Starrs, he'd had to recommend a child for euthanasia because he, too, could have overpowered the natural balance, and he had just placed his college friend on the kill list as well. Connor didn't think he had it in him to recommend another murder in such a short period, and that ended up being the key differentiation: He could not think of Orion's removal as euthanasia or as protection of the civilian population as he had with previous Others; he could view it only as homicide.

In disgust, he deleted his short paragraph on Orion and forwarded the report to headquarters. Since when had he begun to waver on BSI principles? He had sworn to protect the civilian population against Others no matter the cost, even if it meant sacrificing a few extraordinary individuals, and he had made the hard choices before. He had made it with Brian Chamberlain, who had been a young child, and with others who had been unable to control their abilities but had otherwise been blameless; he should not have faltered just because he knew Orion Starr.

He stole a glance at Orion, who was snoring softly in the bed. No jury would convict a defendant if there was reasonable doubt, but the BSI did not work that way; before Eric Dane, every Other had been a time bomb, and so it had been necessary to draw a hard line. What Connor had just done had been an immoral choice, yet he knew that it had still been the right one; he just needed to convince himself of this.

He opened the mini fridge and studied its contents. He grabbed a whiskey miniature, paused, and then took the rest of the bottles, emptying the fridge of its minor stock. As he poured himself a glass to drown the conflicting voices, he mused that his job was turning him into an alcoholic.

- - -

Jack had been galvanized ever since he'd recovered from the initial shock of Pierce Starr's death. The experiment had been a failure because it had not been conducted properly. His child with Evangeline Starr had demonstrated that his abilities could be passed through heredity, and Pierce's children had confirmed the theory, so he had examined the genealogies of all Others he'd identified, tracing any possible bloodlines to see what talents had been passed on and which had developed spontaneously. While Pierce had inherited Jack's ability to drain life force, his children had not, instead developing different traits while still remaining Others, and he was currently researching the root of the disparity.

While exploring the pedigrees of various Others, he was also developing a new experiment. He contemplated marrying Amanda Darling-Whitcomb—whose human bloodline could be considered superior to that of his other subjects— and fathering several children with her; after all, pedigree propagation was what she had originally been raised to do. Acceptance of the marriage proposal would take considerable persuasion, but her hunger for the presidency would be her downfall. He had substantial, important ties to influential people and powerful industrial complexes that she couldn't ignore, even if she didn't trust him, and she would accept the alliance to acquire his power base. After they bred a large enough brood, he could fake his death, and she would initially be happy to be rid of him. She would still be in his power, even if she had no part in his seeming demise, because two dubious spousal deaths begged the label of black widow, and the circumstances of his "death" would provide further leverage against her.

As much as it would amuse him to torment a future Amanda Darling-Whitcomb-cum-Everest, he would most likely choose an Other with a lower profile to dally with. He could not afford to become more notable than he already was, for in the coming decade, he would have to fake his death to start anew and avoid drawing suspicion to his agelessness, and he could safely manipulate the life of a woman, or even make her disappear, if she had never been in the public spotlight. All that remained was to make a choice, which was not easy; there were few identified Others who were not monitored by the BSI or SION, and pre-Dane, it was rare for Others to survive long enough to pass on their genes.

He became aware of a shape skulking in the doorway and knew it was one of his underlings who was prudently fearful to catch his attention. Even though he had not killed the last messenger, his brutal reputation had been reinforced when he'd consumed an entire division of his surveillance team. It had been their job to watch his progenies and keep them from the BSI's sight; the loss of Pierce had been bad enough, but they had failed to stop the apprehension of his grandchildren and had cost him decades of planning and investment. He was not a forgiving deity when angered.

"What is it?" he snapped, penetrating his underling with his intense gaze.

"Good news," the lackey stammered, handing him the sheath of papers. His shaky tone stabilized as he explained that it was Connor's latest report, which differed from the official version. His laptop had been infected with software that logged keystrokes mostly to mine more data on the agency—particularly login information for the BSI database—but in this case, it had captured more than they had intended.

Jack read over the expunged report about his grandson's ambiguous resurrection. Connor's characteristic detailing of the incident appeared alongside what seemed to be an aborted justification to spare him. Connor had afforded no sympathy for his self-proclaimed friend, yet he may have pleaded for Starr's life, and the abrupt shift in tone intrigued him, just as it had with Brian Chamberlain. However, Connor's apparent capriciousness would be analyzed later; he was a consistent reporter, even if he was morally unreliable.

The importance of the discovery lay in his grandson's restoration. He had written off his descendants as a total loss: The only one who could harvest souls was dead, and the other two couldn't even be secured as food sources. Connor's theory changed things. Jack had acquired accelerated healing years ago, but he had never tested its threshold, and he was now fortuitously presented with a testbed for probable curative and regenerative limits. If Orion exceeded his expectations, Jack would risk exposure to acquire his greater capability, but even if Connor had overestimated the child's worth, his discovery was still valuable. His grandson had developed an ability similar to one of Jack's stolen skills, which suggested that his future descendants may also inherit Jack's acquired traits; it would, therefore, behoove him to also explore this possibility.

PART VII
CODE NAME: BHOOT

Sitara Shah was tired of being the one who worked hard and late for "exposure" and a small paycheck, but she didn't have much choice if she wanted to have her art displayed. Besides, she had discovered that she was a talented curator, even if her official position was only that of an assistant to the owner. Félicité was a decent gallery owned by Moise Kabamba, a brilliant artist who specialized in stone and wood sculptures. Though only his works had been displayed when Félicité had first opened, he had begun to exhibit the collections of talented, lesser known artists and had created a following of loyal fans who were eager to see who he'd discover next. His willingness to gamble on newcomer artists was what had attracted Sitara to him in the first place, and she'd accepted her job as the first step toward obtaining her own show.

She did not know what her current standing was toward her goal, but she had progressed up the professional ranks, despite some minor setbacks, and her exposure to other painters allowed her to tweak and perfect her techniques. She was not classically trained, having simply picked up a brush out of sheer boredom during her reclusive teenage years, and had taken only a handful of classes, so she was grateful for her progress and the networking she had accomplished.

She heard giggling and running footsteps behind her and shook her head. "Billee, don't run inside," she scolded without looking up from the checklist on her clipboard. "You need to behave just a little while longer, and then we'll be able to go home and play," she promised, flashing a slight smile in his direction before heading into the main construction room.

Mr. Kabamba had managed to purchase more space, so Félicité was undergoing a partial renovation to join it with the lot next door. The south wing had been closed, and they were still in the early stages, removing art installations from the walls and ceiling and trying to preserve whatever moldings and appurtenances Mr. Kabamba wanted to keep. The wood floor was going to be torn up and replaced, so no one had bothered to protect it, and it already had scuff marks from furniture and scaffolding.

"Are you almost done?" she asked, looking up from her clipboard. She walked the floor frequently, sometimes checking on patrons or displays but mostly for her own pleasure, and she liked to try to multitask. Her inattention to her footsteps often caused her to bruise a hip on a corner or bark her shin several times, but her work stroll was a practice that she intended to continue. This time, however, it caused her surprise as she noted that there was only one laborer on the scaffolding when she thought there should have been at least three. "Oh my God!" she exclaimed. "Are you the only one here, Otis? Shouldn't someone be holding the uh…" She gestured helplessly toward the planks that had been loosely laid over the interlocked metal framework, both of which looked suspiciously rickety at the moment.

"Don't worry about it, Ms. Shah," replied the older man. He slammed his foot down on the slat beneath him several times, earning a solid echo and a nervous grimace from Sitara. "This thing is pretty solid, and I was just finishing some stuff up before I headed home for the night," he reassured her. "I'll come get you when I'm done so you can lock up," he promised, turning back toward the wiring that secured the sculpture to the ceiling.

"Okay," she replied uncertainly. "Don't be long. I want to go home soon," she added with a teasing smirk and then continued on her rounds. After ensuring that no lingering patrons remained, she headed back to her office to reread the latest draft on the displays she needed to submit for publication on Félicité's website.

There was a sudden cacophonous crash, like a muted thunderstorm on a tin roof, and she realized, to her horror, that the scaffolding had collapsed. She raced across the gallery and into the room, dodging rolling paint canisters that had cracked open under the weight of the metal bars and spilled their contents across the floor. She immediately saw the twisted body of the construction worker in the center of the floor and pulled out her cell phone to dial for help. "Don't worry, Otis. An ambulance is coming," she comforted him, navigating her way carefully through the expanding puddle of paint to kneel by his side. Her eyes searched frantically for her brother, but she relaxed when she felt his arms wrap around her and his face nuzzle her neck as he started to cry. She embraced him, relieved, and began murmuring reassurances while answering the 911 operator's questions.

- - -

The drive home from Scotts Ridge was sepulchrally silent as Connor found himself locked in deep thought. Orion, for his part, was satisfied with staring out the window at the passing landscape when he wasn't delivering driving directions, and Connor tried not to look directly at him.

Connor was an agent of the BSI, which protected civilians against supernatural threats, and this meant that he had to make hard decisions. Anyone who posed a threat against the population had to be neutralized no matter their age or circumstances. He knew this and *believed* in this, so why had he faltered in Scotts Ridge?

In the privacy of his own mind, he could admit the reason to himself: He liked Orion Starr. He knew him and was familiar with the challenges of his situation, so Connor had lost his critical impartiality with this subject, and his emotions were now affecting his judgment. If he compromised with Orion, who else might he compromise with in the future? Who might those decisions endanger?

He realized that he was only agitating himself further by tangling his line of thought with self-chastisement, and he took a step back to look at the state of affairs from a different angle. There was no clear evidence that the events at Primrose had progressed the way Connor had believed they had; he knew that his perception had been compromised not only visually but also emotionally. The whole episode had been a traumatic experience, from reliving his deployment to having an armed confrontation with his former friend.

To regain objectivity, he had to differentiate between what was documented truth and what he had observed: Orion had extraordinary regenerative abilities, the limits of which had not yet been tested; Sone could generate over two hundred decibels, which was enough to cause catastrophic internal bleeding; and Connor had seen the cracked plaster and debris covering Orion's unconscious body. In contrast, he had caught only a glimpse of Orion as he'd been propelled backward; therefore, he could not be certain that Sone's strike had solidly impacted his chest. It could have been a glancing blow—one that Orion's natural healing could have easily countered—that had forced him into a weakened wall, and there was no need to overreact.

Connor had still been recovering from the day's high emotional strain when he'd drawn his flawed conclusion in the hotel room, so in retrospect, it had been the appropriate decision to erase his report on Orion's alleged resurrection. Since there was no evidence that the natural balance of life and death had been violated, there was no reason to recommend euthanasia for Orion. Connor had acted correctly, but his conscious mind needed time to process the day's events and reach the same conclusion that his instinct had determined.

"Agent Connor?" The sound of his name shook him from his reverie, and he turned his attention to his partner. "I said, 'Thanks for the ride.'"

Connor forced a smirk. "'S no problem," he replied. "I'll, uh, pop in tomorrow to check on you."

"It's not necessary," Orion assured him. "I told you I'm fine."

He stretched his smile wider, straining both his mouth and calm veneer. "Who said I didn't just want to see your happy face?" Orion sighed deeply in response, but Connor knew that he appreciated the attention; it was unfortunate that his subsequent visits would also be to monitor his health and the boundaries of his ability. The younger man shut the car door and headed into his apartment building, and Connor pulled into traffic and sank back into his thoughts.

While euthanasia was not the proper recommendation for Orion Starr, it was often the correct answer for different Others. There were many Others who, like Aaron Grimm, could not control their powers or who, like Brian Chamberlain, were simply too dangerous to be allowed to live. It was clear that Connor needed to review cases of dangerous individuals like these because he had hesitated in Scotts Ridge, even if he had ultimately made the correct decision. Connor needed to be confident in his evaluations and not spend hours second-guessing himself after the fact, and the best way to reclaim his objectivity was through reacquainting himself with the reason he'd joined the BSI.

He returned the rental car and took the subway back to his chartered apartment, where he immediately connected to the BSI database and began downloading the most deadly cases of Other activity. He intentionally skipped Tinder's file, knowing that it would only confuse his feelings and his determination to reinforce his belief in the BSI mission. He decided to begin with the older cases in the bureau's history and work his way forward. Following the Cokeville Miracle, the first subject whom the newly formed BSI had failed to detect had been Ignition, who had spontaneously combusted in a railcar and caught the R6 Ivy Ridge Line on fire just past Cynwyd Station.

The conflagration had killed five passengers, and another twelve had suffered from burns and smoke inhalation. Ignition had been taken into custody, and the Southeastern Pennsylvania Transportation Authority had temporarily suspended travel on the line due to "poor track conditions" while it had repaired the damage. Like many Others before him, Ignition had been euthanized due to his deficient control over his ability.

Connor realized to his displeasure that many failed subjects were pyrokinetics, and unsettled by the similarity to Tinder and Cassiopeia Starr, he elected to avoid reading them now. Perhaps he wouldn't visit Orion tomorrow after all; they both needed a break from the job, and the free time would allow Connor to continue reviewing cases uninterrupted. After a few days of sequestration, the remainder of Connor's doubts would be extinguished, and his dedication to the BSI mission would be rekindled, both of which would be for the best.

- - -

Tom Bryerly paced nervously in the back room of H.W. Pallas & Sons as he waited. He normally didn't venture to Long Island, choosing to stick to the familiar streets of Manhattan, but Mr. Lionhart's operations were based in Astoria, where the solid middle class acted as a buffer for his dealings and where he had access to a wide variety of immigrant populations, some of which were more eager to make illicit incomes than others. In fact, ties to the old country were very useful to Mr. Lionhart—or so Tom had heard.

The shop itself was nice and cozy, appealing to a clientele who may not have worn suits often but who believed that they should own at least one for special occasions. Nikos Pallas, the current owner, was a charismatic older gentleman who had sold Tom a suit the first time he'd visited. He'd offered to tailor it for free and had even taken the time to help him select the cut and color that would be most flattering to his build and complexion. Though Tom had not become a regular customer, he'd kept the store's card in his wallet and had given the business the occasional recommendation. He tried not to imagine how the Pallases had become involved with Mr. Lionhart.

The door to the staircase opened, and a dour man, known as Graves, waved him upward. Tom climbed the stairs reluctantly, as he had done many times before, swallowing and patting his clammy hands on his pants. Mr. Lionhart often kept his business dealings secret, using enforcers to collect his due rent or debts, but he met infrequently with the proprietors who owed him money to intimidate them and remind them who he was, and it was during one of these visits that Tom had first encountered Mr. Lionhart's truly monstrous side. Tom knew from experience that the man could be vicious, even if he seldom physically involved himself when doling out punishments, because Tom had been beaten within an inch of his life with Mr. Lionhart as the unfeeling audience. Tom had also seen the aftermath of one of his vendettas against a rival who had refused to capitulate: The family had been abducted and taken to one of Mr. Lionhart's warehouses, where they had been doused in kerosene and burnt alive. Yet none of this had prepared Tom for the day that he literally stumbled across a desiccated corpse in Mr. Lionhart's office. The husk's face was frozen in terror, but Tom still recognized the victim as another fellow with extraordinary abilities like himself. He did not know what the man had done to anger Mr. Lionhart nor how the latter had transformed him into a mummy. Throughout the meeting, Tom struggled to ignore the corpse.

Mr. Lionhart lounged in an old-fashioned cushioned parlor chair that Tom recognized from movies set in the Victorian era. Much of his office reflected similar tastes, from the wide, heavy desk to the intricately carved cabinets to the antique paintings that adorned the walls. Mr. Lionhart swirled some honey-colored liquor around in a tumbler before imbibing a mouthful. "What do you have for me, Thomas?" he asked in the dulcet tones of his normal urbane accent.

Tom flinched as the dour man took up a guard position at the door behind him, and he averted his eyes from the spot where the mummy had laid. He swallowed again before answering meekly, "I couldn't get in."

Mr. Lionhart arched his eyebrows. "And why not? That is your one job, is it not? Otherwise, what use would I have for you?"

Tom thought to mention the repair shop, which made them both a decent amount of money, but he didn't think it was prudent to correct him. Instead, he licked his lips and wrung his hands as he explained. "The apartment complex doesn't rely on traditional locks. They use electronic slide cards and—" He found himself hesitating, as if the word might anger Mr. Lionhart, and he averted his eyes as he added, "humans for initial security. It's only the apartments themselves that use keys, so I couldn't really enter the building without getting caught."

In Tom's juvenile days, he'd infiltrated moderately secure homes and establishments whose iron locks had been complemented by human beings. Guards provided a deterrence—they were witnesses who could identify perpetrators and discourage less determined criminal elements—but they could still be distracted. It was conceivable that the young man, dressed in his fine suit from H.W. Pallas & Sons, could talk his way past the doorman and then slip into the building as a "guest." Electronic countermeasures were ineffective when they were overridden by their human masters. Realistically, however, Tom would bumble his attempt and be shut out at the door.

"But, uh, I remembered what you said, and I thought that maybe it didn't matter how I did it as long as I did," he stuttered. He was honestly uncertain why Mr. Lionhart had selected him for the job, aside from his affinity with locking mechanisms. The crux of the plan was to kill some man, whose name Tom had purposely forgotten, by filling his apartment with carbon monoxide and suffocating him. Disconnecting tubing in the stove and heaters was not an especially effective plan for an assassination, but it was necessary for the death to appear accidental so that the police would not become overly involved. Stranger still, the victim should not suspect that he had been subjected to a homicide. The whole scheme seemed irregular, as if Mr. Lionhart was setting him up for failure, but he wouldn't dare question the patrician's motivations; if Tom was being sacrificed, then he would accept it quietly because the alternative would undoubtedly be more violent and painful.

Mr. Lionhart made a noise deep in his throat as he finished the remainder of the alcohol in his tumbler. "Go on," he encouraged perfunctorily. Divested, he rose from his seat to remove a crystal bottle from a cabinet behind his desk. He plucked two ice cubes from a polished wood bucket, uncapped the bottle, and splashed his liquor into his refreshed tumbler. He took a swallow, pausing long enough to savor the taste, and turned back to Tom. He nodded impatiently, signaling that the younger man should have continued after all.

Tom cleared his throat. "He doesn't leave his apartment that often, but I did follow him to the grocery store late one night," he continued. He stuttered over his narrative; his nervousness in meeting Mr. Lionhart was compounded by the memory. He was not a violent man—after all, picking locks was technically a victimless crime—and being a small man, he shied away from physical confrontations. He'd made his peace with the suffocation—he was only required to witness the victim's demise, not participate in it—but unfortunately, his new plan had required more of an active role. "After he left, I sorta cornered him and faked a mugging. I sorta stabbed right in the... uh..." He struggled with the word, stopping his fidgeting long enough to circle his torso with his hand. "Stomach... so he might not realize that I was trying to kill him. A few times." He grimaced, feeling his gorge rise, and jammed his hands in his pockets so they wouldn't give away his squeamishness by cradling his treacherous stomach. He'd used a small pocket knife no more than three inches long to puncture the victim's abdomen. He'd immediately realized that the minor wound hadn't caused significant damage, so he'd torn the knife downward and twisted it around the area until he'd been certain that the viscera had been sufficiently torn apart. The victim had fallen backward, slid down the alley wall, and struggled to keep the blood in his body. Tom had retreated behind a dumpster, watching the scarlet pool expand and mix with the grime of the street, until the young blond had stopped jerking and twitching.

"I stood there and watched him bleed out… or I think I did. But he came back to life like you said, so maybe I didn't do it correctly. But no cops were involved!" Waiting had been the worst part; police sirens were constant in the city, and he hadn't been able to tell whether they'd been approaching or moving further away. Though he'd tossed the knife into the dumpster behind which he'd cowered, he'd still had enough blood on his hands to cast him under suspicion if they arrived on scene.

Tom crinkled his nose and then rubbed his eye with his palm. "Then he kinda just brushed himself off and went back to the apartment," he finished. Upon waking, the victim had scanned the alleyway for his assassin, but since Tom had never pocketed the wallet, opting to discard it nearby rather than possess incriminating evidence, the young blond had reclaimed his property from the ground and had gone on his way. Tom had not been brave enough to follow him further and had escaped back to his own residence.

Steepling his fingers, Mr. Lionhart regarded him with a dubious scowl. "I suppose I should give you some credit for your ingenuity," he announced magnanimously. Tom folded his arms in front of him, stifling the impulse to wring his hands as he waited for the patrician's verdict. Mr. Lionhart shook his head with indifference and waved his hand dismissively at him. Tom glanced at the door guard, who didn't move to intercept him, and swiftly fled from the room.

- - -

It took three hours for Sitara to get her brother, Nihar, back to her apartment without detection. The majority of that time had been spent with first responders and explaining the accident to the police while Otis Cole had been carried out on a stretcher. The accident would be hell on the gallery's insurance, and she would need to file a lot of paperwork in the morning, but Mr. Kabamba could afford the increase. Otis, on the other hand, might never be able to walk again, and she regretted that Nihar had played a part in that.

She had managed to lock her brother in a nearby closet before the police had arrived, obscuring his bare, paint-splattered footprints on the floor with her own, and he'd somehow remained unheard throughout the ordeal, despite his traumatized crying. When she'd been released from the scene, she'd ushered her brother into the privacy of the gallery bathroom, where she'd gratefully discovered that all the paint had disappeared. Extended contact with Nihar's skin rendered anything invisible, and she wouldn't have to traverse the city with disembodied feet. With the most noticeable problem solved, she set about comforting her brother long enough to convince him to return home while not allowing him to unbottle his emotions yet; in the end, she had to promise him a sizable sundae and two hours of television to persuade him to calmly travel back to the apartment.

Once they were home, she had to wrestle him into the bathtub, which earned her accusations of lying and being unfair, but she needed to wash the paint and other accumulated grime from his skin. Over the years, she'd learned the rules that governed Nihar's condition: Objects that he sustained contact with would disappear and would then reappear hours after he'd released them; only he remained in a constant state of invisibility. He was still tangible, which she knew from experience after dealing with his tantrums, and he refused to wear clothes or bathe like any toddler, but at least it was not difficult to feed him.

After bath time, there were sundaes and television, and now it was time for bed. She'd given up on convincing him to wear pajamas years ago, so the difficulty lay in moving a hidden, unconscious adult male from her couch to his bed without waking him. By her estimation, Nihar outweighed her by eighty pounds, and since there was no easy way to transport him, she usually allowed him to rest wherever he fell asleep and hoped that she wouldn't trip over him or bark her shins on the momentarily concealed couch in the morning. However, things had to be different this time: Nihar had confessed during his bath that he'd thought the scaffolding was like the jungle gym at the park—to which she'd promised to take him ages ago—and that he'd climbed the metal framework, causing it to tip over. While thankfully he had not been injured, the event had revealed that his current care arrangements were no longer practical. Since she could not place him in a group home or hire a professional to watch him, she'd carted him back and forth to work with her and kept him as entertained and quiet as she could. While he was generally well-behaved, this was not the first accident he'd caused, and she couldn't allow someone else to be injured like Otis.

Moreover, she was exhausted. She had cared for her brother every day since he'd first vanished twenty-two years ago. The police had concluded that his disappearance had been a family abduction, though they'd had no strong suspects aside from distant relatives back in India, and her parents had come to believe that her brother was dead. So when Sitara had begun to play with her new "imaginary" friend—coincidentally named Nihar—she had been forbidden from speaking his name. In time, she'd nicknamed him the more agreeable "Billee," but she had never been able to convince her parents that she knew the real whereabouts of her brother. With no family support, she'd tended to Nihar's needs as best she could, slipping him food from the kitchen, dressing him in her old clothes, and keeping him safe. When she'd grown up and moved out, she'd had no choice but to take him with her.

She felt around for her brother, finding him passed out on the floor in front of the television. She patted his body, finding his arms and folding them across his chest. She slipped her forearms beneath his armpits and around his ribcage, cautiously lifting him and dragging him toward his bedroom. He stirred, moaning in his sleep, and she rested, whispering a lullaby until he again fell into a deep slumber. The move was a painstaking process, but she gradually reached his room, gently laid him on the floor, and covered him with a blanket; she would never be able to place him on the bed without his assistance. She quietly shut the door behind her and then latched the new steel lock she had just installed. She finished by shoving a medium-sized plastic tub across the entryway and filling it with water. She didn't honestly believe that Nihar was a ghost—which had been suggested to her as a teenager—but she still took the precautions against them that her grandparents had taught her to assist with keeping him contained just in case.

Finally, she collapsed against the wall and released a long, relieved breath. Her life had been much easier when they'd both been younger; her brother's childish behavior had been similar to her mind-set, making it easier to tolerate. Once she'd become a teenager, she'd had to balance Nihar's needs with her own, and her life had become more complicated as the years had passed. She knew now that confining him to one room was a temporary solution until she could develop a more permanent one.

- - -

It was a slow night for Isabelle Martin as she made her rounds. Several of her patients had been discharged that morning, and the remainder were recuperating quietly in their rooms. The rest of the patients she'd seen had experienced routine clinical problems, and she'd been able to diagnose and treat them with little difficulty. All that remained were the final two hours of her shift, which would end at around ten in the evening, after which she could go home and get some rest.

When she'd been younger and fresh out of med school, she'd resisted working the evening shift because it would have prevented her from experiencing the nightlife. Raised in a poor neighborhood, she'd initially believed that nothing good happened after dark, but her college years had converted her views and attitude: She'd become more sociable, and she'd come to miss the club scene after she'd graduated.

She now managed her own shifts, switching with other residents, while she finished her internship, but the nightlife began to appeal to her less and less, so she ultimately switched to the mid-shift. It fit her seniority—there was competition for her work schedule of choice, but not too much—and she enjoyed the slower pace and lessened supervision; after a certain time, she seemed to be alone, apart from the nurses and a handful of other residents, though that phase generally started only an hour before the end of her shift.

She was freshening up in the bathroom when she heard her name being paged over the intercom, so she finished up and headed to the nurses station, where she met with Sharon. Though Sharon was a younger nurse, she had many years of practice under her belt, and Isabelle tended to consider her an expert when paired with her on shift. Despite keeping a professional distance, they had grown close over the years, and seeing the twinkle in Sharon's eyes, Isabelle anticipated a good tease.

"You have a gentleman caller at the front desk," she said in a sweetened mock Southern accent. "Carla says he's very dashing," she added, fanning herself playfully.

Isabelle gave a small smile. "Who is it, Sharon?"

"She said he would only give his name as 'Mr. Lionhart' and that he had a very attractive accent."

Bemused, Isabelle cocked her head; he rarely contacted her directly, especially not at the hospital, where there would be many witnesses placing them together. But as it had been several months since they'd spoken, she wondered whether he'd decided on some sort of spontaneous visit. "Did she say what he wanted?"

"Well, he had flowers, so we thought he might be a secret admirer," Sharon explained. "Did you want to go down to the lobby to meet him?"

She shook her head. "No. Have Carla send him to my office," she said, deciding that caution might be prudent. She flashed Sharon a bigger smile. "Have him be discreet," she added coyly.

Sharon grinned. "You got it," she replied as she picked up the phone. Isabelle headed back to her office, which was a small room with a desk just tiny enough to fit in it. While a bit cramped, it was an improvement from her previous accommodations—a subdivided room shared with three other doctors—and before that, she had shared one desk with all the interns. She'd recently taken the time to personalize it with a handful of colored office supplies and a framed photograph of her parents, but there were few other items in the office that truly differentiated it as hers. Behavior like this was where her rough childhood came into play: She had to move often because her parents couldn't afford to pay rent, and they often ditched their personal belongings to avoid landlords and litigation. She had also developed a complex relationship with the police, who had been the boogeymen of her childhood but were now trusted partners in her adult career.

When Mr. Lionhart appeared, he smiled warmly in greeting and embraced her as affectionately as if she were his child, which she supposed was somewhat true. Shortly after arriving at a new apartment complex when she'd started to bud into a young woman, she'd developed a habit of going to the rooftop, where an old woman, one of the building's hoariest residents, kept cages upon cages of plump, docile pigeons. Isabelle had enjoyed lingering there, imagining herself as a bird that could fly away from her life and start somewhere new, and she'd spent much of her free time among the soiled coops, petting the birds while the old woman had taught her how to care for them. It was during one of these excursions that she'd found herself alone, abandoned by her uncaged pigeon friends that had taken sudden flight, save for the blond before her. He had looked then much as he did now: baby-faced with gorgeous, immaculately styled hair and piercing blue eyes that seemed to have seen too much. Short— barely taller than her adolescent self—he had been dressed more casually than he was today. He'd explained to her that he was a philanthropist, and he had chosen to sponsor her: She would finally find stability in her family situation since they would be provided with a small stipend, and he would pay for her college intuition, no matter where she chose to attend, provided she put the appropriate effort into her public school education. While he had never explained why he had chosen her, he'd visited often enough to be considered a distant uncle, and she'd always held some affection for him.

"These are for you, poppet," he said, handing her a bouquet of purple and blue hydrangeas. She took them, commenting on their beauty, and felt her cheeks burn despite the paternal feelings she had for him. He had been the only one to ever give her flowers, and they were nearly always the exotic types that could be purchased only from fancy boutiques. The first bouquet that she had ever received from him, shortly after she'd begun to receive his patronage, had been a lovely combination of flowers that she'd later determined were amaranthus, mignonette, and monkshood. Despite being fond of the draping curtain effect of the magenta amaranthus blooms, she received the unusually shaped purple monkshood on most occasions when he brought her flowers. "I regret to say that my visit isn't merely for pleasure," he said. "I was hoping we could discuss business over dinner, though I suspect that for you, it would actually be lunch."

She'd often met Mr. Lionhart in open spaces to ensure that she was seen with him. She knew of his iniquitous reputation, though he had never threatened her directly, and she believed that being in public view increased her chances of survival. Conversely, she inferred what business he wanted to discuss because he was visiting her at work, and she did not want witnesses to their arrangement; it was difficult to secure privacy in a public restaurant, so she overrode caution in favor of discretion. "I'm afraid I won't have time for an extended lunch."

"Ah, pity," he replied. "I had a nice restaurant picked out; I think you would've enjoyed it." He shook his head regretfully, and she, too, felt disappointment at the missed opportunity. He often treated her to what she knew were mid-range restaurants, but against the backdrop of her impoverished upbringing, they were five-star quality. "Well, it's at your pleasure, Miss Martin," he added, waiting for her permission. Her office was positioned in a crook of a formerly open bay that had been converted into private offices using plywood and attractive paneling, so the likelihood of being disturbed there was low. She nodded, and he continued, "It's about your debt."

Her smile thinned; despite suspecting this would be the topic of discussion, she'd still held hope that their business would never broach this uncomfortable subject. "What about it?"

The corners of his lips turned down subtly, and he folded his hands in front of him, assuming the pose of a reluctant tax collector. "Your payment plan has worked out beautifully, of course, but I'm afraid there's been a change in the conditions."

"Why would that be?" she asked nervously. She wished that she'd had the forethought to record this conversation, but she hadn't been prepared for a meeting, especially not a fortuitous one during which the terms of their agreement could be documented in a manner that might strengthen her position against him. She wrote prescriptions for Mr. Lionhart's minions to get filled, and those medications were then sold on the street for a tidy profit. The arrangement earned her a small commission while yielding a sizable income for Mr. Lionhart, in effect repaying him for his past sponsorship of her and her family.

"As you may recall, I paid your college tuition and supported you through your internship," he began. His tone was apologetic yet firm like a father grudgingly disciplining a child. "This was not a cheap endeavor, and I expect to be repaid for my generosity. Your current payment plan suffices for the majority of recompense, but this month, I require a little something extra."

Isabelle shook her head. Given his reputation, she was certain he was about to make an unreasonable request and she doubted she wanted any part of another illegal scheme. While her current situation didn't complement her preferred plan, their discussion still provided an opportunity for a new bargain to be struck, and she took her chance. "I'm afraid I'm not willing to allow that, Mr. Everest," she said, naming him with a confidence she didn't feel. He appeared unfazed, which unhappily was not the reaction for which she'd hoped. Regardless, she'd chosen this path and pushed forward, hoping it would lead to luckier destinations. "Yes, I know who you really are," she affirmed, knowing that she was now treading in dangerous territory, and plastered a predatory grin on her face; she'd learned on the streets that confidence was everything, and it might prove vital now.

He raised his eyebrows incredulously. "Do you? And what advantage do you believe this grants you, Miss Martin?"

"I could inform the police," she said. "Not only are you blackmailing me, but they would love to have a lead on your nefarious activities." While Mr. Lionhart's pseudonym was never spoken freely, during her independent investigation, she had discovered several outfits similar to her own illicit prescription service across the city, and it was not implausible to speculate that they belonged under the same criminal umbrella, which couldn't have escaped the attention of the local authorities.

"Is that so, Miss Martin?" he asked, amusement evident in his tone and a smirk tugging at his lips. "You would turn yourself in so I might be arrested?"

Her self-assured expression fell as doubt began creeping into her thoughts. "You are blackmailing me into cooperating," she replied, a tremor creeping into her previously calm voice. "And your criminal activities are well publicized. The police would—"

"Miss Martin, stop this foolishness," he snapped, reprimanding her like a child, and she halted mid-sentence. "You would never surrender yourself to the police, and even if you did, your allegations would never stick," he continued, lecturing harshly her as she attempted to regroup mentally. "There is no connection between myself and Mr. Everest, who is a prominent lawyer who would likely sue you for libel. This conversation only serves to test my patience, so I suggest you discontinue whatever scheme you think you have crafted."

Almost reflexively, his harshness softened, further reminding her of their pseudo-paternal connection. "It is not a difficult task I ask of you on a monthly basis, and this request is no worse. If you continue on this path, I will be forced to reconsider your payment plan, and you know you do not want that." There was no warning in his voice—only an ultimatum that she knew better than to challenge. In her investigation, she had uncovered tales of cruelty beyond murder and simple criminal enforcement, and she did not want to become a target, so she tabled her ill-considered plan to disentangle herself until she was better prepared.

"Good girl," he said approvingly when she acquiesced quietly. "Now then, your additional payment," he said. He hesitated briefly, pressing his lips together as he cradled his mouth and chin in his hand; he was clearly choosing his words carefully. "I need you to be the observer in a little experiment of mine," he continued in a pleasant voice. "Well, I suppose you'd actually be the administrator in this case, or perhaps even the control conditions." He paused, smirking almost self-consciously, and added, "But I digress." Strangely, his civil veneer remained as he announced nonchalantly, "I need you to euthanize a subject and confirm his medical death as a clinical state."

Isabelle recoiled, backing against the desk and leaning on it for support. "I can't—"

"Oh, don't worry, love; he's not actually human," he reassured her in the same urbane tone, seemingly rebuking her for her uncivilized response, and she considered that he might have meant an animal, in which case she had overreacted. He continued, "Do you recall those monsters I warned you about?"

She shuddered, remembering the tales he had told her about beings who could manipulate the laws of nature to do their bidding. He called them the Gods of Old, but he had also cautioned her to fear them, particularly the one he called Vampire, a creature that sustained itself by draining the life force out of others. He had told her many tales about this character, and Vampire had slowly supplanted the police as her boogeyman. "Yes," she replied meekly.

"Well, our subject is one of those monsters, and I suspect our little experiment won't actually harm him, so this is really not as morally objectionable as you presume," he reassured her, ostensibly reframing what she would normally consider homicide and the breaking of her Hippocratic Oath as an anodyne in vivo testing. "You'll need to provide the, ah, mechanism to do it as well," he said delicately, "so I'll leave the details up to you. But do not believe that I'll be fooled by some sort of Romeo and Juliet substitution nonsense." His eyes narrowed again, and his face tightened. "You will perform this task as I instructed," he commanded firmly. "Understood?" Speechless, she smiled weakly and nodded, and his affable expression returned. "Good girl," he praised encouragingly and promised, "I'll be by after your shift ends. Cheerio, love."

He kissed her gently on the cheek, for that was easier for him to reach than her forehead now that she was taller, and he departed quietly, leaving her to process what had just occurred. Had she just become an accessory to murder? Or, as he had stated, was she experimenting on one of the monsters of her youth? He had never offered evidence of their existence, but she'd fully believed his stories and felt deep in her chest that they were true. There were monsters, and they were not just the figurative allegories of childhood.

If she held onto that certainty, she could stomach what the end of the night held. She had agreed to assist Mr. Lionhart, and she sensed that she could not withdraw now without unpleasant consequences, but she could still turn the events to her advantage. If she recorded the night and gathered enough evidence, she could implicate Mr. Lionhart and his alias, Jack Everest, down the road for the crimes they committed. She could extricate herself from the situation or even exonerate herself completely. Eager to implement her new plan, she began her preparations.

- - -

John Reeves' desk was buried under piles of folders. Unlike its more successful sister department, the Paranormal Division had been unable to secure adequate funds to convert all of its archives into electronic files, so the majority of the cases were still paper copies kept in heavy, worn folders bound together by strained, rotting rubber bands. He preferred it this way; there was something more real about physical files and feeling the paper between his fingertips as if he were actually connecting with the original investigators. He felt transported back in time to the decades of the Cold War when every department, even his division, had adequate funding and investigation was painstakingly done by hand and in person.

It was a fantasy, as were most things in the Paranormal Division, and it was a pleasant diversion while he transcribed the files, struggling to read chicken-scratch handwriting and faded Xeroxes. He had scoured his usual alternative news sites and forums for the day, and none had turned up any supernatural activity, so this meant it was time to input files into the electronic archive. He had already scanned the folder he was currently working on, but there were several documents that weren't quite legible in PDF and needed to be reproduced manually.

His computer beeped, signaling that it had received an alert from one of his sites, and he welcomed the distraction. The email contained a link to a news article involving a recent accident at a New York art gallery, and its key element was the mention of Sitara Shah as the sole witness. Though the email briefly explained her importance and included speculation about the event, Reeves was already eagerly pulling her file to review it in its entirety.

Sitara Shah was the subject of the 2003 Savannah, NY Haunting, which was exciting because it was one of the first cases documented in the new millennium using modern techniques. The girl, then a young teen, was plagued by an entity she called Billy. Every time she tried to leave the house, Billy would lock the front door, throw objects, and even upturn furniture in an attempt to prevent her from departing. Sitara would often burst into tears, at which point the attack would subside temporarily. She was practically restricted to her house as a recluse for a full year before paranormal investigators became involved, and the footage they caught was startling. Thermal imaging captured a full-body apparition following Sitara around the house, and video caught it picking up objects and throwing them, though other recording devices never picked up a disembodied voice or other electronic voice phenomena no matter how often researchers tried to reach out and speak with the entity. While groundbreaking evidence in and of itself, the ghost also began to shut off all devices when it detected them, indicating that the entity had learned how to interact with the modern world.

Unfortunately, the activity began to taper off as soon as researchers began to seriously observe and experiment with the entity, which they determined must have been a poltergeist or, sadly and strongly theorized, the ghost of the Shahs' elder child, who had disappeared under mysterious circumstances six years previously. One paranormal investigator regrettably mentioned the standing hypothesis to the Shahs, and they shut down the experiment immediately, leaving many questions unanswered.

At the time of the experiment's closure, the activity began to decline, occurring only when the researchers were not immediately present, and this cast doubt on the whole incident, despite the earlier side-by-side thermal and video recordings revealing an unseen entity. Sitara retreated into obscurity and mediocrity, opting for a career that she could pursue from home.

The construction accident at Félicité revealed that the poltergeist had not gone dormant, which was common once the unfortunate subject of its attention completed puberty; Félicité had independently gained a reputation for possibly being haunted because objects occasionally moved themselves, doors opened and shut, and people heard running footsteps while they were alone. To Reeves, this meant that Billy had not been an actual poltergeist and instead suggested the alternative parapsychological theory: The alleged poltergeist was, in fact, Sitara's latent telekinetic powers developing during her puberty. Poltergeists tended to latch onto one individual, tormenting them through pinching, biting, or hitting, but Billy only threw objects and never at Sitara. Likewise, telekinetics focused on levitating objects, which was the phenomenon most often observed with the girl.

True, it did not explain the thermal image detected in her house, nor the sound of the footsteps that were heard at Félicité, but Reeves was more inclined to believe that one of the investigators had accidentally captured himself on film, especially because the entity began to shut off cameras rather than be recorded. This followed the actions of a researcher covering up a mistake that could weaken or invalidate all other documentation.

Had Sitara refined her telekinesis during her reclusive years? While this seemed to be the case, Reeves had no definitive proof, other than a chance news article and a dubiously haunted building, which would not secure him a cent of funding for closer investigation. This left him with only one option: Forward the case to Morgan Connor. Though his colleague hadn't revealed the final details of the Brian Chamberlain case, he'd thanked Reeves for his submission and informed him that it had been a valid lead; the case was now closed. Reeves could only hope for the same result with Sitara Shah: There was enough evidence that she was a telekinetic to warrant investigation—just not on his division's budget.

- - -

Nihar pawed at the door, meowing like a cat. He thought that if he did it enough, his sister would let him out, but he had been at it for a while now and hadn't heard a response. He supposed she might be napping, which would explain the silence, and he wondered why she hadn't let him out to watch television like she normally did. Not that being in his room was unpleasant; there were several wonderful activities to keep him entertained. There were dinosaurs that roared when the batteries weren't dead, a racetrack with cars that zoomed of their own accord, and his ever-expanding Lego set piled in a corner. Right now, the Legos depicted a space fortress with his favorite superheroes, some planes and ships, and lots of assorted townspeople.

Maybe once his sister awoke, she'd take him to the park like she'd been promising. He went over to the window, which overlooked the busy city streets, and squinted, hoping to make out the swing sets in the distance. His favorite part of the park was the sandbox, but Sitara rarely let him play in it because she said it got him all dirty; this was fine with him because getting dirty was the best part about it. She wouldn't allow him to play with the other children either, because she said he was too old and would hurt them, and no matter how much he promised to be careful, she wouldn't relent; he was only allowed to play in the park late at night or in the early morning when they were the only ones there.

He grabbed a handful of animal crackers from the tray his sister had left, shoved them in his mouth, and then turned toward the center of his room. He'd grown tired of playing with his action figures and had accidentally spilled water on his brand new puzzle, so he'd tried to get Sitara's attention so she could entertain him. Since that had failed, it was time to find something else to do.

His sister loved painting, and she'd bought him a set of watercolors in an effort to coax him into sharing her interest. Since he enjoyed it, his supply had been gradually increased to several bottles of washable Crayola paints, and seeing the colorful containers made him think painting might be fun right now. He pulled some bottles from the shelf along with a few sheets of butcher paper and a brush. He uncapped the bottles clumsily and laid them out meticulously so that he wouldn't tip anything over accidentally; his sister would yell at him if he did. When he finally started painting, he thought about how sad his sister seemed lately and realized he could make her a nice present to cheer her up.

- - -

As promised, Mr. Lionhart was outside waiting for Isabelle when her shift ended, and he took her arm, guiding her toward his waiting car. To her surprise, instead of being chauffeured as was customary for him, he opened the front passenger door of the nondescript vehicle and helped her into the seat before getting into the driver's side. Once settled, he turned to her and stated crisply, "I know I said I didn't want to hear the details, but it occurs to me that for this experiment to be successful, I should be familiar with the process. How do you plan to carry this out?"

Isabelle cleared her throat, avoiding his gaze, and retreated into a clinical mind-set, choosing to reframe the coming events as a case study. "In cases of physician-assisted suicide, they use an overdose of barbiturates to induce a coma," she explained. She opened her small purse, revealing a syringe and several vials of premixed solution, and he inspected the contents with interest. "I chose sodium thiopental, which is an anesthesia, since we have a lot of it on hand, and it should render him unconscious within thirty seconds. It will also suppress his respiratory functions to the point that he'll asphyxiate."

"How long will that take?" he asked curiously.

"Three to five minutes. Maybe less at this dosage."

"Marvelous!" he exclaimed. His eyes wandered, falling on her cell phone, which she had purposely overturned at the bottom of her shallow purse, and he retrieved it casually. Her pulse quickened, and she tried in vain to stop him from turning the screen back on. Indeed, even though the device was password protected, it still betrayed her ruse and showed the recording app running when Mr. Lionhart activated the backlight. He frowned, raising an eyebrow, and then sighed as he chastised her. "I am disappointed in you, Miss Martin. I thought you were smarter than that." He snapped the device in half, showing a remarkable amount of strength for his diminutive form, and pocketed the pieces. "All this time, I thought we had a trusting relationship. I guess I was wrong." He shook his head chidingly as he started the car and drove off.

At this time of the night, traffic had eased, as the majority of the population was either asleep or already at their destinations, and it didn't take long for them to cross the city into SoHo. After a few additional minutes, they were standing outside one of the many converted nineteenth-century warehouses. The apartment complexes were brightly lit, allowing her to appreciate the sterility of the prosperous neighborhood. With a reassuring, almost playful smile, Mr. Lionhart tightened his grip around Isabelle's hand, and she felt as if every cell of her body had been pierced by tiny pins. Perhaps her mind was overcome by the sensation, for she suddenly lost her vision as well. As the inexplicable pain increased intolerably, her sight returned, and unaccountably, she found herself no longer in the car or on the street. She glanced at Mr. Lionhart, seeing his jaw set tightly in a grimace, and sought to regain her bearings.

She was in a large, darkened room, and her eyes struggled to adjust to the dim conditions. Light from the streetlamps streamed in through one uncovered window, while its neighbors had their shades firmly shut against the outside world. She could see the faint outlines of a bed, a dresser, and other furniture, and she heard the soft, even breaths of a sleeping person. Mr. Lionhart tightened his grip again, seeking her attention, and then released her hand. Still wearing his mischievous smirk, he brought his finger to his lips in a shushing motion and then pointed to the bed. She approached it quietly.

As her eyes adjusted, the features of the bed's occupant became clearer, and she saw that he was a young man a few years shy of her age. She glanced back at Mr. Lionhart, who gave her an encouraging nod from the foot of the bed, and she tried not to think too much as she moved her stethoscope from around her neck to her ears. For an experiment to be valid, she had to monitor his vital signs and establish his initial condition, which was difficult to do without waking him. Fortunately, she had soft a touch and she was able to determine that he was a normal, healthy man.

She set her stethoscope aside and retrieved the syringe and vials. It was difficult to operate in the dark, but she was able to supplement the dim lighting with muscle memory as she uncapped the syringe and carefully drew the contents from the first vial. She tilted the syringe, collecting the air in the tip, and squinted as she sprayed the excess out; while she was usually more exact, allowing only a drop to be expelled, the gloomy conditions didn't allow for precision. Clinical procedures complete, she turned back to her patient and seized up. The patient was clearly asleep in his bed, helpless and oblivious to his pending death, and she was about to violate the Hippocratic Oath. She recoiled, stepping back into the firm encircling arms of Mr. Lionhart, who cradled her gently.

"Don't lose heart now, Miss Martin," he said encouragingly. "Go on. You're almost there."

She shook her head. "I can't. He's a human being."

His grip on her arms tightened, belying his fatherly tone. "We've discussed this, love. He's a monster. You can do it."

"No. No, I can't do it," she replied, her determination to disobey him undermined by her shaking voice. "I can't break my oath."

He smiled kindly and explained patiently, "You can't break your oath against a nonhuman."

"Even if he were one of those *things*, I still couldn't do it," she insisted fervently. "It's still breaking my oath. I won't do it! You'll have to find someone else."

"You will, Miss Martin," he countered angrily, digging his fingers into her biceps until they were bruised, "because he is a lesser creature, and so are *you*." He pounced as swiftly as a jungle cat, wrapping his free hand around her neck and hooking it beneath her jaw. She felt her jugular vein and esophagus crush under the sudden pressure of his unnaturally strong grasp, and her visceral panic at being unable to breathe was quickly overtaken by incomprehensible agony. She seemed to detach from her physical body, yet she still suffered what felt like her cells individually vaporizing, and after an eternity, the episode ended as quickly as it had begun. She was paralyzed, completely exhausted, and collapsed into Mr. Lionhart's embrace. Although her strength returned quickly, her animal instincts resisted movement, lest she gain the attention of the predator with which she was now trapped.

The force of Mr. Lionhart's loathing retreated as he uncurled his lips and relaxed his brow, setting his face into an expression of assured superiority. He set her back on her feet lightly, allowing her a moment to rest and regain her balance, and then he caressed her cheek after she'd recovered sufficiently. The simple gesture was oddly affectionate, yet she felt utterly violated as his manicured fingers touched her skin. "Do we have an understanding?" he asked genteelly.

She suddenly understood that the monsters of her childhood were real and that she was at the mercy of the worst of them. Mr. Lionhart had told her tales of the terrifying Vampire, and all this time, he had been speaking about himself. She wanted nothing but to flee, but she was powerless in his presence. She nodded deliberately, hoping that her drive to survive would guide her through the situation.

"Good girl," he declared, widening his sinister smile. "Now get to it. We don't have all night." Obediently and with no further protests, she injected her unaware patient with the first vial of sodium thiopental. Though he flinched, he never stirred and she continued until there were no more doses to administer. Then she set the syringe aside, retrieved her stethoscope, and monitored his vital signs. As predicted, his respiration slowed to a halt, and she listened to his heartbeat fade. Though she couldn't see it, she knew that signs of cyanosis had begun to appear on his lips and fingers, and finally, after several minutes, his heart stopped.

- - -

Orion was lost; but although he could not find his way through the strange gray mist, he was not afraid. Suddenly, there were fingers interlaced with his, and he turned to see his sister dressed in a long, snow-colored sundress. She gave him a serene smile and pulled him forward, taking the lead. He didn't know for how long they had walked, nor did he have any sense of direction in this alien place, but he trusted her to guide him safely. A towering, shadowy wall appeared in the distance, and the mist gradually parted to reveal the unremarkable, cookie-cutter façade of his former apartment in Brooklyn. The entryway was dark, like a gaping mouth ready to swallow him, and his belief in his sister faltered. He hesitated, pulling back suddenly, but she urged him forward into the foreboding entrance with a sweet smile and a mild tug. When he continued to resist, she turned to him and gently insisted, "You must."

"Why?" he asked, suddenly suspicious. His sister had still been an infant when they'd left Bay Ridge, and she had no memory of the apartment, so there was no reason to take him there now; she had no attachment to the place, which was becoming darker and more foreboding by the second as if it were gathering shadows around itself.

"Because there is something you must know," she replied. Patiently, she cupped his face with her free hand and continued, "You are afraid, but there is no reason to be. I am here with you." Her touch, blessed by the purity of her affection, washed away his doubts; he had nothing to fear with his sister by his side. He reclaimed her offered hand and took the first difficult step into their former apartment.

He awoke suddenly. He felt as if an electric current was coursing through his veins, and every lungful of air he inhaled was more delicious than the last. While the lights had been shut off before he'd crawled into bed, the streetlamps had provided enough illumination for his dilated eyes to see into every darkened corner, and for one distressing moment, he thought he'd seen a dreadful phantasm. A young woman's face had floated in the dark, distorted by a mixture of wonder, fear, and regret. He had been able to make out the pale outline of a restraining hand on her shoulder, clawing into her skin without breaking its surface, and another at the nape of her neck. The figure standing behind her had truly struck terror in his heart: It had been his father—shorter and a few years older, yet still undeniably him. As soon as he'd made this identification, the figures had faded from view like ghosts fleeing from daylight, and Orion had been left to wonder what had just occurred.

His heartbeat and breathing slowed as the adrenaline drained from his system, and he realized that he must have experienced a nightmare, albeit one that was harder to discern because he did not recall waking a second time; it was the only way to explain the apparition of his father and his female hostage, whose appearance struck an unsettlingly familiar chord.

He'd again dreamed of the strange mist, which had filled him with concern as well as serenity this time. He recognized the dream for what it was, but he couldn't quite convince himself of the same with his father. Impossible though it might be, he was certain that he'd seen his father alive in his room, and it terrified him like a child afraid of the dark. He was tempted to turn on the light to search his room and then the apartment beyond, even though he had vivid memories of the blackened patch where his father had died and the unnerving smell it had left behind.

He sighed deeply, knowing that he was entertaining the realm of foolish thoughts, and he decided to concentrate on another aspect of his dreams: Cassie. He had yet to speak to his sister directly, despite leaving her several voicemails and texts, and he was uncertain how to proceed. He knew that he had to give her time to adjust to her new circumstances, but he missed her and was certain that the feeling was reciprocated, even if she was currently maintaining a rebellious silence. He considered calling her, hoping she'd answer without checking the number, until he glimpsed the early hour and decided against it; it was still a school night, and she rarely slept her full eight hours.

Optimistically, he checked his phone anyway and was rewarded with a pending text notification. While he was initially hopeful that the sender would be his sister, he wasn't disappointed to discover that it was Connor. Despite promises to check in on him, he hadn't heard from the agent that day, and he found that he was actually disappointed by the missed appointment; it was as if Orion had begrudgingly accepted Connor into his daily life. He knew that tomorrow he would recant the sentiment when Connor picked him up for their next case, but looking forward to the visit helped put his mind at ease and allowed him to push his childish fears about his father toward the back of his mind, where they would hopefully remain. His father was dead and could no longer be a menace to his children.

- - -

Connor's knock was a bit more reserved and polite than it had been of late—if he was going to distance himself from his charge, he had to start off on the right foot—and he expected Orion to greet him with minor irritation, as had become their custom, but the younger man was quiet and appeared pale with dark circles under his eyes, which darted across the hallway behind Connor. Orion didn't allow him to close the door, instead electing to lock and bolt it himself before retreating to the familiar territory of his kitchen, where he began wiping down the bar with a towel. Connor frowned, suddenly concerned, and deliberated taking a softer approach, rather than engaging in his usual abrasive teasing, before he remembered that he was trying to reclaim his objectivity with the Starrs. He pushed forward, adopting a wide, supercilious grin. "Mornin', mate. Didn't sleep well?" he quipped, sitting down at the bar. Orion stared behind him, his eyes still on the floor; the young man really needed to learn confidence and eye contact. "Ah," he continued, taking the absence of an answer as an affirmative, "maybe we could grab a cup of coffee on the way. Need you to be performing at your best."

Orion didn't react at all, and Connor couldn't maintain his pretense of detachment. His half-cocked grin fell as he snapped his fingers in the young man's face to gain his attention. When he finally focused on Connor, he could see how unnerved he was; the young man's state reminded him of a few airmen he'd met in the desert. "Come on, then," he encouraged, ensuring direct eye contact. "This is not like you. What's wrong?"

Orion shifted his gaze to an area behind Connor, and he crossed his arms uncertainly around himself. "Was my father really cremated?" he asked quietly.

Connor realized that the young man hadn't been avoiding eye contact with him; rather, he had been focusing on the bleached spot behind him that had been his father's final resting place. "That's an odd question," he said carefully.

"Just answer it."

"Yeah, as far as I know." Because he'd been hospitalized, he hadn't been present for the entirety of the Starrs' visit to the BSI, but he'd followed up on the case and its results, and to the best of his knowledge, nothing untoward had been uncovered about the family. He searched Orion's face, examining the lines of fatigue for the root of the conversation. "Look, if you're worried about keeping his body for experimentation, that's SION bullshit. They might run a test or two, but for the most part, the bodies are cremated with or without a request," he told him. This was mostly true: Deceased subjects were examined, and when nothing else could be learned from them, they were destroyed so that they couldn't fall into the wrong hands. A few were preserved, but this was rare and only occurred when they had extreme scientific value. "Besides, your father wasn't an Other, so there was no reason to keep his body." He leaned closer. "No one's trying to pull the wool over your eyes, mate," he reassured him. "So what's this about, eh?" Orion turned his back to him, finally relinquishing the attention that he had been paying to his father's death site, and he started wiping down another counter. Connor waited patiently, but when Orion didn't answer, he added, "Fine. Keep it close to your chest."

He bit his tongue to stop him from pressing the younger man further; curiosity like that was what had caused him to lose his objectivity in the first place. If Orion wouldn't freely share his concerns, then Connor wouldn't pursue them. His job was to ensure that Orion made the correct decisions regarding his fate at the BSI—that is, to become an asset—not befriend him any more than was necessary to achieve this goal. Orion was a tool in the private war between the bureau and SION—nothing more. Connor cleared his throat as he took out his phone to sift through his email and find the picture of their next subject to show to Orion. "Right, so this is a live one, too," he announced.

Orion glanced back at him and, deciding he preferred the new line of conversation, fell into his normal habit of inspecting his empty refrigerator. "I thought we were sticking to the 'cold cases' for my development," he replied, discarding an empty bottle of mustard in the trash can.

"This one just fell into our lap, courtesy of one John Reeves," he sneered, his voice injecting bitterness when he mentioned his colleague's name. He liked Reeves, but that did not exonerate him for his role in bringing Brian

Chamberlain's case to his attention. "He believes there's a telekinetic on the loose in Manhattan."

Orion scowled. "Shouldn't that be Paranormal's jurisdiction?"

Connor smirked in spite of himself; Orion knew when to question assignments. "You would think," he replied mordantly, "but there's a fine line dividing our divisions sometimes. In this case, it's funding." Realistically, this dividing line existed for most cases: If a case was worth pursuing, but the investigating unit didn't have funding, it would be forwarded to their division, which would, in turn, screen it for relevance to Others. In his experience, most of these cases weren't worth pursuing. "Plus, telekinesis is traditionally a mental power, yeah? Which means she'd be an Other." He shook his head. "That paranormal stuff… really interesting on the surface, but it's nothing but pseudoscience when you get down to it," he scoffed derisively.

He paused; he wasn't exactly being fair. The BSI had been founded to protect the population from all preternatural threats—not just Others—and it wasn't the fault of the other divisions that their focuses simply didn't exist. The bureau was still peopled by good agents who just couldn't produce results.

"Except this guy, Reeves," he admitted reluctantly. "He really knows his stuff, so he knows when he sees an Other." He recalled when he'd first met John Reeves during his first few months as a novice agent. Connor had traveled to Massachusetts on a hunch to investigate a recent sighting of will-o'-the-wisps in the southeastern part of the state, ignoring the local folklore of the Hockomock Swamp and Bridgewater Triangle to focus on the ghostly orbs' increasing encroachment on a city. Despite it being a questionable lead, he had been able to convince the division that the assignment had been worthwhile because the strange orbs hadn't behaved like the traditional phenomenon. While Reeves had felt similarly, he had been unable to secure funding and had been forced instead to make the trip as a "vacation" at his personal expense. It was Reeves who had identified the "spook lights" as foxfire bioluminescence gathered together and set on the wind, and the two of them had been able to trace the fairy fire back to a bored little girl. Reeves had taught Connor some valuable lessons and had created the foundation of his ability to approach Others and their abilities safely.

"He just got assigned to the wrong division," he finished. He shook his head and shrugged, commiserating, "Bad luck."

"So what about this case?" Orion asked impatiently.

Connor smiled lopsidedly. "Well, it's an interesting thing this," he replied.

"It's a bit like your cold cases—based on previous footwork and a dead end—only we're picking up the trail because it's heated up." He explained the supposed haunting that had taken place upstate a decade prior, revealing only the details that pertained to the telekinetic theory, and then he filled him in on the recent accident at the art gallery, which Reeves had surmised was the reemergence of Sitara Shah's ability. Orion asked the appropriate questions, specifically about the existence of any surveillance cameras, and while Connor cautioned him that most Others avoided revealing themselves publicly, he praised Orion's improving investigatory skills and was proud of the younger man in spite of himself.

- - -

Orion's unsettled attitude eased on the ride to Félicité, and though Connor was relieved it had passed, he deluded himself with the lie that his solace was based on the fact that the younger man would now be better able to concentrate on the task at hand.

The outside of the gallery was unremarkable, primarily due to the drab, stony exteriors of the neighborhood, and it wasn't much better once they entered the building. Connor had never understood art, even as a subject in school, and museum visits didn't inspire any additional comprehension. He saw walls covered with paintings, sculptures, and other installations, and they were no more noteworthy than what he'd seen for sale at the local Ikea.

"Ah, welcome my friends!" greeted a booming, lightly accented voice. "I am very much pleased to see you." A handsome, well-dressed man stood in the main hallway, holding his arms wide open. He was a bit older than Connor, and his athleticism was noticeable under his tan suit, which contrasted heavily with the darkness of his skin.

Upon seeing him, Connor felt as if his foot went through the tile, and he staggered, catching himself before playing it off nonchalantly. "Must have been the wet floor," the man explained politely, allowing Connor to save face. "We are cleaning up after the mess, and there are quite a few hazards about, I'm afraid. I'll have someone place a sign. Please be careful of your footing."

Connor nodded, feeling a twinge of a headache commencing at his temples, and regained his composure. He pulled out his badge and introduced himself. "I'm Special Agent Connor—"

"Yes, I know," the man interrupted congenially and then apologized immediately. "Ah, pardon my rudeness, but I make it a point to be familiar with law enforcement. I find that a bit of caution works wonders in preventing any unpleasant incidents." He grinned and offered his hand. "I'm Moise Kabamba. I am the proprietor of this establishment."

Moise's handshake was firm, as if he had nothing to hide, yet Connor felt the seeds of suspicion sprouting nonetheless. "How did you know we were coming?"

"I have my connections," he replied secretively. "But don't worry. I'm not trying to hide anything. On the contrary, I want this investigation over as quickly as possible so that the unfortunate Mr. Cole can finish his claim with the insurance company, and I can open my own." He paused thoughtfully. "Though I honestly don't know why federal agents would concern themselves with a minor accident."

"Oh, it's just routine," Connor replied dismissively. "A bit of quality control, you could say, to make sure everything is on the up and up." Even though Moise knew that they were federal agents, Connor realized that he couldn't know the reason for their visit. Many people had never heard of the BSI, and they were willing to accommodate him based on his Homeland Security status alone, so he could push his authority quite a bit. However, it was worrisome that Moise had been forewarned of their arrival, at least from an agency standpoint: Others should not be alerted to their presence because they might panic and do something inadvisable to prevent apprehension. Fortunately, it didn't appear that this was the case. "We do random samples every few months."

Moise paused, rolling the idea around in his head, and then smiled. "That makes sense," he agreed. Without further delay, he gestured toward the back of the gallery. "If you'll follow me, I'll show you where it happened."

Connor began to follow, with Orion in tow, when his attention was abruptly seized by one of the art pieces on display. The statue was carved from some type of stone—possibly marble, though it looked more like a common material, such as limestone—and the subject was an ordinary house tabby. The details were arresting: The cat's hackles were raised, the individual hairs standing on end along its back, and its tail was puffed out like a bottlebrush. Its delicate ears weren't quite pressed against its head, and its mouth was wide open and hissing; Connor could almost feel its breath as it spat angrily. A second wave of vertigo washed over him, but he shook it off with some difficulty and commented, "This statue's pretty lifelike, isn't it?"

Moise stopped, turned, and grinned when he saw the piece being admired. "Ah, yes. That is one of my first successful works," he declared. He took a few steps back, joining Connor and sinking into nostalgia as he admired his handiwork.

Connor stole a glance at Moise, squinting at him as if the thought he'd just lost would return, and asked, "You did this?"

"Yes," Moise confirmed and then smiled self-deprecatingly. "I know it's a bit vain, but Félicité was paid for by my art, so I thought it would be appropriate to display it here in the main entrance." He indicated the rest of the foyer. "All of these pieces are mine. The other artists are further into the gallery."

"This is incredibly detailed," Connor remarked, turning his attention back to the statue. There was something strange about it, and he couldn't put his finger on it. It was supported by a pedestal, putting it at eye level, and its placement invited closer examination. The subtle bands of color in the stone mimicked natural fur pigmentation, and if not for the dull, dead look in its eyes, Connor would have believed that the animal was alive.

"Thank you, Agent Connor."

Connor felt there was something under the surface—something important that he was missing. "It's almost like…" He trailed off as his words failed him.

"Like it is living," Moise finished, amusement bubbling into his tone. "Yes, that is a compliment I have heard many times, Agent Connor, and I never tire of hearing it," he continued proudly. "It is very flattering, and we artists have very sensitive egos."

Connor continued to falter, his mind grasping desperately at strings he couldn't catch, and he could not construct the line of questioning he desired, nor could he even justify his sudden change in direction. Surprisingly, it was Orion who spoke up and steered the conversation back on course. "I'm sorry, Mr. Kabamba, but you were going to show us where it happened."

"Of course, Agent…" Moise fumbled. "Ah, I did not catch your name."

"Starr," Orion replied. Connor noted that Orion had not corrected him on the erroneous title, and he smiled to himself; his student appeared to understand that it was sometimes necessary to allow their subjects' assumptions to work to their advantage.

"Agent Starr," Moise corrected himself. "My apologies. They did not tell me you would be accompanying Agent Connor. Please follow me," he said and ushered them into the south wing. Though Connor spotted several more of the uncannily intricate statues along the way, he did not allow himself to become distracted again, and when they viewed the scene of the accident, he noticed immediately that the floor had been mopped and the water was still drying.

"Please excuse the mess," Moise apologized, his arm sweeping the room. "We were in the process of cleaning it up when we were notified that you were coming and that you might want to see the scene." He shook his head and gestured toward the pile of metal and wood that had been the scaffolding. "I'm afraid it is not well preserved because of that," he explained.

"Don't worry. We'll get it sorted," Connor replied, noting the state of the area. Several footsteps—most likely those of the first responders—led from where the accident had occurred, and a number of them had been erased by the diligent efforts of the janitor, who must have started from the front entrance and worked his way back. A part of the lake of paint had also been wiped clean, and the remainder was still tacky, providing a partial reconstruction of what had been repositioned following the accident. Much of the metal and wood had been stacked against the wall, with white footsteps confirming this, and the emptied tins had been collected and stashed in another corner. There was blood mixed into a gentle rose hue where it met the dye surrounding the body, and the paint provided a misshapen and slowly shrinking halo where the victim had lain.

Connor turned to Moise, still certain he was missing a connection. "Tell me, were you here when it happened?"

"No, I was at home," he replied, and Connor knew from his body language that he was being honest, so that was not the reason he felt uneasy with this man. "The only one here was Ms. Shah," Moise continued, unfazed by Connor's scrutiny. "Unfortunately, she's not here. She took a sick day." He glanced at his watch. "Now, if you'll pardon me, I'm late for an engagement, and I must leave you," he announced. He reached into his suit jacket and pulled out a small engraved silver case, from which he retrieved a card with elegant script on expensive coated stock. "If you have any questions, here is my card, but I suggest you wait until tomorrow to speak with Ms. Shah." He hesitated, providing the opportunity for Connor or Orion to interject, but they declined the invitation for the moment; Connor would have to let his impression of Moise percolate, and he could better focus on the case without him present. "Have a good morning, gentlemen," Moise concluded before taking his leave.

Connor watched him depart, hoping to catch a detail he'd missed previously, and when nothing revealed itself, he turned to Orion and asked, "Now, mate, what can you tell me about this scene?"

Orion remained in the entranceway, his eyes tracing the same path that Connor's had a few moments ago. "That paint tells you a lot about the aftermath, but it's not going to tell you anything if it's really telekinesis, right?" he asked, markedly with more confidence than he'd had during their previous cases. His eyes settled on the camera in the corner facing them. "Maybe the cameras could, though," he suggested.

"There's a good lad," Connor said. He crossed over the threshold into the accident scene and confirmed what he'd suspected: The cameras had been removed for safekeeping during the renovation. "There aren't any cameras in the room anymore, so we're not going to get much recording of the event," he told him, pointing to the corners where the cameras had previously been installed. As he walked back toward his partner and crossed into the other display room, he examined the positioning of its two cameras. Though they were focused on their displays, they might have captured the incident to some degree from their respective angles. He didn't believe the images would be of much worth; it was likely they would have only captured images of the floor in the other room, if anything at all, and while it was worth checking out, it would not be of primary concern or assistance at the moment.

"They might've captured something if she had been was foolish enough," he allowed, "but I think we might have to just do things the old-fashioned way if we can't find any real evidence." He smiled wickedly, causing his partner to reflexively frown in dread.

"Interview?" Orion guessed, disappointment evident in his voice; he anticipated that he would be the one conducting it.

Connor's expression shifted toward empathy while retaining its mischievous edge. "Come on, now. Don't be like that," he said and clapped him robustly on the shoulder. "You're doing much better." He nodded behind him at the scene, adding, "And we're here now, so we might as well get a look around before we take off. We don't want to miss something." Connor didn't believe that they'd find anything additional, because, as Orion had observed, telekinesis didn't really leave physical evidence, but it would allow the younger man time to compose himself and create interview questions. Despite needing preparation, his social anxiety had decreased appreciably as his confidence had increased.

The younger man nodded and knelt down, examining the few footprints that remained. He slowly worked his way back toward the main puddle, combing the area studiously, and Connor was proud that the young man had learned so much. While his technique wouldn't yield anything this time, the practice was important, and he was creating his own routine and procedures. Connor retreated quietly into the south wing, intending to head back to the main entrance. "Where are you going?" Orion asked, cocking his head curiously as he stood.

Connor shrugged. "Don't worry 'bout it," he assured him. "I'll be right back." While he did see the faint outline of what appeared to be bare footprints on the wooden floor, instead of following their path, he found himself drifting back toward Moise Kabamba's main exhibit to see whether he could recall his misplaced thought.

- - -

Orion was understandably irritated that Connor had implied that he'd be conducting the interview, but he was also visibly relieved when Connor revealed that he'd only be observing. While holding Orion in suspense hadn't been necessary—it had been a little thrill that he'd allowed himself—the suggestion had spurred preparation, and that had been the point of the exercise; Orion would eventually question people on his own, and he needed practice whenever he could get it. The only reason he wasn't taking an active role this time was because the younger man had never seen Connor interview a subject whom he already suspected was an Other, save for his sister, and he doubted Orion had been taking notes then. While Connor relied heavily on body language, the strategy he employed with Others varied: With elementalists, he tried to trick them into revealing themselves by baiting them; with Sitara Shah, he needed to craft probing questions that would trap her into a confession. It was also a dangerous game: If he didn't properly assess his subject's triggers and control limits, he risked injury or death.

Sitara Shah was a slight woman with light skin, dark hair, and the distant gaze of someone who hadn't slept well for several nights. She was polite but firm when she answered the door, insisting, like any good New Yorker, to see his identification before allowing him entrance to her spartanly decorated apartment. Like her employer, she had questioned the involvement of the federal government and had accepted the tenuous explanation that insurance industry oversight had provided. She offered the two men refreshments as she showed them into her sparsely furnished living room, which smelled faintly of eucalyptus, and they took a seat on what appeared to be a secondhand couch, whose questionable odor briefly overpowered the scented air freshener. Once settled, Connor retrieved his notepad from his jacket pocket and reviewed his notes, while Orion sat quietly next to him sipping water.

"We just have a few details we'd like to go over, if you don't mind," Connor said, poised with his pen in hand while watching her closely.

Sitara shook her head. "Of course not," she replied amiably. "I'd like to help Otis and Mr. Kabamba in any way I can." Her smile was unsteady yet genuine when it appeared, and she clasped her manicured hands in front of her as she set her wide, doe eyes on him.

He nodded sharply, indicating the beginning of the interview. "First, where were you when this all happened?"

"I was in my office reviewing some paperwork when I heard a crash, so I ran to see what had happened," she answered. "That's when I saw Otis buried beneath the scaffolding." She cleared her throat in a low murmur and averted her gaze, wrapping one slender arm around herself. Since that did not provide enough comfort, she began stroking her bicep, tracing small circles with her fingers as she returned her attention to Connor.

While he immediately recognized the signs of someone still distressed from recent trauma, he was not equipped to deal with it, nor did he have the inclination; that was left to professionals, and due to his own deficiently beneficial experience, he had a dubious opinion about the effectiveness of their efforts. "Was there anyone else present?" he asked, pressing forward, and he paid careful attention to her mouth, eyes, and fingers, which were the first body parts to display signs of deceit.

"No," she replied quickly and cleared her throat again. "I'd just swept the floors and cleared everyone out. I'd actually thought there were more construction workers there, but they'd already gone, and Otis said he was just finishing up before leaving like the rest of them."

"Has anything like this happened before?"

Her eyebrows knitted together in confusion, and her fingers slowed their massaging and then came to a standstill. "What do you mean?"

"Accidents, of course," he replied, slipping facetiousness into his voice. "I mean, I saw in the report that this was the first such incident, but we both know that not everything's always recorded."

He winked cheekily, hoping that by intimating that he approached his job in a relaxed fashion, he would encourage her to open up. It evidently didn't work, as she replied blandly, "As far as I know."

"What about here at home?" he inquired, briefly scanning the room for unsecured objects. Several paintings, all in the same artistic style, adorned her walls, while her tabletop and coffee table held no decorations, save for one photograph of a handsome couple who he assumed were her parents. However, he noticed that the secondhand quality of her couch also extended to her other furniture, with her coffee table in particular showing signs of repeated abuse. It seemed odd, given her respectable position at Félicité, but he was cognizant that an opulent workplace didn't necessarily correspond with an appropriate paycheck.

She scowled. "I'm afraid I don't follow."

"You know, things moving of their own accord," he explained casually, insinuating a hidden layer to the conversation. She grew uncomfortable, shifting in her seat and fidgeting until she fixated on one of her chipped nails. "An unattended cup falling off a counter or a picture falling off the wall," he suggested, gesturing to the nearest painting. He stressed his final word, hoping to incite a reaction: "'Accidents.'"

"What are you implying?" she responded, holding steady.

"Nothing, Ms. Shah," he replied dryly. "It was just an observation about your colorful childhood."

Sitara flushed. "That has nothing to do with what happened to Otis," she declared. Fleetingly, her eyes darted away from his, and she covered her mouth as she softly cleared her throat, delaying the conversation briefly as she recovered.

"Oh, I'm not implying anything of the sort," he insisted smugly, making notes on his pad.

"Then why bring it up?" she asked crossly.

"You're right. That was inappropriate," he apologized, fixing his face into a suitably remorseful expression. "Please, tell us more about that night," he insisted, inviting her to resume her testimony in a reasonable, professional tone. She continued, with Connor interrupting only for clarification, and he recorded any discrepancies for later follow-up. While she was clearly lying, she didn't dive heavily into details that could trip her up, nor was she too vague. In fact, Connor couldn't discern what she was lying about, and he intended to corroborate her entire story, but he was certain that she wasn't an Other, despite her adverse reaction to the mention of her childhood haunting.

He concluded the interview, and they left the apartment, catching a train back to the city center. Although the train was fairly populated, no one paid them any special attention, and Connor turned to his protégé to discuss his perspective of their visit. "What did you observe?" he asked at a conversational volume.

Orion sighed deeply, crossing his arms and pressing his lips together; he had known that this was coming, yet his frustration didn't appear abated. Connor thought that he'd progressed as an instructor, sharing his insights openly during the last case, so he didn't understand his partner's apparent dissatisfaction. "Well," Orion replied, "last time we had this conversation, you said I needed to observe body language. She appeared irritated, and you made it worse." He paused, adding pointedly, "On purpose. Which means, I think, that she was lying."

Connor nodded approvingly. "Your observational skills are improving," he said. "Do you know what she was lying about?"

The younger man mulled over his answer, watching the tunnel walls zoom by for a few seconds before saying, "No."

"Neither do I," he admitted with a shrug and a short, clipped chuckle. "But I don't think she's our Other." He paused, breathing deeply as he reexamined what they had discovered so far. He trusted Reeves' opinion, knowing that he performed good research and fieldwork, and though Sitara had proven to be a dead end, he strongly felt that they had missed something; perhaps Reeves was onto something, but had just pointed them in the wrong direction. "I think we should head back to Félicité and see what else we can dig up there."

Orion shifted in his seat, turning so he could see Connor's face better. "I thought you didn't think it was worthwhile."

"I didn't say that." Connor leaned back, sinking into the threadbare cushions. It was difficult to relax on the subway, especially when it was crowded, and his nose picked up the scent of everyone's collective body odor or their efforts to conceal it. "I said we should do things the old-fashioned way," he continued, choosing instead to lean forward to rest his forearms on his spread legs to ensure the least contact between him and his malodorous surroundings. "Which we have, and it's not turned up any results, so it's time to follow that other lead you suggested." A wicked smirk grew on his face as he leered at his partner. "It's going to be a long night watching all those videos, though," he teased, knowing full well that Orion was imagining a night full of his jibes and wisecracks; but, in truth, Connor was picturing another confrontation with Moise Kabamba. Although the artist proprietor had been polite and had given no reason for suspicion to be cast on him, Connor wanted to restart his investigation of Félicité by focusing on him.

- - -

Of all the guests, dignitaries, and donors she'd hosted for breakfast over the years, Amanda Darling-Whitcomb preferred the company of beneficiaries the most. Like most of her meal companions, these individuals spoke at length about themselves, their accomplishments and dreams, and what her donation meant to them. But they also came with the bonus gift of flattery, and Amanda enjoyed having her ego stroked as much as the next person. Moise Kabamba was a pleasant variation on the theme.

Moise was a self-made man—his wealth had been derived from natural talent—and she was certain that his good looks improved his commercial capability. He filled his suit nicely, and though most men shied away from baldness, he embraced its early arrival and shaved his head; this complemented him, deducting years from his face in return. While his accent and diction were odd—not typical of his native country, in her experience—they resonated with his timbre to create a cumulative uniquely pleasant effect.

She'd eaten lightly this morning, as she did with the majority of her meals, though this time, her dearth of calories was to make up for a missed gym visit. Her nutritionist and fitness instructors would both have disavowed her decision, reminding her that she had made a technically unhealthy choice, but she knew that one had to make sacrifices for one's public image. She'd already seen what an inconvenience an illness could be on the campaign trail, and she'd hate to see what a few pounds would instigate among both her constituents and opponents.

She placed her fork on her plate delicately, folded her hands in front of her, and smiled charmingly. "I apologize again, Mr. Kabamba. It seems Mr. Everest will not be joining us this morning," she expressed regretfully. "Normally, his firm sends their regards if they cannot make a meeting."

"It is no problem, Mrs. Darling-Whitcomb," Moise replied. "I am just happy to meet even one of my benefactors. You have no idea what this means to me."

She smiled, knowing he meant that it was easier to secure funding from her than a personal loan from a financial institution. Moise's collateral was his artwork, and while it was valued highly now, this might not always be the case, and banks liked to hedge their bets. "I like to cultivate personal ties to the city to show my support for our people, and I must say that your dedication to exposing up-and-coming artists is inspirational."

"It is the least I can do after someone took a chance with my talent," he replied, being genuinely modest. "But this new addition is what is most important to me." He explained that the gallery had been named after his "aunt"—the wife of his godfather—who had helped to raise him after he'd fled persecution in Zaire. Even though he had no blood ties to this woman, she'd cared for him as passionately as any natural mother. The gallery's new wing, adjoining the original south wing, would initially display installations of motherhood and eventually transition to support immigrant artists, and a portion of the admission would go toward assisting others to escape the Congo. "And you helped make it happen."

Amanda knew that an influx of immigrants would be unpopular in the current political climate, yet it would help her establish her credibility with the international community and, therefore, develop her résumé for her future presidential run. Besides, Moise was a tremendously popular artist, and he was making his own influential connections. In fact, he'd contracted Milton, Chadwick, and Waters and had secured Kevin Chadwick's donation independently; Jack Everest had been due at their morning meeting as the firm's customary representative only because he liked to remind her of their regrettable connection. "I do what I can," she replied magnanimously, managing to make the platitude sound sincere. "Mr. Kabamba, I hope it's not too personal, but you only mentioned your godparents," she said in an attempt to cultivate familiarity; she needed to nurture their rapport if she wanted to access his connections or use his star power in the future. "What happened to your mother and father?"

Moise, who had politely stopped eating when she had, reclaimed his fork and pushed his food around his plate like a child reluctantly finishing a meal. As Amanda was about to interpose an apology, he finally spoke in a low voice. "I am afraid I do not know, and I have been trying to discover that myself for several years," he replied solemnly. "I was taken out of the country in secret by my godfather, and they did not have enough currency to pay passage for everyone. My father was likely an enemy of Mobutu and spent time in his prisons, if he was not outright executed." He shook his head. "I know less about the fate of my mother."

"I'm sorry I brought up a painful memory," she replied remorsefully.

"No. I do not remember much of them, but I remember their sacrifice." He fell into a somber silence, which Amanda respectfully kept until he gently took one of her clasped hands. "Ah, I must apologize for darkening such a nice meal," he said, the timbre of his voice lightening as his expression relaxed. "This happened many, many years ago. You are burdened by a great many things in your position, and I have only this one." He kissed her hand in a gentlemanly fashion, and temporarily nonplussed as she did not understand this peculiar change of tone, she let him lead.

"You have a public face to maintain," he continued, "and it must be very tiring to give special attention to so many people. Let us speak of happier things." Yet, he asked about her, and remarkably, she found herself opening up to him in a cathartic confession of her more public frustrations. While he may not have actually cared about them, she found the unexpected release gratifying and his interjections enjoyable enough that she considered adding him to her rotation of regular breakfast partners.

- - -

Sone waited patiently in the canteen. It was emptier these days, with patrons lingering no longer than was necessary, and even though there was nowhere else on the compound to eat comfortably, many opted to grab their meals, wolf them down, and leave, if they tarried at all. This SION complex was small, crowded into a disused basement, and overflowing into sewer and electrical accesses beneath the streets, so space was premium. It was for this reason that the medical clinic was located off the canteen: It promised cleanliness as well as convenience. But unfortunately, the arrangement was proving problematic since they'd acquired their most recent refugee. Naught, for all her expertise, was unable to contain Aaron's episodes to her designated space, and they had spilled into the common area.

Sone was present during the initial incident, which occurred only a few hours after Aaron arrived. Sone saw the creeping shadows slither through the cracks and around the corners and pool in the center of the room, although they advanced no further. Instead, an almost corporeal dread, heavy like lead in the stomach, permeated the area and choked the minds of anyone unlucky enough to be in attendance. He'd been harkened back to the Primrose Bed & Breakfast and his secret battle. It had been insinuated in the pharmacy news reports that the victims had seen their greatest fears, and he'd expected to see some tangible terror, but he'd instead been gripped by an existential panic. His mother, all that his father had aspired him to revere, had appeared in a bleak, spectral form with nothing for him except chastising words of disappointment. She'd listed his failures and had been unable to accept that she had wasted her life for him. Eventually, when he had been unable to stand any more of her callous diatribe, he had retreated inward, allowing his combat mind to reawaken and seize control. He hadn't spoken about his vision to anyone—not even to Naught—and had swallowed any shame associated with the incident. He had planned to forget that it had ever happened. But the memory had been reawakened by Aaron's fit entirely too soon after the original wound had been opened.

The compound episode was brief yet amply distressing, and word quickly spread that no one should linger in the canteen any longer than was necessary. Despite the fleetingness of the few occurrences, it was understandable that no one wanted to risk experiencing them for themselves, and everyone steered clear of the area.

Finally, Naught entered, having left her hollow for food, and Sone pounced on her immediately. "Do you have a moment, Doc?" he asked, matching her sluggish pace as she walked across the room.

She smiled and shrugged. "Sure," she replied as she gathered a tray, dishes, and utensils from various stacks across the counter surface. "Just grabbing some food for me and Aaron." She looked exhausted, and it was little wonder; she'd rarely left Aaron's side since he'd come to join them, save for the few excursions to get him medication. Since SION did not have the resources to acquire his medication legally, Naught used her extraordinary speed to sneak into pharmacies and abscond with their stock, and she'd collected a wide selection to give herself treatment options. Sone did not think that she'd slept since Primrose; yet, she was still in good spirits.

"How's the treatment going?" he asked neutrally in an attempt to ease her into the conversation; her attention had become so focused on treating Aaron that she had lost sight of the larger picture, and she needed to be reminded what else was at stake. Casually, he leaned against the counter, resting on his palms, and crossed his ankles.

"Eh, as well as it can," she answered, sighing deeply, but there was still a trace of her normal playfulness in her tone. She went over to the dingy refrigerator and paused to review its contents before diving in. Her voice was thick and slow, and she took care to project it while she scrounged. "I think I've determined the correct medication, but it'll take a while to figure out the dosage. He doesn't remember how many milligrams he was taking, and he never took it consistently, so I have to increase the dosage slowly until he's stable and comfortable." She shook her head unhappily as she resurfaced from the fridge. "That'll take a few months because the medication needs to build up in his system before it's even truly effective," she continued clinically, talking to him directly while leaning on the refrigerator door. "It makes it harder to judge the right dosage and frequency, so it's a sort of trial-and-error situation, especially since I'm not a psychiatrist." Her grimace was exaggerated, as if she was doing it for humorous self-deprecation, but he could see that she was frustrated with her lack of qualifications.

"That's still pretty good, though," he assured her sincerely; even though she hadn't finished medical school, her expertise had made a difference in their lives and would continue to do so if her research ever received funding. "But," he said, drawing the word out cautiously, "do you think you can keep him contained in your clinic? His episodes, uh, leak into the common area, and it's unsettling the others." He gestured to the deserted canteen, which was empty apart from the two of them.

She finally absorbed the misplaced quiet and exclaimed, "Oh, I'm sorry! I didn't realize that was happening." She smiled sheepishly, revealing a few more lines that age had carved into her face and that hadn't existed a few weeks ago. "He's technically still having psychotic episodes, but the intensity has dropped off significantly now that I have him on the correct medication." She scowled, looking troubled as she admitted, "I think I technically overdosed him to get him back on schedule and at the levels he should be, but I've got him grounded in reality again. It's nothing like we saw in Scotts Ridge with the kneeling and cowering and stuff—more just sweats and panic attacks—so I didn't think he'd been projecting. I'll try to keep him engaged so his subconscious doesn't get out of hand."

He nodded. "Thank you." She smiled again and then buried herself in the refrigerator once more. He knew that the refrigerator offered a variety of ingredients, though he wasn't certain who shopped or how frequently, and he often chose to reheat leftovers or prepare an instant meal. Given her distaste for the bags of withered vegetables in her hands, she wasn't impressed with the selection either. Nonetheless, she carried them over to the cutting board and separated the worst offenders from the rest.

Sone took this moment to reflect on the situation. He knew what his plan of attack would be once he engaged Naught, and he strategized on the words he would use and how he might deflect any protests. But the reality of putting his plan into action was still difficult. His original acquaintance had been with a compassionate yet actively disengaged individual; nevertheless, she had been the one to volunteer to go on the mission in Fission's place, and she had aggressively defended Aaron against the BSI. She was a different person from the one he'd met in the beginning, and going forward, he needed to handle the situation delicately. "How long do you think it'll be until he's well?" he finally asked.

"He's regained cognizance pretty quickly, and like I said, his episodes seem to be easing. They're also becoming less frequent, though, from a clinical perspective, I don't know how often he normally had them. I believe that having a steady supply of medication and a real support system will help him greatly," she answered. She stopped slicing, placed her knife on the board, and turned to him, crossing her arms in front of her body. "I think he'll be ready to enter the general populace in several weeks… maybe a month if I push him," she continued, shaking her head to indicate that she wouldn't. "And then there'll be another adjustment period. He's still pretty uncertain about the existence of Others." She grinned roguishly, though the smile didn't make it all the way up to her eyes. "It makes it kinda hard to differentiate between reality and fantasy when reality itself has been redefined, but I couldn't really ease him into the truth of our situation. The first time he sees one of us use our abilities, he'll immediately regress, and we'll lose any progress we've made."

He nodded. "How long until he can train with the Vanguard?" he asked carefully.

The smile, real or not, fell from her face, and she tilted her head and narrowed her eyes. "Why would he do that?" she asked suspiciously, her eyebrows arched.

"He needs to learn how to control his ability, right?" he replied in his most persuasive voice.

She shook her head, and her arms tightened around herself. "No," she answered firmly. "I don't have all the right equipment to create a good metric, but as Aaron's mental state improves, I believe he'll utilize his ability less. It's a defensive reflex of some kind—the result of trauma and an inadequate coping strategy. I think once he's recovered sufficiently, his ability will never manifest again."

He straightened, returning to his feet. "So you think his ability is a direct result of his mental state?" he asked pointedly, digging at her motivations.

"Yes." While her tone was certain, her body belied her confidence; she could meet his eyes for only a flickering moment before they dropped to the floor to search for an answer there.

"I don't think it works that way, Doc, and I don't think you do either," he said, scolding her softly. He took a step forward, closing the gap between them, and rested one hand on the counter beside her. He used the other one to emphasize his point as he made his argument in a quiet yet assertive voice. "In any case, his ability to project visions is a powerful one. We need a weapon like that if we're going to win against the BSI."

She clenched her jaw and let her arms fall to her sides. "We're not at war, Sone," she replied in a low, tense voice. "We're just trying to survive."

"Sometimes survival requires going on the offensive."

"I'm not going to let you use him as a weapon," she hissed. She tightened her fists and broadened her stance, taking a step backward, but not in retreat.

He caught a movement out of the corner of his eyes and noticed that the shadows had acquired a depth they hadn't previously had. However, he was not going to be intimidated by this development; she was not its source, and it only reinforced his belief that Aaron's ability needed to be honed. "That's not your decision to make," he argued, and while having her on his side would make it easier to recruit Aaron, she wasn't a necessity; all he needed was for her not to stand in the way.

"I'm not going to let you bully him either," she asserted, as prepared to fight him as she had been the agent at Primrose. The stakes might be lower, but she was no less protective of him. "He's very sick, and he needs help. He's been through a lot, and he's seen plenty of death—more death than any of us." She stuck her finger in his chest. "I'm not going to let you put him in a position where he might experience that again."

"Doc—" he began, but his protest was cut short when his breath was caught in his throat. He felt his whole body tense and then coil like a spring, and his blood rushed through his ears. Stubbornly, he struggled to maintain eye contact with her, feeling that a failure meant acquiescence, but in the end, animal instinct won over, and he glanced about the room, searching for danger.

In contrast, she appeared largely unaffected and waited, hands on her hips, until Sone was little better than a jackrabbit anticipating an owl swooping down from the sky. "The answer is no," she maintained, and after staring him down, she sprinted from the canteen to her room. Moments later, Sone could breathe easily again, and he collapsed, barely catching himself on the counter. He smiled weakly, amused by the ironic thought that Naught's immovable mind-set meant that she would have made an excellent member of the Vanguard after all.

- - -

Much to Connor's surprise, Félicité proved to be as popular as its promotional materials claimed, yet Moise Kabamba was still able to meet them personally, and according to him, the current volume of customers was lower than normally expected, a deficiency that he attributed to a new exhibit opening across town. He was more gracious about the decreased patronage than Connor had expected, as the latter honestly believed that small business owners in New York were cutthroat, given the current economic climate. After taking a few moments to excuse himself from the main floor, Moise led the two agents back to his office. While one would have believed that hosting a social gathering every night would be stressful, Moise instead seemed contented, and he happily offered them drinks.

"I am surprised to see you again so soon," Moise said, pouring himself another glass of wine. He extended a second offer of refreshments, which was again declined, and he continued, "I thought perhaps you would be satisfied with the earlier walkthrough since you were gone when I returned."

"There were a few things we wanted to check out based on Ms. Shah's story," Connor explained and began pacing, gravitating toward the office entrance. He had previously refused a seat for this express purpose. Like Félicité's entranceway, Moise's personal space was decorated with his own work and ostensibly his favorites. Each of his pieces portrayed small yet incredibly detailed subjects, and while they were typically the delicate blossoms of a flower, the displays of insects showed his true talent: There were beetles, fragile casings lifted and poised for flight, while the wings of butterflies were almost translucent with their shaved slimness. Clearly, Moise had a steady hand and a lot of patience.

Moise raised an eyebrow, and his jovial expression diminished slightly. "Ah, you saw her today," he concluded, his eyes following Connor as he made his measured circuit around the room. Orion remained at the entrance, watching Connor with growing confusion: His posture had relaxed—he no longer appeared as rigid and anxious as he had in previous interviews—and he seemed to be growing into his role of authority. He hadn't expected Connor to conduct an interview since they had only come to review the security tapes.

Connor lingered in front of one of the larger displays, which depicted a butterfly, struggling to shed its cocoon, along with several of its brethren in various stages of emergence. One imago stretched its wings, drying them so that it might take its first flight, but the subject that caught his eye was the one set furthest back in its labor. The surface of the chrysalis expanded slowly, a thin veil separating the pupa from the outside world, and the slightest breeze in the room could disturb the cocoon and cause it to sway. It seemed to Connor that the rigidity of the material—in this case, some type of wood—should not allow that motion, but he couldn't be positive that a fishing line or some other malleable material wasn't in fact supporting the chrysalis.

"You have quite a talent," he interjected, temporarily shifting the discussion toward art. "I was reading your biography," he continued, turning his back on the display, and he gestured toward the other installations, which had been shaped from woods and stones of varying hardness. "You exhibit this kind of talent across several mediums. How did you get so good?"

The brightness returned to Moise's face. "It's a trade secret," he replied and then chuckled. "Practice. Years of practice."

"Yes, of course," Connor allowed. He called upon his few, feeble years of study in public school and any documentary he might have caught on television to create a semblance of knowledge of the art world. "But don't most artists only specialize in one medium?" he asserted, hoping it was true. "Like the difference between stone and wood has to be as vast as the difference between oil and water, eh?"

Moise nodded. "A bit. But I have dedicated my life to improving my skill."

Gently, he caressed the base of the butterfly statue; even though he was suspicious, he had to respect the mastery of the piece. "This reminds me a bit of Hephaestus," he said casually while his keen eyes swept back to, and kept careful focus on, Moise's face. "They say his skill with metal was so good that he could bring his creations to life like little automatons. It almost seems like your creations could do the same."

The grin on Moise's face widened so much that it could have outshone the moon. "You pay me a great compliment!" He laughed before continuing, "I told you this morning that artists survive on their egos."

If Connor was expecting another reaction, he was disappointed, but he was not ready to concede defeat. He believed that he had discovered Moise's weak point—a tactic to force him to expose himself—despite his conjecture having no substance; they were not even certain that an Other was involved in the construction accident, let alone what Moise's part in it might have been since his alibi placed him off the premises. Nevertheless, he pushed forward, pursuing his implausible lead. "You ever thought they were real?" he asked, assuming an appropriate mesmerized, distant tone. "You know, late at night when no one's around, maybe one of them moves." He shrugged and smirked, acting facetious while insinuating that he might have been sincere. Moise politely maintained his smile, though he shifted his eyes questioningly toward Orion, who was less poised and clearly perplexed by his partner.

Having failed to invoke any response, Connor continued after a beat as if the tangent conversation hadn't occurred. "We wanted to check out those surveillance videos after all," he explained, all pretext gone from his voice, as he turned away from the sculpture and paced back toward the center of the room. "See if we missed anything." He shoved his hands in his pockets and winked at Orion, signaling that the digression had been a ruse. "Don't worry; it's just a formality, and then we'll wrap up."

"Ah," Moise replied, breaking eye contact as he crossed his hands in front of him. Regretfully, he added, "I would like to cooperate, but I'm afraid there aren't any videos of the incident. The cameras in that room were uninstalled that afternoon as part of the renovation efforts."

"We noticed some cameras facing the room."

Moise shook his head. "They would not have captured anything. They are meant to focus on their respective displays. I think you will find their view is obstructed."

"We'd like to view them just the same." He shrugged, adding, "Just to be thorough."

"Of course," Moise agreed, clasping his hands. He gestured toward the doorway. "Please. After you, Agents." Connor exited first, followed by a bewildered Orion, and Moise brought up the rear, directing them toward the video room. After introducing them to the security guard, who showed them how to operate the playback system, he left them to their own devices while the security guard excused himself to make his rounds.

"Did I miss something?" Orion asked when they were finally alone. He had occupied the lone seat in the room at Connor's insistence; the latter preferred to stand, as it gave him a better view over the bank of screens. It also placed Orion in a better position to operate the system.

"What do you mean?"

"It's just that you seem awfully interested in Mr. Kabamba instead of the case we're on," he replied as he worked. He glanced up toward him. "Do you think he's the Other?"

"It's a possibility," Connor revealed, deciding to keep his full opinion in reserve; informing Orion that he was operating on a hunch would only confuse the younger man, who was supposed to be learning proper investigative procedures.

Orion knitted his eyebrows. "What about Ms. Shah?" he asked curiously. "I thought you trusted Agent Reeves' opinion."

"I'm not discounting her entirely either," he said. "It's just that something is going on here that I can't quite place my finger on, so I'd like to follow all leads." If he allowed himself to explore his feelings, he'd characterize his suspicion of Moise Kabamba as similar to what he'd felt in Pierce's presence. Before the fateful encounter with him in the Starrs' apartment, he'd passed him in the hallway—a chance meeting that he'd only recognized in retrospect—and he'd felt a brief tug in his direction, as if the man had his own gravitational pull, but he'd disregarded the strange feeling offhand. It was the same with Moise Kabamba, though the nature and intensity of the sensation were different, manifesting instead as a nebulous, nagging impression driving Connor toward recklessness. Pierce Starr had not been an Other, but Connor had to pursue the queer instinct to its end, even if it developed into nothing, because he could not forgive himself if he discounted it and another violent encounter ensued. He had been uncannily fortunate during his confrontation with Pierce, and it was unlikely that a probable victim would have equal luck.

When Orion frowned, Connor recognized it as an expression of his frustration, and he knew that this snit was about his supposed lack of communication skills. This prompted him to reluctantly offer, "When I have something, I'll tell you. Right now, it's just a gut feeling."

The younger man sighed, seemingly satisfied with the promise for now, and brought up the footage from the previous evening. "Ready?" he inquired snarkily, reminiscent of his sister and perhaps even Connor himself.

As they watched the night's silent surveillance recordings, it became obvious that Sitara was not a telekinetic as Reeves believed. Pictures and objects would move ever so slightly out of their places when no one was visible, and as Sitara passed through the area, she would straighten every askew object as if she knew instinctively that they'd been put that way. While her actions built a strong case for an ability, the movement happened whether or not she was present in the area, and she didn't always make a circuit through the affected areas.

Once, one of the pieces was knocked from its pedestal onto the floor, and it levitated back to its place, albeit moments later and not in the same position; Sitara was in her office at the other end of the building during the incident, coincidentally fixing another misaligned artwork.

"Do you think it's actually a ghost after all?" Orion asked, trying to explain the apparent lack of causation.

Connor snickered. "No such thing," he derided scornfully. The video continued onward into late evening after everyone in the building had gone home for the night, leaving Sitara alone with the construction worker. Sitara briefly entered the room, momentarily casting doubt on her testimony, and then departed, retreating toward the office. As Moise informed them, the angle of the cameras prevented any real coverage of the incident, so it was entirely possible that there was a completely mundane explanation for the accident: Sitara herself, who subsequently claimed innocence.

Then the accident occurred off camera, signaled by a lone paint canister that rolled into the frame as it spread its contents across the ground, and Sitara turned on her heels immediately, reacting to a sound the playback hadn't recorded. As she made her way to the accident, a strange thing happened on the main cameras: Paint-laden footprints manifested, leading away from the expanding puddle, and it improbably seemed that a pair of disembodied feet attached to a single leg were the source.

When Sitara approached the scene, she immediately drew her cell phone to call the emergency services. The call had been recorded by the dispatch center, so her lie had not been about the accident itself as Connor had suspected. She headed into the scene, disappearing as she waded into the spill toward the downed construction worker, and the phantom footprints, which had fled the scene in the opposite direction, turned back. The change in perspective further obfuscated what the video showed: The leg, which had only been covered in paint down the side, appeared flat, while the feet appeared hollow. The cameras also picked up two floating, paper-thin palms, which had been obscured by the comparable whiteness of the wall against which the image had initially been caught.

As the exposed phantom returned to the scene and moved out of camera range, Connor realized what Sitara had been hiding. She was not an Other, nor was she followed by a poltergeist she called Billy; he may have even solved her brother's disappearance.

- - -

One of the advantages of owning an art gallery was the guarantee of a reserved private area in which to work. Moise could have utilized his former studio to the same effect, but he appreciated the convenience its collocation offered; he could duck out of the gallery to create a new piece whenever he was inspired, and he was inspired often these days by the more attractive clientele his displays drew.

When he'd been an art school student, Moise had discovered Carrara marble—the same white marble that had been used by the ancient Romans. Since then, he'd endeavored to surpass the master sculptors of the age, especially their ability to simulate cloth, and he had drawn flattering comparisons due to his delicacy when depicting the more fragile aspects of life. While *Metamorphosis*, which the federal agents had admired earlier, was the epitome of his efforts, he had first invited attention with the intricate fur he'd formed, which had caused one critic to be stunned that the hairs did not flex or soften when he stroked the sculpture.

His career was all a lie.

Art school had imparted mechanics: how to pose a subject, ratios for proper proportions (which was useful but often superfluous for his method), and that art was created to instill emotions. While this foundation of tradition allowed him to better align his aspirations with the community, he had no natural talent. He could not chisel stone into a recognizable shape or whittle wood without wounding himself. He couldn't even select quality materials.

Instead, the root of his artistic ability was a supernatural talent that he had unlocked years ago and slowly harnessed over the interceding decades. Moise could transfigure material from one state to another and transmute it at an atomic level. As a child, the skill had nearly gotten him killed, inciting an angry, superstitious mob, and the gift had languished in secret for years, withering until he'd found the courage to tune it. *Ferocity*, the beautiful tabby at the front entrance, had been his first true success, but many others had swiftly followed.

However, he had reached a creative plateau. It was no longer exciting to capture the essence of his subjects; the exercise no longer tested his limits, which was why his latest piece strived to portray motion with the same subtle intricacy. Moise meticulously set up the scene: a cherry suspended over a petite pool of water. On his mark, the fruit would plummet into the container and rebound with sufficient force to lift back up from the liquid. If all went according to plan, the cherry would be balanced atop its drop impact and would be surrounded by the corona ripples—all frozen and reinterpreted into wood. His previous trials had involved a high-speed camera, which had encapsulated the event as it had happened and had allowed him to strategize. All that remained was the live attempt, and if it did not succeed, he would have wasted almost a day of dry runs and a week of planning. Conceivably, his ability would allow him to transmute the materials back into their original forms to allow for a second shot, but he knew that his heart wouldn't be in it; he had to get it right the first time.

The result was not quite as he'd envisioned it: He'd reacted an instant too soon, leaving the cherry partially submerged in its rebound column. But after deliberation, he decided that he preferred the fault; the asymmetry made it seem more organic, which was an observation he found ironic. Satisfied, it was time for him to decide where and how to display the new piece.

With the reopening of the south wing delayed, he could presumably release the new sculpture to sustain interest, but it could not be a part of the main exhibition. Despite the tenuous connection that he could draw between the cherry and ovaries—or perhaps even conception—he felt that its inclusion would detract from the wing's purpose. However, it brought a new dilemma to light: Patrons would expect his own contribution to the exhibit, and he could create nothing less than the centerpiece. So what would capture the essence of the new wing?

An idea formed out of his professional jealousy: If he truly wanted to surpass the masters, then he needed to create a work that exceeded Giovanni Strazza's *Veiled Virgin*, which was his benchmark for realism. Costuming would be a concern; he needed to determine which fabrics could be translated satisfactorily into marble and how to drape the material over a form for maximum effect. He also needed to figure out what style of dress his subject would wear, and it would allude to the most famous mother, the Virgin Mary, and all the works that she inspired. However, the major stumbling block would be the subject herself.

He had never worked with a human subject before, but his education prescribed that she should be a classical beauty who was full of grace, mystery, and sensuality. A woman like Grace Kelly or Audrey Hepburn would be ideal, and it was a shame that he could no longer suspend them in their prime to preserve their splendor for later generations.

He'd seen many human models over the years, and all had fallen short of the ideal in some manner. Many had been too young to be considered mothers, and some—particularly one model—had destroyed any air of mystery the moment they'd opened their mouths to speak. Worse, none of them had had that intangible *je ne sais quoi* that made the aforementioned movie stars irresistibly charming.

He expanded his pool of candidates to women whom he met in his everyday life, including his assistant, Sitara Shah, and he rejected each of them in turn for the same lack of sophistication and allure until he considered Amanda Darling-Whitcomb. The former senator's wife had the poise of New England aristocracy and the charm of a fifties housewife while maintaining the sharp mind of a pioneer suffragette. She had grieved publicly with grace while keeping enough cognizance to use the subsequent national sympathy to launch her own career, and she'd expertly countered any attempt to paint her as inexperienced. In her few years in office, she had become quite a formidable force.

She also fit the definition of a classic beauty, using makeup to subtly enhance her natural good looks, and while she was on the thin side, she had developed enough of a matronly figure not to be mistaken for a girl. Even her personal style, from her hair to her wardrobe, was meant to reflect an earlier era.

In short, she was the perfect subject. Now, however, came the planning stage, and he would have to be both crafty and precise to accomplish his goal.

- - -

Sitara appeared to have recovered somewhat from her ordeal when she opened the door. She looked refreshed, any dark circles beneath her doe eyes had been concealed by subtly applied makeup, and her dark hair was neatly pinned into a chignon. She was half-dressed, wearing a chiffon blouse in combination with plaid pajama pants, and she was barefooted. Her delicate smile fell slightly as she recognized her guests. "Officers," she greeted with the forced politeness of an experienced host.

"Good morning, Ms. Shah," Connor said with his winningest grin. "Can we come in for a few moments?"

Her lips turned further downward before she caught them, and self-consciously, she glanced behind her into her apartment. "I'm getting ready for work."

"Won't take long, love," he assured her. "We just have a few follow-up questions we'd like to ask so we can put the finishing touches on our report." He retrieved his notepad from his jacket pocket and waved it at her, trying to be as disarming as possible.

Sitara composed herself, smiling faintly, and nodded. "Alright," she agreed and stepped aside to allow them entry. She didn't offer them refreshments this time, opting instead to show them to her living room immediately, and she took a seat across from them. At first, she crossed her hands over her lap, and then, becoming embarrassed by her state of partial undress, she shifted them to her knees; the effect was a somewhat more dignified pose while shielding her worn, stained pajamas from view. She had mopped and dusted since yesterday, somehow making the already meagerly furnished apartment seem less cluttered, and now the air smelled of lemon and bleach in addition to eucalyptus, creating a sharp, almost offensive scent.

Orion settled into the couch next to Connor, forcing himself to relax to reinforce his air of authority, whereas Connor propped his elbow on his knee as he pretended to skim his notepad. Dramatically with his pen in hand, he sniffed and began, "Now, I know you said the gallery was empty, save for you and Mr. Cole, but is it possible that you missed someone on your sweep?" Sitara inhaled. She was already starting to formulate a misleading response when Connor cut her off; he wanted to keep her off balance and make it harder for her to invent a plausible lie. "I'm asking because we came across something a bit odd," he explained. "You noticed the spilled paint, of course. Well, unfortunately, it got tracked all over that nice floor by you, the paramedics, and anyone else who was there."

She shifted uncomfortably, clearing her throat. He'd seen a woman's heels tracked from the coagulating lake and overlapping the mysterious bare feet, but her feet were too small to truly obscure the other prints, and in his haste to investigate Sitara's employer, he'd disregarded the clue that she'd left behind. But his head had cleared after he'd viewed the surveillance tapes, allowing him to spot the traces of her tampering as they left Félicité; if he had acknowledged the trail that the video tapes had revealed sooner, they wouldn't have run in unnecessary circles wasting time. "It was cleaned up, but that actually made it easier to see some bare footprints that had been made as well," he continued seriously, watching her. "We think the owner of those footprints is the one who caused the accident."

She leaned back, sliding her hands up her thighs before wrapping one arm around herself; the other hand went to the nape of her neck, stroking it as if she were searching for stray strands of hair that had escaped her updo. "I suppose I could have missed somebody hiding in the bathroom."

"Of course. Can't expect you to catch everyone. That's the security guard's job," he said with an understanding, sympathetic smile. "Do you have any idea who this person could have been?"

She shook her head. "We have a lot of traffic during the day," she replied.

She put her finger to her slim mouth as she thought, and then she offered, "I could check with the security guard... see if he saw anything suspicious or expelled anyone that day. It doesn't happen very often."

He grinned wolfishly. "As it happens, we already spoke to the security guard," he said in a mock-helpful tone. "Well, more like reviewed the tapes, and—"

He was unexpectedly interrupted by a rhythmic knocking from one of the back rooms. He turned, trying to better understand the noise, which sounded like a closed door being repeatedly shoved against the jamb and strike plate. It was followed shortly by a soft, un-feline meow that continued like a cat demanding egress, and Connor gave Sitara a sidelong glance, eyeing her suspiciously.

She reacted quickly, asserting, "Oh, that's just the neighbor's television. I've made complaints, but these walls are so thin." Unfortunately, her explanation was immediately discredited by an ill-timed utterance from the back room that sounded faintly like a whimpering of her name.

He smiled sardonically. "I think I'd like to investigate just the same." He rose, quickly crossing from her living room to the rest of her apartment, and Orion scrambled off the couch to follow him.

"You can't do that!" Sitara protested, her small stride struggling to catch up to his. The hallway adjoined the bathroom and what might have been her bedroom, and the doors to both were ajar. There was also a third room that had been barred with an impressive new deadbolt. Connor scowled at the plastic tub of water that was stretched across its entryway, and Sitara deftly leapt in front of him, admitting sheepishly, "Alright. I never stopped being haunted by the poltergeist." She smiled nervously, a petite hand gesturing toward the container while she stopped him with her other. "Please don't move that. It's the only thing keeping him in that room."

Connor rolled his eyes; even if he'd understood the superstition she'd referenced, it wouldn't have deterred him. "Either you open that door or I will," he threatened, ready to invoke probable cause, but she relented unexpectedly. She slid the tub aside, splashing its contents across the floor, and reluctantly unlocked the door to reveal a child's room. The walls were decorated with peeling decals with a hodgepodge of Disney characters, superheroes, and other popular children's shows, and toys were scattered across the floor, along with puzzle pieces and several sheets of construction paper. A Lego tower dominated the far corner, and several paint bottles were strewn across the floor; at some point, their contents had been spread across the walls and subsequently scrubbed away.

"See?" Sitara said weakly from beside the door. "It's just an empty room. I use it to appease the ghost," she added, trying to explain the worn toys that had unmistakably been played with. "I think he's a young child."

Connor raised an eyebrow. "We'll see about that," he remarked cynically. "Starr, stay in that doorway, will you? And don't let anything pass." Orion moved into place, flashing Sitara an apologetic look as he moved past her into the threshold. Connor conducted a measured circuit around the room, examining it for further corroborating evidence. The scent of eucalyptus was overpowering, as if it had penetrated the thin wallpaper and seeped into the cheap walls, and he wanted to open a window to air out the stench, but he hesitated; the window had been sealed shut with nails and paint. He glanced back toward Sitara. "You know, love, this is highly illegal," he scolded disapprovingly. "I could cite you for this." Declining to provide an explanation, she looked away and tucked a stray strand of hair behind her ear as she licked her lips nervously.

Connor reached the doorway, having completed his search, and raised his eyebrows expectantly at Sitara, affording her a final chance to come clean. She didn't move, frozen in anticipation, so he shrugged indifferently, reached into his pocket, and pulled out a Ziploc bag containing flour. Theatrically, he coated his hands in the fine powder and then blew it in a steady arc over the entire room, covering everything in a layer of dust and revealing their concealed quarry. The shape was hunched down, hiding near the foot of the bed as if they were playing a game, and was very close to Connor himself. Before the agent could assign any significance to the scene, Sitara pushed past Orion, knocking him into the doorframe, and went to her brother's side. Connor sighed heavily and declared, "That's what I thought."

- - -

Connor herded them back into the living room, where Orion took the recliner, and Sitara and the partially visible figure sat on the couch. It was disconcerting staring at the revealed Other: The flour had accumulated only on the horizontal surfaces, revealing mostly his shoulders and back, and powder clung to ill-defined tufts of hair and eyebrows. Orion could see through the space the man occupied, as if his shape were a crafted illusion, and even with the flour's assistance, he couldn't distinguish any features. Sitara encircled her brother protectively with her arms, and Orion was reminded of his bond with his sister.

Connor remained standing, dominating the room. "See, I knew Reeves was onto something, but he was following the wrong subject," he told Orion. Even though he'd already made it clear that he considered paranormal activity to be a hoax, his disdainful tone continued to underline his contempt. "Sitara's older brother disappeared, alright, but he didn't die. He just couldn't reappear, so he's been 'haunting' her ever since because she's the only one who could help him." He turned to Sitara. "Isn't that right?"

She stroked her brother's hair, dislodging some of the flour and dispersing it across herself and more of his body. "I know he looks like a man, but he is just a child," she said softly, almost pleading for clemency. Orion wondered whether she'd discovered the BSI's mission or whether she would have made her appeal regardless. "He has a developmental problem. You cannot blame him for things."

The corners of Connor's mouth quirked, and his face became expressionless. "I'm from an agency that helps people like your brother," he informed her. He shifted his weight to one side and tucked his hands into his pockets. "Tell him to turn visible again, and we can all discuss what'll happen," he commanded, his voice flat and emotionless, as his gaze transferred to Nihar's shape.

She hesitated, biting her lip with downcast eyes. "He can't," she admitted regretfully. "That's why we've lived like this for so long." She returned her focus to Connor and, her face showing the slimmest glimmer of hope, asked, "Can you help him with that?"

Connor nodded gradually, glancing at his feet as he pursed and licked his lips. "Yeah, we can," he promised. He crossed the distance between them and forced a crooked smile as he patted her reassuringly on the shoulder.

Orion watched silently as Connor made arrangements for the custody exchange. As they waited, Connor gave a broad description of the bureau and the training it had provided Eric Dane, but he refrained from describing any specifics to Nihar's case. Although Sitara asked probing questions like a concerned parent, Connor was skilled at answering evasively and she eventually settled for his approximations about treatment. They spent the remainder of the interim in awkward silence disturbed occasionally by Nihar's various childish needs.

The other team was on their doorstep within a few hours. The man was dressed in a suit, much like Connor and himself, but the woman wore a form-fitting jumpsuit that was padded in strategic places by heavier material; it counterintuitively seemed to be some sort of tactical uniform. In the dark-skinned woman's presence, Orion felt a blanket cover his senses, as if his cells had become encased in molasses, and when she entered the apartment, the cloak concealing Nihar fell away.

Nihar was older than Orion had expected. He was senior to them all in age, but the bright, goofy grin on his face belied his physical maturity. He was covered in patches of grime, despite obvious attempts to cleanse them, and his hair was shaggy, uneven, and matted. He was naked, save for the tattered remains of a pair of cartoon-decorated briefs, and he was sprawled contentedly across his sister's lap. When it was time to leave, his sister took his hand, and he followed her from the apartment unquestioningly, asking excitedly if they were going to the park now. Although she answered in the affirmative, Sitara had been told that their escort would take them back to the Plum Island facility for final assessment and processing.

Orion and Connor didn't linger much longer after Nihar's departure, though Connor delayed long enough for the dark-skinned woman's distressful effect to recede from his senses, and he found himself wondering whether Connor's consideration for his comfort was genuine concern or a pretense of compassion. The agent accompanied him back to his apartment, possibly expecting questions about the case, but Orion wasn't ready to speak with him yet and instead began collecting his thoughts on the events of the day. Connor tried to goad him into conversation, ostensibly to entertain himself, but Orion managed to ignore him. Despite Connor's mastery of irritation techniques, Orion didn't budge on his silence, and the agent instead amused himself by manipulating his phone wordlessly. He knew that Connor's intent was to create discomfort with his presence—another method to coerce conversation—and he chose to combat his new approach by preparing dinner. The agent would nonetheless stay, and Orion's preparation was mindless—almost meditative—as his hands moved in practiced familiarity. With his body occupied, his mind was free to wander, and he was better able to articulate his grievance and discontent.

By the time dinner was served, he was ready to confront Connor. They ate at the island, with Connor sitting on a barstool while Orion chose to remain standing. He was leaning casually against the surface of the island in an effort to encourage self-confidence. "Why did you lie to Ms. Shah?" he asked, locking eyes with Connor as he'd seen the agent do when he wanted answers.

"Eh? What do you mean?" he asked as he cracked a self-assured smirk, but Orion was starting to see people's body language for what it was, and he noticed the sudden tension hidden behind Connor's egotistic expression.

"About euthanizing her brother," he said, and Connor wasn't quick enough to hide his surprise as it flashed across his face. "I'm not stupid, you know," Orion continued disdainfully. "I have been paying attention. I read BSI guidelines."

Connor regained control of his mask and smiled disarmingly as he shoved his plate out of the way. "No one's said—"

"'An Other is a threat to public safety if he cannot control himself'," Orion quoted. "That's what the guidelines say, right?" he demanded, emboldened by the agent's lack of adequate resistance. "And her brother certainly can't, so why did you lie to her?"

Connor's smile twitched and then fell, and he sighed deeply. "My job is to facilitate the processing of Others," he replied, his voice suddenly burdened. "Sometimes that means omitting less-than-savory information."

"You mean lying," Orion declared accusatorily.

Connor forced a bitter, twisted grin as he admitted, "Yeah, I mean lying."

Orion took a step back, swallowing to prepare himself for his next question; he really didn't want to know the answer, but it was something he needed to know. "Have you ever lied to me?" he asked, leaning against the counter and staring Connor down. Connor broke eye contact, just as Orion was afraid the agent would do, and then scowled at the kitchen tile as if he'd find the answer there. He chewed his bottom lip as he considered his next words, and Orion decided that he didn't need to hear them; Connor's actions had told him enough. "I can't believe it!" he exclaimed, slamming his fists on the counter. "I can't believe you! All those visits, those conversations..." He turned away, tearing at the roots of his hair as if they'd reverse time and salve his sudden heartache. "I thought you actually cared," he spat.

Connor seemingly leapt over the island, seizing Orion by the front of his shirt, and narrowed his eyes, boring his sudden rage into him. "Look here, mate! I may have not always told you the whole truth, but I've never lied to you," he hissed, baring his teeth like a wild animal. "Who told you the truth about Tinder? About your sister?" He shook him to emphasize his points, draining Orion of any confidence he'd manufactured, and the younger man felt like a terrified child in the agent's grip. "If I were you, I'd look to myself and my own survival instead of that damn self-righteousness because it helps nothing."

Then, perhaps revealing more than he meant to, he added, "Cooperation is your only choice here if you want to live, so you'd best straighten up and stick to the job!" His voice cracked, and though it seemed anger was the culprit, his eyes glistened and his mouth, already stretched wide in a grimace, contorted as it strained to express whatever emotions he was feeling.

The agent stared at Orion for a few more heartbeats, menacing him with his anger, and then suddenly shrank away, releasing him and shoving him back. Connor swallowed, bowing his head and refusing to look anywhere but at the floor, and he retreated back to his stool, where his jacket lay. "I'm gonna go now," he declared gruffly, though his voice wavered traitorously, and he quickly concluded, "I'll see you tomorrow." He left, slamming the door behind him, and Orion sank against the bar.

While Connor's outburst had terrified him on a primitive level, it had also served to confirm Orion's fears: The agent's friendly overtures had only been an act to secure his cooperation as if his sister's continued safety wasn't enough of an incentive. Now more than ever, he needed to determine a way to extricate himself and Cassie from their present situation and disappear.

PART VIII
CODE NAME: GORGON

Cassie had given up on normal. All the years she'd tried to emulate her peers became a wasted effort once the universe threw her its latest curveball, and her homicidal father had also turned out to be a serial killer. No more would she strive for the top tier of the cheerleading team or to win swimming medals. If she was going to stand out, she was going to do it on her own terms and not through society's approved avenues. She'd chopped off her long hair, dyeing the remaining red locks black and changing her hairstyle to a jagged-edged, flattened pixie cut. She abandoned New York's upscale brands for ripped, dark garments that openly displayed her discontent. After her transformation, she discovered the irony that her new recalcitrant and cavalier style took as much effort to coordinate and maintain as her previous prep attire.

She also ditched the former "in crowd"—she didn't want to expend the energy necessary to be accepted into their circle—in favor of the fringe groups, only to discover that they weren't as delinquent or iconoclastic as their projected reputations. The worst rebellious behavior they undertook was drinking at a secluded location, which was an act that she entertained only because she knew it would anger her brother; she didn't even consider her caretakers' reactions. A few claimed to do drugs, and she knew which ones were potheads and which ones did meth; she stayed away from the latter because she was rebelling, not trying to ruin her life, and she could still hear Orion's scolding voice in her head, much to her annoyance.

Her new friends did not know about her or New York, and her lack of disclosure kept them at a comfortable distance. Her cover story acknowledged the Vickers as her legal guardians: They were distant relatives who were watching over her until her parents returned. She never indicated from where her parents would return, which initially gave her an air of mystery until one of her classmates accused her of being overly dramatic and claimed that she'd been abandoned or that her parents were in prison. She allowed the story to stand because there wasn't much she could do to counter it, and she didn't care about her parents' legacy, no matter what was said. This even extended to the idea of her parents; she didn't have anything in common with them except genetics, and their appalling behavior didn't reflect on her, so there was no reason to defend them.

With fewer distractions available, she couldn't avoid putting effort into her schoolwork, and her grades improved, though only marginally. She wasn't going to attend college like her parents or her brother because it hadn't worked out for any of them. She'd put in the effort to prove that she could, and once she'd made her point, her grades had again deteriorated to an acceptable average.

She also hadn't experimented with her pyric abilities since her arrival in Pennsylvania. She'd completed the BSI's training course, which had helped her hone her self-control and discipline and had further dampened any interest she'd had in developing her talent. It was no longer a game—the agency's stringent guidelines had assured her of this—and her previous solitary forays had attracted the wrong sort of attention, so she wanted nothing further to do with that side of herself. Unfortunately, it put her slightly at odds with her new clique, who were exploring their pyromaniac side, but she also tolerated their childish pranks and experiments because even though she was determined not to be popular, she still needed to "belong"; they were her new group, and she needed to show them loyalty if she wanted to be accepted.

- - -

Lawrence Johnson worried the toothpick, chewing it squarely on the left side of his mouth until it splintered. He then deftly rolled it to the other side and spit out the offending shard before continuing. Like many of the long-term Plum Island staff, he lived in the nearby village of Greenport. He could easily have finished his report in the morning or from the comfort of his living room, but he had no one waiting for him at home nor any significant connections outside work, so he continued writing it in the scarce company of late-night coworkers who didn't want to go home to empty houses either.

It hadn't always been like this, although he couldn't remember where it had gone wrong. He'd had a girlfriend in college and plenty of friends in the service, and over the years, he'd slowly lost each one until he'd gotten to the point where he spoke only to his mother on holidays. Perhaps it had been his ambition and his passion that had driven everyone away, and now he only interacted with his coworkers during custody transfers and the irregular meeting. Antithesis was his most frequent companion, and he would never consider her more than a tool—a weapon in the war against Others. While some might believe it to be a lonely existence, he knew that it would be worthwhile as long as the mission was accomplished.

His cell phone rang, tugging him from his introspection, and he answered it automatically, "Special Agent Johnson." He never received personal calls.

There was a pause at the other end of the line and the rough clearing of a throat before he heard the abrasive tenor of his associate, Morgan Connor. "Hey, yeah, Johnson, are you back at headquarters yet?"

Subconsciously, Johnson checked the lower right-hand corner of his computer display for the time. "We've been back for a few hours," he replied. He'd driven the van while Antithesis had observed Nihar Shah and his sister in the back. It had been an uneventful but noisy trip as the man-child had frequently demanded entertainment before Antithesis had dosed him with a mild tranquilizer and he'd curled up contentedly in his sister's lap. Processing into the facility had gone much more quietly, as Sitara had gently encouraged her brother's cooperation, and they'd been shown to a cell for the night. There would likely be a battery of tests tomorrow to assess whether Nihar could control his invisibility before a final determination would be made about his condition, but Johnson believed that he'd be euthanized. While invisibility was potentially a useful skill, letting a child wield it would be foolhardy.

"Thought so," Connor replied, disappointed. "Look, I think I have another Other on my hands."

"Another already?" Johnson exclaimed, genuinely surprised. "You do work quickly." Being partnered with the BSI's primary escort, he knew firsthand about Connor's impressive acquisition rate, but he'd never seen such a short time frame between his discoveries.

He heard a hiss, like air passing through clenched teeth or a vocalized grimace. "Not quite yet, mate. It's more of a hunch," Connor admitted reluctantly. "Do you think you could turn around and maybe head back our way?"

Johnson hesitated, chewing on his answer as he sat up straight and leaned into the phone. The bureau's best-kept secret was the fact that Morgan Connor was an Other, which was information so crucial that it was never entered into the database and never mentioned to anyone below a certain clearance.

Nevertheless, all field agents knew to defer to Connor's instincts, as he was usually right when it came to detecting more of his kind. This placed Johnson in a bind, as he was obligated to keep Connor in the dark—the BSI bent over backwards to conceal the truth from its prize agent—while still following the bloodhound's intuition. "I'll have to requisition some funds for the trip, Connor," he replied carefully, trusting that his associate had more to share. Since Connor's fieldwork was typically thorough, it had been assumed that his uncanny knack for finding Others had been pure talent, until it had proved to be statistically implausible. "That'll be difficult to do based on a hunch."

"I'm hoping to have something a bit more solid on him by tomorrow evening. I just need the time to dig up the evidence," Connor told him. His haughty, insufferable attitude crept in as he added, "Catch him in the act, so to speak." He could hear his conceited grin, and he wondered whether the agency's ostracism was a contributing factor to his irritating personality. Since he wasn't a true agent—Connor was an Other, after all—his peers distanced themselves from him, treating him as an outsider, but Connor probably believed that the treatment was due to professional jealousy over his prolific career.

"And if you don't, I'll be in the lurch for a couple hundred bucks," Johnson countered.

"I'm good for it."

Johnson smirked, recalling the shabby suit that Connor typically wore, and he wondered where Connor's money went, as they earned similar salaries. Regardless, Connor's simple comment provided him an opportunity: If he framed his assistance as a favor, Connor had no reason to question his return to New York City. "I'm not sure you are," he teased, "but if I were a betting man, I'd have to put money on your track record." He purposely stretched out the silence, sighing for dramatic effect, and added, "Antithesis needs her rest, so we'll have to head out tomorrow morning."

Connor grinned. "Thanks, mate. I owe you one."

"Yeah, you do," Johnson agreed. "Just get the evidence," he commanded and hung up the phone. He tossed the device onto his desktop and leaned back in his chair. It wasn't over yet; Connor still needed to provide proof of some kind so that it wouldn't be suspicious when Johnson apprehended his target. Johnson glanced at his computer, the dark cursor in his unfinished report still flashing rhythmically against the white background, and he realized that he should have asked for a name so that he could do his own research. Perhaps

Johnson was more fatigued than he thought, and he decided to head home for the night. Connor and his conundrum would still be there in the morning.

- - -

Orion was suddenly awakened by a short, clipped noise that he imagined was a scream. He clutched his sheets closer, pulling them up to his chin, and waited for the sound again. It did not come and was instead preempted by a crash and several loud thumps. Overcome with the curiosity that fear sometimes inspires, Orion crept from his bed and stole through the dim, empty house searching for the source of the disturbance.

A heavy form suddenly slammed into him, knocking him to the floor and drawing the shrillest, most terrified cry he could muster. The figure, disoriented by the perplexing obstacle, clasped a hand around his tiny arm and held tightly until a light was switched on. Orion bawled louder: The woman who had become his captor had a deep gash through her face and into her skull, and the remains of one bloody ear sagged against her shoulder. She was bleeding profusely, and the blood oozed down her neck and arm and even down onto Orion. The stranger didn't hesitate, seizing the smaller Orion and clutching him close to her bare chest. He could hear her ragged breathing and feel her heart thumping rapidly against his ear.

She hadn't taken more than a step before the two of them toppled to the ground, upended by an unknown force. He tumbled away from her motherly embrace, her fingers reaching for him desperately as the distance widened, and her already fearful face twisted into horror, as if she were suddenly more worried about his well-being than her own. His small form was swept into another hold—a firm security that was somehow cold despite the human touch—and he wished that he could help the prone woman. Though he could no longer move, he reached out to her through the life he felt draining from her and attempted to reverse its flow and restore it to her.

Orion awoke again slowly, with no starts and to no strange noises, and yet he still clutched the sheets tightly against the sudden chill in his bones. He had experienced another nightmare, nothing more, and he quieted his breathing as he tried to recall the details. He'd once read that nightmares were the result of unresolved issues that manifested while one slept, and while it seemed true— he often dreamed about losing his sister and, more recently, about his father's murder spree—he was uncertain how to interpret his most recent experience. He wanted to understand; it was the best way to dismiss the emotions his dreams created, and this one had disturbed him deeply, making him question his early life at Bay Ridge. The woman bore a familiarity and did not seem to have been created by his subconscious, yet he could not recall meeting her in the waking world.

Once more, his mind drifted toward his sister and the lack of communication between them, and though he knew it was either a late hour or early in the morning, he nevertheless called her; it was time to end the inexplicable silence between them, even if he had to pressure her into it. The phone rang repeatedly, continuing on to voicemail, and his second try yielded an immediate banishment. She was awake and did not wish to speak with him, so perhaps he should wait until she was ready; harassing her would only encourage her stubbornness. Reluctantly, he tossed his phone back on the nightstand and turned over to go back to sleep.

- - -

It was one of the rare mornings when Amanda Darling-Whitcomb's schedule was clear and she could eat by herself. She used these silent meals to rejuvenate, and she fell into an almost meditative state as she watched the three flickering television screens, giving none noteworthy attention. There would be plenty of stress later in the day following meetings, decisions, and mini crises, so she soaked in the peace while she could, keeping the serenity in reserve for later use.

She heard heavy footsteps behind her and didn't immediately recognize them as belonging to one of her aides, so she assumed it was a bodyguard. However, a deep voice spoke, and she identified its owner as Moise Kabamba. "Mrs. Darling-Whitcomb, I apologize for the interruption," he said softly. "Your staff said it would be all right if I spoke to you briefly." Her private area was on a platform raised slightly above the rest of the establishment, and he stood at the bottom of the stairs, his hands folded politely in front of him.

She smiled, inviting him closer, and he joined her at the table. "I have a few minutes. I'm just finishing up breakfast," she explained.

Moise smiled, slowly nodding his head appreciatively, and took a moment to collect himself. His fingers went to his lips, idly revealing his lack of a marriage partner, and his head tilted as he leaned toward his hand unconsciously. "If I do not sound too forward," he carefully began, "I would like to invite you to my flat this evening, or whenever you are free, to express my great appreciation for your donation. I do not believe a simple breakfast adequately conveyed my gratitude."

Her experience with diplomacy enabled her to flawlessly freeze her convivial expression as she absorbed the invitation and its implications, and her hesitance to answer drew out the silence. She could feel his eagerness pouring out from him in waves, and while she often felt this in the presence of her staff and a few enthusiastic constituents, his eagerness had a different flavor—a strange undertone that was reminiscent of desire or desperation. As the mayor, she never ate with the members of her voter base unless they were particularly influential—a term she freely interchanged with "affluent"—but Moise had proven his ability to make connections, and the distinctive eagerness he generated gave her pause.

Fortunately, Moise did not oblige her to answer. "Ah, I have made you uncomfortable," he continued, clasping and rubbing his hands in front of him apologetically. His subsequent grand gestures suggested that he might make an excellent public speaker. "Allow me to explain this awkward situation," he offered gently. "My gratitude is a very special gift. I created my first human statue, and she is carved in your likeness. I would very much like your opinion before I reveal her to the public."

His grin widened while taking on an air of self-consciousness, and he diverted his eyes briefly before leaning in and admitting, "I could do this at my gallery, but the truth is that I very much would like to also prepare dinner for you. It is a pleasure to cook for a beautiful woman, and I hope you will grant me that honor." While his expression was charming, she also felt his emotions ramp up in anticipation of her answer.

Amanda found his offer sweet, and more importantly, she felt her cheeks burn between his words and his sincere passion. She heard common adulation and praise from her staff, business partners, and constituents, and her stylist often complimented her beauty, but she could not remember the last time she'd flirted, and she actually felt flattered that someone would try. While she was by no means old or even seeking a partner, her focus on her career was such that his overeager, almost hungry attention was gratifying.

What was a date anyway but harmless fun? She needed the practice—it had been too many years since she'd had an enjoyable, nonbusiness-related dinner, even before Johnathan's untimely death—and the rendezvous would help her establish the rapport that she desired to have with him. She might even lead him on for a bit, as she found his unexpected formality regarding dinner strangely attractive, and she knew that there was no risk involved; she could later manipulate him in such a way that her gentle rejection wouldn't affect any burgeoning loyalty. "I may be able to clear my calendar this evening," she replied coyly.

Moise laughed; it was a low, rumbling sound like liquid sloshing in a barrel. "You have made me a very happy man, Mrs. Darling-Whitcomb, and I will not disappoint you."

"Under the circumstances, you would not be remiss in calling me Amanda."

He echoed her small but sincere smile with his own, but his grin was wide enough to split his face. "I did not want to presume, especially since this meeting has gone so well."

"You have made quite the impression, Moise." She then added teasingly, "If I may?"

"It is only fair," he allowed. "I am only at my best because you brought it out of me. And that is why I must repay you."

Her smile grew, softening the subtle aging lines of her face as her cheeks reddened; she was like a schoolgirl again, and it was refreshing, if a bit embarrassing. "Well, when you put it that way..." She leaned toward him, crossed her legs, and awaited his next verbal riposte.

Surprisingly, he withdrew against the seat back and shifted slowly in his chair. "I'm afraid I must excuse myself," he said apologetically, eliciting unanticipated disappointment that their interaction had already come to an end. "I have many preparations to make, and I have already taken much of your time." His face lit up with another grin as he took her delicate hands into his and kissed her thumbs softly. "I will see you tonight," he promised.

- - -

"Why are we doing this?" Orion asked sulkily.

"You said you wanted to stick to your 'cold cases.' This is called investigation." Connor glanced at him with a smart sneer and added snarkily, "It's what the analysts do back at headquarters and what you'll do between cases." The two of them sat at Orion's kitchen table; Connor was directly in front of his weathered laptop, and Orion was seated slightly to the side. The agent had entered the encryption key for the BSI database, and they were waiting for the network connection to complete so he could download pertinent files and teach Orion how to piece together information when building a new case file.

Connor had affected his usual pseudo-enthusiasm when he'd arrived earlier that morning, but Orion's sullenness had been so impenetrable that he'd dropped the pretense and had allowed it to infect their interaction. He didn't have the energy to deal with a childish tantrum, especially when the subject in question didn't appreciate what had been placed on the line for him.

Orion scowled. "They're not my 'cold cases,' and I meant Mr. Kabamba specifically." He crossed his arms petulantly. "Why are you so fixated on this guy?"

Connor sighed. "I told you before that there's something off about him, and now that our case is closed, I can focus more on him. See what he's hiding." Orion narrowed his eyes as he twisted his mouth skeptically, and Connor suppressed the urge to roll his eyes. "You can doubt me all you want, but I'm the senior agent here." He smirked, remembering that Orion hadn't corrected Moise's assumption about his federal status, and then he added vindictively, "In fact, I'm the only real agent, so we're going to do things my way."

Orion shook his head and muttered, "Whatever."

"You shouldn't be so impertinent. It doesn't suit you," Connor chided, causing Orion to sink further into his brooding. He'd explained the purpose of the database before, but only in bits and pieces, and as the system loaded, he took the opportunity to describe its function and capabilities in greater detail. The database had been filled with details of any suspected Other activity from the modern day stretching back to antiquity, when it had first been created. The intent was that the background information would allow researchers to better predict how subjects would behave. When there were instances of activity that could not be explained, a profile was built for the perpetrator, and the case was tagged with key words. While it was an extensive database, it was not perfect; it was restrained by the flaws of human programming and human observation. Some cases were not connected until years later, creating a plethora of one-off events, and these were the kinds of assignments that Connor and Orion were originally supposed to work on: read up, do legwork, connect the dots, and hopefully apprehend the culprits. This was actually step one of the process, but Orion hadn't been ready for it when they'd begun training, so they'd started somewhere closer to the middle.

Connor initiated a search, starting simply with Kabamba's name, and while they were awaiting a response from the system, Orion's cell phone rang. The younger man excused himself, stepping a few feet away to the landing to speak in quiet, solemn tones, and Connor immediately assumed that the call concerned his sister.

When the database returned nothing regarding Kabamba, Connor changed his focus to instances of material manipulation, primarily that of stone or wood. The few results he received were either associated with Others who had either died by an uncontrolled outburst of power or had already been apprehended and euthanized, including a member of the Vanguard. The single unresolved instance of dendrokinesis was unsubstantiated and provided him with no valid leads. He broadened his search, casting a wider net that would hopefully uncover cases that were more germane to his investigation, but he was instead rewarded with complexified, irrelevant data. The glut of information only further obscured his search, with nothing matching the profile that Connor had constructed for Kabamba, and his frustration grew. Despite his certainty that Moise was an Other, he couldn't uncover any evidence either at Félicité or in his agency's own data banks.

Tetchily, he pulled up his email account to draft a request to the analysts at headquarters. When Orion returned to his side, his pale face was drawn with worry, and his lips were a thin line. His eyes remained downcast, almost submissive rather than socially anxious, and his tone was respectful. "I need to leave for a few days."

"Why's that?" Connor asked casually, shifting to look at the younger man.

"I have some business to take care of."

"Yeah, and what's that? Would it be about your sister?" He was severe, almost caustic, and he eyed Orion eagerly, waiting for his body language to give something up. Orion flinched almost imperceptibly, as if he were a dog anticipating a beating, and Connor slouched deeper into the wooden chair, digging his heels into the floor as he crossed his hands in his lap. "I recall telling you the onus is on her to succeed," he lectured. "That means in life, too. You can't just go running off to help her every time she's in trouble."

Orion drew confidence from some hidden reserve and dared to reply, "If you want me to trust you, you need to let me go."

"You want to talk about trust?" Connor's face twisted, barely suppressing the sudden rage welling up inside his chest. "That's real rich considering the circumstances." Surrendering to an inimical impulse, he added unkindly, "Did she set fire to something again, and you're running to cover it up before we find out?" He regretted his words instantly, having implicitly condoned her execution, but he stubbornly refused to retract his comment.

Surprisingly, Orion didn't yield or submit to his own anger. Instead, he humbly requested, "Please."

Connor could see the pain he'd inflicted in his eyes—his dilated pupils struggled to maintain a determined focus—and despite his erstwhile toughness, his posture was still subservient as if he'd realized that he'd better achieve his goals through diplomacy than acquiescence or confrontation. He was currently begging, but Connor knew that he'd take the first opportunity he could to rush to his sister's aid. As his supervisor and de facto handler, Connor didn't want to make an enemy of him or place Orion in a situation in which his status with the BSI would be threatened.

Even though his sister was his weakness, Orion was intelligent enough to mitigate risks on both their behalf, and if Cassie had broken the terms of her parole, he knew it was better to inform Connor than try to resolve it himself. Therefore, Connor should give the kid a break; they were only going to clash until some distance had been created from last night's argument and its inception at Primrose.

"Fine," Connor relented, huffing as he jammed his hands onto his hips. "Get it sorted, and get back here. Your whinging is just going to distract me anyway."

Orion smiled slightly, ambiguously in relief or amusement. "Thank you!" he replied, already heading toward the doorway. Realizing he needed more than just himself, he quickly trotted up the stairs without waiting for his response.

"Yeah," Connor muttered cynically as he turned back toward the computer. He was already questioning whether he'd made the right choice, and he immediately silenced the disbelieving voice by diving back into his work. He became absorbed in his email, being only vaguely aware of Orion's farewell and subsequent departure, as he tried to cover every angle he could conceive. Since Moise's name had returned no results from the database, it was possible that Moise Kabamba had not always been his legal name. Connor requested a deeper probe into his background: name changes, locations close to unsolved Other activity, and known associates. This opened another avenue: his family. While it had not been proven that genetics could influence the development of abilities, the existence of the Starr siblings validated its possibility as a factor, and a similar connection might be made to Moise. Finally, he applied for permission to place the target under twenty-four-hour surveillance; it was a long shot and a request that he expected to be denied due to a lack of both staff and evidence, but he couldn't devise any other plan of action. If these inquiries also returned negative results, then he had followed the peculiar lead to its end, and he would have to be satisfied that he'd done all he could.

- - -

Jack Everest relaxed in an armchair in his modern flat. He did not approve of contemporary amenities with their unnecessary plushness, believing that they nurtured softer citizens than in his time, but he understood the value of appearances and had hired a talented interior designer to create a tolerable living space that would impress his professional colleagues. At least the decorator had good taste in tumblers and stemware, the latter of which he was currently using to drink cognac as he reflected on what he had learned from his experiment.

He had witnessed with his own eyes the death and resurrection of his grandson, Orion Starr, and it had been confirmed by a medical professional that the boy had returned in completely good health. It had been a peaceful death, as he'd slipped quickly into unconsciousness, and he wondered if the boy had experienced pain upon the moment of his passing. In his younger years, Jack had nearly expired from starvation, and each moment had been filled with a gnawing in his stomach until his appetite had finally been sated. He still experienced aches and stings whenever he was harmed, so it could not have been different for his grandson when he'd passed.

However, pain was an obstacle that could be surmounted with enough determination. Jack's reluctance to fight stemmed from a fear of death, not injury, so he'd only ever engaged the enemies whom he knew he could overpower. Absorbing Orion's ability would bring something new to the table—a certainty that he could not be defeated. True, he could still fall, but now it was only a matter of time before he'd resuscitate to reassess and redirect his plan of attack. He would be emboldened—no longer held back by the final restraint.

Yet, there was still reason to stay in the shadows. An immortal could still be entombed or otherwise incapacitated, which meant the BSI and its sister organizations remained a threat and he needed to circumvent them wherever possible. He also did not yet know whether he needed to continue to hunt his fellow Others for sustenance; if he were lucky, Orion's ability meant he would only need to consume Others as an occasional delicacy. Regardless, he needed to elude Operation Blackout's attention by maintaining a shroud of secrecy, albeit one that did not need to be as carefully constructed.

Of course, his newfound immortality hinged on the procurement of his grandson. Without him in hand, all of his plans were placing the cart before the horse, so he needed to focus on Orion. The boy was under the watchful eye of the BSI, but it did not have a firm grasp on him; Connor was only a leash, and like all humans, he was fallible. With the proper motivation, Orion could slip his collar and disappear long enough for Jack to acquire him. All he needed to do was manipulate his grandson's other leash, and he would come straight to Jack.

- - -

The flat, featureless road stretched out before Orion, seemingly elongated by his anxiety. The radio, which was tuned to some talk show, played softly in the background, and though it created the illusion of company, he was still alone with his thoughts, which were far louder than any background voice. Cassie had not been returning his calls since she'd gone to live with the Vickers, and while he'd tolerated it in an effort to give her time to settle into her new life, he wondered if it had been the correct decision after all. Charlene Vicker was aware of his sister's "uniqueness," so when she'd called about a suspected arson, she'd immediately reassured him that Cassie hadn't been responsible to ease his mind. However, the Vickers were unfamiliar with how often his sister lied; she was not very good, as he'd learned to distinguish her "tell"—a term that Connor had taught him—but that didn't stop her from nevertheless attempting it, and the Vickers weren't as experienced as he was when it came to dealing with her.

Arson. Cassie and a handful of her new friends had been arrested by the police, processed, and held long enough to frighten them and instill a lesson about breaking the law. Thankfully, none of it would go on an official record, as the damage had been done to an abandoned property in the woods, and Timothy Vicker—who had, mercifully, been one of the arresting officers—had personally persuaded the owner not to press charges. Nevertheless, it was a dangerous game that Cassie had played, one that she could have lost easily if the Vickers had contacted the BSI instead of him. Connor's earlier remark had cut deeply: If it had been determined that she'd violated the terms of her parole, she would be euthanized. Orion wanted nothing but to flee with Cassie and go into hiding, but Connor had cautioned him against what he'd called a foolish action. Moreover, despite the current friction between the two men, the agent had released him on his own recognizance, and inexplicably, Orion didn't want to disappoint him. When his business with his sister was complete, Orion knew that he would return to New York and his training.

By the end of the four-hour trip, Orion's nerves were frayed, and yet he had formulated nothing wise or even suitably reproachful to say to his sister. He parked the rental car in the driveway, exchanged polite but clipped greetings with the Vickers, and headed back to Cassie's room, where she was to be restricted for an undetermined amount of time. The grounding might have meant something to her back in the city, but here in Waynesboro, it might not have made a difference.

Cassie was seated at the foot of her bed, staring sullenly at her smartphone; while Orion would have confiscated it, the Vickers felt that they should not restrict her access to her brother, even if she never contacted him. His eyes drifted upward, scanning the walls, which were clad with posters of classic punk bands that she had never heard and would never listen to, including the Ramones and the Sex Pistols. These had been placed alongside posters of more recent bands, movies, and sentiments with which he was unfamiliar, and he noticed a distinct hostility to the bedroom's décor, in contrast to the welcoming vibrance of her room at home. She'd never invited him into her room, but at least he hadn't felt like an invader there.

He was also surprised by the change in his sister's appearance, and though the Vickers had forewarned him, it hadn't been adequate preparation. He'd been so used to her long locks and expensive wardrobe that seeing her dark transformation was like walking in on a stranger. It wasn't that the new hairstyle, makeup, or even the overly theatrical attire bothered him, though he didn't necessarily approve of it; rather, he was disturbed that the drastic makeover had occurred at all. Since becoming a teenager, his sister had been obsessed with fashion and had taken vindictive pleasure in adopting new styles before her peers; in contrast, this girl didn't seem like she'd be concerned about trends other than to challenge or contradict them. What had happened to his sister?

Steeling himself for the conversation ahead, he walked across the room and sat on the bed next to her. Without missing a beat, she stood and repositioned herself several inches away from him without diverting her attention from her phone. He suppressed his urge to sigh in exasperation, instead reaching inside himself for a stern voice and asking, "Cassie, what happened?"

Though she was turned mostly away from him, she shifted again so her back was to him while somehow managing to keep her phone screen covered. Her fingers had remained still since he'd entered the room, so he didn't believe that she'd been texting. He wondered how many of her New York friends she'd retained after the identities of the Bramble Butchers had been released; he'd have to ask her about it once communication was reestablished between the two of them. Since she wasn't texting, she might have been reading, and he wondered what the subject might be; between her arrest and her new uncouth style, he fretted that she might be browsing more iconoclastic literature, which would only exacerbate her obstinate attitude toward him.

"Tell me what happened with the fire," he demanded, his voice bolstered by his recent experience in cross-examination; at least his compulsory position with the agency was being put to some good use.

"Why should I?" she grumbled, sinking further into her smartphone. "Charlie and Tim already did."

"I want to hear your side of it," he replied, using the same reasonable, soothing voice that Connor had taught him how to cultivate during the Scotts Ridge case. She made a deep noise—almost a dismissive growl—that came from her throat, and then she shifted again, propping herself up against the headboard while apparently texting. He tried to stare her down—another technique he'd learned—but he was thwarted by the lack of eye contact, and he folded. "Please, Cassie," he insisted. "Help me understand what happened."

Reluctantly, she looked up from her phone, and yielding to the idea that she wouldn't be rid of him until she answered his question, she sighed heavily and rolled her eyes. "Fine," she agreed petulantly. She sat up, pulling her ripped-stocking-clad knees closer to her chest, and tossed her phone onto the pillow beside her. "Whenever we ditch, we go out to this shack by Route 316," she explained. Orion scowled reflexively, but he knew that she'd been prone to skipping classes; she'd just been smarter about it in the past. "Tyler and Felix decided they wanted a smoke, and one of those idiots dropped the lighter, trying to be cool." She then injected all of her annoyance into her final statement, spitting, "That's it."

"Why didn't you try to stop it?"

"Why would I?" she scoffed, glowering at him with her arms crossed. "You already think I started the fire, and I'm not stupid enough to run into a burning building." Although Orion had meant extinguishing the fire with her ability, he could see the caution behind her lack of action. Despite having worked alongside an agent, he didn't know how the BSI detected or tracked Others, so he agreed that it had been prudent of her not to use her ability in a situation in which her involvement might be questioned. He stood up and went to her side, pulling her into a tight embrace. He'd assumed that she'd lied about the event and had perhaps even started the fire out of juvenile spite, and he was grateful to be wrong. He shouldn't have doubted her, as she was often more intelligent and responsible than her peers, a few incidents notwithstanding, but weeks of one-sided communication efforts had disheartened him and warped his perspective of his sister.

"Get off me!" Cassie suddenly pried his arms loose and shoved him away from her, shattering his enjoyment of the reunion. He was surprised by the vehemence in her voice; her anger seemed so deeply rooted that he knew that it was not related to her being scolded or grounded. "Cass, what's wrong with you?" he asked, failing to disguise the hurt he felt. His sister simply crossed her arms and pointedly kept her attention focused away from him, but she didn't answer. Hastily recovering from his shock, he resumed his stern approach and said warningly, "Cassiopeia."

She leaned away from him, ostensibly regretting the failure to move earlier, and gave him a sideways glance of ire. "First, my name is 'Cassidy,'" she snapped. When she'd been placed with the Vickers, he'd also had her name legally changed to Cassidy Green to further elude media attention. The agency had initially suggested the surname Evans, after their mother's maiden name, but Orion couldn't stomach the idea and instead chose Green after one of his sister's favorite authors.

"I thought you might like it," he mumbled defensively.

"I hate my name, Ryan! It's dorkier than yours."

"I'm sorry," he apologized. He'd never been bothered by the uniqueness of his name, and the derivative "Ryan" was in common usage. Conversely, he thought that the astral connotation of his sister's name was less apparent, with some people only recognizing the constellation's Greek progenitor; he also believed her fortunate not to have been called Andromeda, Virgo, or a more conspicuous name that couldn't be disguised by an innocuous diminutive.

"It's close enough that I thought it'd make transitioning easier," he explained. His rationalization didn't seem to satiate his sister's wrath, and she continued to glare at him, unmistakably trying to place some distance between them without actually moving. While he wasn't offended, her posture was bordering on ridiculous, especially as she tried to keep her balance. He suppressed an urge to smile as he turned toward her. "What else?" he encouraged.

Her scowl deepened as she threw her arms into the air melodramatically. When he failed to understand her gesture, she motioned toward the front of the house, and with a finality born of exasperation, she clarified, "Charlie and Tim."

"You don't like them?" he asked, frowning. Though she'd expressed nothing but contempt for her new guardians, he'd assumed that the antagonism would pass once she'd settled into her new and infinitely more stable life. He'd interviewed the couple, who shared his outlook and values, and he'd left the meeting with the impression that she'd experience the normalcy that she'd desperately craved for so many years. If he'd miscalculated and she actually disliked the Vickers, then he wouldn't hesitate to relocate her to another household, but if that were the case, he wished that she would have communicated it sooner, as her transition was meant to be as smooth as possible.

"That's not the point!" she retorted.

She clenched her jaw and tightened her lips, but no hostility was redirected at the Vickers; instead, it remained on him in the form of her physically trying to leave the conversation. She scooted across the width of the bed, snagging her phone along the way, and then went to stand in a corner, turning her back to him. He gave her a moment to continue before he rose as well. "Then what is it?" he asked, stopping several inches away from her to give her space. She pretended not to hear him, burying her head inside her phone again, and he stretched out the moment, staring at her expectantly. She turned even further away, still facing the corner, but she glanced furtively toward him and eventually relented under the pressure of his silent gaze.

She continued to face away from him as she slowly unwrapped her arms from around herself. "I didn't care about Mom and Dad's deaths, but as soon as it happened, you dropped me off with a pair of strangers," she admitted quietly, shivering as she released her pent-up emotions. "That wasn't supposed to happen. It's been you and me against the world for as long as I can remember." Her fists tightened as her eyes began to water, and she tried and failed to reclaim her composure. "I knew things weren't going to be the same after they died, but I didn't think you'd abandon me, too."

Orion's heart sank, and his face burned as he berated himself for failing to foresee her reaction. While he'd stopped seeing his parents on a regular basis at age ten, his sister's memory of them at her age was murkier; as far as she was concerned, they'd never been around for any extended period. He immediately closed the distance between them and wrapped his arms around her, pulling her into an affectionate embrace that she didn't resist. "I'm so sorry, Pickle," he apologized, stroking her feathered hair gently before kissing the top of her head. "I was trying to do what was best for you. I didn't know how long the media circus would last, and I didn't want you to experience that," he explained as he began to cry, too. "We've never been normal, even though you've tried so very hard, so I wanted to give that to you by sending you to the Vickers."

He squeezed her tighter, cradling her face in his shoulder, and he kissed her again. "I love you, Cass, and I didn't mean to hurt you. I just wanted you to be safe." His voice broke as his mind returned to their apartment, where their father had attacked them, and to its reenactment at Primrose. He'd spent the majority of his life watching over her, attempting to shield her from harm, but twice in the last few months, he'd failed at that duty, and though the latter incident had been only a vision, its disturbing impact on his psyche was significant enough to still count. Perhaps it had been the best choice to place his sister with the Vickers in spite of the emotional damage it had caused her.

Heedless of his reproachful internal reflection, the outside conversation continued. "I can take care of myself, asshole," she murmured, but now there was no venom in the sentiment.

He smiled into her hair, injecting appeasement into his tone. "I know, Cass," he lied. Though he knew that she could handle herself against a bullying peer, the incident with the mugger had proven that she was still a child in spite of any façade, and he would be remiss as a brother if he had not tried to protect her.

He held her closer for a moment before taking a step back to look her in the eye. Her tears had streaked her eyeliner, undoubtedly also staining his shirt, and she met his gaze expectantly despite her red and puffy eyes. "Look, this wasn't meant to be a permanent solution," he began. "When I'm done with training, I promise I'll try my best to set it up so you can join me, but you have to promise me you'll behave." Sternly, he added his conditions, "That means you'll have to actually do well in school and obey a curfew and come home at night."

"You're gonna kill my social life," she complained, but the faint twinkle of a smile in her eyes suggested that she was secretly pleased. A new arrangement would suit him as well: The apartment was cavernous without her, so she'd bring some life back into it, and he would especially need the company if they moved to a new place.

Gradually, he released her from the hug, and they parted, moving separately toward her bed. Though she took a seat, he chose to remain standing in an effort to maintain the momentum of his confidence, but he still faltered and dropped his gaze to his feet. "Hey, Pickle, there's something I've been meaning to ask," he announced hesitantly, massaging the back of his neck. He noted that his hair felt greasy, which meant it would become even more unruly if he didn't wash it soon, but he dismissed this line of thought as a distraction; he knew that he didn't want to continue and was finding a reason to avoid the topic. "I've got Mom and Dad's ashes, but I haven't done anything with them yet. I was wondering if you wanted to get rid of them with me." While he'd received his parents' remains almost immediately after they'd been cremated, he'd placed the box that contained their ashes on a high shelf in the closet because he'd been ambivalent about their passing. Though they had given him life and provided for him, it had been up to him to raise himself and his sister, and his parents' crimes had guaranteed that there would be no public ceremony to give him closure. He'd delayed granting them their valediction, as he imagined his sister had also done, until he could better articulate the emotions he felt at their passing, and while he understood them no better, he believed that it was closer to the appropriate moment to address the situation.

"Maybe even tonight," he suggested. The locale he had in mind for their final resting place was back in the city, which meant he'd be commuting for the majority of the day, but it would be worth it to finally be liberated from their parents' shadow. Besides, his sister would be present with him for a portion of it, allowing them to catch up on the time they'd spent separated.

Cassie gave him a dubious look, crossing her arms as she repeated suspiciously, "Get rid of them?"

"It's exactly what it sounds like," he assured her. "Dispose of the ashes. No ceremony. No catch. Just the two of us."

He could see the conflict in her face. He'd never spoken directly to her about their parents, save for his occasional reminder that he and Cassie were their offspring and should, therefore, respect them. Based on her behavior and the derogative terms she used to describe them, he'd drawn the conclusion that she disliked them, but though she'd never expressed any fondness for them, she'd regularly withheld affection from him as well. He could only assume that she felt no real attachment to them—seeing them as strangers who visited on weekends and holidays—but she appeared to feel as ambivalent as he did. She must have come to a conclusion, for she slowly began to smile. "I think I might be okay with that."

- - -

Little Italy was a shell of the historical neighborhood it had once been. Formerly an insular village, it was now a tourist destination peopled by vacationers who wanted to touch living history during their breaks between visiting New York City's larger attractions. It was also the terminus for citizens who couldn't afford the higher rent of SoHo, which was why Morgan Connor's studio apartment was located off Mulberry Street. Since Orion Starr's training was to take place in familiar territory, headquarters had determined that it was more fiscally sound to lease a fully furnished, extended-stay residence than to continue renting a single hotel room nearby. Upon entering the apartment, the first thing that Johnson noticed was that although Connor had lived there for months, there were barely any signs of habitation, let alone any attempt at adding a personal touch.

Initially, Antithesis flanked the door, taking a position against the wall before settling uneasily into one of the chairs. Johnson scanned the room and scowled. "Where's Starr?" he asked.

"Don't worry about it. He's on an errand," Connor assured him, urging him into a seat as well. "What have you got?"

Chomping on a toothpick, Johnson gave him a sideways glance before he sat down on the pristine couch and pulled out his phone. Connor would receive the data via email shortly as well, if he hadn't already, and Johnson had been tasked with explaining the information, so he began without delay. "I've got some bad news. There wasn't much time to research between last night and now, but nothing they found was encouraging." A preliminary inquiry into Moise Kabamba's background had traced his origins back to a village near Dekese, so analysts had searched the archives in the hopes that their Zairian counterpart's data had been saved. While the records had been copied prior to the nation's dissolution, they had proven to be of little use. Zaire under Mobutu had bred corruption, and even those charged with keeping Blackout had not been immune. There had been plenty of references to *enfants sorciers*— child witches who had been accused of causing droughts, famines, and the like whenever a village had suffered—and unfortunately, the allegations had become so common that the majority of the *enfants sorciers* had simply been unlucky children used as scapegoats, and not actually Others.

The Zairian files had been so unreliable that they still had not been transferred to the electronic database; instead, they had been kept by hand, and two references could be found. The first was to a Kabamba who was a deserter or escapee from Mobutu's army and who may or may not have been related to the target. The second related to an incident that had occurred in Moise's tiny village. The first was still being retrieved, his record having been misfiled or lost, while the second referred to the sudden petrification of a decades-old Okoumé tree. A major panic had been avoided by the immediate declaration of an *enfant sorcier*, an eight-year-old boy who had subsequently been exorcised. Unlike the traditional Catholic rite, the child had been starved and beaten in an attempt to secure a confession of witchcraft, and during the third week of this abuse, the child had died. If Moise Kabamba had lived in the village during this time, it was understandable why he'd fled, but his presence alone proved nothing. The Okoumé, which had transformed overnight from a living tree into a twisted stone chimera, had been burnt on the same cremation pyre as the boy, so no hard evidence of the event had remained.

"That's it then," Connor nevertheless insisted, indicating the passage regarding the tree.

"How? It doesn't prove a thing," Johnson replied sternly; it was a coincidence at best, even assuming that the account was accurate.

"It proves enough to bring him in for questioning, doesn't it?"

Johnson shook his head. "It's a tenuous lead," he reasoned begrudgingly; it would be difficult to plausibly follow Connor's instinct based on the information at hand. "Do you even know what his ability is?"

Connor scowled, drawing his lips into a thin line as he looked away, and Johnson was inwardly disappointed. How could Connor not realize that he had an extraordinary ability? Connor been with the agency for three years, and his rate of identifying and capturing Others hovered around twice that of normal agents. No one else was that skilled, even if they were well trained in detective techniques, and while Johnson wasn't aware of what sort of mechanism Connor used to perceive Others, he certainly should have noticed a difference between himself and regular people.

Johnson sighed. "So, what's the next step?" he asked, looking toward Connor. Even if he weren't here under the pretext of a favor, Johnson didn't know how to proceed; investigation was a part of Connor's skill set, not his.

Connor rose from his seat beside Johnson and started pacing, ostensibly to get his blood flowing. He muttered to himself, counting off ideas on his fingers and recounting aspects of the case that he'd witnessed or researched, and then he suddenly halted. His eye twitched and then closed, and he immediately pressed his palm against the offending orifice. After a sufficient pause, he appeared to shake it off and seemed ready to soldier on. He then resumed his thoughtful pacing. "I don't know," he admitted. Then another jolt of pain struck him mid-step, and he stumbled.

Johnson leapt from the couch to catch him before he fell on the table or otherwise hurt himself. "What's wrong?" he asked with concern. The other man stiffened, despite leaning hard against him, and Johnson lowered him onto the cushions.

Connor seemed dazed, and his eyes rolled backward, but he managed to answer after a moment. "I've just got this seething headache," he hissed, cradling his head even more gingerly than if he'd had a hangover. "It's like… It's like I've got a fire in my brain."

Johnson instantly recognized the indicators of a reaction to Antithesis' suppressive field, and he realized that he needed to separate the two of them. Although he needed Connor to finish his investigation, it was also important to ensure that Connor didn't perceive the fog that she created over his ability; prolonged exposure should, therefore, be avoided. "Why don't you lie down for a bit?" he suggested, improvising. "Antithesis and I will head back to our hotel, and you can give us a call when you feel better."

His instrument—though he supposed that he should technically refer to her as his partner—stopped tapping her fingers like a cat irritably flicking its tail. While she wasn't heartless, she was impatient and single-minded while in pursuit mode. "What? Why?" she demanded impatiently. "Just because of a headache?"

It occurred to Johnson that Connor shouldn't experience such an intense reaction to her field. His ability was to *sense* Others, so if anything, he should have felt only a blanket over that mechanism; only Others who attempted to use their abilities while Antithesis was nearby tended to suffer. However, Johnson didn't have the luxury of time to consider the implications, as it was still his duty to conceal the truth from Connor, which, at the moment, meant swift departure. "We have no evidence that our target is an Other," he told her. "We must wait until we're reasonably certain before we can apprehend him."

"We drove two hours! How is that not reasonable certainty?" she exclaimed, crossing her arms petulantly as she locked her jaw and glared at him.

Johnson mused that the tension of the situation would be assuaged if Connor weren't inexplicably susceptible to her suppression field. He wondered what difference the current circumstances had made; he'd performed custody transfers with Connor present in the past—most recently with Nihar Shah—and Connor hadn't experienced an adverse response to her company. He released his grip on Connor, whose distress seemed to have eased, and faced her with a stern scowl. "What's our job?" he asked, casually removing the toothpick from his mouth.

She met his eyes, staring back at him defiantly, before she broke contact and looked away. "Apprehension and escort," she recited obediently.

"What's his job?" he continued, his hands confidently on his hips.

"Investigation," she mumbled.

"So… ?"

She huffed, uncrossing her arms and throwing her fists to her side. "If he doesn't have evidence, then we can't move," she admitted, pouting. The young woman tensed her body, stomped twice, and then relaxed, her frustration ebbing away. Her Plum Island caretakers wanted to encourage her to express herself, more specifically through articulation and extended dialog, but Johnson found that he could wait out or dismiss her tantrums if he didn't acknowledge them. Regardless, it would do her a lot of good if he placed her on Moise's trail as soon as possible so that she could disperse her excess energy.

He smiled at Connor, who'd turned over onto his back on the couch. "We'll see you in a couple hours, Connor," he promised, the dispute now settled with his charge. "We'll do a bit of digging ourselves. Maybe we'll find something you missed, or maybe we'll be lucky and they'll find something in the archives." The other man, who was only partially listening, nodded and gave him a dismissive wave as he pressed his hand over his eyes and settled into a comfortable position on the couch. Johnson nodded toward the door, and Antithesis followed; even if their excursion didn't uncover anything, she'd be occupied for a few hours until Connor could recover.

- - -

When Moise had moved to Brooklyn, it had still been a popular spot for artists in residence, and this had undoubtedly helped him establish himself in his community. It had also allowed him to meet his first patron, who had assisted with bringing his talents into the spotlight, and the diverse community had also assuaged any vestigial homesickness he may have felt. However, a decade's worth of growth and conscientious rezoning had altered the borough's landscape, increasing its worth to private business investors, and the subsequent increase in rent and living costs made many residents consider relocation. Moise was not among them, and he instead used his wealth to purchase neighboring vacant apartments to convert them into one unit.

Moise met Amanda at the door, greeting her with compliments and kisses on her cheeks, and then escorted her to the table, where he graciously seated her and poured some wine. She was impressed by the setup; she had never been in a residence smaller than five thousand square feet, and Moise's significantly smaller condominium seemed cozy rather than claustrophobic. His home was simple: It was lightly decorated in a way that suggested creative intent over meager funding, and the furnishings had a subtle Mediterranean motif that was indicative of an interior decorator's guiding hand. Acanthus leaves adorned the crown molding, and a mosaic in the foyer hinted at a classic Greece style. While there were several raised stone designs, including a few sculptures, none of his designs were on display as they were at Félicité; perhaps even an artist could tire of viewing his own work.

He had a lavish table set in anticipation of her arrival. He'd selected a Schweitzer tablecloth and Waterford dishes, and battery-powered candles faintly illuminated the table, where a bottle of Domaine de la Romanée-Conti and two glasses sat. The wine selection itself offset any unfavorable impressions about the size of his dwelling.

Moise himself was casually dressed in a honey-colored button-down shirt, which emphasized the light specks in his eyes, and he'd generously applied Clive Christian cologne. Explaining that dinner would be several more minutes, he offered her a plate of olives, cheese, and crackers, but she politely declined the hors d'oeuvre in deference to her slim figure. Only then did he take a seat across from her.

"Dinner smells lovely," she commented, initiating conversation. She had been raised to believe that etiquette dictated that the host should encourage and guide discussion with the guest. However, she'd also maintained her decorum when courting potential donors and benefactors, and as a politician, the use of such skills had become a natural habit. A large part of her profession entailed being likable, and involving others in her conversations contributed significantly to this goal, even if she didn't personally concern herself with their responses. With Moise, she was courting him as a prospective sponsor, while he was potentially courting her as a future partner, and smooth dialogue facilitated both of their goals. "Do you cook often?"

"It is an acquired skill," he replied, lapsing into nostalgia. "My aunt loved to cook, but she did not really enjoy my assistance." His surrogate parents had been hard workers, and both had held difficult jobs that had kept them employed for long hours. His aunt had found relaxation in preparing familiar Zairian cuisine—when she had been able to find the appropriate ingredients on the market—and in learning new dishes, especially region-specific fare from their adopted home. Moise had wanted to assist her, as any child desires to please their maternal figure, but he had often proved to be more of a hindrance, burning dishes or adding too much flavoring. However, her patient tutelage had borne fruit over time, and he'd developed excellent skills, which had been honed while he'd tried to survive his early hardship in the city. "Now I can afford a personal chef, and she does not like my interference either," he explained, beaming in amusement, "but I do make an occasional exception and cook for myself."

She returned his smile and replied coyly, "If you cook as well as you speak, I may also make an occasional exception and forgo my personal chef." He chuckled, his booming voice echoing off the walls, and his delight spiked momentarily, prompting her to read his emotional state. It was duplicitous to do so, especially on a date, but as a politician, she did it so often that she didn't think twice before reading him. His excitement was elevated and intense, surging like an incoming tide, and like his eagerness at breakfast, it was tinged with something else—desire or perhaps even arousal—that she could not positively differentiate. She not only felt flattered, but her confidence also increased; his state meant that she would have the upper hand in negotiations—if that had been the reason they had come together.

Instead of exploiting his obvious interest, she was judicious and diverted the conversation away from flirtation; it was better to maintain her class and an air of mystery than to act unmistakably coquettish. "Since we have a few minutes, why don't you show me this statue?" she suggested.

He gave a tight-lipped smile that had a touch of mischief. "She is a mystery, Amanda, and I do not want to ruin her surprise too early in the evening," he answered secretively. "Like any beautiful woman, she will shed her mystique when the time is right."

She thought that his response had been phrased oddly, but he had proven to be a bit of an eccentric. She observed amusedly, "You like to speak in riddles."

His grin grew wider, lighting up his eyes. "I'm afraid it is one of the burdens of being an artist: We are only straightforward when we speak about price, if we care for money at all," he replied facetiously, and she laughed in spite of herself, her own smile growing to match his. He reached across the table and, tenderly caressing her hand, continued, "I promise the wait will be worth it. Allow me to savor the time leading up to the moment."

She acquiesced as he poured more wine into her glass, and she found herself relaxing into his gentle banter. They skipped the traditional talk of the weather and traffic and eschewed discussion of their respective jobs. Instead,

Moise guided their conversation toward minor anecdotes about the city and their lives. Gradually, they transitioned into tales of their childhood, and she discovered that he had been raised further north than she had assumed in the proud city of Boston. Even though he hadn't acquired its distinctive accent, the Olde Towne had imparted to him a love of classical music, live concerts, and reading, the latter of which had helped him master the English language. In turn, she shared stories of her upbringing and her mother's narrow, antiquated view of a woman's place in the world. She had been an obedient child and a shockingly dutiful teenager—a mind-set that hadn't actually changed until she'd discovered her abilities—but that hadn't precluded her from having rebellious periods in her youth, even if they'd been relatively minor offenses. After she had grown sufficiently comfortable—and perhaps even a bit tipsy— she recounted the time she'd switched places with Barbara Flanders on a school trip to New Haven, as Barbara hadn't wanted to go to see the then-President Bill Clinton. Amanda had slipped away from the tour to support her friend at his first music venue. Although neither the band nor the relationship had lasted, she had experienced an enjoyable and memorable afternoon.

Moise had a way of placing her at ease and persuading her to open up, and during the meal, she'd spoken more freely than she'd meant to. Even if a romantic relationship was off the table, the wine was beginning to make her believe that a true friendship was possible. "I think it might finally be time to introduce my beauty," he announced during a natural lull in the conversation, and she grinned; it was charming that he kept referring to his statue as a woman. To her, it indicated an appreciation not only for the work but also for the artistic process itself.

"My dear Amanda," he continued, standing as he took her gently by the hand and drew circles in her palm. "I am afraid you are quite underdressed for this occasion," he informed her regretfully. "I have a more suitable gown available, if you would be so kind as to change into it," he added as if it were a gracious offer.

Although his tone had been polite, if a bit overdramatic, the absurdity of the situation cut into her intoxication and dredged common sense back to the surface of her thoughts. She was wearing a custom-made Ralph Lauren coatdress, and while it was considered a bit old-fashioned for the modern day, the style suited her, and it was by no means inappropriate for this informal event. She noted his hand, which had migrated to her upper arm and was poised to firmly guide her away from the dining table, and she scrutinized his emotions. Lust or desire—she wished now that she'd learned to better differentiate between the two—colored his excitement, whose level had not been abated by alcohol consumption, and she wondered whether he'd tricked her into drinking while he'd abstained. Her adrenaline increased, nearly sobering her completely, and in spite of it, she remained calm and diplomatic. "I must decline, Moise," she replied, lowering the warmth in her voice to a more neutral tone. "I don't think it's in my best interest."

His large hand twitched, as if he might have used his strong grip to compel her movement, but he released her instead and stomped over to the butcher block, where he seized a chef's knife. "I'm afraid I must insist," he said. Despite his actions, his voice was strangely reasonable as if the night hadn't taken a sharp turn. "It will only be for a little while, and I believe you'll find the gown suitable and to your liking."

If he expected her to cower or yield, she would happily disappoint him. She was constantly protected from threats as a precautionary measure necessitated by her august position, and even without the mayoralty, she would still have chosen to be accompanied by a bodyguard, but this didn't mean that she was entirely helpless. While she sometimes lacked the subtleties of exactitude, a sledgehammer did not need to be precise to perform its job, and she released a fear-producing pheromone that flooded the area near her. Instantly, Moise dropped the knife and took the quickest path away from her, which led into a corner created by one of his leaded-glass countertops and the terrazzo wall. Panicking, he briefly attempted to scramble up the barrier before he settled into an alert crouch and watched her warily with large, saucer-sized eyes.

With the situation now in her favor, she leaned against her chair and considered her situation. She must have lapsed into shock, for the first thing that came to mind was damage control. Moise Kabamba had been the recipient of her favor, and she'd even consented to a private meeting with him; she didn't think her presence at his residence would precipitate a scandal, but her first phone call should be to her public affairs aide. The police also needed to be notified; he'd attempted an assault, even if she couldn't characterize his full intent.

What would she tell the police? Jack Everest had assured her that she was not alone in her abilities, but their existence was not public knowledge. A scandal would undoubtedly unfold if she disclosed that she had the ability to manipulate others with chemical signals from her glands, even if their use had been in self-defense. She'd visited Moise unaccompanied by her customary detail, and her diminutive, fragile physique begged the question of how she'd overpowered a man who was more than twice her size.

She'd have to render him unconscious, improvise, and then hope that her account was convincing enough not to elicit a second look by the authorities. She crossed her arms as she studied his cowering form; the whole night had been a pretext—though for what, she didn't allow herself to consider—and because he'd manipulated her emotions, awakening her girlish wistfulness, she would exact recompense. With a thought, her glands ceased secreting fear and instead produced a paralyzing allomone. As the new chemical wafted through the air and surrounded him, Moise stiffened, and his breath intensified as his body tried to resist the toxin, but he ultimately succumbed, collapsing onto his side in the fetal position. Aware that it was now safe to approach him, she grasped the empty bottle of Domaine de la Romanée-Conti firmly in her hand and smashed it against his head; the bottle shattered, but he remained cognizant, distraught, and in pain.

She searched the kitchen and, seeing the unwashed frying pan, seized it as well and struck him across the temple. This time, the blow produced the intended effect, and he lost consciousness as his blood began to spread across the laminate floor. Despite inflicting a grievous wound, she still felt spiteful and kicked him squarely in the stomach. Her husband, Johnathan, had often selected her outfits, also insisting that she had been unsuitably dressed for an occasion, and he had once controlled her every move and thought, having inherited the role from her overbearing mother. Amanda wouldn't tolerate a successor now that she'd thrown off their yokes.

Her petty indignation sated, she phoned the police and mentally began to construct her story as her pheromones dissipated.

- - -

Aaron's eyes were unblinking as he lowered the tiny piece closer to the main body of the model. It was only a small detail, an antenna that some technician had glued on just before the original had gone on set, but it had looked good on camera, so it had become canon, and hobbyists like himself painstakingly replicated it. As he drew closer to the ship, his hand twitched, and the fragile wire snapped. He swore and seized the offending hand with his other to massage the palm; the tic hadn't been from mere carelessness and was appearing more frequently.

He stood, licking his lips and working his tongue to stimulate saliva for his dry mouth, and he decided that it was time for a break. He paced the moderate length of the room, now made smaller by his tools and scattered modeling supplies, and thought to sit on one of the many beds. Three of them were reserved for patients and one for the doctor, but the remaining handful of cots were stacked against the wall and ready to be pressed into service when needed. He decided instead that he'd made enough of a mess of the supposed clinic, and he began tidying, starting with the corner nearest the door. He straightened the folding chair, stowed the odd belonging he'd acquired, and tried to figure out how to actually clean up without ruining whatever chaotic storage system was already in place. There were a lot of medical supplies, primarily cotton and gauze, but without enough cabinets, they were stacked in boxes against the wall or beneath standing beds, and they were kept separate from his table and a second one. The latter table was covered with opened medical supplies of various sorts, such as vial racks and a centrifuge, and while it had decidedly been set up for research, it had fallen into disuse.

The door opened, and Sam entered with a tray of food. She greeted him with a warm smile and handed him the glass of water first before shutting the door and setting the tray down on another chair. "Thanks," he said. He downed it in one gulp and found himself looking for more; Sam, anticipating this, handed him another glass before unloading the tray to serve him.

He supposed he should be grateful that she was so thoughtful, but he took everything with a grain of salt. Ever since they had left Scotts Ridge, she had practically kept him prisoner, never allowing him to leave the room and never leaving him unattended for long. Then there was the matter that "Naught," as she told him she was now called, barely resembled the Sam who had left him in the middle of the night. She had the same blonde hair, thin frame, and impish wit, but her face had become weathered and was framed by several locks of white. Though it had been only a few years since they'd parted ways, she appeared to have aged at least ten. No matter how much Naught assured him that she wasn't a hallucination, he couldn't believe her.

She cleared one of the overbed tables for their use, transferred their plates, then set down two mismatched chairs, and invited him to join her. He obliged, and after he sat, he asked, "When can I go home?" She hesitated, avoiding his gaze, as she took the seat opposite him. He knew that she would because they had already had this conversation, but he had hoped that it might go differently this time. Yet that was the definition of insanity: doing the same thing over and over again and expecting different results.

"Of course," he said and huffed sharply. "I forgot. I can't."

"We've been over this, Aaron," she replied gently, chewing on her lower lip. "You can't go back to Scotts Ridge."

He nodded. Pinching his nose, he repeated her explanation wearily. "Because there are evil government agents who will kill me if they capture me."

"Aaron—"

"No, I get it," he continued, raising his head and looking her in the eye. "I've developed full-blown psychosis, just like Dr. Kowalczyk warned could happen." He twirled his finger, encompassing the modest area that served as her clinic, and then tucked his hands into his sides. "This, uh, is a new reality to compensate for my previous trauma. You're here because I had unresolved issues with you leaving." He scowled, thinking of the damp smell, the cramped space of his cot, and the slight chill in the air. "Could have better accommodations, though," he quipped. If he was going crazy, he might as well have a sense of humor about it.

Naught smiled faintly in spite of herself. "Aaron," she said, leaning forward and taking his hands within hers. "You wouldn't be cognizant of a shift if that's what happened. You're getting better. The medication is helping, it's just that..." She trailed off, trying to figure out how to best explain. He already knew what she would say, and she was still a better companion than the shadow children. She didn't follow him around silently to menace him at work; rather, she actively tried to improve his life and how he felt, even if she had altered his surroundings to this drab basement. "Reality has also changed," she continued tactfully, choosing her words precisely. This was the other reason he knew that Naught wasn't really Sam; the latter woman was never careful in speaking, even when she tried to be. "You've peeled back the surface of a conspiracy that's been going on for decades. It's going to take some adjustment."

"It feels more like paranoia," he disputed, "which is something else Dr. Kowalczyk warned me about."

Naught allowed her smile to escape and blossom affectionately. "Aaron, I'm real," she stressed and stood so she could kiss his forehead, which was supposed to certify her tangibility. She walked around the table so she could kneel by his side, and she laid her hands on him in gentle, reassuring caresses as she continued. "This is real, and trust me, you weren't able to make this kind of differentiation when you got here. The medication is helping, and I think you know that." She bit her lip as she continued, "You're just doubting yourself because it's been so long coming." She broke eye contact suddenly, looking at the floor and then resting her forehead on his arm.

While it was true that he'd felt more coherent since he'd arrived at her clinic, he couldn't take the sensation at face value. The shadow children felt real when he was enveloped in their anger, and he often struggled to remind himself that they were only a construct of his guilt and not the manifestation of the vengeful dead. He had to ground himself in facts—the things that he knew were true—but in this clinic, there was nothing familiar that could help him reestablish reality. Even Sam's existence was dubious because she had changed so much. "Then why haven't I seen anything outside these walls?"

She sighed deeply and met his eyes again. "We'll leave if you want to. Anytime," she promised. "But I am trying to protect you from the BSI and, if necessary, from SION, too, and we need to make sure you've recovered before you're exposed to any additional stress." She stood, cradling his head against her chest, and he leaned into her, listening to her heartbeat. "I just want to protect you, Aaron."

"Then let me leave, Sam," he entreated her quietly. "It's been a week. If I'm not crazy, I need to prove it to myself." He pulled away, first looking up into her lined face and then standing to give him equal footing. "I need to see Scotts Ridge," he declared resolutely. "I need to see Primrose. I need to see anything that's outside the reality you've given me if you want me to believe that this isn't another fantasy." His lips quirked as he added, "You know, independently verify?" She smiled faintly in response; she had once accused him of making the latter his catchphrase, even though he didn't recall using it often. By the time they'd met in Scotts Ridge, he was no longer a cop, but the habits he'd long developed had nevertheless persisted, and he'd often collected evidence from various sources when making a decision no matter how nominal it might be. Then his had condition worsened, he'd started to miss work when he'd chosen to self-medicate with alcohol, and his meticulousness had been one of the first casualties; it was difficult to verify anything when everything could be questioned.

Still, if Naught was willing to let him leave, and he was able to authenticate his apparent recovery, he had to give her the benefit of the doubt when it came to other things. Hesitantly, he added, "Especially if I'm to believe in this Other nonsense."

Her grin broadened. "There you go acting like a cop again," she said and pulled him into a tight embrace. "I love you, Aaron Grimm."

"I love you too, Sam," he said, holding her close. He could smell the lavender from her shampoo, as well as pungent chopped onions, likely from dinner, and the scent helped reassure him of her existence. He never recalled all senses being fooled by a hallucination, and he desperately hoped that she was real.

- - -

The severe headache confined Connor to the couch long enough for him to drift off, and the pain had subsided by the time he awoke. Its onset had been sudden: One moment he had been reviewing the details of the case to strategize his next move, and then the next he'd felt as if his synapses had been exploding. He had never experienced a headache of such intensity before, and he prayed he never would again. Fortunately, he was able to concentrate once more, so now it was time to get back on track and uncover the evidence that would have Moise escorted back to the holding facility.

Johnson implied that the petrification account was exaggerated, if not entirely fictitious, and that it should be dismissed from consideration. However, Connor was convinced that Moise was an Other, and a lead was still a lead no matter how unsound it appeared. He might be desperate at this point, but he could still be methodical about following the trail.

Presupposing the veracity of the event, the next assumption he made was that the accused *enfant sorcier* had been innocent, and this meant that the unidentified perpetrator had never been caught. This was confirmed by the absence of similar incidents in the area, and while it was possible for the Other to learn control, it was far more likely that he or she had simply left the village in response to the turmoil. Still operating on conjecture, Connor figured that if Moise were that missing Other, he could extrapolate his ability from the original record.

The tree had petrified, which meant living tissue had spontaneously circumvented a mineralization process that was millions of years long to become stone, and he didn't believe it was simply a case of mistaken identification; the report specified that a part of the very same tree was still green and struggled to remain alive. He thought back to Félicité and the displays of realist sculptures depicting various animals, from simple insects to more complex domestic creatures. He remembered *Ferocity* with its intricately carved fur whose strands could be individually recognized and how the stone's inherent bands of color were employed in such a manner that they resembled fur pigmentation. The animal's semi-flattened ears had been delicately shaped by a steady hand, shaved to the fragile slenderness of reality, and even portrayed inflamed veins whose pathways could be followed subcutaneously by gneissic lines. The work had even been praised for its lifelike appearance, so it was not a stretch to assume that Moise had the same skill that had petrified the tree, as both subjects were now stone. Perhaps Connor had erred in comparing the artist to Hephaestus; unlike the Greek deity, he did not create life from inanimate materials but rather stole it.

Unfortunately, Moise did not work in mineral mediums only, so it was possible that Connor was still chasing a misguided lead; the artist also worked woods, and Connor vividly remembered the detail of *Metamorphosis*. As with the feline statue, the insects appeared to have been captured in the middle of life—in this case, it was the emergence from their cocoons—and while the fine facets were masterfully shaped, it seemed to him that the paper-thin butterfly wings should have snapped rather than allowing themselves to be sheared into translucence.

While it was theoretically possible for Others to have multiple talents, it had yet to be recorded in the database; Moise being able to transmute living creatures into two different inanimate materials stretched this premise to impossibility when placed in the context of Connor's numerous other suppositions, so he was again left with no substantial evidence—only untenable conjecture.

His thoughts circled to Orion and how his instruction would proceed if he were present, and he was instead unexpectedly overwhelmed by an unbidden vision. The young man's face was distorted by agony, his teeth were bared like a cornered animal, and his skin was a brownish gray—not pallidly ashen like that of the ill—and was stretched across his bones by an unseen force. It was as if he were shrinking and the moisture was being siphoned from his body, aging it thousands of years in moments. He caught another flash: a young, blond man—similar enough in appearance to Orion to be mistaken for his father or another relative—with his diminutive hand wrapped firmly around someone's throat. His grip was clenched tight, obstructing the air pathways of his victim, and his handsome face was calm and impassive as a final death rattle was croaked.

Then Connor felt as if he'd slammed into a wall, yet the churning fluid in his inner ear convinced his body that he'd reemerged into freefall. He grasped the couch to reassure himself that he was stationary as his body reacquired its equilibrium. It had been an intense hallucination—powerful enough to immobilize him—and though he'd never experienced a seizure, he would still characterize the episode as such, especially due to the rocky transition back to reality. In spite of the disorienting nature of the vision, his primary concern remained for his partner, and he immediately retrieved his phone to dial Orion. The phone rang repeatedly and then proceeded to voicemail, but as he listened to the prerecorded message, Connor realized how foolish he was behaving; it had been a waking nightmare, nothing more, and any action he took based on it was irrational.

However, the vision served to reinforce the difficulty of the conundrum he faced: Orion Starr was a BSI asset, not a true partner, and Connor needed to remain detached from him lest his objectivity regarding Others become affected. He should not have let Orion leave on personal business; that had been a failure of accountability, which he would have recognized if he'd acted as his trainer instead of his friend.

As he acknowledged unhappily that he'd never reclaimed his objectivity with the Starrs, he also lamented the lack of alcohol in his accommodations; he was not in a hotel but an extended-stay residence, and if he wanted liquor, he had to procure it himself. Perhaps the addition of whiskey to the mix would allow him to clear his mind of his concern for the Starrs and focus instead on the case at hand; at the very least, a long walk might help him articulate the intangible reason he believed Moise Kabamba was an Other.

--- --- ---

The interrogation room was cold and bare, and the sickly light of the fluorescent bulbs lit every corner. Moise remained dignified, sitting squarely upright in the hard wooden chair while his lawyer sat across from him reviewing the charges. The room had a wall with a one-way mirror like in the movies, but no one was observing them to his knowledge; he was unable to secure true privacy to speak with his lawyer elsewhere, so they had been given this space. However, it would not surprise him if the police circumvented the confidentiality between his lawyer and himself, considering the former had recently dismissed the interrogator politely but firmly without allowing an interview. Evidently, the detective had not anticipated Moise's lawyer arriving so quickly, nor his prominence. While the incident with Amanda Darling-Whitcomb had eliminated his chances of being represented by Milton, Chadwick, and Waters—her primary backers—it hadn't precluded him from soliciting assistance from a rival firm.

His lawyer, Nelson Wright, removed his reading glasses with a long sigh.

"Your situation is dire, son," he drawled, giving him a stern, almost fatherly look. "I think it's best if you start from the beginning so I can piece together a defense."

"How can it be a 'dire' situation?" he asked curtly. Shock was setting in, washing away his former disbelief in the situation and replacing it with active denial. "That is why I hired you. This is a case of my word against that of a hysterical woman," he insisted. "She overreacted to a simple misunderstanding."

Nelson's nose wrinkled as his lips twisted into a frown. "Be that as it may," he said slowly, "that 'hysterical woman' happens to be the mayor, so her word carries more weight, especially in her territory." His words came slowly, and he tugged at his ear as if it generated speech for him. "You're a relative newcomer." Moise huffed; he'd moved to the city a little over ten years ago, predating any political aspirations by the former senator's wife. Nelson continued, "And there's a heavy political climate about this case that you just don't understand. That's why I need to know your story to build a counter-narrative."

Moise didn't regret choosing Amanda Darling-Whitcomb as his subject, but he reproached himself for his arrogance and inadequate planning; he should have used eloquence to persuade her to change into the gown instead of resorting to brute force when her intoxication had failed to immediately facilitate her cooperation. The disparity between his preferred timetable and the reality had been unfortunate: He simply hadn't been able to afford adequate preparation, especially not if he'd wanted the exhibit to be present at his opening, and he had been overcome by a passion for the project that had circumvented any caution. Even if he'd had infinite time and resources, his ideal process would not have sufficed; he could not have befriended the mayor and persuaded her over a long friendship to practice poses for the statue without eventually soliciting suspicion of some nature, particularly when she later disappeared without a trace. It had been better to strike quickly and decisively, as he already had, except he should have acted more prudently during his attempt to capture her essence.

Of course, he could not divulge the genuine story to his lawyer—aside from appearing fantastical, it would also admit his guilt, and he did not intend to be convicted—so he lied. He fabricated a sequence of events in which Amanda had propositioned him for sex, citing that she had helped fund his gallery's new wing, and he'd refused her. Although he knew that it thinly stretched his credibility—the mayor was a popular, attractive woman, and he was only a "newcomer," as Nelson had established—it was still within the realm of possibility. While she had not been publicly seen with a male suitor since her husband's death, she had occasionally attended closed meetings, and his had been the first during which she hadn't been accompanied by a bodyguard. His narrative generated enough doubt to be plausible. He asserted that the current fracas, from the assault in his apartment to the charges that had been pressed, was reprisal for his rejection of her.

Nelson nodded as he listened, taking notes in chicken scratch, and he furrowed his brow as he leaned back. "That's a hard angle to play, son, and she's likely to turn that around and say you propositioned her," he cautioned him. He twirled his reading glasses in his left hand, wiggling a loose temple tip. "The jury is more likely to believe that no matter the truth." He breathed deeply while shaking his head regretfully. "You got the short end of the stick here."

Moise snorted, wondering why he'd bothered to employ Wolfram and Murdock; they clearly weren't the rivals that Kevin Chadwick had proclaimed them to be if this man was the best they could provide him. "The woman must have drugged me," he declared. "How else do you explain a woman knocking out a man twice her size?" Thinking back to the moment, he could not remember anything except fear—no details, no inkling how it had gone wrong. "She assaulted me!"

His lawyer cradled his chin in his hand, tapped his cheek a few times, and leaned forward abruptly, jamming his glasses back onto his chubby face so he could take more notes. "When they took you to the hospital, did they draw any blood?" he asked, scribbling furiously; it appeared he was recording references to scrutinize later in greater detail. "Right, no hospital," he remembered. "We can still have them draw blood now since it's been less than twenty-four hours. See if we get a result that'll support your side of the story."

Moise had difficulty remembering the evening, believing for a moment that he might have gone to the hospital after all. Aside from the fear and unexpected unconsciousness, he had few solid memories; everything was a blur. He had been treated by the paramedics and dosed with some sort of pain reliever. He'd also been escorted to the back of a police cruiser instead of the hospital because the wounds hadn't been deemed too serious, despite the fact that he believed that he had a concussion, and he realized that he'd mistaken the sudden brightness of his overhead kitchen lights for those of the emergency room.

Nelson cleared his throat as he put down his pen and folded his hands in front of him. "Now, son, I'll try my best because I believe you're innocent, but the situation here is more complicated than just criminal proceedings," he declared gravely, scowling over his glasses. "As I said, she's got politics on her side, so she's desperate to make her narrative work because it gives her more public sympathy," he said, alluding not only to her original mayoral campaign but also to her rumored upcoming bid for the presidency.

"Now, if you lose on these charges..." He indicated the original list that the detective had surrendered before he'd left them alone, and though it was not a long list, all four charges were felonies. "... you'll be deported back to the Democratic Republic of the Congo." Nelson explained that even though Moise had never been a citizen of DRC—it had only come into existence after he'd lived in America for several years—he could still be deported there because it was Zaire's successor. Once convicted of a felony, Moise could never return to the United States, and it was likely he'd be barred from entering other countries once they checked his criminal background.

However, due to Moise's reason for departing Zaire, Nelson suggested that he take a plea bargain for lesser charges from the New York District Attorney. While he would still be convicted of a crime and, therefore, subject to deportation, they wouldn't waste effort on a trial, and Nelson could instead focus on the subsequent immigration court held by the Department of Justice. In his appeal, he would explain the complicated political situation leading up to Moise's conviction, and citing fear of deportation and the unpopularity of Moise's family with Mobutu, he could make a case for wrongful conviction and request asylum. Nelson admitted that it was a gamble, but he believed it was his client's best bet for a favorable outcome under the dismal circumstances.

Alternatively, Moise could go to trial and try his luck with a possibly hostile jury. He could conceivably win, and if he did not, he could petition to be deported to the United Kingdom or the European Union, citing a failure to secure asylum in the United States. Despite the present refugee crisis, both entities had previously been amenable to accepting Congolese refugees rather than allowing them to return to their motherland. Regardless, Nelson cautioned against this plan, as a felony conviction almost guaranteed a decline of his application.

Moise was miserable; he had to choose between a bad option and a worse one, and while it was possible that he could build a life in his former country—after all, he had no living links to his family—he desired the familiarity of America, where he had been raised and had experienced the most memories. He weighed his options, taking into consideration what Amanda might be able to prove and what his word was worth, and he decided on the least risky choice: the plea bargain, which represented his best chance of staying in the United States.

- - -

The evening's excursions had not proven fruitful, and Johnson's thoughts kept him awake as the clock began its final countdown on the night. After departing Little Italy, they'd headed to the gallery for a follow-up investigation, and while he didn't believe that they'd discover anything new, he'd needed to occupy his charge for a few hours or she might have blown a fuse. Antithesis was a delicate instrument, fine-tuned for a single function, and she was permitted to leave Plum Island for only that purpose, so she consequently became distressed and even choleric when she did not perform it. The visit to Félicité had not helped to improve her mood: Johnson had insisted that they examine every display for clues, particularly those by Moise Kabamba, and she'd become increasingly exasperated by the combined lack of progress and her own incomprehension of art; the latter seemed to have agitated a memory of the deficiencies of her sheltered childhood. Nevertheless, he'd shepherded her onward until she had become exhausted and her patience had worn thin.

While they could have surveilled Moise's residence, Johnson had believed it to be more prudent to feed his charge, and he'd reluctantly released Antithesis to her hotel room when he hadn't been contacted by Connor at the end of dinner.

Accountability was a deceitful process. Two of their instruments—Angel and Antithesis—had been raised and kept in controlled environments, so the original procedures had been simple, as neither subject had known more about the modern world than the BSI had necessitated. As technology had evolved, so had the BSI's ability to track their assets; last year, the two had been allowed to possess simple flip phones during their missions. Each had been equipped with GPS capability—something neither of them had recognized—but the phones had also been misdirection from the true tracking devices, which had been sewn into their pants and had been charged between missions. However, the agency was currently in the process of developing new procedures, as Echo—who was due to enter the field within the next year—was far more technologically savvy and did not need to rely financially on the bureau, so she would be a verifiable flight risk if she ever became disenchanted with their mission. Orion Starr had served as their testbed for a new protocol, and Johnson despised it because it functioned primarily on trust; trust might have worked with Connor, who'd had the motivation to cooperate, but Connor had also been unaware of his true nature, and Johnson doubted the two additions would become as amenable to the agency's draconian culling processes. It would be better to keep them under constant surveillance—like all identified and controlled Others—than to pull back and entrust them to return on a daily basis. At least they still had leverage over Starr if he fled because he could not abscond easily with his sister.

The current accountability process was simple: A handler would inspect the phone for its charge level and to ensure that all the important numbers were still in the phonebook; aside from assigning misdirected importance to the device, it also provided a distraction while the handler used his or her smartphone to check the functionality of the GPS tag in the subject's clothes. This happened in the field nightly, regardless of how many handlers were available, but it was imperative tonight, as Johnson had made a critical oversight: In his enthusiasm to collar another Other, he hadn't accounted for an overnight trip, and therefore, no support team was available to watch Antithesis while he slept. Normal government guidelines dictated separate quarters for different genders, and especially for Others, and he didn't feel particularly comfortable about them bedding down in the same room.

However, this was not the reason Johnson was still awake. Johnson was still awake because Connor had not called the whole night, and while it did not appear this would change, he still held out hope that he might and that they would subsequently execute a late-night apprehension. If Connor was circling Moise Kabamba, then he was an Other, even if there was currently no proof, and Johnson was anxious to detain him. While all agents foundationally believed in the mission—protect the civilian population against supernatural threats at all costs—Johnson's enthusiasm had grown into zeal when he'd delved deeper into the archives and uncovered pre-Dane incidents that had been suppressed or rewritten in the public record to eliminate widespread panic.

In particular, the true account of the Tunguska Event disturbed him: Cheko, then an insular hundred-year-old village, and the surrounding taiga had been mysteriously leveled and the town's existence erased from public record to keep the peace when the destruction had been traced back to a strange, bluish column of light that had momentarily outshone the sun. Decades later, scientific testing of the area had detected incredible levels of background radiation, and researchers had determined that Cheko had been destroyed by a nuclear explosion, though not by a bomb that predated the first official use in WWII; the culprit had been an unidentified Other, and worse yet, the BSI had categorized a Vanguard called Fission as his or her spiritual descendant. While the BSI might believe that a percentage of Others could live safely among the population, Johnson's passion was to terminate the most threatening of them before eliminating the ones who were deemed harmless and then the very last ones—their assets, even Angel and Antithesis.

Given the notoriety of Connor's track record, which included his instrument-partner, he doubted Moise Kabamba fell into the harmless category.

With his unexpended energy building uselessly and serving only to keep him awake, he decided to suffer through some late-night television in an effort to stupefy himself to sleep with infomercials. Instead, he was greeted by the midnight review of the top headlines, the foremost of which was the arrest of celebrated artist Moise Kabamba for the sensational attempted murder of the city's beloved mayor. It was perfect news: Since Moise was only a permanent resident and, consequently, still subject to immigration laws, federal jurisdiction for the case could be established under the DHS, and Johnson could, therefore, escort him to headquarters, where they could better scrutinize him with impunity. Once secured on Plum Island, abilities could be manufactured and delivered to Connor to avoid arousing his suspicion, and Johnson could revise the final report when Moise's true skill was determined. Eagerly, he grabbed his coat and set off to collect Antithesis from her room.

- - -

The cell in which Moise waited was cleaner and afforded more privacy than he would have expected, and he wondered whether he'd been purposely placed into isolation or if the precinct in which he'd been detained experienced a lower arrest level than the rest of the city. His lawyer, Nelson Wright, was negotiating with the judge over his bail amount. The amount would already be significant with four felony counts, but the additional factors of his supposed victim and the fact that he was facing possible deportation apparently caused the judge to consider him a flight risk and deny him bail. Nelson was trying to demonstrate his client's close ties to the community and his lack of a criminal past in order to convince the judge to reconsider and set his bail at a reasonable rate.

It was possible for Moise to leave the country as soon as bail was posted and flee to a non-extradition country, but he was not desperate enough to ruin his chances of continued American residency. He had faith in the legal system, which had helped him stay in the country so far—after all, his application for a green card hadn't drudged up his lack of legal status, nor had the original student visa he'd filed; his asylum had been granted with the incomplete data that he and his family had provided. With that kind of luck, he should be able to stay in the country indefinitely, especially when Nelson used his fear of deportation as part of his defense: No man fearing a return to a war-torn country would risk committing a crime that would certainly send him back there.

Moise used his previous run of good luck to bolster his belief in the American legal system. He couldn't return to the DRC, even if it was no longer Zaire. His legal guardians had kept apprised of their former country's situation, and he knew that the corruption and instability still remained, even if the country had taken steps to recover. While he had retained the ability to speak French, he doubted he remained competent enough to communicate effectively with his fellow countrymen, let alone make connections with a land to which he no longer had any emotional ties. He was an American by assimilation, if not by birth.

His concerns addressed the practicality of returning to the DRC, but they failed to capture the true root of his reluctance. The country was a den of superstition that had nearly killed him. If crops failed, if financial ruin visited, or even if general bad luck struck, children became labeled as *enfants sorciers* and were violently exorcised, killed, or cast out of the village to fend for themselves. The surviving children collected in the larger cities, where they were exploited—sometimes sexually—and nearly all of them died in the streets from malnutrition, disease, or violence at a young age.

When the old Okoumé tree in the central square had suddenly petrified overnight, it had been a clear sign of witchcraft and a herald of disaster to come. Moise's friend Eshele had been the first person to be accused, and Moise's father had quietly spirited his son away from the square before the forming mob had been able to place their focus on him as well. His father and mother had argued that night over what was best for Moise and the family and whether to shun him or risk an exorcism, and his father had stood his ground: Moise would leave the country because his father had feared what would happen to him when the exorcism didn't work. In the early light of the next morning, his father had revealed that he had also shared the burden of being a "witch," and he'd instructed Moise to conceal his gift from Mobutu and his government, who would have used him for their own gain; his father had learned this the hard way and had escaped servitude in Mobutu's army, though his freedom had come at great personal cost.

It was the fear that Moise remembered—the intense pain of separation from his parents coupled with uncertainty about his future. Even if Mobutu was no longer in power and no one alive knew that Moise was a witch, he wouldn't be able to walk down the streets without onerous anxiety that someone would discover his secret.

He had faith in the American legal system because the alternative was to face the depressive possibility of returning to that corrupted, fearful land.

- - -

The Hudson River itself was a New York landmark. It was home to Bannerman's Castle and the Sing Sing Correctional Facility and provided a backdrop for Poughkeepsie and Hyde Park. It had cultivated its own fame over the years, from its importance as a major transportation canal to the daring landing of a jet on its surface. As long as one didn't examine the water's hue or depth too closely, the river also provided many scenic views, from Riverside Park to Paulus Hook and the Empty Sky Memorial, and some might even claim that Liberty Island owed its beauty to the river.

But this spot was not one of them.

The two of them stood at the end of a random pier in Greenwich Village. The sun was setting over the estuary, briefly painting the sky red and orange to create the only pleasant portion of their evening. People, including families, dog walkers, and couples on romantic walks, passed them on the boardwalk, but no one paid them any special mind. They might as well be alone, isolated in their moment.

Orion gave Cassie the honor, as she had fewer memories and a lesser connection with their parents. She held the box aloft and dumped it over the railing, barely catching the empty cardboard before it, too, fell into the water. The wind caught the ashes and whipped the lighter particles into the air, but the majority fell into the river and sank or mixed with the steel-gray water. She tossed the box to the side, where it fell on the cement with a thud, and though he should have scolded her about littering, he refrained because her carelessness with their parents' funeral container created the appropriate ambience for the two of them.

There had been no ceremony for his parents, but the moment that the siblings shared made him feel lighter, as if the memories of their parents had been a burden to be discarded. No words were exchanged between them as they returned to the rental car—not even to inquire about their next destination— and Orion wasn't certain where he was heading until he was halfway to Central Park. While the traffic made him regret renting a vehicle, he'd had little choice in the matter if he'd wanted to visit his sister, and fortunately, there had been a parking garage within convenient walking distance.

He bought her a hotdog on the way, and they ate in comfortable silence as they strolled along the route to her favorite place in the city. He'd introduced her to Umpire Rock after a local festival almost a decade ago, and she'd fallen in love. He'd been too meek to attempt to scale the rock, even with offered assistance from community enthusiasts, and while she'd initially made several futile attempts, she'd eventually decided to admire it from afar, asking to make a detour anytime they'd been in the park. To his knowledge, she hadn't outgrown her fascination with the formation, though she hadn't taken up bouldering either, and she didn't comment as they found a spot under a nearby tree. The ground was damp, gradually saturating his jeans, and he offered her his hoodie as a meager seat; she accepted, sitting beside him and laying her head on his shoulder.

She remained quiet as he rested his head on hers and listened to her breathing. She'd been right; it had always been just the two of them, and even though she'd frequently tested the boundaries he'd set, she'd always known that she could rely on him to rescue her from her bad decisions. He'd been her father as well as her brother, and it was now obvious to Orion why she'd taken offense to her new custodial arrangement.

Despite being rid of the last physical reminder of their parents—the apartment belonged to the siblings, no matter who had paid the mortgage—his heart was still heavy with residual guilt, and he sought absolution from the one person from whom it'd have meaning. "Did you ever suspect them?" he whispered, irrationally afraid that a louder volume would summon the ghosts of their parents.

For a long time, she didn't move, and her low breathing ceased. As the pause stretched out, he considered repeating the question, but then she sighed deeply. "No," she replied softly. Though she tried to infuse her voice with incredulity and derision for the question, beneath her bravado, he heard the same doubt that he was experiencing; perhaps she, too, felt that she'd failed to detect obvious behaviors and clues and had, therefore, been inadvertently complicit in their parents' crimes.

He closed his eyes, feeling the soft tickle of her feathery hair against his cheek. "I think I was a witness," he murmured. He felt her shift beneath him and he moved, allowing her to sit up. Her brown eyes, hooded by a knitted brow, focused on him, and he quickly averted his gaze from her scrutiny. While the siblings had shared many secrets over the years, and his sister was the individual with whom he was most comfortable, he still had difficulty with sustained eye contact, and he feared that her opinion of him might change as a result of what he had to say. "I keep having these dreams… nightmares really," he said quietly. "There's this woman. Her face is…" He hesitated, recalling the horrible vision. The blow had missed its mark and skidded down the side of her head, cleaving her face and shattering her cheekbone. Her eyelid had begun to swell, possibly in an effort to protect the uninjured eye from harm, and blood had flowed freely, matting her hair and obscuring the wound. Cassie did not need to know the specifics. "Bloody," he decided, his voice becoming strained as he continued; he hoped that she wouldn't notice the difference in tenor. "It's like it's been slashed open. She needs help, but I can't help her. I'm too scared, and I don't even know what to do, if I can even do anything. Then I'm dragged away before I can even try."

She shrugged and then resettled her head on his shoulder. "It's a nightmare," she replied easily. "What makes you think it's a memory?"

"I was having this other strange dream at first." The gray mist had made an appearance only thrice in his unconscious mind, but each encounter had been carved into his memory, granting it greater significance. There was an abnormal quality to his sister in these dreams—as if she were a doppelganger or changeling—and he didn't want to contemplate what her surreal part as his guide meant, so he chose to omit any description to focus on the nightmares. "I ended up at our old apartment in Bay Ridge, and that's when these nightmares started," he explained. "It's always the same woman, the same screaming, the same running. All in our old living room." He shook his head and wrapped his arm around his sister, more to comfort himself than her. "I can feel her terror, like she's running for her life, but I'm helpless. I'm a hindrance." He sighed deeply. "When I wake up, everything about it seems so real, and I can't shake that feeling."

He expected her to respond, to be either supportive or more likely sarcastic, but she refrained, and as the silence grew, he tore his attention from the single faded leaf on the ground in front of them to look at her. Her brow was still furrowed, and she gnawed at her bottom lip. "What?" he asked, concerned.

She sat up, leaning against the tree trunk fully, and looked upward toward the city lights. She sighed deeply before slowly and quietly answering. "The police think they'd been killing for a few years before they began working in the observatory." Orion scowled with disapproval. The whole point of her living with the Vickers was to shield her from the sins of their parents; if she'd discovered more than the fragment she'd witnessed, then she'd rendered her foster placement purposeless. "They refined their technique over the years, so by the time they started working in Mason, they were impossible to catch." Her gaze didn't leave the skyline, and her voice droned onward as if she were reciting a report in front of a classroom rather than her personal history. "Everything about them is a cold trail. Johnstown seems to have been one of many dump sites because they've yet to find a whole body there—only pieces of several different people—and they haven't identified any victims, except for that runaway." She paused, drawing her lips together, and something about her expression made him wonder if she felt a kinship with the victim. The runaway girl had been young, closer to his age than Cassie's. She'd had no one to turn to, save an older sibling who hadn't been aware of her situation and who'd later publicly expressed regret that the victim had ended up on the street instead of turning to family for assistance. Perhaps Cassie had also considered leaving home at one point to stay permanently at a friend's residence to escape the turmoil at home and realized that the victim could have been her under different circumstances.

Regardless of her thoughts, she pressed forward. "They're all John or Jane Does—people no one would report missing. The observatory had a whole room dedicated to…" She trailed off; despite being frank about the murder spree, she couldn't bring herself to name their pinnacle crime. He'd heard the same rumor about the slaughter room repeated endlessly during the brief media circus and had immediately discounted it as false; if it had been true, how had their parents not been discovered early in their criminal careers when they'd occasionally shared a workspace with other astronomers?

"What I'm saying is that it's possible they did murder someone in our apartment." Cassie swallowed and then rubbed her palms on her raised knees before resting her head on her hands and looking him in the eye. "If you think it'll help you, we can go drop by the old place and see if it jogs your memory," she offered, chewing her lip.

Orion's frown deepened as he considered how much she appeared to know about the murders, and he scolded himself; she knew how to utilize the Internet—probably better than he did—so he should have realized that she'd conduct research on her own. He slid his hand beneath her chin, cupping her fingers, and he gave her a comfortable squeeze. "No," he replied, and relieved, she relaxed imperceptibly. He was morbidly curious, and though he knew that a revelation about being a child witness would do him no favors, it was his sister's discomfort that concerned him more; he'd failed to spare her the terrible experience of many things, but this was in his control, and there was no concrete reason to proceed. "No," he reiterated, "I think we've spent too much time on them already."

He'd recorded his thoughts about the Bramble Butchers in a journal with the intent to share them with his sister later. His mind had been a jumble of emotions: betrayal, anger, and even an irrational fear that he might become like them someday. Later, he'd also written scraps of his memories—moments when he might have noticed their unusual habits. He assumed that Cassie would experience the same troubled thoughts, and he wanted to reassure her that she was not alone in her uncertainty, but after their conversation, he realized that the journal would do more harm than good. He flashed her a reassuring smile, which she affectionately shared, and he pulled her into a close embrace and kissed the top of her head. Their parents were dead, and they were not, so they should live their lives out from beneath their shadow.

- - -

The lock failed to provide the anticipated resistance as Orion turned the key and opened the door to his apartment. It was midmorning, yet he was only somewhat surprised to find Connor sprawled across his couch with his unbuttoned shirt hanging open; his paisley tie was draped across the arm, and an empty bottle sat on the floor next to a glass containing what he assumed was melted ice. He sighed heavily and hesitated before quietly shutting the door and placing his keys on the counter. At least the agent had chosen the couch to occupy rather than one of his beds, though Orion wished that he knew why Connor hadn't spent the night at his own place.

Connor stirred, startling Orion as he leaned over to retrieve the glass next to him, and his yawn turned into a self-satisfied smirk. "Ah, I see you're back. Enjoy your trip?"

"Didn't I lock the door?" Orion asked, determined not to be baited or allow his partner to ruin the good mood generated by the visit with his sister. He took the bottle and glass into the kitchen, where he placed one in the recycling bin and the other in the sink.

"No, mate," he replied, rising to follow him. He casually propped his elbows up on the bar and leaned heavily against it. There were shadows beneath his eyes, which were marginally bloodshot, and Orion could smell the alcohol on his breath if not his person. "How about a bit of breakfast? I'm a bit peckish."

"And I bet a bit hungover, too," Orion quipped, eyeing his disheveled appearance with disapproval.

Connor chuckled, grinning wider, and began buttoning his shirt to reestablish a semblance of professionalism. "I see your sister's rubbed off on you. Glad the visit did you a bit of good." He scowled abruptly, as if a dark thought had flitted into his mind, and he sharply buttoned his sleeves before tucking in his shirt. He forced a new smile onto his face and reclaimed his nonchalant position against the bar. "Need you to stay focused," he said, his reproval spiced by unconvincing affected superiority. "You made it home right on time. The case has been solved for us." He pulled his scuffed smartphone from his pocket and showed Orion the fine print on its screen. "I was right. Kabamba was an Other," he explained. Despite having been proven correct, he sounded a bit disappointed. "I've been waiting to share the case notes with you, and it took you long enough to get back." He nodded behind Orion and suggested, "Why don't you make us something while I read it aloud to you?"

Begrudgingly, Orion accommodated him by pulling cereal and bowls out of the cupboards. If his sister had still lived with him, he might've had more substantial fare, but since living alone, he'd been less motivated to grocery shop and had subsisted on more basic meals. Connor didn't complain, laying into the bowl like it was a feast instead, and Orion contributed his enthusiasm to the hangover.

Connor's demeanor was slightly off as he recited the case file; it was as if he didn't quite believe it himself and Orion was serving as a sounding board for credibility. The agent described the afternoon following Orion's departure—which didn't amount to much explanation, as Connor had spent most of that time laid out by an awful headache—and then he relied on Johnson's own narrative. The other agent had left Little Italy with his partner for their own inspection of Félicité, whereupon they'd found a modicum of the evidence that Connor had sought: On each of Moise's pieces, there had been a single smooth spot like polished glass, which had often been well-hidden. While the disparity had meant nothing out of context, it had gained meaning as the night had progressed, and the petrified Okoumé incident had been later reexamined.

Through a series of events better kept discreet for the sake of those involved, Moise Kabamba had been arrested for the attempted murder of the mayor, and his booking had recorded an outlandish method of assassination: an attempt to turn her to stone, which had been foiled by the accidental transformation of a chair in her stead and her subsequent disabling of him with a heavy object. The incident had been flagged by the BSI as soon as it had been entered into the system, much like Cassie's mugging, and Agent Johnson had been able to establish federal jurisdiction and had escorted Moise back to headquarters, where a battery of tests had confirmed his preternatural ability. The mayor had been politely informed that she could not press charges—as this was now a matter of national security—but she had been assured that her assailant would be punished, and Blackout had been maintained.

It had all fallen into place, and this appeared to trouble Connor deeply. While the agent hadn't examined the entire surface of Moise's pieces, he was confident that his thorough inspection would've detected the same flaws that Johnson had found, and he expressed skepticism about the coincidental nature of the apprehension. "It seems to me like it'd be hard to keep a lid on Blackout with such a high-profile victim, eh? You'd think she'd be calling for a more thorough investigation or begging for a better grasp on what's going on."

Orion shrugged. "Maybe they forced her to sign a nondisclosure agreement?"

Connor shook his head. "An NDA isn't going to do much to stop chin wagging, especially when you're looking for answers," he refuted. "How did you feel the first time you figured out you and your sister were Others? You did research, and when you didn't find anything, I bet you were frustrated you couldn't find anyone to ask questions." He raised his eyebrows persuasively, tilting his head. "She's got more resources than you, so she's more likely to dig."

After a moment's reflection, during which he most likely recalled Amanda Darling-Whitcomb's perfect face beaming from billboards scattered throughout the city, he added, "Though the mayor doesn't seem to be the sort who'd serve jail time, so maybe staying out of prison is her incentive to keep silent."

Being an outsider, Connor wasn't familiar with the mayor's background, and he made an incorrect assumption about her character. Orion believed that her charming personality was genuine and not rehearsed, but her PR rep constantly carted her around to homeless shelters and galas for photo ops and kept her approval rating at a phenomenal eighty-one percent, and he fully believed that no judge would place her in prison if they even bothered to go to trial; as she liked to remind her constituents, she was heir to the Connecticut Darlings, and they seemed to get away with murder. While a federal judge might challenge her prominence, he doubted the government would heavily pursue charges unless the damage she caused was catastrophic, and it seemed, in his limited experience, that the BSI was well accomplished in burying the truth, so there'd be little point in calling more attention to any security lapse that her testimony might produce, as it would only exacerbate the problem if the story made national news.

Orion didn't have much to add to the conversation. He had to defer to Connor's expertise, and when the seasoned agent expressed suspicions, he couldn't do much to refute them, which he inferred Connor desired him to do. Orion believed that the agent's fixation on Moise Kabamba had been inappropriate until he'd proved to be an Other—and a dangerous one at that—and despite Connor's skepticism of Johnson's report, neither of them had been present for Kabamba's capture. Even though he hadn't read any of Connor's reports, his access to Tinder's file had demonstrated that case summaries weren't always comprehensive, and it was perfectly possible that the coincidences that Connor saw in the Kabamba case were, in reality, a flawed narrative; the fact that it was a preliminary report supported this conclusion.

Connor stared at him over the island, clearly expecting further input, but he remained quiet, instead looking into his empty bowl and refilling it. The agent shrugged, took the cereal box from Orion's hand, and replenished his own helping. A look of unpleasant contemplation suddenly crossed his face, and he slammed the box on the counter and angrily shoved a hearty spoonful into his mouth. He seemed to chew with antagonism, or perhaps he no longer enjoyed the taste, and then he swallowed. In a low, sour voice, he said, "So, Starr, I've been meaning to have a talk with you about that incident the other day." He might have smiled then, except the expression instead emerged as a grimace. "Actually, it's been going on quite a while." He paused, cringing as appropriate words failed to precipitate, and he seemingly struggled as he announced, "It's not that I don't like you, mate, but I can't do what I do and be your friend. I need to remain objective."

Connor rose suddenly, the stool shrieking as it scraped across the tile, and as he entered the living room, he turned abruptly, as if he'd forgotten his objective, and started pacing instead. "What if you join VSION? Or go off the deep end?" he said, possibly speculating aloud as he gestured with his free hand; the other was thrust violently in his pocket. "What am I supposed to do about that?" He hesitated briefly, perhaps soliciting an answer to what must have been a rhetorical question, and then he pressed forward before Orion could formulate an answer, if he'd even had one. "It's better for both of us if we just keep a bit of distance," he declared in a reasonable tone and grinned winningly to emphasize his point.

Despite the care with which he'd attempted to frame their work relationship, Orion felt a stab of renewed grief: For all of his flaws and annoyances, Connor had been the first person to take an active interest in him in several years, and he begrudgingly considered him a friend, albeit a conceited, self-important one. However, he'd started acting distant after Scotts Ridge, which had culminated in their fight at his apartment, and this conversation accentuated their false comradeship. "Is that how it is then?" he asked, pulling himself out of his slouch to lean aggressively against the counter. The acid in his response matched the bitter, half-cocked grin he'd acquired from his not-partner.

Connor's smiled faltered, fleetingly exposing the doubt he may have felt before turning brighter. "Oh, don't be like that," he teased cheerily. He ceased pacing and faced Orion broadly, holding his palms out in an act of appeasement. "It's a job, and my job is to make sure you're ready to do yours."

"Fine," he agreed cynically; regardless of his personal feelings, he still had to work with Connor until his training was complete. "Then how am I supposed to trust you?"

Connor's expression became suitably somber as he tucked his hands in his pockets and looked Orion in the eye. "You have my word of honor." Orion gave him a dead stare in return, skeptically raising his eyebrows and crossing his arms, and Connor scowled sourly, reproachfully amending, "You just are."

The answer, no matter how sincerely it had been offered, did little to reassure Orion, and he intensified his scrutiny. Their whole relationship had been based on trust—his sister's continued well-being, his own personal safety, and his belief that cooperating with the BSI had been the correct course—which now appeared to be misplaced. He'd had reservations about his cooperation with the bureau, and it had been Connor who'd assuaged them; at the time, he'd believed Connor's heart-to-heart had been genuine concern, but he now began to question his motives.

Connor's gaze slipped to the floor. "Look, I know it's not easy," he admitted quietly. He hesitated, focusing on the polished tile for several moments, and then he sniffed sharply, sauntered back to the island, and casually retook his seat. "I had this buddy—right git he was. He couldn't even be trusted to fry an egg. Don't know for the life of me how he made staff sergeant." His lips twitched, hinting at a smirk, but his face remained set in a scowl, and he didn't look Orion in the eye as he usually did when he was going to be facetious;

instead, he was focused intensely on the spoon that he was twirling on the counter. "He was a terrible influence—messy uniform, poor hygiene, bad attitude—anything to push our lieutenant's buttons just for the hell of it. But when it came down to it, he didn't hesitate to sacrifice his life for me. Not for one second." His movement ceased, save for blinking back his denied tears, and he seemed to become lost in thought. Orion remembered seeing him like this before when they had worked their first case together; Connor had thrown cutting jibes at him when he'd inquired about his personal history, despite him asking the same of Orion only a few minutes prior, but he'd still revealed more intimate details than he'd intended that night. The tiny crack in his otherwise mordant bravado had been the first stepping-stone toward deepening their superficial relationship, and the reappearance of it had meant that there had indeed been something genuine about their interaction.

The agent sniffed again as he resurfaced from his reverie. "He was terrible at his job, but he could still be trusted, and just 'cause I'm doing a job doesn't mean you can't also trust me," he said, and this time Orion believed him. "You can."

Orion nodded slowly. He didn't know the circumstances behind his earlier outburst or the inimical words he'd uttered recently, but he was reassured that deep down, he could trust Morgan Connor. Despite his flaws, the older man had given him advice and information beyond what was required of him, and his wellness checks were superficial only in the fact that they were awkward and tactless, not paltry attempts at camaraderie.

Connor clenched his jaw and attempted a reassuring smirk that didn't quite make it to his eyes. "There's a good lad," he commended, clapping Orion on the shoulder.

PART IX
CODE NAMES: PENUMBRA & SINGULARITY

Cassie despised public transportation outside the city. In most places, like Waynesboro, it was so inefficient that it might as well not exist, and the more time she spent in the sprawling cities, the more she realized the value of a driver's license. She considered obtaining her own, although she doubted the Vickers would lend her their car, and she knew that her brother wouldn't buy her a car if he didn't own one. Like most people in the city, he didn't have use for one because the bus and subway provided affordable transportation. Since a handful of her friends could borrow vehicles, she didn't often concern herself with travel arrangements, but the night's activities had been canceled by the group, so Felix had invited her over because his father would be working the night shift. Though he'd pretended that the reason she was coming over was to study, she had a feeling that he had something else in mind, and while she didn't fancy him, his house provided a better hangout spot than her temporary home. The two of them would probably end up watching a movie until it was time for her to leave.

She didn't bother knocking, instead letting herself into the trailer. Felix's father would likely return in the early morning hours, and his mother had unfortunately passed away several years ago, leaving Felix to care for himself while his father worked. He never cared about personal safety, which she supposed was normal behavior when one lived in the outskirts of a town with a relatively low crime rate, and he rarely locked his doors. However, she was entirely surprised when she entered the mobile home to find that Felix was not alone.

The dour-looking man was well dressed in a suit that had been properly tailored to his frame, yet its uneven, worn appearance revealed its age; there were several spots—particularly the abraded lapels—that had been cleaned asymmetrically, implying a concentrated effort to scrub those areas. Though he was not a large man, his frame was sturdy, and he projected power. His eyes looked tired and worn, but they held resigned determination as he pointed the pistol in her direction.

Cassie froze, immediately harkened back to the confrontation with her father. She felt the initial impact and experienced disbelief that she'd been shot. She knew that she should have felt burning pain and the warmth of her fleeing blood; instead, she was numb, wondering if she'd imagined the gun's report echoing off the walls and filling her ears. Her equilibrium failed, and the delicate balance keeping her in shock was lost. As she fell, she felt the heavy molten weight of the bullet burrowing through her chest, and the pain came all at once, shrinking her world to distressing sensations.

Felix, who knew nothing of her frightful experience with firearms, apologized immediately. "I'm sorry, Sid," he said, using her newly acquired nickname. His hands were in the air, clearly visible beside his head, and he was shaking, no longer the macho anarchist he played at school. With a bloodied lip and disheveled clothes, he looked like he might've taken a beating before he'd contacted her. "He threatened my dad. He said there'd be an 'accident' if I didn't text you," he explained desperately. "He said he just wanted to talk."

Cassie reexamined the stranger, trying to determine whether she knew him. The dour man was not related to any of her New York friends, whose fathers and brothers wouldn't have allowed their suits to become visibly damaged, and he was not a frequent customer at Hallowed Grounds because she knew everyone by name, and the few who didn't enjoy the kitschy niche café never returned. He was no one she'd met during her brief time at Plum Island, where all the agents wore a universal, bland design, and the staff wore business casual, save for a handful of instructors. Finally, he was not one of the two individuals from SION whom she'd met that fateful night. She did not recognize this man and, therefore, had no idea what he wanted from her, but she was also unwilling to find out.

The BSI's training regimen focused on control by extinguishing a fire once it had been summoned, assuming Cassie would be its source as well as its solution; it was not concerned with the fine-tuned manipulation of the flame itself, which was a skill that she'd developed with guidance from her friend Sone prior to her apprehension. As much as she loathed her ability, she saw it as a self-defense mechanism, and proficiency with it was necessary to avoid another incident in which someone died. The trailer was small and full of ignition sources, and though she'd used the incandescence of lightbulbs before, they were inferior to actual living fire. The quality of the pilot light was preferable, and she drew the small flame toward her, stretching it into a ribbon to be wrapped around the stranger. It took a wide arc around the man, converging on his firearm, which she intended to superheat until he released it and thereby negate the threat he posed with minimal harm.

However, things did not play out the way she envisioned. A thick, mucous-like substance manifested from the dour man and encased his weapon and his skin. Her flames licked its surface, but the material absorbed the heat, and ultimately, no damage was done as her fire smoldered and snuffed out. Once the threat was gone, the dour man reabsorbed the viscous fluid. Though the gun had been aimed at her, the stranger smoothly switched targets to Felix and immediately fired his weapon as if nothing had occurred. She watched helplessly as his head exploded, splattering gore over the small confines of the trailer.

Cassie screamed, backing away, and the doorknob slammed into the small of her back. She had not managed to gain control of the situation; she'd only worsened it by getting Felix killed. She recalled the canister of pepper spray she kept in her bag despite its ineffectiveness against the Vanguard, and she dismissed any thought of using it; she doubted it would prove any more effectual against the stranger, and she shouldn't risk angering him further if she wanted to survive. She was defenseless and at his mercy.

The dour man cleared his throat as he reacquired his bead on her. He smiled lopsidedly, seemingly to place her at ease, but the result was forced, as it came from a man who was never amused. "Mr. Lionhart cordially invites you to join him in New York City," he announced, his thick Brooklyn accent and prior actions undermining the courteous tone he affected. "I regret to inform you that he will not take 'no' for an answer." He nodded toward the door, and Cassie had little choice but to obey.

- - -

Orion sighed heavily, slouching into the chair he'd pulled up beside Connor. "Why are we doing this again?" he asked. Despite his uninterested tone, the younger man was in better spirits this morning and had been for the last week. Something must have worked between his visit to his sister and his heart-to-heart with Connor to inspire an attitude improvement: He'd gone grocery shopping, finally refilling his cupboards with appropriate sustenance, and had even prepared breakfast in anticipation of Connor's arrival.

"I told you, it's good for you," Connor laughed, secretly pleased that the rapport between them had been mended; it made it easier to pretend his objectivity wasn't an issue and that Orion was a normal human partner. "You'll be doing this sort of work back at headquarters."

"But this is all we do," he complained. Compulsively, he began stacking the breakfast plates so he could place them in the sink. He'd probably grab a dishrag in a few moments to start wiping down the counters if he didn't start washing the dishes instead. Connor had recently come to realize that Orion's cleaning habits weren't just to avoid eye contact and social interaction; his anxious need to keep everything immaculate traced back to either his care for his sister's environment or to a deeper neurosis.

Connor held up his index finger. "Wrong," he corrected. "I've taught you the basics. How the organization works, how it fits under the government, what to do when you encounter an Other…" He grimaced, knowing that none of their engagements had gone by the book. "How to handle yourself when a confrontation goes sideways… But most of it's been lessons in administration and not actual fieldwork, apart from watching me. And I know how much you like that." He flashed him a cocky grin and looked him in the eye. "How many cold cases have we worked?"

Orion shrugged. "All of them?" he replied flatly. Connor's expression told him that he was mistaken, so he counted them off using his fingers and amended the total. "Four."

"Two," Connor said, "and I wouldn't exactly count the last one since we stumbled across him." Even then, Orion hadn't actually worked the case; while he might have been present for Connor's initial suspicions, he'd left New York far too early to have made a contribution toward solving it. "We've been working active cases, which is an entirely different skill set, and you need to develop this one," he asserted and offered a smirk as commiseration. "It's right boring, but you need to get it down."

"It's interviewing people," Orion replied unhappily. If it were the only skill needed, Connor would have petitioned his boss to reassign Orion. Despite rapidly improving his techniques, he knew that it placed undue stress on Orion's social anxieties, and while normal career paths would promote that sort of difficulty as an opportunity for personal growth, Orion would never advance higher in the ranks, so putting him through it was an unnecessary discomfort. Fortunately, there was more to his job; interviewing was only a small aspect of it.

"Yeah, and you've got that down. You just need a bit more polish," he said, complimenting the younger man despite himself. "But there's also analyzing clues and following leads, and we haven't had much luck with those." He chuckled sharply, rolling up his sleeves. "Or maybe we've had too much luck since it's been so easy, like following a trail of breadcrumbs."

Connor's career had been oddly charmed. There had never been any close calls with his personal safety, despite confronting Others who had dangerous abilities; he always knew how far to press his limits, and he never crossed the line. The incident with Pierce Starr was the only snag in his run of luck, and that could be written off as being in the wrong place at the wrong time. As far as locating Others was concerned, he'd worked cold cases in the past and had always been fortunate enough to select a subject just as the Other's ability was making a resurgence. The other agents weren't as lucky, having a much lower success rate, and it might have been a better choice to pair Orion with one of them so he'd have more firsthand experience in the work that cold cases required.

Connor placed his arms on either side of the laptop, which was still making its connection to the database. Once it was secure, he'd run a filter that would confine their searches to the New York area, and then he would have Orion take over so he could familiarize himself with the system. He didn't know what kind of access Orion would be allowed, especially since both Starr siblings were already in the database, but he assumed it would be restricted rather than inefficiently forcing the younger man to go through an intermediary.

"What am I really going to be doing?" Orion asked straightforwardly.

"I told you." Connor's self-assured grin fell as he looked into the younger man's face, which was a mixture of pitiable distrust and blatant cynicism. He had already been too honest with Orion, setting a precedent based on which the younger man expected the truth from him or he would sulk, and rather than deal with the latter and the subsequent damage to their rapport, Connor decided to be candid in spite of himself. His boss, William Terrance, hadn't deemed it necessary to share the full plan with Connor, so he blended what he knew with his own conjecture. "They're not going to send you into the field like Angel and Antithesis. You're a new kind of asset, and they're not going to risk you in a confrontation, though you've done well in the odd dustup."

Though Connor had been otherwise occupied when Orion had stood up to his father, both the report and Orion's own account indicated that he'd kept a level head and had done his best to keep the situation contained; it wasn't his fault that he hadn't had the training to keep it from accelerating out of his control. He'd also stayed out of Connor's way when they'd confronted Lena Malmkvist, allowing the agent to talk her into surrendering peacefully. Connor might have even made a case that he'd handled himself well during the Phobos episode, utilizing his regenerative abilities to keep himself alive, if he chose to acknowledge Orion's near-death experience and Connor did not.

"No," he continued, dismissing the event in Scotts Ridge from his mind. That needed to be put behind them, which was probably the reason he was being so outspoken now; he needed Orion to trust him to make their relationship work. "They're more likely to use you in cleanup, and when you're not doing that, you've got to earn your keep, so you'll be analyzing old case files." He nodded toward his weathered laptop. "That's why we've got to develop these skills."

Since they were speaking candidly, Orion decided to ask the next difficult question. "Am I still going to be able to see my sister?"

Connor inhaled deeply, glancing back toward his screen. He attempted an egotistical smirk that was meant to reassure his protégé, but he instead adopted a more ambiguous expression. "That's what they promised, isn't it?" he replied, injecting enough mockery into his voice to be mistaken for confidence, and Orion seemed to accept that he wasn't lying. But the truth was that Connor didn't know. The other two assets—three, he corrected himself—on the books resided at Plum Island, while any minorly talented candidates were released back into the general population after training. In his opinion, Orion wouldn't require the same level of supervision as Angel, Antithesis, or Echo, but it wasn't his decision to make. Perhaps he could put in a recommendation for Orion to live with his sister in Greenport, where the facility staff lived and he himself maintained an apartment.

The arrangement wouldn't necessarily create a conflict of interest: Most of Connor's job was spent on the road, traveling from one site to another for his investigations, and the apartment wasn't his primary residence. Legally, that honor belonged to his mother's former house in Ohio, one of the few ties he'd maintained with her, as it was also the only link he had to his father. The newlywed couple had bought the house during happier times, and when his father had died, his grandmother had moved in to help pay the mortgage and had eventually assumed both the loan and the title. The house was currently rented out to a nice family and would remain so until Connor was ready to make it his permanent home. His mother had no legal rights to the income or the property.

In contrast, his Greenport apartment was a home of convenience. It was fully furnished yet able to sit empty for weeks at a time, and it would be ready to receive him without advanced notice. When he had to report back to headquarters or had no cases to work, he resided comfortably in the mostly empty duplex. It could be a nice change of pace to have friendly neighbors, and it would allow him to more easily keep in touch with the Starr siblings.

He decided to push the thought from his mind and concentrate on the task at hand. He nodded toward his screen, where the connection had finally completed. "Now this time, you'll be the one selecting the case," he continued. "When I picked Succubus, I'd filtered out several factors to make it easier to teach you, but that didn't work too well, yeah?" He chuffed. "So, this time, you're going to pick the case, and I'll guide you." His grin widened as he watched Orion shift uncomfortably. He couldn't characterize why his partner's agitation amused him; perhaps he'd missed out on having a little brother to torment, so Orion had become his surrogate. Nevertheless, his duty was to train the younger man, and the best way to learn was to throw him in the deep end while holding a lifesaver.

Orion stood, reluctantly switching places with him, and settled into his new seat. Connor reviewed the utility of the database features, particularly the search function, and allowed Orion to explore on his own. Unsurprisingly, he filtered out any incident that implied the involvement of a pyrokinetic, and he tried to restrict the flagged activities to a single borough. Connor made the recommendation to select an apparent serial offender as that kind of profile provided more opportunities to train Orion; several linked incidences increased the chances of clues and witnesses left behind by the perpetrator and therefore improved Orion's likelihood of formulating a good lead.

Moments later, he was relieved that Orion had accepted his recommendation, as the first unsorted result was an unsolved case from 2012. The passage of Hurricane Sandy had caused the East River to overflow, flooding several nearby areas with raw sewage and dredging up garbage from the city's deeper recesses. Along with the debris an anomalous desiccated body had appeared. Modern forensics had refuted the possibility that it was an ancient mummy, as had the preliminary inquiries with local museums. Yet, the apparent mummification of the body had still been deemed unnatural and not due to accidental environmental conditions. Given the state of the city at the time, the curiosity had been noted, filed, and forgotten by authorities, save for the bureau. The details should have brought to mind Jody Barles and her ability to remove life from her victims, but instead, his mind jumped to his vision of an agonized Orion being drained of color, and he was eager to dismiss the case to work on something less troubling.

The next few sorted results were more amusing. One was a man who'd filed multiple times for disability, citing limb amputations following industrial mishaps over the years. These accidents—each with a different company—had been substantiated, as had his medical claims. However, each disability application had listed the same right arm as the casualty appendage, which was why the initial data entry clerk had flagged the individual. However, Connor and Orion agreed that the construction worker was most likely committing insurance fraud rather than being the beneficiary of extraordinary regenerative abilities.

Their next rejection was a slew of exotic animals appearing all over the city, from subway tunnels to the Waldorf Astoria Hotel. Animal Control had confirmed that the wayward beasts had escaped from city zoos, but they had been unable to explain how the fugitive animals had appeared in such diverse locations over the years, particularly when there had been no witnesses, and none of the parks had ever reported a break-in or even suspicious activity. While the two of them agreed that the case was strange, there were not many clues to follow, and they gave it a pass.

Instead, Orion settled on a seemingly innocuous but outrageous accusation against an unidentified Flushing pedestrian who had used a tree to kill a passing motorist by impaling her with a branch and then crushing the vehicle she was driving with the crown. This incident had been tenuously connected to an eyewitness account from over a decade earlier that involved a man being skewered by a sapling after threatening a teen who'd run into him. Both accounts had alleged that the arboreal growth had been rapid and that the offending trees had not previously existed.

Orion scowled. "Why wasn't this better investigated?" he asked derisively, scoffing at the lack of comprehensive detail in the report. He was being rudely introduced to the inadequacies of open case files after his expectations had been unreasonably set by Connor's high closing rate.

Connor casually pointed at the top of the screen, indicating the date of the most recent incident. "Busy year?" he observed sardonically. "Or maybe because there were 'probable tornadoes' that could explain the vehicle crash. It's only one man who's making a claim to the contrary, and the same can be said in 1997." He chuckled cynically, which was reminiscent of his derisive attitude toward the paranormal. He'd interviewed a fair share of nutjobs throughout his career, but he'd always been careful to prescreen his interviewees to keep out the true crazies. His witnesses had always been seemingly normal, well-adjusted people who'd seen one abnormal event that had been supported by outside evidence. Though this case was strengthened by two separate accounts, it didn't give off the correct vibe, and Connor remained skeptical. "Are you really going to believe a real-life Poison Ivy is going around mugging people when there are actual crimes out there to be solved?"

Orion regarded him with confusion. "But you know there are Others."

Connor shrugged. "Yeah, but that doesn't mean we have an unlimited budget," he replied reasonably. "That was the year of Deepwater Horizon. We spent most of that year chasing down the Vanguard." The younger man's frown deepened with concern, and Connor nodded, confirming VSION's involvement. From his understanding, it had been a long, exhausting year, and he was almost certainly glad that he'd been in the process of enlisting rather than working for the bureau at the time, because things had only gotten worse. He began ticking off his fingers. "After that, it was Fukushima, and then it might have been a rogue tornado or something…" His subsequent grin was dripping with arrogant condescension. "VSION keeps us quite busy when we aren't chasing down Others. That's why you've got to learn how to do this so you can work during the down time."

Orion rolled his eyes, and Connor snickered as he rose and poured himself a nonalcoholic drink. It would take some time to study the few photographs, locate persons of interest, and plot their next move. Unless one of the witnesses revealed a groundbreaking secret, he believed the case would be another dead end, but that was something that Orion had to determine on his own.

- - -

The sun had set several hours ago, and dinner had long grown cold. Charlene and Timothy had already eaten, the latter having prepared the meal on his day off, and the dishes had been washed and put away. It was not unusual for Cassie to miss meals—she was a brooding teenager who was looking to rebel—but the time for their wayward child to return to the house was drawing near.

Charlene knew the night scene in Waynesboro was incomparable to the city to which Cassie was accustomed, but the young woman still pushed her boundaries and found activities to occupy her time. Orion's curfew for her had been midnight, but the Vickers had reduced it to eight, and Cassie seemed to appreciate the structure and discipline, because she rarely broke it. She'd returned even earlier in the evening following her visit with her brother. Overall, Charlene was unconcerned about the teen's whereabouts. Nevertheless, she kept an eye on the time as she went about the house preparing it for final closure for the evening, tidying the living room, and preparing her bag for her daily commute to Washington, D.C.

When curfew came and went, Charlene decided to give her charge a generous grace period of a half hour before becoming angry; trust was important to maintaining a relationship, especially with a teen, and Cassie's good behavior of late should be rewarded. However, this did not mean she wouldn't find out where Cassie was or why she'd been delayed in the interim.

She retrieved her password-protected work phone from her travel bag and dialed the on-shift surveillance team. Like every other graduate from the BSI training program, Cassie was followed on a daily basis by professionals who monitored her behavior; if she had a relapse or, worse yet, an incident with a civilian, their orders were to contain the situation and remove the threat to Blackout by any means necessary. This team was how she'd known that Cassie hadn't started the shack fire, and she'd taken the opportunity to foster trust with Orion Starr—their newest asset—by pretending to contact him first to express her concern over the incident. He'd remained ignorant of her close connection to the BSI and her secondary duty as his sister's handler.

When the surveillance team failed to answer, Charlene's concern began to rise, though it was not yet more than mild unease. She decided that the grace period had ended and called Cassie directly. Predictably, her charge behaved normally and ignored the phone call, so Charlene utilized her secret weapon: She'd downloaded a locator app onto Cassie's phone, which was the real reason she had been allowed to keep it after she'd been grounded; it was easier to track a wayward teen when the device they always carried could be altered to remotely broadcast their location.

The cell phone reported its location as Eden Avenue, which was the residence of Felix Buchanan, her fellow internee for the shack incident. Since she knew Felix's father worked the night shift, she didn't want to disturb him just yet over a minor misstep and opted to phone the son directly to give him a chance to explain. Felix also ignored his phone, and when she called Cassie a second time, she used the signal Orion had taught her: Call, text, and then call again. It told Cassie she was needed urgently and would be in serious trouble if she did not answer the second repetition. When she again failed to answer, Charlene's motherly instincts kicked in, and she redoubled her efforts, phoning the surveillance team more insistently.

She tried to reassure herself that Cassie was behaving like a normal teenager: She was out late testing her curfew and had relapsed into her previous city behavior. Orion repeatedly apprised them that his sister had a habit of sleeping over at a friend's house without asking permission first or informing him but that his connections with parents allowed him to keep accurate tabs on her. While Waynesboro might not be as exciting as the city, similar behavior wasn't out of the question. It was also equally possible that Cassie had finally noticed the tail that headquarters had placed on her and had ditched them, either realizing their purpose as government operatives or, given her run-in with the Vanguard, assuming that the team was trying to forcibly recruit her.

When Charlene failed to contact the on-shift team through the primary number, she opted to call the alternate line and was connected with the off-shift leader within seconds. "Special Agent Parker," he answered.

Charlene smiled, hoping her apology would translate over the line. "Hey, I know you're not on shift anymore, but I can't get a hold of Ayala or Foster," she said. She sounded like a suburban housewife, which she supposed she was in a way, and she hoped that her worry was unwarranted. "Do you think you can give them a try?"

Parker yawned. "Sure, give me a minute," he replied. She could hear the quiet beeping of his personal phone and its subsequent ringing over her connection. "Having trouble with the girl again?" he asked casually.

"Yeah," she replied more calmly than she felt. Perhaps it was only maternal instinct that encouraged apprehension to gnaw on her subconscious, but it was more likely because the night was venturing toward memory and déjà vu. They had been unable to locate their son, who would have been Orion's age by now, after his graduation celebrations, and after a long night of missed phone calls and search parties, the police had discovered his totaled car in a ditch. While she doubted the same situation had been visited upon her foster child, the memories still crept into the fringes of her mind and colored her thoughts. "She's breaking curfew," she continued lightly. "I think she's over at the Buchanan boy's house, but I want to make sure before I head over there."

Parker made a noncommittal noise as he waited for his call to complete.

There was silence on the line for several minutes until he commented, "That's weird." His voice was suddenly deeper, a cross between annoyed and perplexed. She could hear more electronic noise, implying that he was still using his personal phone and might have been texting. "They're not answering me either," he explained. "Give me the address. I'm gonna collect Agent Barton. We'll check it out and get back to you."

Charlene forced her smile to resurface; the short exchange had only worsened her increasing fears. Nevertheless, she stated the location given by the app and hoped for the best.

- - -

Fear is a powerful thing. It can hold a person in place, making them absolutely immovable, or it can pump one full of adrenaline and allow the impossible to happen. Cassie experienced both ends of the spectrum during her ordeal. The dour man walked her to the car and then coated her wrists and ankles with his disgusting gel, which felt surprisingly insubstantial despite its rigidity and refusal to permit any play with these restraints. She was stuffed in the trunk, where the initial helplessness of the situation kept her immobile and the darkness invited her to release her emotions. She'd seen another man shot, close enough that she'd felt his blood drying against her fair skin. She could not voluntarily remember the first time she'd taken a bullet as well—it was just a blank space in her mind when she tried to consciously recall it—but now that it had occurred again, she didn't think she could ever forget. Felix was the third person she'd seen injured in front of her in less than a year, and he'd been her friend, which deepened and personalized the trauma even further.

She cried for a long time, feeling the car bump along a road at high speeds, and when she'd exhausted herself, the car's motion lulled her into an uneasy sleep. When she awoke, she was sore yet refreshed, and her mind had cleared: She would not be a victim; she would fight back. She determined that she could not escape her situation immediately. She wasn't certain that she was entirely immune to fire, and her training at Plum Island had failed to address this possibility, so reaching into the engine block to manipulate it into combusting the vehicle would be a poor choice when she was trapped within its trunk. Even if she were fireproof, she couldn't be certain that the vehicle would come to a safe stop, and a crash would almost certainly kill her.

Instead, she focused on what she could do after being freed from the trunk. She couldn't run until she was freed from the strange viscous fluid, and she knew that her ability wouldn't directly work on her captor; instead, she'd have to be alert for an escape opportunity and take it when it was presented. She could use her ability to cover her flight, despite its initial inability to protect her.

Two men removed her from the trunk: the dour, mostly well-dressed man who'd abducted her and a tall, lanky man with a goofy grin who leered at her. She shivered, briefly overcome by greasy uneasiness in the latter's presence, and then she forced herself to concentrate, focusing on her surroundings instead of on him. She'd dealt with perverts at Hallowed Grounds, and she told herself there was no difference now.

There were rows upon rows of metal shipping containers stacked tall to obscure the skyline, and despite the cover, she knew she was back in the city. There was no mistaking the familiar sounds and smells and especially the lights reflecting off the smoggy haze to create a second horizon, but it was difficult to precisely determine her location. She was led to a warehouse and noted its number even though it meant nothing to her now.

The interior was sparsely lit, and several people milled about the warehouse stacking and moving boxes under the watchful eye of a short man in a suit. He must have heard their entrance, for he turned their way and smirked handsomely. "Ah, wonderful! I see you have been successful," he said by way of greeting. He gestured at one of his underlings, signaling them to take over supervision, and he approached the trio.

The boss was a stranger, yet he was not unfamiliar. His short blond hair was combed and styled in the same fashion favored by her father, and the shape of his face had the same sculptured chin and cheekbones that Cassie and most of her family possessed. Despite having piercing blue eyes, the resemblance was uncanny, and the smooth tones of his voice also echoed those of her father. She had never known her grandparents—Madeleine had disowned her blood relations, while Pierce had only ever mentioned a deceased mother—and she wondered if this stranger was a long-lost uncle or other relative.

He studied her in turn, taking her chin into his manicured hand and turning her face gently from side to side. "Remarkable," he commented. His intonation was reminiscent of the British Isles, though subtly different from her father's Americanized accent, and it reinforced the conclusion that the two men might be related. "You look exactly like a woman I once knew," he continued, his voice a mixture of nostalgia and controlled anger. "She had a ghastly temper. She used to return home absolutely reeking of alcohol, and she'd beat me if I hadn't earned enough money that day." He smiled bitterly. "Sometimes she'd do it even if I had."

Despite her renewed determination, Cassie trembled as his hand left her face and cradled a lock of black hair for closer examination. She refused to shrink away, tolerating the touch as best she could, and the man frowned subtly, his eyes glinting with disapproval. Yet, the expression failed to take root, and he remained convivial. "My friends have said you've a mighty temper as well. I hope you don't plan on using it while you're here."

His smile widened magnanimously as he released her and stood up straight; he was barely her height. "I wouldn't worry your pretty head," he reassured her. "Your ordeal will be over swiftly, provided your brother follows directions."

Her feistiness suddenly revived, temporarily driving back her fear; she was not the commodity the BSI had reduced her to—some leverage to be held over her brother. Orion had always come to her rescue, bailing her out of sticky situations, mundane though they may now seem, and the last time had forced him into the service of a shadowy government agency. It might have been the two of them against the world, but she was not going to be used against him; she would find a way out of the situation without endangering her brother. Since she had no plan, she fell back on her contingent strategy: biting sarcasm, which she could wield to cut him down to size or at least fill herself with temporary gratification.

Her intentions must have shown on her face, for though a caustic remark was on the tip of her tongue, the Brit preempted her with an amused laugh. "Ah, now that temper won't get you very far," he scolded her softly, "and let me show you why."

He was fast—too quick for her eyes to track—when he pounced on her. Absently, she felt her feet leave the ground, but the observation was lost in the chaos that her senses reported, as was the pressure around her throat. Her skin burned, her nerves screamed, and it seemed like even the very molecules that made up her body were in flux, abandoning her to create a new bond with something foreign. The ignition sources around her faded, vanishing from view as if they would no longer deign to service her, and she felt her connection to them turn brittle and begin to break.

Then her torment ceased, draining all of her energy, and even her mind was weakened. She fell into the stranger's outstretched arms as he suavely caught and cradled her limp body; it was if she had fainted. "Graves," he said, addressing the dour man, "please escort our guest to her accommodations." He gently raised her back to her feet, and Graves supported her weight, though control was already slowly returning to her limbs.

"Now, love, you are a clever poppet," the boss continued, his tone sweet and genteel as if he hadn't just preternaturally tortured her. "I would hate to see further harm come to you, so please be a dear and behave yourself while you remain under my roof." He gave her a wide, paternal smile that chilled her despite its outward friendliness, and she remained silent and complacent, declining the opportunity to accidentally antagonize him again.

- - -

Connor tried his best to keep normal work hours; this proved convenient for potential interviews and kept him on the same schedule as restaurants, stores, and other service industries. However, in the "City that Never Sleeps," he had little incentive to maintain that timetable, and his habits slipped to a semi-nocturnal predisposition. Of course, Orion had resisted, having his own schedule centered around the needs of his sister, but in time, he'd also faltered toward setting his own hours and had married his schedule to Connor's. The agent also rarely worked eight-hour days, performing labor as much or as little as necessary, and since neither of them had particular obligations, it was easy to work into the wee hours.

It just so happened that the shift in their schedule serendipitously accommodated their first witness, an elderly man named Hank Lester, and they made the trip up to Queens to catch him before he set off to work. He was an odd gentleman: short, a hunched posture, silver hair shaved at his temples, and a smile that was missing more than a few teeth. He released a whole set of deadbolts to allow them entry into his apartment, which was so crowded with junk that only narrow passageways remained, and he cleared dog-eared magazines from a worn couch to offer them a seat. Orion declined, clumsily hiding his disgust, but Connor nonchalantly shrugged and plopped down on a discolored cushion. His expression was subtly patronizing, despite his forcibly polite smile, and he opened his notepad and placed it on his knee. "Your rodeo," he said, cueing his partner.

Orion cleared his throat, shifting his weight between his feet before settling into a comfortable position, and he reviewed his own notes carefully. He inhaled quickly, giving a false stutter start, and then took a deep breath, closing his eyes and relaxing himself. Calmed, he began again. "Thank you for seeing us, Mr. Lester," he said.

A high-pitched giggle bubbled out of the old man. "My dad's 'Mr. Lester.'"

Orion's carefully arranged poise was easily dislodged, revealing his sudden discomfiture, which had been caused by the interruption. "Could you review what happened in…" He broke eye contact briefly to squint at his notes, also utilizing the opportunity to wipe his sweaty palm on his pants. "March 1997?"

The old man's pleased air deflated. "I thought you already knew," he said, his disappointment palpable. "I mean, that's why you're here, isn't it?" His faded eyes swung between them, taking note of the contrast between their suits, and then came to rest on Orion's tidier jacket. "You people investigate things like this." He simpered and added sullenly, "Though it took you long enough to come see me. The cops wouldn't take me seriously and file the report."

"Uh… In your own words," Orion floundered, trying to reclaim the momentum he'd meant to establish. "We've read the report, but we like to hear the victim—" As Hank flinched, shrugged his shoulders, and almost snarled, Orion quickly amended his statement, "—*witness* describe the events."

The old man's mood switched to excitement almost immediately. "Man, I cannot believe you're really here," he gushed, and then he broke into another fit of giggles. "It's all like I said. I was coming home from work—"

They were interrupted by a chirpy, generic ringtone. Orion sheepishly took the offensively loud phone out of his pocket and set it to vibrate before respectfully returning his attention to their interviewee. "You gonna get that?" Hank asked, his lip curled in a sneer, and the younger man shook his head, smiling an apology. "I wouldn't either. Microwaves in your brain. They'll cook it," Hank informed them helpfully before relaxing again. Connor involuntarily shook his head with incredulity, but he managed to pass the movement off as simple agreement about the dangers of cell phones.

"Anyway," the old man continued. "I was working over at Worksman Cycles—" He suddenly shifted gears, sitting on the edge of his seat and becoming even more animated. "You know, they make the best bicycles, but that's not all they make," he said, addressing Orion directly as if his lecture was a life lesson. "They started out making the wheels to those little vending carts you see all around the city."

The subtle buzz of a vibrating phone reached Connor's ears, and he noticed his partner check his device discreetly. His brow furrowed immediately as he read its screen, and he quietly excused himself, picking his way carefully through the precariously balanced jumble lining the corridor to make his exit into the hallway.

For his part, Hank redirected his monologue seamlessly toward Connor as if there had been no change in audience. "Marvels of technology, they are. I used to spin the wires for the spokes by hand. By hand!" He grinned proudly. "Do you know what kind of craftsmanship that takes?"

Connor stretched his half-amused smile, hoping it didn't appear as condescending as it felt. He leaned forward, resting his elbows on his knees in a posture that expressed interest, even if it was the sentiment furthest from his mind. "I'm sure it takes a lot of skill," he interjected in a patient tone of voice, "but that's not why we came here, Hank. Can I call you that?"

The old man released a titter that was more worthy of a preadolescent girl. "It's like we're friends," he agreed eagerly.

Connor suppressed the urge to roll his eyes. "You were going to tell us about your extraordinary experience."

"My *extraordinary* experience?" he repeated proudly.

Connor hesitated, taking note of the odd weight introduced to the statement. The case file was already unconvincing, and the witness' strange behavior served only to exacerbate his skepticism. The incongruous emphasis tweaked his suspicion, and he began to scrutinize the old man's body language more closely. "Yes," he replied, continuing his polite rapport. "You reported to the police that afternoon that you'd been attacked."

"Yes, of course," Hank confirmed, his eyes darting behind Connor and back toward the door as if he'd suddenly been distracted. "By the subway rat—" His voice, which had been full of conviction, suddenly cut off as he rectified his testimony. "Oh, but I wasn't coming home from work that day. I was actually coming from uptown to pay my friend Sal—"

As his narrative threatened to meander again, the geniality of Connor's smile became strained. "Hank," he said reasonably, "when we called, you said you had to work this evening. I'd like to get to the point before you head out." He wrenched his cheeks and lips into an apologetic expression. "I don't think we'll be able to drop by again anytime soon," he added, infusing his voice with enough regret to make the lie seem credible. The doubt he felt hadn't receded, and the old man's inability to stay on topic grated on his nerves.

"Oh, yes, of course," he replied, crestfallen, and then he perked up suddenly. "What if I had evidence?"

"Evidence of the attack?"

"Yes. I kept the branch he stabbed me with." Hank's wide grin was accompanied by a manic, triumphant cackle.

Connor scowled, muttering, "Of course you did."

"It's, uh, around here somewhere," Hank promised, but his inconsistent body language had already given away his disingenuousness, and Connor was ready to leave as soon as his partner returned. He watched the old man rummage around his apartment, toppling a stack of magazines and newspaper clippings, and his subsequent scramble to reorder the pile before it scattered into too much chaos. Though Connor could have assisted, he didn't feel obligated to help a false witness, and when Orion reentered the room, he flashed him a look that was meant to convey both his relief and a forceful suggestion to leave. However, it quickly disintegrated into one of concern when he noticed his partner's pallid complexion, wide eyes, and otherwise blank expression. He shoved past Hank, who was still fretting over his assorted paper scraps, and quickly joined his side.

"Something's come up," Orion whispered before he could speak. "I've got to head out. I'll see you tomorrow." His words were quick, rolling off his tongue like lightning, and Connor wasn't having any of it. The younger man avoided even fleeting eye contact, which would have given him away even if he weren't already a terrible liar.

Intending to confront him, Connor grabbed his shoulder and instead slipped into a different reality. Orion's youthful face became distorted by pain as his skin shriveled against his skull, yet black determination shone in his eyes, and before Connor could make sense of the invasive hallucination, his legs failed him and he was sharply returned to real life. His body could not process the contradictory sensations his nerves were emitting—whether his skin was crawling with electricity or he'd swallowed a cold boulder that had solidified the contents of his stomach. He tried to close his grasp around Orion to steady himself and impede his fall, but his hand would not obey, and he collapsed, dropping his full weight onto something hard. He felt a foreign object jab his rib, leaving a sizable bruise to develop tomorrow, and he avoided knocking his head against the ground only because Orion's reflexes saved him.

"Help me get him into the hallway," Orion said commandingly. Before Connor knew it, his numb arm was around Orion's reedy neck, and the slender man was dragging him through the narrow passage, upsetting its delicate balance and obliterating the path behind him. Hank became caught in the cave-in, making floundering attempts to reach them before he gave up. "I'll get some water," he declared, trying to be helpful, as he turned back.

Orion set him against the wall just outside the apartment door and crouched beside him. He removed Connor's jacket and loosened his tie before he began fanning him. "What happened?" he asked, his fraternal instincts surfacing.

Connor moved to shove him away but hesitated before making contact, unwilling to touch him for fear of sparking another vision. Vexed, he allowed his newly obedient arms to fall to his lap, and he insisted darkly, "Nothing."

Orion frowned sternly. "You collapsed. I don't think that—"

"Why don't you tell me what happened to you instead?" Connor snapped, unwilling to engage in a discussion about his health and the questions it would raise. A second vision was not only unwelcome, it was inconvenient; he could silence his thoughts only while alone, with copious amounts of alcohol, or both.

Orion recoiled; Connor's venomous reaction seemed to persuade him to temporarily shelve his troubles. "It's nothing," he said quietly. "It can wait until later. I think—"

"Bollocks!" Connor exclaimed, anger hastening the return of his sapped energy; it was an easier emotion to manage, so he embraced it to drown out his fears, and he redirected it as his reticent partner. "We've been over this, Starr: You have a tell. Now *tell*, or I'm going to beat it out of you." Heedless of his previous aversion, he reached forward and seized the younger man by the lapels, bringing his face within an inch of his own.

Orion fell forward onto his knees as his submissive nature resurged, expunging the lingering strength he'd drawn from being a caretaker, and he quickly and meekly surrendered, "Cassie's been kidnapped, and if I tell anyone, they'll kill her."

Connor felt the rage drain out of him, and he released his grip. "What?"

Orion rocked back on his heels, crossing his arms around his knees and pulling them into his chest as he sank to the ground, claiming a spot next to Connor. "Cassie just called. She's terrified," he said. He'd already averted his gaze, but now his eyes became unfocused, and his shoulders slumped. "They wouldn't let her talk for long—only to say that I needed to come alone."

Connor softened his tone. "What did they ask for?"

With perfect timing, Hank stumbled around the corner cradling a faded, chipped plastic novelty cup. Fortunately, it was equipped with a lid, for he tripped, barely catching himself on the doorframe, and then shrieked. Connor gave him an icy glare, and the old man quickly abandoned his notion of trying to assist and instead retreated into the safety of his apartment.

Orion shook his head. "Nothing. They just said to come alone."

Connor slammed the back of his head against the wall, expressing his frustration in an explosion of passion. "So you weren't going to tell anyone?" he exclaimed, chastising him with an incredulous scowl as he cursed Orion's infuriatingly meek nature.

"They said they'd kill her if I did," he explained timidly. His voice was small, shrinking as his anxiousness grew, and panic began to set in.

"That's what they always say," Connor growled, trying to sound reassuring while still giving him a dressing down. "That doesn't mean you don't. When they tell you to 'come alone,' it usually means they're going to try to double their investment and demand a ransom for you, too, or they're going to carve you into a pretty corpse." His mind immediately re-conjured the phantasm he'd glimpsed only a moment ago, and he snarled, shaking his head aggressively to banish it again. The subsequent displeasure leaked into his voice as he added cynically, "It's a trap."

"I have to go," a breathless Orion declared suddenly. He jumped to his feet, halting as Connor caught his sleeve.

"Well, you're not," the older man declared, somewhat undermining his own authority as he pulled himself up using the wall for support, and he tried to reinforce his influence over the younger man by puffing his chest out as he slapped on an overconfident grin. "Not like this. Not into a trap."

Orion yanked his sleeve from his grasp and turned to face him. "It's my sister! I have to go!" His pale face was flushed from the exertion of wrestling with conflicting emotions, but he set his jaw, and it seemed to help him draw strength while the rest of his body was still undecided. His fingers twitched, alternatively clenching and convulsing with nervous energy, and he was panting, bordering on hyperventilation. It was obvious that he was not thinking clearly.

Connor dropped his grin, becoming more appropriately stolid, and calmly took a step back, letting his hands fall naturally at his sides. "Look, this isn't the place to be having this sort of discussion," he suggested reasonably, hoping to mollify his partner into rational thought. "Why don't we head back to your apartment and talk it out, yeah?" Then despite himself, he couldn't prevent the small, wry smirk from appearing on his lips, and he quickly injected a healthy dose of stern criticism into his voice to counteract it. "Maybe we can come up with a plan that doesn't involve you stupidly sacrificing yourself."

Orion glowered, but his challenging gaze didn't last long. The tension drained from his body as his initial wave of adrenaline ebbed, and he closed his eyes in resignation. "Fine," he agreed sullenly.

- - -

The conference room was cozy as well as functional. The original facility had been hastily annexed to house Eric Dane, and as the new training program had grown, it had gradually absorbed wings from the former owner until the USDA had been entirely evicted from the site. On paper, Plum Island remained an animal research center to allow for expansion of the site without drawing suspicion from the locals and to conceal its true purpose. The room was a remnant from those early days; it was perpetually slated for renovation but never received it, and it had adapted over the years to the limitations of its confined size. A hardy table was centered in the room, providing a focal point for prominent attendees to do their business, and plenty of chairs lined the walls to allow individuals to listen or take notes whenever the table was full.

There was no need to be concerned about space that night, as only three people were in attendance: William Terrance; his boss, Jocasta Summers; and the containment supervisor, Nick Sable. They were joined via teleconference by Charlene Vicker and the two surviving surveillance agents. No one was happy tonight, especially not Summers, whose already severe face was distorted by displeasure. She was no taller than the rest of them, yet she seized the center of attention and, by doing so, seemed to grow in height. Her hair, which was normally pinned into a French twist, was a frizzy mess, and Terrance imagined that she'd hastily restyled it after receiving the call at her Greenport house and immediately reporting back. The rest of her appearance was immaculate, and her grim expression dared someone to disappoint her.

"Tell me the full situation," she demanded. She spoke rapidly, as if she had little time to spare for this meeting, but Terrance had experienced her indifferent method of speaking in the past; she had much on her mind and often tried to hit everything on a long internal list without accounting for the extra time it might take to fully explore or explain the items. In this case, every minute counted, as it placed them further behind the perpetrators, and she was due to explain the situation to Washington, D.C. shortly. Although Charlene Vicker worked for headquarters directly and could relate the account to her superiors, it was Summers' responsibility. "What have you found? What are your leads?"

Charlene spoke first, explaining how Cassiopeia Starr had broken curfew and her escalating attempts to locate the missing subject, and when she reached the end of her narrative, she passed it onto Parker, the senior agent in his partnership. Spurred by 9/11, he'd enrolled in a nascent Homeland Security degree program once he'd graduated from high school, and he'd worked his way up the ranks over the years before transferring to the smaller BSI under the promise of concentrating on a unique threat to national security. In contrast to his partner, his field experience was limited, despite extensive training, and his years of service, as well as his familiarity with the department's procedures, placed him above Barton, who was a former Ohio police officer and relatively recent hire. "We split up when we arrived on scene," Parker explained. "I took the house while Barton checked on the agents."

Summers crossed her arms. "You checked the house?" she asked in a critical voice. His actions were technically against protocol, as Parker had risked exposing the operation by contacting the subject directly. If the subject had taken note of his appearance, she might later recognize that he had been following her.

"I had a plan to impersonate someone," he assured her, "but it didn't matter. The door was ajar." Parker explained that he'd announced his presence as a federal agent as he'd drawn his weapon and entered the trailer, where he'd immediately seen the remains of Felix Buchanan. His voice was marked by disgust, ostensibly by the recollection of a teenager's splattered brains, but his composure remained admirably intact as he described clearing the remaining rooms. He hadn't found anything significant, aside from the subject's purse— left behind on the counter—which held her cell phone and their only means of tracking her.

Summers scowled, deepening the lines of her otherwise plain face, as she addressed Sable. "I noticed in the file that it was the only tracking she had," she remarked reprovingly. "Why is that?"

"Ma'am, it is standard procedure for—"

"She's a flight risk, is she not?" she interjected. Terrance wouldn't characterize the subject's risk of disappearing from the BSI's custody as her own initiative; by her own admission, she'd almost been abducted by VSION and had resisted because it hadn't felt like a wise decision to leave with the Vanguard. However, BSI was using her as leverage against her older brother, and consequently, more precautions should have been taken. Terrance surmised that Summers would have insisted on employing methods similar to those practiced with assets, and while he wouldn't disagree in principle, he didn't think strapping a rechargeable GPS to the subject would have been practical.

"So shouldn't closer accountability techniques have been used?" Summers demanded, confirming his thoughts. She'd entrusted her department heads to run their sections without her interference, but tonight she undoubtedly regretted not having micromanaged their decisions.

"It was suggested and rejected, ma'am," Charlene explained. "Both Cas—" She immediately corrected herself, as BSI designations were meant to dehumanize subjects, making it easier to deal with them objectively; Connor was the only exception to this rule, and this was only because it was necessary to keep his secret. "Supernova and her brother are too educated for the old techniques. She knows too much about technology to be fooled by simple misdirection."

"That's why we're developing new accountability procedures," Sable clarified. He then added, "She also lived with a BSI employee, so the risk was deemed low. In fact, if she hadn't cohabitated with Vicker, we might not yet know she went missing." While the statement was true because deceased agents couldn't report movement, it didn't help his case.

Nevertheless, Summers gave a reluctant nod and moved on. "Barton, what did you see?"

As Barton spoke, Terrance envisioned her grim expression and curt nod. "While Parker searched the trailer, I went to check on our agents," she began. Normal procedure was to observe the subject from a distance, which had been accomplished in this case by following her to the Buchanan place, parking two to three blocks up the street, and watching her through binoculars. Though troubled by the lack of contact with the team, Barton initially believed that the two of them had simply been complacent—even negligent—that night. The missing agents had parked their car in a pool of shadow between two streetlamps, and she'd called their phone again as she'd approached the vehicle in the hopes that they'd answer and confirm their status. Once again, they'd failed to answer the call, and she'd become unsettled as she'd drawn nearer and had been able to make out their unmoving silhouettes. "I drew my weapon and approached the car slowly," she said, slipping further into a detached tenor, and her voice became more intense. "The first thing I noticed was that the passenger-side window was down. Foster was slumped in the passenger seat. It looked like she'd been shot through the forehead at point-blank range."

Terrance closed his eyes. Foster had recently returned to duty after maternity leave. She'd asked for an easier detail—one that would have allowed her to be home more often to continue nursing her newborn—and he'd promised her that he'd arrange it as soon as a position became available. Waynesboro had been that assignment.

"Ayala didn't do much better," Barton continued. "He tried to pull his weapon, but it looks like the door and the steering column got in the way, and the suspect got the drop on him." Terrance briefly wondered if Ayala would be still alive had he been right-handed, but he discarded this line of thought; his grief didn't need to be fed by what-if scenarios.

"Whoever the perpetrator was, they've definitely killed before, but I wouldn't exactly say they were professional," Barton speculated, voice discolored by disdain. "We're working with the local police to canvas the neighborhood. Someone had to have seen or heard something."

Summers narrowed her eyes. "It's one thing to lose an asset; it's entirely different to find our agents assassinated. The perpetrators were professional," she asserted vehemently, "in and of the fact that they knew where our agents were and eliminated them." She inhaled deeply, clenching her jaw tighter. "Could it have been VSION?"

Terrance grimaced. "They were after the girl before," he agreed quietly.

"We haven't found any evidence of abilities being utilized," Parker answered. Unhappily, he ticked off signs of known Vanguard abilities, rejecting the presence of their owners. "No excessive breakage, water puddles, or even unexplained scorch marks from the girl."

Barton cut in angrily. "We didn't have a Geiger counter handy, but I doubt it would have detected anything," she spat. "Our agents were shot. VSION hasn't used guns in a confrontation yet." Her antagonism was unexpected, yet Terrance recalled a minor detail from her file: She'd left the police force after being caught in a shootout during the pursuit of a robbery suspect. Moving up to the federal level had reduced the likelihood of her being caught in another violent confrontation despite the BSI's sustained standoff with the Vanguard, and she was undoubtedly distraught that she'd been unable to protect her fellow agents.

Summers sighed as she pushed air through her clenched teeth, resulting in a hissing sound. "Could it have been the girl?" she asked, resigned to hearing an affirmative answer that would end the subject's life and their secure hold on her brother. "Could she have done this, with or without help?"

"We were always careful to hang back. She never noticed us," Parker contended. "No close calls. Nothing."

Summers nodded briskly, convinced. "We need to get her back," she declared, placing emphasis on each word. "Penumbra's continued cooperation hinges on her." Then, reverting to her clipped tone, she turned to Terrance.

"Call Connor. Tell him to watch out for her trying to contact her brother, strange behavior… anything that might be a clue."

"Yes, ma'am."

"But under no circumstances is Connor to let Penumbra know we lost her," she commanded, again stressing the importance of secrecy. "Parker, Barton, continue working with the local police," she commanded. She set her jaw again, working the muscles in lieu of staring down the absent agents. "I don't like this one bit. You scout that crime scene, and then you scrub it clean," she barked. "If Others were involved, I don't want any outsider finding out." In a deliberate voice, she added, "Keep this contained." Continuing her momentum, she switched gears, and if she'd been in the room, Summers' attention would have instantly shifted. "Vicker–"

"Yes, ma'am?"

"I know you don't work for me, but we'll need your help on this." Summers' tone softened to a level that was appropriate for requesting a favor, but she was still in control, and it would be difficult to refuse her. "Can your husband be brought on board?"

Though Charlene hesitated, she did not allow silence to coalesce, and she hid her discomfort well, allowing her voice to waver during only the first sentence. "He's the head officer working the case," she answered. "He knows I work for the DHS and that there's something special about Cassie." Terrance noticed this time that Charlene hadn't bothered to correct herself, and he made a mental note to follow up with Sable about the Vickers' continued suitability. It had likely been a misstep caused by frequent everyday references to her real name, but it still merited an investigation; as Supernova's de facto handler, he could not afford to have Charlene lose her objectivity with the subject. "I can have him sign an NDA and explain the situation and our mission. I think he'll help us suppress evidence in the name of national security," she offered, sounding more confident.

"Good," Summers replied, satisfied. "Parker, Barton, deal with Vicker's husband exclusively if you have to," she said. "None of this goes anywhere higher than a kidnapping or possible runaway. Got it?" The three of them agreed, and she didn't give much time for additional comments as she ended the call abruptly. Summers had little time for pleasantries.

She straightened, having leaned over to be able to better project her voice for the call, and crossed her arms as unease slyly crept into her features. "I don't like this at all," she opined; it was likely an aside not meant for them, as she immediately leveled the two of them with her disapproving and now hostile gaze. "How the hell is she not being better tracked?" she demanded of Sable.

"Well, ma'am—"

She silenced him, cutting his explanation off. "Do you know what losing a subject means for your program?" she rebuked him. "Jarvis has been pushing to euthanize all non-assets, and after this fiasco, I'm inclined to agree with him." She let her statement hang menacingly in the air for a moment, staring him down and letting him know that he was on thin ice, before she continued. "This is terrible, especially since she's an elementalist," she added heatedly. "Do you know what kind of damage she can do?"

He flinched, countering weakly, "She passed the training program with flying colors. She's the first elementalist to do so."

"I don't care," she snapped. "That's even worse, because now it means she's a *smart* bomb." Her anger wasn't directed solely at Sable, which was a fact that Terrance soon discovered as her focus shifted and her brusque attitude steered her aggravation toward him. "Are we sure about Connor?" Harshly, she demanded, "Why the hell did you partner an asset with another asset?"

It had been a joint decision by Sable and Terrance—one that had been made following several hours of debate—and the choice had not been made lightly. The Starrs had presented a unique situation, with Penumbra's valuable ability necessitating special handling, and the circumstances of their apprehension had created obstacles. Unlike Antithesis, they had not been isolated from modern society, so it had been impossible for them to be misled by ignorance or misdirected from the fetters that the BSI exploited. New techniques would have had to have been created in the short and long term, and when Connor's inquiries had been channeled up to Terrance, he had embraced the opportunity and acted on it.

Terrance cleared his throat. "They established a rapport, however minor it may have been, and Connor was present for Supernova's incident with her father," he explained, outlining his logic. "Penumbra *chose* to save his life and, in doing so, revealed his ability to us." Connor had followed up immediately on the Starrs as soon as he'd been released from the hospital, evidently invested in their well-being as a result of gratitude for having received their aid. This should have been a disqualifying factor for a partnership, and Terrance had known that Connor would be treading a thin line. "If I'd denied Connor's request after that, he'd have started investigating the reason why, and we didn't want him looking too closely, did we?" he asked, meaning Connor's case files and his own dossier. Handlers were mandated to be objective with their subjects, and though Connor had demonstrated a personal interest in the Starrs, this connection was understandable, and Connor had since established that his objectivity had remained uncompromised. If Terrance had used this mitigatable factor to deny Connor's request to be partnered with the new asset, he might have turned his detective skills on the situation and uncovered his significant disqualifying factor.

"He wouldn't have figured it out from one case," Summers replied skeptically.

Terrance shrugged. "I didn't want to risk it, and as I said, Connor already had a rapport with him," he countered. He shifted, taking a more comfortable posture, and used his hands to emphasize his points as he defended his position. "You know how most of the agents regard the assets... even Connor—a supposed 'field agent.' That's not going to make a kid warm up to the idea of helping us voluntarily." Even though Connor was afforded the same benefits as every other agent—access to files, department resources, and unrestricted facility areas—he was basically shunned by his peers, none of whom wanted to become attached to an asset who might be euthanized someday.

"He's basically here under coercion, but we want his willing cooperation," he continued. "We're not going to get that if he's partnered with someone who hates his very existence." Lawrence Johnson immediately came to mind; his distaste for Others colored even his personal interaction with Antithesis, who felt similarly about her kind. "At least Connor still treats them like humans, and we know he'll make the hard decisions."

Summers nodded slowly as she absorbed his words, hopefully agreeing with them; Terrance knew that, if necessary, he could fall back on Connor's decisiveness in the Chamberlain case. Evidently, he didn't need to strengthen his justification, for she moved on, turning back to Sable. "Where are we on Echo?"

Sable released a long, deliberate sigh that seemed to invalidate her as an alternative avenue via which to locate the missing Starr girl. "She's not progressing," he replied, clearly frustrated. "She's refusing the training based on the fact that she's not 'one of them.'" He pulled a face as he mocked her delusional rationalization. "The visions that led her to Others were tools sent to aid her mission, not a mutation, and it's an ironic attitude since those very senses told her that both Penumbra and Connor were others." He shook his head. "She asked about them, about their status, when she was processed."

Terrance's gut clenched. "I didn't hear about this," he said, worried. "Did she mention it to Connor?"

Sable shook his head dismissively. "It was in the examination room after they'd left," he explained. "If she mentioned anything to them at all, it would've been about Penumbra. She recognized immediately that he was an Other, but with Connor in a position of power, she needed reassurance that we weren't all Others. Then she started doubting her senses and needed clarification of Connor's status. He confused her, and we told her an appropriate fabrication to obfuscate his existence." He sighed deeply. "But to my knowledge, she never mentioned it to Connor himself."

Terrance relaxed somewhat as Sable readdressed Summers. "I asked Angel to speak with her Other to Other, but she won't accept any advice or comfort from him," he continued. Angel's assistance had been crucial to molding the guileless young Emma Braddock into Antithesis, helping her come to terms with the arrests of the adults in her life and her sudden transfer from her childhood compound. His words had eased the transition as she'd come to accept her new status as an Other and her transformation into a containment tool. Contrastingly, Echo had apparently rebuffed his efforts. "She avoids him and Antithesis, treating them with as much disdain as any of the agents would."

He paused, considering an idea that had just occurred to him. "Since she's in such deep denial, maybe we could reassign her as an agent like Connor," he suggested, but he immediately discarded the notion with a sharp shake of his head. If he hadn't, Terrance would have directly denounced the proposal as ill-advised and desperate; Echo already knew that she was an Other, even if she hadn't accepted this fact, and the knowledge itself might taint her actions as an agent.

Summers' severe expression tightened. "You'd better figure it out and come to an understanding with her, because if she doesn't train, she's not an asset—just a drain on our resources," she warned him and continued into an ultimatum. "I don't really want to capitulate to Jarvis, but this debacle with Supernova is going to make us take a hard hit, and if Echo doesn't appear to be a good investment, then she's the first on the chopping block. I don't care what her ability is." She jabbed her finger at Sable. "Get it sorted!" she barked and left the room without allowing further comment.

- - -

Cassie's fire had gone out. She'd been terrified the night of the mugging, acting on instinct in the moment and then retreating into childhood behaviors for comfort after the fact. Her brother had tried to console her, but he'd provided only an unwelcome reminder of their inhuman nature. When Sone and the Vanguard had come to collect her, she'd maintained a level head and escaped the situation as soon as her "saviors" had been distracted; fear had never entered her mind—only confusion and concern. Even her father's great sin against her brother and herself had only inspired feelings of rage rather than terror; Pierce had never respected his children, so he shouldn't have dared threaten them in their own home, and she'd consequently taught him a lesson for his presumption.

But this was not the case tonight with this familiar stranger. Every time she thought she might have a handle on the situation, the floor was ripped from beneath her feet, and her fearful mind was compressing everything to a single point—the present—as fear seeped deeper into her brain. While the sophisticated stranger was like them—and she'd been prepared for the existence of Others by the BSI—the dread she felt at the possibility of him reusing his ability was even more intimidating than any physical cage could have been.

She again contemplated setting her surroundings alight simply to put an end to the entire affair. She knew she'd get only one chance; the filaments of the substandard industrial fixtures wouldn't burn well enough to ignite anything more than a single target, so she'd have to merge the individual sources into a single kindling pile if she wanted a useful blaze. This, of course, presented the same conundrum as the car: Since she might be only superficially fire resistant, her escape plan might instead transform into a suicide mission. It might be worth it to destroy her dreadful captor if it worked, but she had no guarantee that it would; her limited knowledge of her kind handicapped her ability to plan, and she fleetingly regretted cutting off contact with Sone.

She also had to consider the impact that her actions would have on her brother. If she survived the blaze, then she would have to pay the price for breaking established BSI guidelines, for which the punishment was permanent restriction to Plum Island. But she'd gleaned from the staff via avoided eye contact, awkward phrasing, and reading between the lines in various conversations that the penalty was likely far more severe. Her actions, whether or not she lived, would result in a lose–lose situation, and though she had been selfish as a teenager, she didn't want to invalidate the sacrifices that Orion had made for her over the years. She cared deeply for her brother and for everything he'd ever done for her, and she knew that her death would devastate him and there would be no one left to comfort him when she was gone.

- - -

The ride back to Orion's apartment served only to exacerbate his condition; the clock continued to tick while he was trapped in a long metal tube. He was like a druggie on a bad cocktail, crawling out of his skin with nervous energy one moment, only to sink into traumatic depression, and there was no way to delineate when either mood would peak and the pendulum would swing the other way. Connor could abide anger, and he could mold fear and even panic into a facsimile of it, but he didn't know what to do with despair other than to drown it, and there was no alcohol in the apartment. He'd have to somehow redirect the younger man's energy into something constructive—and soon.

Connor forced Orion onto a barstool and corralled him, leaning on the bar and keeping his forearms within easy distance of the younger man in case he had to shake some sense back into him. "Right," he said in a sufficiently somber tone of voice; he greatly wished that he could be facetious—it was his own way of coping—but it was not appropriate in this situation, so he kept focused. "So, start from the beginning." Orion shuddered, catching his breath at the back of his throat, and Connor quickly snapped him back into the moment. "Take a deep breath," he coached, exaggerating the motion of a large lungful of air.

Connor painstakingly drew the story from the younger man, gently guiding his partner toward calm with his voice whenever Orion's composure started to waver. Cassie had made the phone call at the behest of her kidnapper, reading the message under duress, and Orion's responses had been relayed via speaker, as he had been able to hear the faint echo of his own voice but little else. It had been a short conversation, and no demands had been made. Too tangled up in fear for his sister, Orion hadn't questioned the lack of ransom, assuming that negotiations would take place after he'd met with the culprit. However, the threat on her life had been explicit: Orion should inform no one, especially not the BSI—which had been mentioned by name. The kidnapper had graciously allowed him to set a time for them to meet, and he could not be late to that appointment.

"You can't go," Connor declared. The provision regarding the BSI had put him on edge; public knowledge of the agency was vague and vanilla to the point of inducing torpor, so for someone to know its personal connection to Orion proved that the person had insider knowledge. This meant that VSION or their ilk were involved. "It's clearly a trap."

Orion clenched his fists. "Well, what else—?"

"You can't handle this on your own," Connor insisted. He grabbed the younger man's forearms and spoke calmly, ensuring their eyes met to confirm that his message was being received. "We've got to involve someone higher, if nothing more than for your protection." His preference was to involve the BSI to avoid complications; if Cassie or Orion used their abilities, there would be no need for a cover-up. However, he was willing to deal with local authorities simply for expediency, and he'd take the inevitable hit from his boss with pride if it meant that the girl was safe.

He scowled as his phone rang, interrupting the momentum he was building. He glanced at the screen just in case and then wished that he hadn't; it was his boss, which meant that the call was important and he would have to salvage his argument after the fact. "What timing," he groused before answering. "Special Agent Connor."

Orion's eyes widened. "Don't—" Connor silenced him with a look and shook his head sharply, causing the younger man to back down. He also flashed Orion a reassuring grin; while he might inform the agency of the situation, there was no need to let Orion suspect that he would.

"Is Penumbra there with you?" He recognized Terrance's deep bass.

"Yeah," he responded, holding his smile.

"The whole evening?"

"Yeah," he repeated, his brow furrowing slightly despite his efforts to the contrary. "We just got back from an interview."

"Good. Don't let him out of your sight," Terrance said. There was a hush— the way a crowd quiets when a stunt goes wrong and everyone is waiting to see if the stuntman has survived—and then he spoke with the confidence of a man who'd recused himself from a situation. "There's been an incident involving his sister. She's gone missing."

Connor had difficulty maintaining his unconcerned veneer and disguised its lapse by sustaining eye contact with Orion. Maintaining a separate and duplicitous narrative for his partner was not a part of the job he enjoyed. "What do you mean?" he replied in a neutral voice.

"It's not important," Terrance assured him in an attempt to forestall the inevitable line of conversation. "We need you to watch out for any strange behavior and let us know about it immediately."

Connor chuffed, unsatisfied. "I kinda need to know what I'm looking for." He was fishing for information, and there was no guarantee Terrance would take the bait, but surprisingly, his boss caved easily. Connor wondered if this meant that the agency was desperate for information or whether another factor was in play.

"Someone made a major move against us," Terrance replied, speaking more carefully than the curt, no-nonsense manner to which Connor was accustomed. "The sister's surveillance team was assassinated, and we're not yet sure if she had a hand in it. We're chasing down a few leads, but if Penumbra's been with you, it probably means he wasn't involved."

As soon as Connor recognized that Orion might overhear something he shouldn't, he casually strolled out of earshot toward the foyer, keeping his eye on Orion. He kept his attention divided between the conversation and his monitoring of the younger man to prevent him from absconding to meet the kidnapper. "VSION?" he surmised quietly.

"We don't know," Terrance admitted gruffly. "There's not enough evidence either way."

Connor grunted unhappily. As far as he could tell, Terrance wasn't lying or withholding information—no purpose would be served by keeping the Vanguard's involvement under wraps—and Connor was unsettled by the reminder that the agency was still constrained by human limitations; it was easy to forget this fact when the BSI so often dealt with preternatural latitudes. If they were dealing with Others, then it would be advantageous to let Connor know so that he could better deal with any threat. "So, what do I tell him?"

"Nothing."

He scowled. "He has a right to know."

"Not for the purpose of his continued containment." Terrance's tone was cold, and Connor knew that his supervisor had made more difficult decisions in the past than he had, but this knowledge didn't make his rationale any easier to hear. "She's our primary control for him, and with her missing, he loses all incentive to cooperate. He might even try to reacquire her on his own." It was ironic that Terrance didn't know how right he was, though Connor believed that his boss was overestimating Orion's capabilities; Orion was an overprotective older brother, not a commando, and Connor was in no danger of losing custody of him to an ill-advised rescue mission. "No, you're not telling him a thing until I give you further instructions."

"When's that gonna be?" he asked acerbically. Just because a sound decision had been made didn't mean he had to agree with it.

"Most likely when the situation is resolved," Terrance replied icily. His deep voice became critical and almost dangerous as he addressed Connor's perceived insubordination. "Connor, do we have a problem?"

"No, sir," he replied, infusing the words with enough sarcasm that he almost sounded sincere. "I'm just a little concerned he'll figure it out on his own. That won't jibe well with the friendly image we're trying to project here."

"I have the confidence you'll figure it out," Terrance told him; his tone didn't leave room for argument. "Lie to him if you have to."

"Yeah," Connor agreed resentfully. He ended the call hastily, no longer willing to be reminded of his unfortunate responsibility, especially in the midst of trying to handle the unfolding crisis. He turned his full attention back to Orion, who must have overheard at least a part of the conversation despite Connor's best efforts, as the younger man had wrapped his arms around himself and was kicking the barstool footrest semi-aggressively. Connor tried to force a blithe smile as he placed his phone in his pocket and sauntered back to the bar, but he found that it wouldn't stick on his face. Instead, he leaned heavily against the island, folded his hands, and pulled a long face as Orion watched him expectantly.

He couldn't do it; he had to be honest. "This is a lot more serious than you realize," he said slowly, bowing his head; he found that using his fingernail to fiddle with the grout in the island tile made it easier for him to continue. "When your sister graduated from Plum Island, a surveillance team was tasked to keep track of her. They were killed when your sister was taken." Involuntarily, he twitched into a taut smirk. "'Assassinated' was the term they used." He returned his full attention to his partner, his eyes full of concern. "Whoever took your sister meant serious business, which is why you can't go meet them alone. We need backup of some kind."

Orion's eyes went wide at first, and then the nervous energy drained from his limbs as he decisively tightened his jaw. "You've got a gun," he asserted as he stood, nodding toward Connor holster. "You can watch over me."

Orion's suggestion was naively resolute, and Connor felt ashamed that the younger man had so much confidence in him, especially since the agent had to bitterly acknowledge to himself that his firearm never did much to aid him: A human had once shot him with his own weapon, and an Other had rendered it useless during his last confrontation. "I mean someone with better expertise."

Orion suddenly drew himself up. "Notifying the police takes time," he stated, speaking with an assertiveness that was fueled by the dire nature of the situation. "I've listened to you because you're my friend, and you might know what to do, but all you've done is waste my time. If this is what it takes to protect my sister, then I'm going to do it, and I'm leaving whether or not you're going to help me." He displayed the same confidence that Connor had briefly glimpsed at Hank Lester's apartment when he'd collapsed; it was that of a man who'd identified a situation, knew what to do, and was taking decisive ownership of it. Orion strode to the foyer, where he retrieved a heavy jacket for the colder weather, and he began donning it with little regard for the older man's reaction.

Although Connor was impressed by the historic transformation of his partner's demeanor, it didn't change the fact that Orion was making a stupid decision, and he was going to stop him. "Orion Starr, you are not going out that door," he growled authoritatively, banking on his tacit dominance in their relationship to arrest his partner's building momentum.

To his great surprise, Orion did not yield to his commanding influence. "Yes, I am," he replied with finality and left.

- - -

The hour grew late, and the evening seemed to stretch on forever. It had all started so simply with a teenager missing her curfew—an event that happens daily to parents all over the world—and had deteriorated into an abstract composite of a military operation and the painful memory of the night Charlene's son had died becoming a new construct of stress, anxiety, and mixed emotions.

It had been difficult to isolate Timothy when he'd been conducting a search and leading the team through the trailer park in which the Buchanans lived, and even more so to get him to keep his voice down when Charlene had finally been able to reveal the existence of Others to him. But he had taken the news well, considering the child he'd taken into his home had been classified as a living hazard, and after he'd recovered from the initial shock, he'd asked probing questions about the BSI, its mission, and Others whom she had met. Her work at headquarters had been primarily administrative, dealing with the bureaucracy of the government, as well as navigating the complex political climate of D.C., so she had been unable to provide him with many solid answers, but she had still been able to impart the importance of Operation Blackout, including its significance to international relations. Even though Timothy had signed the bureau's nondisclosure agreement and had consented to suppressing evidence in the name of national security with no resistance, she'd felt that she may have failed to convince him to adopt a BSI-sanctioned viewpoint.

The conversation had regrettably drained the last of her reserves, and she'd crumpled to the ground, folding her legs beneath her once she'd placed the NDA safely in her purse. "What's wrong?" her husband had asked as he'd crouched on the dried grass beside her in concern, rubbing her back reassuringly.

Her duty completed, her thoughts were free to turn dark again as she remembered another endless night during which she'd searched for her lost child, Shaun. Cassie might not have been her biological daughter, and she'd been a poor fit for the hole that had been left by Charlene's son, but she'd nevertheless developed affection for the child in the short time that she'd been in their care, and her mind drifted back to the ditch where they'd found Shaun's body. She was terrified that the same fate had befallen the girl. Cassie had been abducted—the violence at the scene had left no doubt about that—and Charlene worried about her safety. Would Cassie return to her in one piece, or had that morning's breakfast been the last time she would see her? Like Shaun, she'd taken Cassie's ongoing presence for granted.

Then there was the matter of her queer biology. Cassie had only been placed in their home because she was an Other and Orion Starr had believed that the Vickers were good parental candidates. When she'd become Cassie's foster mother, she'd acquired the additional duty of monitoring an Other. She'd received additional training centering on the control procedures for Others and how to disable them, and while she had not enjoyed the experience, it had instilled in her the importance of the mission. The BSI manifesto dictated that Others were to be kept under strict control or euthanized, and Charlene feared that this incident would reflect poorly on Cassie. If fortune smiled on the siblings, Cassie would only be transferred to Plum Island, where she would be closely monitored, but it was the alternative that weighed heavily on Charlene's mind. The BSI did not believe in gray areas, and Cassie had escaped their authoritarian control, however brief or unintentional the action might have been.

"I don't want Cassie to come back," she admitted suddenly, surprising even herself. Timothy's brow furrowed, and he strained to keep his expression neutral in an attempt to conceal his deepening concern; perhaps he thought she'd lapsed into shock and was expressing it in an outlandish fashion. "I'm afraid if she comes back, something bad will happen to her," she explained, wondering if she should clarify her meaning by revealing the BSI's euthanasia policy, but she instead paused when a worse thought occurred to her. "But if she doesn't come back, then something bad has already happened to her."

The burden she carried suddenly became a crushing weight, and she bowed her head against its might. Shaun had been only eighteen—he would have turned twenty-two this year—and Cassie was even younger. She remembered the Jaws of Life tearing apart the shell of his Ford Escort and paramedics rushing in to treat her son before they'd determined that his broken body had been too far gone. She remembered the panic she'd felt all the way to the emergency room as it had risen to consume her future, as well as the numbness that had descended when he'd been pronounced dead. Despite a significantly weaker bond between herself and Cassie, she knew that she'd be no more able to bear the burden again; her mind would break.

Timothy held his composure, holding her through the sobbing and wiping her tears away, and this was why she loved him; he'd been her rock after Shaun's death. However, in this moment, he failed to find comforting words and instead focused on solving the problem. "It's starting to look like a kidnapping," he said, his voice solid and earnest. "A neighbor saw a strange car departing Eden Avenue around the time of the murders. It matches the description of a suspicious car that had been seen hanging around the high school." Hindsight undoubtedly told him that the vehicle sighting should have been better investigated when it had been originally reported, but he hid his anger and frustration well. "The license plate on that vehicle had been reported stolen, so it was a dead end."

He became quiet, holding his breath, and Charlene pulled away from his embrace to look at him. His brow was furrowed, mirroring the frown on his face, and he looked exhausted. He shook his head, adding dolefully, "These guys staked out our house, figured out Cassie's schedule, and followed her to Felix's. They must have realized no one would be home at the Buchanan's and figured it would be a good opportunity to ambush her."

She sat up, her heart in her throat. Despite being concerned for her foster daughter's safety, she also suddenly felt violated and wondered what the perpetrators had seen, when they had been near the house, and whether she'd seen them and had failed to take note. "So what do we do?" she asked, ill at ease.

Casually, Timothy continued to stroke her back, and he gently restored some of her calm with his touch. "We wait for the kidnappers to make contact," he answered confidently. Disapprovingly, he added, "Your friends are trying to make a good case as to why the FBI can't take over, and I have to say I disagree. They're the experts in this sort of thing, and it'll only help us get her back quicker." He shook his head and sighed, looking at the darkness around them. Several individuals were still using flashlights to search the wide yards between trailer homes, but their numbers had dwindled, and Parker and Foster had joined the cluster of people at the Buchanan place to make their petition.

"In the meantime, we'll continue looking for clues and see if we can figure out who these people are," Timothy finished, sounding startlingly optimistic.

Charlene couldn't quite yet buy into his positivity. "What if they don't ask for a ransom?" she asked, thinking of all the things that went wrong in the movies. If the police were notified or got too close, the victim suffered, losing their limbs or even their life. Sometimes the abductee was being forced into slavery or a murder dungeon as part of a larger operation. At other times, even the abduction itself went wrong, and the victim was accidentally killed during transportation. In real life, things were more likely to go wrong, and with the innumerable unsolved cases around the world, she was afraid that tonight might be the end of the road for Cassie and that there would be no closure for her.

"They will," he replied with certainty.

"But what if they don't?" she insisted. "Cassie would put up a struggle, but you said she didn't. What if something went wrong? We'd never hear from her again!" The knot in her stomach tightened, and she was thankful that she was already seated or her legs might have failed her.

Timothy was silent, looking into the distance rather than meeting her gaze, and after a moment, he stretched an encouraging smile across his face. There wasn't much he could say to reassure her, so he pulled her closer and whispered soothingly into her ear. "Don't worry. We'll find her," he promised and kissed her head.

- - -

Regardless of his personal feelings on the subject, Connor had an obligation to catch up to his partner, who had displayed surprising strength that had heretofore been unrealized in the younger man. Orion refused to yield to Connor's normal tactics of irksome behavior, and despite having to fall back on supercilious browbeating, Connor was the one who eventually surrendered and reluctantly accompanied the younger man to his rendezvous.

The address directed the pair to a string of warehouses near the docks, and the taxi driver wouldn't venture further into the district, instead dropping them at the avenue entrance and forcing them to proceed on foot. There were a handful of dingy streetlamps, faintly illuminating the warehouse numbers as they counted down to their destination, and Orion insisted that Connor wait a few buildings up the street so that he would not be seen. The distance was too great for Connor's comfort, as he could barely see in the dull, dingy amber light provided by the scant lamps. But Orion was immovable, and Connor watched from the shadows as the younger man continued alone.

Connor doubted he could even hit a target at this distance, given his limited training. He pressed himself hard into the metal siding and, realizing his form would nevertheless remain conspicuous, slid around the corner so its cover would provide both concealment and protection. He hadn't seen or heard anyone since the cabbie had left, but he knew that at least one person must be lurking in the area to meet Orion, and he drew his firearm as a precautionary measure.

The combination of sights, sounds, and smells sometimes made it difficult to differentiate anything in New York, but Connor felt a creeping sensation that an intruder was in the immediate area. As the hairs on the back of his neck raised, he caught a glimpse of movement out of the corner of his eye and spun around immediately. His attacker caught his wrist, impeding the proper deployment of his weapon, and pulled him deeper into the darkness between the two buildings. Connor reluctantly relinquished his gun as his arm was repeatedly beaten against the wall and pressure was properly applied to his grip. He pushed back, lashing out blindly in the hopes that pure adrenaline would be his ally, but it let him down instead. His attacker shoved his knee into his abdomen with enough force to make him double over in pain and finished the assault by clubbing the back of his head with his fists. Connor saw stars and defeated, he recovered breathlessly on the ground as another man claimed his firearm.

The lanky man clucked his tongue, detaching the weapon from the useless leash, and chuckled. "Didn't do you much good, did it?"

- - -

"I told you that would happen," Parker said as they exited the Buchanan trailer. Barton waited at the bottom of the stairs for him to join her, and they walked down the short lot that served both as a driveway and a parking space. There was a thinning group of searchers lingering near the north corner of the mobile home. Barton hoped these people were only stragglers and that the main body was still out conducting its hunt for the Starr girl. She made a mental note to speak to Timothy Vicker about them. She remembered a statistic from when she'd still been on the force—that the first forty-eight hours were crucial to solving a crime and that every hour thereafter diminished their chances of success—and she deemed time an especially important factor in this case, so no one should have called off the search yet. Cassiopeia Starr's disappearance wasn't an ambiguous question; a crime had occurred, though time would tell whether she'd been a victim or a collaborator.

They'd already uncovered two clues in the short period following the discovery of the crime scene. The first had been the partial imprint of a man's dress shoe found in the tacky mud next to the stairs, and it had been used to estimate the general weight and height of its owner. It had already been determined that the footprint did not belong to Mr. Buchanan, and its size eliminated Cassie's brother as a suspect, though it did not absolve him of being involved just yet. Forensics were already working on determining more about the shoe itself, including the manufacturer and where else the owner might have traveled.

The second lead had been provided by a neighbor in the form of a probable getaway car. The description had sounded familiar, reminding the two agents of a suspicious vehicle they'd seen when following the subject during her daily rounds. Its driver had been a lanky man with slicked hair and a sleazy grin, and at the time, they'd reported him to the local authorities because they'd seen him take pictures of the student body using a zoom lens. In retrospect, Barton wished that she'd paid closer attention to him; perhaps they could have prevented the kidnapping. He was too lean to have been the man who'd left behind the footprint; nevertheless, an all-points bulletin had been placed on him, as it was possible that he was an accomplice or a person of interest.

"The FBI has clear jurisdiction in the event of a kidnapping," Parker continued to lecture her. They'd reached the end of the short driveway, which was blocked by police cars and equipment, as well as a grieving Mr. Buchanan and his extended family. Parker appeared uncertain where to head and turned toward the street, trying to isolate their conversation from casual eavesdropping. "Unless you wanted to bring up terrorism charges, we didn't have a chance of taking the case from them."

"Maybe we should," Barton replied grimly, letting the insinuation hang sinisterly for a moment. She watched Mr. Buchanan embrace his mother while his teary-eyed sister looked on; her husband hung back, possibly unsure how to comfort his wife and in-laws. "VSION previously went after the girl," she reminded him, establishing precedence of terrorism.

"You don't believe they were involved this time," Parker replied soberly, calling her bluff.

"Maybe not, but it'll give us jurisdiction," she said, glancing toward the temporary incident command post that the police had set up and the FBI had taken over. The trailer's phone line had been redirected to the tent because the mobile home was an active crime scene, and a negotiator waited tensely for a call, but no one had made contact yet. "Maybe I'm changing my mind." It was an idle threat—one that had been made to alleviate the helplessness she felt—to seize jurisdiction under false pretenses because Parker would never allow it, but available evidence made the list of probable perpetrators exceedingly short. The Vickers had no known enemies, so the subject's kidnapping had nothing to do with them. The alternative was that her alias had not been as well constructed as previously believed, and this left two possibilities: VSION or the Starrs. While the Starr couple's crimes had been horrendous, most of their victims had remained unidentified, and it was unlikely that anyone would target Cassiopeia Starr for retribution, especially since her adult brother lived openly under his legal name. It was far more likely that VSION was the culprit, even if Barton didn't believe that they were behind the abduction.

"You bring terrorism into this case, and it'll accelerate out of our control," Parker warned her; they were the same age, but his stern tone reminded her of her drill-sergeant father. "You heard the chief: We need to keep this contained."

She sighed heavily, hearing his words and then absorbing them, as she remembered their conference call. She was angry and would remain this way; they'd lost good agents tonight, and someone would pay. "We'll keep it contained, but I'm not going to just stand here," she promised, retrieving her gun from its holster and giving it a function check. Although she wasn't planning on starting a conflict, she hoped that one of their leads would pan out soon or that she'd find an Other to confront.

- - -

The stench of the dim warehouse was repulsive, overpowering the ordinary briny ammonia stink of the docks, and Connor detected a strange scent of rancid meat among the intermingling odors as Orion and his escorts herded them into the center of the building, where a small group of people waited.

The ache in Connor's head already required a fraction of his attention, as did the several new bruises that were blossoming across his body, but they were washed away by a sudden wave of vertigo. His dizzying headache grew, slowly consuming his sight and concentration, and he couldn't help but massage his complaining temples. However, as he sought relief behind closed eyes, he was instead revisited by his unwelcome vision, and he realized, to his great dismay and incomprehension, that this well-dressed criminal boss, who had them at his mercy, had also been the pitiless blond murderer he'd inexplicably imagined.

Between complications from his physical state and mental shock, Connor lost his balance and fell flat on his face. The lanky man who'd disabled him snickered before picking him up off the cement, which also left its mark, and held him steady.

When Connor's sight and faculties had fully returned, he reexamined the manicured blond. He did not recall the man from his hallucination in any great detail, only the impression of the Starr family resemblance. He, therefore, could not accurately compare their features, but this man bore the same similitude. In addition to Connor's rising confusion stemming from an inexplicably accurate hallucination, his equilibrium was further disrupted by an invisible tug toward the man, except that the flavor of his metaphysical gravity also broadcasted a danger resembling the insidious ergosphere of a black hole.

Jack granted him a wide, charming smile. "Ah, so the bloodhound has shown some loyalty after all," he observed, stirring up disturbing thoughts that had been deep within Connor's mind; there was an insight he was failing to comprehend, and he conceded hazily that he might be rejecting whatever it was. However, he did not linger long on the sensation, allowing the handsome stranger to keep his attention. "Fascinating," he continued in a tone that held traces of both amusement and patronization.

He gestured behind him to where a small table had been set with several courses. A single man stood to the side; attired similarly to his boss and guests, he was dressed in a suit, although his was not custom-fitted and appeared to have been inadequately maintained. He had a serviette draped over his arm, much like the waiters in fancy restaurants, and the combination of the pattern and condition of his ensemble and his unenthusiastic expression made the unfortunate man appear to be an unwilling choice of servant.

"As you can see, we've set up quite the feast," Jack continued in his gentlemanly manner, this time addressing Orion directly, and Connor took the opportunity to steal a look at his partner. Nothing about Orion's manner implied he recognized the stranger, but he couldn't miss the family resemblance and the younger man's brow was beaded with sweat despite holding his ground.

"Your sister gave us an idea of what you might like." The quality of Jack's smile transformed from hospitable to benevolent. "I'm not as savage as my reputation suggests," he asserted, prompting Connor to question the man's identity. It was clear from the kidnapping and warehouse arrangements that the man was a professional criminal, but he would have recognized his face if he'd been on the evening news. "In your case, I believe a final meal is appropriate."

Connor turned to his partner in disbelief. "You knew it was a trap," he deduced, and suddenly, his reluctance to formulate an appropriate plan made sense. However, Orion shook his head fervently; the sudden look of fear on his face indicated that he had been just as unaware of their captor's final plan for the evening.

"Ah, no, he did not," Jack interjected, "and I apologize, Agent Connor. I didn't know you would be joining us tonight, or I would have accounted for you as well." He bowed his head in regret, and Connor felt a twinge of fear, as if the handsome man's metaphysical gravity had intensified and his simple words had contained a cryptic threat. "Pity, since our arrangement was only just beginning to bear fruit…"

Now it was Orion's turn to regard his partner with dread. "What are you going on about?" Connor demanded. His mind swirled with an overabundance of questions that this interaction had raised: Why had a hallucination conjured the image of a real person? Did anything else that he'd seen have any bearing on reality? Why did this man seem to know who he was? What insight skulked in the shadows of his own mind?

He did not have long to ponder these alarming thoughts, as Jack continued seamlessly and with elegance, as if Connor had never interrupted him. "Now, now, there's no point in standing on ceremony at this juncture," he said, striding toward the set table; the reluctant waiter automatically pulled out a chair, his face revealing the apprehensive respect that he had for his boss. "The two of you will be dead soon, and I doubt you want to spend your last minutes gaping at one another. This food is quite sumptuous, and I'd hate to see it wasted on this lot." He briefly gestured toward his underlings and his contempt for them had crept into his voice with this last comment, but it was easy to overlook due to the congenial demeanor he employed. "So please, have a seat, and enjoy yourselves."

Orion swallowed; he was surprisingly resolute as he spoke, drawing on that same hidden reserve. "I only came for my sister. I'd like to see her."

"Yes, of course, but we don't have to get down to business just yet," Jack suggested affably. "I'm sure neither of you have eaten, knowing your schedules, and a short delay won't affect the proceedings." He shook his head regretfully. "I didn't take your sister into account either, but that omission was by design."

"Please," Orion replied firmly, though Connor detected a slight tremble.

Jack nodded affably. "As you wish," he conceded with a dash of disappointment. "Graves," he bellowed. Seconds later, Cassie was led out by a dour-faced man who kept his meaty fingers lodged in her shoulder. She was wan, her eyes were downcast, and though she perked up when she laid her eyes on her brother, melancholy still clung to her. Her eyes flitted toward Connor, pleading with him to act, to interfere, and when he appeared unable to help, she chewed her lower lip as her mind turned to devising its own plan.

"Cassie!" Orion shouted, smiling for her benefit. "Don't worry," he added reassuringly. She shook her head, seemingly as a warning, but she spoke only his name in response, forcibly remaining with her guard.

"As you can see, the girl is alive and mostly unharmed," the handsome man stated, closing the distance between them again. The lanky man holding Connor took a step back, dragging him with him, and Jack shed a kind smile as he stood toe to toe with Orion. "All that is required for her to remain that way is one little thing from you..." He reached upward, seizing the younger man by the throat, and squeezed it like he intended to wring blood from a stone. Orion grasped the man's forearm with both fists, clawing at them as he tried to pry open his grip. The air moved around them, darkening distinctly as its flow circled Orion like water caught in a whirlpool, and then it surged toward his assailant, who seemed to absorb the strange breeze through his pores as it streamed around him and disappeared. "Don't struggle," Jack told him in his charming voice. "It'll only hurt more if you do, and this needn't be messier than required."

Cassie screamed in furious grief, reaching toward her brother, and Graves dug his fingers deeper into her shoulder, splitting the space between her clavicle and her rib cage. She gritted her teeth and grabbed his hand as she appeared to consider fighting, only to reassess her options at the last moment.

The plastic slats hanging far above them splintered, freeing the heat and light of the filaments within, and they converged on one point—the grapple at the center of the warehouse. With independent illumination gone and his eyes slowly adjusting to the now dim conditions, Connor found it difficult to follow the ensuing action. While the plasma appeared to strike true, there was no subsequent inferno to confirm success; rather, the flames snuffed out, leaving them in abject darkness, and Cassie screamed again, this time emitting an overwrought wail.

Connor's guard was disoriented by his lack of sight, but he, having learned his lesson, did not try to attack his captor directly. Instead, he wrenched in such an angle that his guard's unprepared hand could not keep its rigid grip, and he ducked before the lanky man's blind pawing could capture him again. Connor had little time to formulate a plan and, knowing from the aches in his body that he could not put up another fight while disarmed, he did the one thing he thought would help. He reached into his pocket, retrieving the small Zippo lighter that had resided there since he'd first met the Starrs, and he snapped the flint wheel, giving its sparks life. The fueled flame grew, bursting from the eyelet like a newborn sun, and encircled the warehouse like a hungry wolf stalking its prey before its final strike. He could feel the flames licking his skin and the heat flashing across his face, but as the fire engulfed their captors, he felt no pain nor even sympathy as he heard their panicked cries in the dancing light.

- - -

Orion was engulfed in incomprehensible pain; he could feel the necrosis of his cells as some intangible part of their cores was being torn from them. He tried to resist the attack, reaching deep inside himself to hasten cell division to replenish the deceased ones and to monitor the replacements for detrimental mutations. While this stemmed the tide, his strength would not last; the agony grew with each evaporated bond.

He heard his sister scream, and her expressed pain bolstered his resolve; he was the only family she had left, so he had to survive to protect her. He was cognizant of his own essence at the cellular level and could normally sense those around him. Now locked in a deadly dance, he'd become isolated from the others but not Jack Everest: As the older man used his ability to detach Orion from the world, forcing a disturbing intimacy between them, he also exposed himself to easier biological manipulation, and while Orion might not comprehend the reality of what was happening to him, he could still defend himself.

His connection to his ability was intensified by the isolation, and with it, he reached deep inside Jack's body, passing through his flesh and veins to his heart. The vital organ was sturdy, beating like a war drum, and Orion arrested its electrical impulses so that the muscle would remain in contraction, but the heart resisted and continued on like a coursing river. He tried again, this time weakening a tiny section of the aortic wall to allow it to bulge and eventually burst from arterial pressure, but his victory was again denied: The wall repaired itself, returning to normal as if he'd made no incursion.

He felt the kiss of scorching heat, and a flicker of bright light flashed across his distant vision, but his mind was focused elsewhere and was soon distracted by pinpricks joining the subjugation of his cells, making him feel like he was composed of static and white noise. None of this mattered as he probed desperately for a weakness in the notable hardiness of his foe.

Jack's constant barrage eroded Orion's strength and stripped him of his life; his body mass had decreased by nearly a quarter, consumed like the outer layers of a star being siphoned by a black hole. Despite his resolve to survive for his sister's sake, he knew that he would not last much longer, and his determination to wreak revenge deepened.

If he could not attack the cells, perhaps he could turn them against their master; he redirected his efforts to smaller dimensions, diving deep into Jack's bone marrow. Being the blueprint of the body, DNA was resistant to direct alteration, with the exception of the faulty copies made during cell division. It was here that Orion focused, attempting to short-circuit the hematopoiesis process by speeding up cell reproduction and increasing the chances of a malignant error occurring during duplication. It was a difficult task to complete successfully, but the result should synergize with his attacker's extraordinary ability and ultimately destabilize the healing process.

As Orion felt the last of his consciousness buckle under the onslaught, he was blessed by one final bright point: His leukemic cells were being accepted by Jack's body, and the cancerous agents had been released into his bloodstream. Jack's inhuman regeneration, recognizing the dangers the insidious cells posed, attempted to attack them while producing faulty replacements. Knowing this chain would cascade out of control now that the metastatic process had commenced, Orion relinquished his willpower and let the last of his substance be absorbed.

- - -

A single column of white-hot flame burning as brightly as the sun was the sole source of illumination now that the fixtures had been shattered, and stillness had descended on the warehouse. The other men had died from various degrees of burns, save for the one presently burning like a candle, and Connor sought to end his misery with a bullet. He picked up a discarded weapon—it might have been his, but it could just as easily have been one of theirs—and shot squarely into the glowing pillar at approximately chest level. The intense heat was a shield, destroying the bullet before it penetrated the outer layer, but the inferno soon died, and Graves' corpse toppled to the ground. He was not blackened as Connor expected; rather, he was covered in a disgusting, thick, semitransparent substance that dissolved once the column dissipated. The man's nose and mouth were scorched, and some sort of dried white substance dotted the latter; these were the only outward signs of his demise.

Connor initially spared no thought for Cassie, as the girl had demonstrated remarkable resilience in the past, but he knew that assumptions would only lead to catastrophe, and he could afford a second to check on her. He was immediately glad that he did, noting her pale face and wide eyes. She did not move, except to sink to her knees and whisper silently to herself. He patted her gently, squeezing her shoulder reassuringly, and then her allotted time ended. He could not comfort her when her brother was still in danger.

Muted light shrouded the murky scene and prevented Connor from taking precise aim. He could make out the white of Orion's teeth, bared like those of a cornered animal and its stretched width advancing toward rictus proportions. The younger man shriveled, becoming even thinner—almost emaciated—and the shadows continued to eddy around them. Connor acted decisively, aiming for center mass, and emptied his magazine into the dark. He disregarded bystander safety, certain that Orion could heal their wounds, but he was disappointed to hear the sharp ping of ricocheted bullets skipping off distant metal.

Connor might as well not have tried to interfere, as Jack casually discarded Orion's newly desiccated corpse, dropping it at his feet as if it were no more than a disposable wrapper. Connor felt nauseous; he could not even recognize his partner. The dangerous blond grinned devilishly as he turned his attention to his remaining audience. He regarded the scattered corpses of his deceased gang impassively, as if their deaths were no more than an irksome inconvenience. "What a waste," he observed, his charming veneer reestablished by his urbane mannerisms. "Graves and Javier had such useful talents." He shook his head regretfully. "Ah, well. That's what I get for trying to have my cake and eat it, too." He chuckled politely, as if the joke had been told at a society dinner rather than at the scene of mass death.

Jack stole a glance at Cassie, noting her dispirited form crumpled in front of Graves' untouched body. She had not moved since Connor had checked on her, and she seemed no closer to cognizance of their present situation. The blond turned back to Connor, asking brightly, "Which of you would like to be next?" His eyes slipped down to Connor's hands, and though he would have bluffed, the empty slide locked to the rear denounced him before he had a chance. Jack looked back up, meeting Connor's gaze meaningfully. "You or the girl? I'm afraid I cannot let…"

He trailed off, suddenly losing his staunch footing, and he wobbled slightly as a new shadow formed over his features. He inhaled deeply, clutched his chest momentarily, and then reclaimed his civility and charismatic smile. "Pardon me. Perhaps it's indigestion," he continued, making light of the situation despite being faintly unnerved. "As I was saying, I'm afraid—" This time, he could not disguise his distress as a wave of unexpected exhaustion spread over him, and he stumbled, finally taking a dignified knee, as he addressed his inner turmoil. Abnormal masses bubbled to the surface, manifesting as tiny, irregular growths, and they spread through his veins like metastasizing vessels. Jack cringed as he tried to regain his footing, placing the majority of his weight on his supporting leg, but he did not move, instead becoming sheet white as the effort drained the blood from his formerly handsome face. Lurching forward, he made another attempt that ended in disappointment and a violent coughing fit. Despite his determination, Jack could not make it to his feet, but though he fell prone, he did not surrender. His pain seemed to fuel his willpower, bolstering his effort, and he crawled toward Connor.

Whatever malady afflicted Jack, its uncontrolled proliferation fed on his insides and birthed its offspring as identifiable tumors. The agent watched him, mesmerized by horror, as he inched forward. Instinctual desire to avoid disease broke the spell over Connor, and he retreated prudently, keeping an adequate distance between himself and the suffering man. The invasion swallowed healthy skin, warping and converting its surface until Jack Everest became unrecognizable. It sapped his strength, for he no longer made any meaningful progress, and when he fell, he did not raise his head again. He convulsed briefly and then lay still, expelling his last breath in a rasping croak.

Connor watched the fallen man for several minutes, telling himself that he was confirming his inertness, and then he roused himself to action. Claiming a new pistol from one of the other goons, he approached the corpse cautiously and emptied the entire magazine into the back of Jack's skull, hoping that this time, it would make a difference. The bone shattered, splattering blood and hair, and he heard a satisfying, solid impact with flesh and the floor beneath it. He didn't know what had occurred previously— there were no entry or exit wounds in Jack's torso—but he knew that he couldn't have missed that many shots. He tossed the useless weapon aside, letting it clatter to the cement, and moved to his next task unenthusiastically.

He knelt beside Orion's crumpled form. His resolve faltered, his mind treacherously evoking ancient memories he'd rather remained buried, but he forged ahead, angrily banishing thoughts of Stern's death and any associated emotions. He needed to focus now. Though his partner's flesh felt like parchment, Connor optimistically felt for a pulse. But there was nothing—not even a feeble beat. He rested on his haunches, sighed deeply, and closed his eyes. Perhaps the miraculous resurrection at Primrose had been only an illusion caused by high emotions, but he nevertheless prayed for an encore.

- - -

This time, there was no lingering in the mist. Orion's sister led him gently yet firmly down the now familiar path toward Bay Ridge, and he was not disturbed to see its dark profile take shape and its gray stone steps appear beneath his feet. Nevertheless, its entrance was foreboding, and he used every ounce of his sister's reassurance to enter its dark mouth.

The atmosphere of his former home was dark and oppressive, and he struggled to find the light switch, only to realize that muscle memory was dictating its position as far higher than it was in reality. Once he recognized that he was an adult and not a toddler, it was easy to locate the toggle, and the overhead fixture illuminated the living room, although it did not lift the mood.

Orion's heart stopped, and he froze as he beheld his otherworldly apparition in full light. The young woman couldn't be much older than he was now, but the copious blood that obscured her recently hardened features accumulated in the dirty lines of her face and attempted to give it new contours. Her ear had been sliced away, attached by only a thin layer of skin that had been filleted from her skull. He could see now that she had defensive wounds on her forearms and hands—chunks of flesh that had been raked by a cleaver or other sharp implement—and she was entirely naked, as if she'd disrobed willingly. Her exposed body was not yet bony, the streets having only begun to work their famine on her, and it revealed stretch marks and scars that hinted at her personal history. One eye was swollen, attempting to protect itself from her shattered cheekbone, while the other possessed a profound sadness.

His gaze wandered—not from inattention but rather due to shame—and he noticed the crimson stain in the carpet on which the woman stood. He recalled the bare square cut into his living room floor, the confusing reprimand that he'd received for experimenting with fire in the apartment, and the cheap throw rug that had been used to disguise the blemish until they'd left Bay Ridge. While he had no memory of his supposed offense, he knew that the rug concealed a rust-colored stain in the wood beneath it.

As he watched, the woman's wounds closed, knitting shut in the swift fashion that only he was capable of inducing, and she smiled brightly, reminding him more of a mother than Madeleine ever had. However, feeling trepidation over the proceedings, he clutched Cassie's hand tighter, and this silenced the unease he felt when the stranger became clothed in the same snow-white sundress that his sister was wearing.

"Who are you?" he asked, curious yet afraid to know the answer. She had haunted him for weeks, and despite her gruesome appearance, she had never been accusatory—only concerned for his safety. In his nightmares, he was responsible for her death: If she had not paused to rescue him, she might have escaped.

She smiled beatifically. "That detail doesn't matter," she assured him in a soft, maternal tone that filled him with reassuring comfort like snuggling under a warm blanket next to a fire. "You never knew. The better question is about what you remember... or rather, what you do not."

In spite of her kind words, uncertainty still held its clutch on his heart, and he hesitated. "I don't understand."

He felt a hand caress his cheek, and he turned to see the supportive smile of his sister. "Yes, you do," Cassie insisted patiently, taking his chin into her hands. "Don't be afraid. I am here with you. You can remember safely." Reassured by her hallowed touch, he relaxed as he closed his eyes trustingly and released the reins on his mind that he'd forged from fear years ago.

The dream had indeed been a memory, but it had been incomplete: Pierce, fueled by anger that his prey had escaped and the sudden alarm that their dark secret might be exposed, had tackled the woman with the intent to finish her off swiftly, and Madeleine had quickly reclaimed her child to safely remove him from the scene and protect his innocence for a few more hours. However,

Orion had refused to simply abandon his new friend, with whom he'd felt more kinship in a few moments than he'd experienced throughout his entire young life with his parents. He'd struggled frantically to escape his mother's grasp so that he could go to the stranger's aid. He'd felt an extraordinary power awaken deep within himself, and he'd directed it toward the vagrant. Pierce's executing blows had been arrested once he'd witnessed the broken shards of his victim's skull extending toward one another in an attempt to reunite and become whole and her skin mending faithfully to heal the gaping wound. Unnerved or simply pragmatic, his father had resumed his task and had struck her several times with his machete, ensuring that her slender neck had been severed and that her life had ended. When he'd glanced up, covered in blood splatter and wearing a look of annoyed inconvenience, his frightful visage had been enough to forever imprint fear into the heart of his vulnerable child.

"You shouldn't blame yourself," the decedent told him, gently wiping away his tears. Cassie no longer held his face, having surrendered that role to the woman. "You were only six, and there was nothing you could do; yet, you let your guilt color you for the rest of your life." Her smile expanded warmly as she shook her head, reassuring him. "I never held a grudge against you, and it is time for you to forgive yourself."

Orion's subconscious challenged the idea of the dead maintaining a grudge, temporarily removing him from the tranquility of the situation, but the moment was fleeting, and his doubt was quickly erased by the soft, restorative kiss that the woman imparted on his forehead like his mother never had. She faded from view, as did the rest of Bay Ridge, leaving him alone with his sister in the peculiar mist.

"Are you ready to go home?" she asked, her kind voice taking on a saintly patience and equanimity. Orion was surrounded by gray dimness, and no mysterious looming shapes threatened to manifest in the mists. He was ready—there was nothing left to bind him to this place—and he took her offered hand willingly. Yet, a faint nagging lingered in the back of his mind as if there was something that did remain—if only he could remember.

- - -

The sound of the ringing phone roused Terrance from his restless slumber. Like most Plum Island staff, he'd remained at the facility until it had become evident that little else could be done that evening, and he'd headed home, where he'd fallen into a reluctant and troubled sleep. He pounced on the device, cleared his throat, and answered confidently, "Terrance."

"Starr is dead," Connor stated. "I'm going to need—"

Terrance bolted upright, swinging his massive legs over the side of the bed so quickly that he bashed his ankle into the nightstand; this did not improve his tense mood. He clasped the injury and, through gritted teeth, demanded, "What the hell? How did that happen? I said to watch him for strange behavior!"

"It's a long story that I don't feel like getting into at the moment." Connor's voice, which was stretched thin like the last intact thread of a frayed rope, threatened to break with every word. Then it rebounded, becoming flat and lifeless as he completed the request he had begun to make at the beginning of the conversation. "I'm going to need a cleanup team ASAP. Make sure Antithesis is on the crew. Maybe even bring Angel along for the ride." Surprisingly and without missing a beat, he added, "And a doctor—preferably the one who did the autopsies for the Chamberlain case."

"Whatever you say, Connor," Terrance replied reassuringly, his mind questioning what had rattled his subordinate. This was the man who had tried to make a status report from inside the back of an ambulance, and though he wasn't always well-mannered or polite, Terrance respected the man who he knew wasn't easily shaken and could maintain his composure under pressure. "This *is* about the girl, though, isn't it?" he asked, trying to confirm his suspicion.

"She's alive, so don't worry yourself too much. I'll bring her back once the scene's secure, and I'll make my report then," he promised. He sounded as if he was being straightforward—no trace of his normal condescension—and he nearly made it to the end before his voice cracked, spilling a dark, acrid laugh. "Maybe I should be a little more specific about the team, yeah?" he continued, bleeding incongruent bitter anguish into his tone. "This bastard's able to siphon the life out of you, and he consumed Starr. I think he's dead, but I sure as hell would like Antithesis to make sure."

Nothing in Connor's reports had ever made Terrance reconsider his partnership with Orion Starr, but the raw emotions he was displaying gave him pause; had Orion survived, he would have finally reviewed the arrangement. As it was, Connor was high-strung and volatile, and it was possible that his reaction was due to whatever events had transpired and not to an overly personal connection. "It'll take a few hours to get there," he replied, greatly regretting the distance between the two cities; urgency could not alter bothersome geography, and though traffic cleared by the late hour, the time it would take to assemble the team ultimately meant that no gain would be made.

"Do you think you can make it that long?" he asked. If the agent could not, there was little Terrance could do, except hope that local law enforcement could keep its composure when it responded to Connor's request for backup.

"'Course I can," Connor assured him brightly. "Just a few minor scrapes and bruises, and the girl's practically comatose, so she won't be any trouble." Terrance could hear the forced smile in his pause. "I'll hold down the fort," he continued cheekily. "Maybe I'll even squeeze in a good nap."

Although the sarcasm and marginal insubordination had returned, Connor's sudden reversal and the absence of the other emotions worried Terrance. "Connor, you don't sound so good."

His agent chuckled cynically. "That's just the adrenaline talking. I'm fine," he replied smoothly, no unsteady trace betraying that he was not as collected as he portrayed. "Though I'd love a drink when you get here. Do you think you could have them pack a Jameson for me?"

"Yeah, we can have them do that," Terrance agreed grudgingly. Connor seemed to be struggling with early signs of psychological shock, a condition to which he was already prone due to his service record. There was not much Terrance could do for him now, and though he'd sat through numerous seminars, he was not prepared to deal meaningfully with it; he'd have to leave that to the professionals, and he'd ensure that one was placed on the requested team. "Hang on, Connor," he said.

- - -

Connor shoved the phone into his pocket, barely registering that it clattered to the cement instead, and limped back to Cassie's side; now that his adrenaline high had begun to recede, he felt the soreness seep back into his body and he knew the pain would increase overnight. Though the girl had still not budged from her spot, she'd at least fallen silent, and he wrapped an arm around her inexpertly. Cassie flinched at his touch—which he certainly understood, as he had no experience in consolation—and then exploding into tears and rage, she rejected his gesture. "This is your fault!" she shouted vehemently.

"Yeah, I know, love," he accepted softly and pulled her into an embrace. Despite her outburst, she didn't resist, receiving succor from their shared grief, and she buried her face in her hands as she slumped against him. He shifted slightly, shielding her brother's body from view, and though he should have kept watch over Jack's corpse to validate its continued inertness, he was relieved to banish both forms from his sight.

As Cassie sobbed, he considered what would happen to her now that her brother was gone. While it was conceivable that she'd continue to live with the Vickers—they were the last legal guardians whom Orion had authorized—it was more likely that she'd be shipped back to Plum Island. Orion had once scoffed at the idea of Cassie living with relatives instead of foster parents: Pierce's single mother had died decades ago, and her English parents, who were practical strangers to the siblings, were too old to care for another child, while Madeleine had cut her family entirely out of her life. Cassie would turn eighteen within two years and was set to inherit a fortune, but Connor wondered if she would ever make it that far.

Cassie was responsible for five dead bodies, and though she might have killed the warehouse workers in self-defense, he doubted this argument would protect her for a third time. Her probation would be revoked, her case file reviewed, and his passionate endorsement of her for government work would certainly be dismissed. She would be recommended for euthanasia because even if the BSI accepted his proposal to use her to fight fires or assist in arson investigations, she had taken too many human lives.

Why had he offered to escort her back to Plum Island? He could have lied and said that she had died like her brother, but his brain had already taken refuge in the comfort of autopilot and he'd provided an accurate report. He'd offered her up for the good of the population; she was like a loyal guard dog who'd bitten the wrong victim.

He was telling himself a lie, and he knew it; it was one that he couldn't even swallow this time. It was his duty to save as many lives as he could, and Cassie should have been one of them; she was not a destructive force but a child in unfortunate circumstances. He was failing to protect her, which meant he was invalidating the sacrifice that Stern had made for him. Connor was losing his right to continue living.

Stern's memory stirred another disturbing thought. He'd never received visions of Stern's demise, and he desperately wished that he had, for then, he might've been able to prevent it. Stern had meant as much to him as Orion had—perhaps more—so experiencing a premonition was not a matter of friendship or intimacy. Alternatively, maybe Connor should be considering why he'd received these visions at all.

The hallucinations might have centered on Orion—first, the confrontation at Primrose and now his lost battle with the parasite—but he was not all they revealed. To Connor's knowledge, he had never met their captor before tonight, yet he'd accurately visualized his similitude to the Starr siblings. Moreover, Jack's words upon greeting them had seemed oddly au fait, as if he'd known more about Connor's secrets than he did himself. While this alone was disquieting, it became much worse when placed in context: The vertigo that he'd felt in Jack's presence echoed two earlier occasions when he met new people—Moise Kabamba, a proven Other, and Pierce Starr, whose enviable hardiness made a good case for preternatural ability—and, most damning, he'd been incapacitated by a severe headache during Antithesis' last visit. Only Others reacted to Antithesis' suppression field, and while he'd never experienced an adverse response to it before, his well-timed headache became admissible evidence for the realization he was trying to resist. Perhaps it wasn't luck guiding his phenomenal Other apprehension rate.

He did not have long to consider his troubling line of thought before it was mercifully interrupted by the loud, dry gasp of a man who'd completed his first marathon. The sound also drew Cassie's attention, and she looked up from her mourning in startled surprise and fear. Her tears, which had stained her cheeks with ruined mascara and foundation, had now run dry, and her puffy eyes seemed to shoulder the bulk of her emotions, widening in anticipation of a new threat. In contrast, Connor took the new development in stride, scowling ambivalently despite his extensive relief; Orion's miraculous recovery complicated things, as it confirmed the original problem he'd identified at Primrose.

Orion appeared entirely unharmed and rose to his feet eagerly, intent on only one thing: his sister. "Cassie!" he exclaimed, happily sweeping her into his arms. However, his reunion would not be as smooth as he might have hoped and instead became a maelstrom of emotions. At first, she grinned, readily returning his embrace with the same elation, but as her joy peaked, a shadow moved over her face as her mind began to sift through her feelings. She shoved him away violently, shouting, "Get away from me, you freak!" She could not presently reconcile her relief at his apparent resurrection with her deep-seated rejection of their supernatural natures, and the latter seemed to be currently in control, also distracting her from the upsetting thoughts that had previously caused her to passively withdraw. It seemed that, like Connor, she coped better with anger, and he could appreciate the unhealthy strategy.

Her brother's face fell, the shadow of uncertainty creeping across it as well.

"Cassie…" How much memory had he retained? Connor had never been able to debrief Orion on his experience at Primrose, even after Connor had badgered him, and had instead focused on validating the younger man's continued good health. Did Orion realize that he'd been attacked or that his sister, traumatized by the idea of losing her brother, had conducted her own assault to rescue him?

Cassie had already taken a few steps backward, tears forming in her eyes as she clenched her fists, while her brother nervously wiped his mouth with his hand. Connor decided that he needed to intervene before the siblings became too involved in their argument. "Hold on, love," he said, preempting her words, which were on the tip of her sharp tongue and ready to be launched. "Before you get in a row, there's something a bit more pressing I need to speak with your brother about." He managed a cocky grin, drawing her attention and hopefully her ire; she'd have been irate at his interruption anyway, so there was no harm in acting like a lightning rod for the rest of her resentment if it would grease the wheels for an easier evening. "Do you think you can handle holding off a bit? You can have at me later if it makes you feel better," he added smugly, cementing certainty that her anger was redirected toward him. She glared daggers at the agent, confirming the success of the ruse.

Connor took Orion softly by the arm and led him a short distance away—far enough that their quiet voices weren't likely to carry. He caught the younger man's chin in his hand, turning his face side to side in an attempt to examine him in the dark, and he quirked his lips; Orion appeared fine—not even flinching as he was being handled—and his throat bore no ill signs or even any bruising. Nevertheless, voicing his concern, he asked, "Are you okay, mate? Everything intact?"

Orion's gaze flitted momentarily toward his sister before he sighed heavily. "I'm fine," he replied unconvincingly. His eyes dropped to the cement, though they did not remain still and traced a path along the string of bodies illuminated by the distant ambient city light. He scowled as understanding dawned, and when he again looked past Connor at his sister, he seemed to have aged visibly.

Connor nodded slowly. "If you say so," he agreed solemnly, and he wished that he had time to confirm Orion's statement. He'd conducted several cognitive tests on his partner after Primrose, and Orion had shown no adverse effects from the experience, but this didn't mean that it would hold true this time. He flashed a conceited smirk, switching gears to grant him some distance and conserve his nerve. "You're indestructible, eh?" he teased nonchalantly, earning broken eye contact and a deeper, more troubled frown. *So, Orion might remember after all...*

As tantalizing as the possibility was, Connor couldn't press him for details if he was going to follow through with his plan. "Look, we don't have much time," he said, maintaining his illusion of control. As the words tumbled from his mouth, he could not believe that he was betraying the BSI mission, but he knew that it was the moral choice. As with his Primrose report, he had to have faith in his instinct. "I called headquarters. I didn't know you were coming back." Orion tilted his head, poised to interrupt, and Connor forestalled him with a blithe smile and a wave of his hand. "Don't think about it too hard, mate. You'll drive yourself mad," he quipped, burying his actual concern in customary glibness.

He let his insouciance float between them for a few moments, allowing himself a chance to reconsider because he had not yet crossed the line, and when he did not, his face twisted sourly. "The point I'm trying to make here is that you need to take her and leave, soon," he urged him. "When the containment team rolls up in a few hours, your sister is going back to Plum Island, where they'll euthanize her, and there'll be no staying of this execution." He felt drained; it had to be hours after midnight by now, and he was exhausted from the evening's events.

He glanced behind him, checking on the young woman. She'd sunk back into her stupor, arms wrapped tightly around herself like a blanket. He shook his head, malcontented, as he turned back to his partner and added regretfully, "She's had a hand in too many deaths."

The lines around Orion's tired face deepened. "Why are you telling me this?" he asked, warily searching Connor's face. "What happened to protecting the populace and preserving the public good?"

Borderline angry, Connor chuckled acridly; after all they'd been through, he still hadn't regained the younger man's trust. "Didn't anyone ever tell you not to question a gift horse?" he chastised him. Then he forced himself to relax, trying to release the tension that he'd built up throughout the evening, but he knew that it would take him a long time to recover from the night's events. It suddenly became easier for him to study a spot on the ground, and he bowed his head, placing his hands squarely on his hips. "Now get out of here before I change my mind," he murmured reluctantly, though he was secretly relieved that he'd managed to spit it out.

Suspicion gave way to sincere gratitude as Orion realized that Connor hadn't been making a crass joke; the agent had been speaking with disguised candor. Unexpectedly, he wrapped his arms around him, pulling him into a tight, emotional embrace. Connor greedily reciprocated in spite of himself, indulging for a moment before breaking contact and shoving Orion away. "Go on, then," he urged, suddenly biting back tears.

Orion nodded silently and went to collect his sister. Cassie started at his touch, and then she pounded her anger into his chest. He whispered something to her, drawing her face close to his. Connor couldn't catch his words at his distance, but they clearly had a palliative effect. Cassie clung to her brother's form, squeezing him as tightly as he had embraced Connor moments before, and as he led her from the warehouse, Connor couldn't resist giving him one last piece of advice.

"Don't head off to SION for help. They say they help Others, but they're not the type of people you want to be associated—" He cut himself off, realizing that he was only prolonging their departure. "Just take my word for it, eh?" he warned, taking the edge off with an impish expression.

Orion matched him with an earnest look. "Thank you, Connor."

He nodded, acknowledging the final kind gesture between them, and turned his back on the siblings; it was easier to concentrate at the task at hand than to watch them leave. He still had a scene to contain, and there would be a lot of questions, especially with the Starrs missing. He'd undoubtedly face criticism, a few write-ups, and perhaps even a demotion, and Connor mused cynically that it might be time to start a new career.

- - -

A column of thick, black smoke rose into the air, blotting out the horizon like a stain, and the sky grew brighter as the BSI caravan approached its destination, painting everything orange with the occasional splash of red to give it variation. A police barricade blocked its path, and no amount of credentials could get the agents past the perimeter line—not now. Johnson wanted to pressure the cop minding the cordon to grant them entrance, but fellow agent Danvers held him at bay and preached prudence: The call had been for containment and had made no mention of an inferno. They needed to find the agent who made the call, debrief him, and then proceed; if containment required commandeering the scene, especially because Cassiopeia Starr had violated her probation, the decision would be made at that point.

Fortunately, Connor was easily found sipping cocoa in the back of an ambulance. Despite the seriousness of the situation, he appeared quite pleased with himself, and the cozy blanket wrapped around him only covered the extent of his injuries; his wrist was bandaged, and his outfit was in more disarray than normal, with his suit jacket and tie missing entirely. He was also sitting alone in the back of the only ambulance, which meant that their target was missing.

Although Johnson was eager to begin the hunt, anticipating that Cassiopeia Starr had escaped custody, Danvers was the ranking agent and, therefore, held the authority to debrief Connor. Nevertheless, she asked Johnson to accompany her so that he could hear the information firsthand and facilitate more informed decisions when it came time to deploy Antithesis, who had remained at the caravan with the rest of the team. Johnson stood at the rear bumper while Danvers took a softer approach and sat next to Connor after introducing herself. As expected, Connor didn't seem too impressed with the sociable gesture. "Can you tell me what happened?" she asked.

"'Course I can," Connor replied. He sounded a bit hoarse, as if he'd been delayed in his flight from the warehouse, and now that Johnson was cued to look for it, he noticed that the visible portions of his coworker's shirt had become desaturated by smoke and sweat. Danvers waited patiently, staring at Connor until the silence grew uncomfortable, and he smirked. "What, now?" he quipped irreverently. "Well, alright then," he agreed, placing his cocoa on the cold, laminated floor beside him. "Where do you want me to start?"

Danvers was unfazed. "How about the beginning?" she suggested, adopting a tone that was simultaneously professional and cordial. "You didn't say much over the phone—only that you needed a cleanup team and Antithesis. What are we walking into?"

Connor chuffed. "Nothing now," he responded and immediately amended, "The aftermath." He gestured casually toward the warehouse and its towering inferno; though the blaze had been a multi-alarm fire, the crew had been able to gradually coax it under control, and it was now only a matter of time before it was snuffed out. "That right there is the result of the second skirmish. The first..." He smiled bitterly, contorting his face into a grimace. "You'll be glad you missed that one, too."

He only briefly described the events leading up to the warehouse: The kidnappers had contacted Orion directly, preventing Connor from intervening until his only option had been to tag along, and he'd attempted to act as backup, observing the proposed exchange from a secret location, but the goons had discovered him anyway, and he'd been captured. From there, his narrative became a bit fuzzy, and it wasn't from Danvers' lack of trying to understand him; rather, Connor remained fixated on the unidentified Other and constantly redirected the conversation back toward him to emphasize how dangerous he was.

"Agent Connor," Danvers interrupted delicately, having somehow not allowed her patience to wear thin. In contrast, Johnson was agog with the prospect of confrontation, especially after such a long drive; he was similar to his inhuman partner in this respect. "We understand this man is dangerous," she said. "However, this isn't the end of the story, and we need the entirety of the picture to ensure the safety of our agents."

"Antithesis will neutralize the threat," Connor answered facilely, scowling disapprovingly as if her statement wasn't worth their time. "That's why I asked for her."

Connor was displaying the secondary cause for his isolation from his peers—his abrasive, often sarcastic attitude—which Johnson had learned to ignore over the course of their frequent collaborations. Surprisingly, Danvers retained her composure, letting his condescension slide for the moment. "What about the fire?"

"It was Supernova," Johnson assumed.

Connor winced, stretching his mouth wide and tilting his head. "Yes and no," he replied evasively, as if the answer physically pained him. "If you recall, I reported that she was practically comatose," he continued evenly, relaxing his face as he looked to Danvers for confirmation; she met his eye and nodded encouragingly. "She was a bit traumatized, what with her brother being dead and being the victim of an attempted murder. There wasn't much I could do for her until you lot showed up, so we just sat there." Casually, he reached back into the ambulance to reclaim his cocoa, which must have gone cold by now, and Johnson wondered whether Connor had been more unnerved by the situation than he was letting on. If that were the case, he was performing admirably, but he also didn't believe that the incident could have been as disturbing as Connor maintained; the mystery subject had only "fed" on an Other—not on a fellow human being.

Abruptly, Johnson's mind latched onto another detail, and as it occurred to him, he asked, "What happened to the other guys? The humans."

Connor was perturbed by the interruption. "I told you: They were taken care of," he replied dismissively.

Johnson frowned; it was not at all clear what had happened during the firefight, including the actions that his coworker had taken. The only thing that was clear was that Connor and the girl had remained alive by the end of it. "How—?"

"In any case," Connor said, urgently resuming his account; Johnson thought he might've flashed him an irritated sideways glare as he replaced his cup on the floor and turned back to Danvers, resecuring her attention. "Less than ten minutes after I made the call, VSION decided to show up," he continued, baring his teeth in annoyance. "I don't know how they found us, but they were determined to take the girl." He shook his head regretfully, adding, "She didn't take too kindly to it." He nodded toward the warehouse, where the roaring blaze was dying slowly, and then took offense when Danvers appeared to write down the allegation in her notebook. "Hey now, it was self-defense," he snapped, offering vindication indignantly.

"You know the rules," Danvers replied coldly, not even looking up from the paper as she finished her personal remarks, and Johnson agreed with her decision; circumstances might mitigate a sentence, but it didn't eliminate penalties altogether. "This was her third strike."

"It's not the girl's fault that she was the target of two wild kidnapping schemes in the same night," Connor admonished her, his voice like a keen knife. Then his angry disgust dissolved, turning sour with remorse. "Not that it makes much of a difference."

Danvers raised a bushy eyebrow. "Why not?"

"Well, she's dead," Connor announced impassively, seemingly shrugging off the remainder of his emotions. "I shot her in the head before they could make off with her." Danvers leveled a skeptical gaze at him, though Johnson kept his opinion in reserve; while Connor seemed too emotionally invested with the subjects under his care, he'd also metaphorically signed the death warrant for a six-year-old several months ago, so for him, the extrajudicial execution of the Starr girl was still in the realm of possibility.

Connor returned the scowl reproachfully, as if he didn't appreciate his integrity being questioned obliquely. "Just because I sympathize with her doesn't mean I can't still do my job," he grunted. "I wasn't going to be able to get her back, and I couldn't let her fall into their hands." He looked away, breaking his domineering eye contact with Danvers, and then added cynically, "The solution to that was rather simple, especially if you were going to euthanize her anyway." As he hesitated, his face twisted wryly and he bit his bottom lip. "It's also why the inferno got so bad," he admitted faux-sheepishly, quirking the corner of his mouth, and his dark eyes twinkled mirthfully as if he weren't taking the state of affairs seriously. Knowing Connor's psychological profile, this was likely an illusion of detachment—a mask to protect his inner self from whatever he was feeling. "Without her around anymore, it just sorta raged out of control." He fixed his gaze on Danvers' notebook. "I just want it posthumously recorded that she defended herself."

Danvers lowered her head, deliberately overlooking his glibness, to express her commiseration, but she did not revise her comments. "You made the right decision, Agent Connor," she said, because the company manual instructed them that it was sometimes necessary to reassure agents of their moral authority. Judging from Connor's abrupt changes in demeanor, he could be suffering from situational stress or even doubting the mission, so it was a safe bet to verbally support his difficult choice.

"I know, but let's not focus on that, yeah?" he replied blithely, rejecting her sympathy. His easy expression hardened as his eyes flitted back to the warehouse and then tightened, exposing every wearied line that had been carved into his face. His eyes narrowed as he continued in a more sober manner. "We need to focus on finding that body." It was not a suggestion; it was an order, and it was one that Johnson felt compelled to obey due to the gravity in Connor's voice. "After what I saw, I want to make sure he's dead."

Danvers nodded gravely. "We will," she assured him steadily. "You made a good decision with your requests." She redirected the flow back toward the mission, revealing her endless patience, and inquired about probable threats. "Are they still in the area?"

"VSION?" Connor confirmed, evidently needing a reminder that hazards existed outside of his new menace. "No, they cut their losses and cleared out about the time everything went to Hell," he replied critically and then laughed uncomfortably. "Good thing, too. I was out of ammo."

"Alright," Danvers breathed, bringing the conversation to a close decisively by standing and reclaiming her position at the center of focus. "There's not much we can do until the fire's out. I'll go talk to the incident commander to see if he's willing to turn the case over to us before they get a forensics team in here."

Connor's expression darkened as he pulled the blanket tighter around himself. "Why would they need a forensics team?" he asked with concern.

"A fire this big could be arson, so the city will want to conduct an investigation," Danvers explained matter-of-factly. "I'd rather have our professionals on the site and in control. Cleanup is much easier when we have direct access to official files."

Connor's sharp exhalation sounded like a vocalized wince. "'Course," he agreed, likely remembering protocol. It was seldom needed for him to become involved in cleanup, particularly in the less noble necessities of falsifying official documents, so his memory lapse was understandable.

As Danvers walked away to command her team, Connor firmly clenched his jaw shut, chewing his inner cheek aggressively, and Johnson wondered what had prompted his odd response to the inclusion of a forensics team. Before he had a chance to inquire, Danvers summoned him to the van so he could prepare his preternatural instrument, and the trivial observation was forgotten.

- - -

Though it had been several weeks since the incident on the waterfront, Connor was still finding it difficult to resume a normal life. Returning to Greenport had not been easy; his apartment had seemed cavernous, even though he'd always resided there alone, and it had taken some time to readjust to the silence. He'd missed the cacophonous hum of Little Italy, even the constant din of traffic far into the evening, and the days had become hollow now that he'd been deprived of someone to share them with— or, more accurately, a tolerant target for his well-intentioned harassment.

Headquarters had been a hive of chaos since Connor's return, from the angry buzzing of Danvers' cleanup team, who had to battle locals over jurisdiction, to the nervous skittering of a borrowed and blended forensics team comprising NYC locals and BSI personnel. Under Summers' intense scrutiny, the BSI tried eagerly to piece together the identities of those who had perished in the fire, and it became steadily obvious to Connor during the ensuing aftermath that it wasn't as difficult to conceal the bizarre nature of Others from the public as he had been led to believe. Alternatively, it could have been that the BSI's detection techniques were not as ubiquitous as publicized.

Though the thought of a professional investigation of the warehouse fire had initially made Connor uneasy, its threat was mitigated by carefully applied bureau interference. Summers pressured the forensics team to disregard the role of accelerants in the blaze; the speed at which the conflagration spread undoubtedly pointed at some sort of accelerant before any chemical analysis had been conducted or other evidence had been studied by the team, and the bureau reasoned that closer examination unnecessarily risked the possibility of civilian authorities discovering the existence of Others when no trace of a mundane accelerant could be found. Fortunately, the bureau was unaware that the speculated accelerant was in fact of mundane origin: Connor had discovered kerosene stored in a back corner and had poured the drums' contents over the gathered bodies, ensuring that the inferno would destroy the most ephemeral evidence. While his actions had obfuscated the number of Others who'd been present in the warehouse, it had not fully eradicated the identities of those involved.

Connor had taken for granted that the kerosene fire would be hot enough to partially cremate the remains, and despite the precautions taken, he hadn't considered the possibility that all six bodies might be recovered from the ashes—only that some might be. Though their names would need to be determined via dental records—a process that would be thwarted by the sheer number of possibilities and no dependable leads—he had not realized that gender could be established based on skeletal structure, thereby revealing that Cassiopeia Starr's body had not been among the deceased. When Terrance confronted him with this fact, he could offer only a dubious explanation: Following her death, the inferno under her control must have consumed her first, leaving nothing but ashes, and while Terrance seemed to accept his rationalization, Connor knew that he was treading on thin ice. Her brother's body hadn't been properly identified either; the bureau relied on Connor's testimony that the two bodies with damaged faces belonged to Orion Starr and the unknown dangerous parasitic Other. Knowing that his build was similar enough to Orion's, Connor had placed a bullet in the back of the lanky thug's head to obliterate his dental record, and then he'd claimed that the body belonged to his partner. As long as Connor's credibility as an agent was undamaged, the Starrs would remain safe; it, therefore, became his duty to be incontrovertible.

It was not as if Connor had much of a choice but to remain with the bureau. He had not obtained many skills from his stint in the military, and though he'd developed and honed investigatory expertise in the field, he wasn't certain that he could parlay his aptitude into another career. He was too comfortable in the familiarity of the BSI, even if the office and its agents seemed more distant and alien nowadays, and he had no true motivation to change. He was alone in life, drifting with no central purpose—the true reason he'd joined the BSI—and it had been Orion who'd sparked a shift in his attitude and outlook. With his partner gone, Connor had no personal connections and, therefore, no motivation to improve himself or to try something new.

But as Connor sat at his desk reviewing the database for a new case to pursue, as he had done many times in the past, he knew that he was ignoring a crisis of conscience under the guise of protecting Orion Starr and his sister. If Connor were indeed an Other, as he was starting to believe, should he be hunting his own kind rather than asking to be quietly transferred to a different department? Two of the three BSI assets had reconciled their dangerous nature with the difficult decisions of the mission, but Connor was doubtful that his capability to do the same had remained undamaged. His time with the Starrs had shaken his convictions, and he knew now that euthanasia wasn't the only answer; yet, it was the BSI's default verdict when it came to protecting the civilian population. He didn't think that he could make the hard decisions anymore—not without considering who else they might affect and, therefore, allowing his judgment to be compromised.

Conversely, if his credibility became doubtful, the Starrs would be put at risk. Protecting them meant that he had to stay the course, but perhaps there was a way to assuage his conscience as he navigated the morally questionable waters in which he'd found himself.

It was undeniable that there were Others who should be euthanized: As much as it pained him to admit it, Brian Chamberlain was only one example of the handful Connor had discovered who posed an active threat to the public good. Connor's other, more benign discoveries had undergone mandatory training so they would not become a danger, and while he'd initially kept in touch with many of them, Connor now suspected that some had been euthanized because they hadn't completed the training, despite him being informed otherwise. A few may have even been executed because their very existence had posed a threat to Operation Blackout, as Samantha Anderson would soon prove. It was to these individuals whom Connor felt that he owed a debt—one that had started with Jacob Stern.

Morgan Connor had survived due to the actions of an Other, and he'd originally set about repaying this debt by finishing college and then trying to find a new purpose in life to justify his continued survival. At first, he'd thought that he'd found it in the BSI mission: Protect the civilian population against the dangers posed by Others. But his exposure to the Starr siblings had realigned his axiom: Others themselves were not always a danger; sometimes they, too, needed protection. Perhaps the best way to repay his debt to Jacob Stern was to continue to separate the wheat from the chaff; but he had to continue to sift through the wheat to isolate specific grains and prevent the compulsory registration of those Others who posed no danger because if they remained undocumented by the BSI, they would be safe from euthanasia. Concealing the survival of the Starrs was only the first step in his new mission, but it would not be the last: From inside the BSI, he could ensure that harmless Others escaped notice.

CONNECT WITH THE AUTHOR

Connect with the author at:
J.L.Middleton.Author@gmail.com